FALLING

ALSO BY **CHRISTOPHER PIKE**
PUBLISHED BY **TOR BOOKS**

The Cold One
Sati
The Season of Passage
The Blind Mirror
The Listeners

BOOKS FOR YOUNG ADULTS

Alosha
The Shaktra
The Yanti

FALLING

CHRISTOPHER PIKE

FORGE® A Tom Doherty Associates Book
New York

FALLING

Copyright © 2007 by Christopher Pike

This book is printed on acid-free paper.

A Forge Book
Published by Tom Doherty Associates, LLC
175 Fifth Avenue
New York, NY 10010

www.tor.com

Forge® is a registered trademark of Tom Doherty Associates, LLC.

Library of Congress Cataloging-in-Publication Data

Pike, Chirstopher, 1961–
    Falling / Christopher Pike.—1st Hardcover ed.
        p. cm.
    "A Tom Doherty Associate book."
    ISBN-13: 978-0-765-31718-6
    ISBN-10: 0-765-31718-4
    I. United States. Federal Bureau of Investigation—Fiction. I. Title.
    PS3566.I486F35 2007
    813'.54—dc22

                                        2006033707

First Edition: March 2007

Printed in the United States of America

0   9   8   7   6   5   4   3   2   1

FOR ABIR,
MY KELLY

Pain is old . . .
        it has seen a million dawns.

                        —ANONYMOUS

CHAPTER ONE

The first sensation Matt Connor felt when he awoke that morning of all mornings was pain. For a long time he had come out of unconsciousness to a feeling of loss in his chest, and he had come to accept it as inevitable. It was ironic that the pain was quickly followed by a wave of love. Thoughts of her smile and hair caught forever in a yellow ray of sunshine. He still loved Amy Techer, always would, and he hated her more than words could say.

That morning was special because it was the start of the day Matt planned to fake his death and disappear from the face of the earth. A bold plan, and he was not by nature a bold man. Yet Amy had changed him into something he was not.

He had set the alarm for six but his eyes opened at five. He closed them and rolled over but sleep was lost. He felt unsettled on top of his pain. When he left his bed, he would never return to it. He would never see his apartment again—his *stuff*. Not that he had much. Thirty years old to the day, he thought grimly, and how little he had to show for it.

The brief reflection hardened his resolve. His stomach was knotted and his heart pounded but he would go through with his plan. If he could not have love then she would not have it either. He wondered how many other men throughout history had come to the same conclusion.

Matt got out of bed and took a hot shower. Tonight, if he was not careful, he would suffer a cold bath. He was an excellent pilot but an inexperienced skydiver. Of course, not many people riding a parachute to earth were required to hit a boat at night in the middle of the sea. Yet that particular challenge did not daunt him as much as others. Those other tasks would come later, after he was dead to the world, when he could no longer be blamed. Until then he just had to be systematic—do the job and not think.

Still, he thought of her, of Amy. The name alone was a curse.

He had scarce food in his apartment: a carton of milk, a loaf of bread, two overripe bananas. He made toast and spread jam and butter on it and wolfed down the milk while he dialed his mother. She lived in

Santa Barbara, ninety miles north of his Santa Monica apartment. His mother had always hated that he never chewed his food. He supposed he had a streak of impatience in him, along with other things.

Although early, his mother answered on the second ring. She was unhappy that he wouldn't be arriving for his birthday party until seven that night. The insignificance of that particular concern troubled him deeply. His mother would never see him again.

"Why do you have to finish your scuba lessons today?" she asked after they had talked a minute.

"I've wanted the certificate for a while. To get it on my birthday makes me feel like things are coming together for the next decade."

"You already have everything going for you, Matt. Now that Cindy's in your life. Should I expect her early this evening?"

"I'm not sure. I'm going to call her in a few minutes."

"She didn't spend the night?"

His mother was being coy. She liked Cindy, much more than she had liked Amy. None of his friends or family had cared for his ex-girlfriend. They saw what she had done to him; they thought they saw.

He liked Cindy Firestone as well. A nice girl, but made of papier-mâché when touched by his wretched hands. He could not really care for her because she was not Amy. It was so unfair to her, but he continued to date her even though he saw she was falling for him. She was his insurance; she provided extra cover for his plan. He had a girlfriend, the police would say to themselves, he had a *life* for godsakes. His death would be seen as an accident, nothing more.

"No. She didn't spend the night," he replied. He didn't know what to add. At this point, the less he said, the better.

"How are you two getting along?"

"Great." He had to take a breath to lie. "I care about her a lot."

"She's excited about your party. She struggled over what to get you. You're going to be surprised."

"I like surprises." He added suddenly, "I told you about that bathroom I have to finish in Orange County? I better get going."

"You shouldn't be working Saturdays. On your birthday, of all days. You have to have more fun. You won't be young forever."

"I'll have fun soon." He had a lump in his throat. The last time he would hear his mother's voice. She'd had him late, at forty, and his father had passed away the previous year. He had no brothers or sisters. He was the center of her universe. She had a weak heart—his death could kill her. He had thought about that endlessly. Yet the thoughts had not halted his plan. His pain cut deeper than blood ties. He had to say goodbye. He added, "We'll have fun tonight."

His mother might have heard something in his voice.

"Take care, son," she said quietly.

"You too, Mom."

He set down the phone and closed his eyes. His heart no longer pounded. Inside was cold. The icy sting of the ocean tonight—should he hit it—would be welcome. He deserved to suffer for the suffering he could not bear.

Cindy slept late on Saturdays but did not mind being awakened. He had met her three months earlier at a coffee shop in Santa Monica. One of those late-night encounters that usually held more promise than substance. She was studying architectural diagrams, ones she had designed. They struck up a conversation about the Los Angeles skyline. Her knowledge of the city's major buildings was impressive. He did not remember who said hello first, but when they parted she was the one to offer her number. She liked to take risks. Later, she told him she was intrigued that he might be a dangerous character. The remark had amused him.

It was rare that women hit on him. Six foot and well-built—with a shock of choirboy brown hair and intense dark eyes—he supposed he was handsome enough. But he was very shy; he did not invite casual attention. Cindy was the opposite. She would find out where the busboy who cleaned the table went to school. It was important for her to connect to people. She felt they were connected. But she was still trying to understand why they had not been intimate yet. She suspected Amy was a lingering problem. Matt had been vague when describing what had happened.

Like his mom, Cindy was quick to answer the phone. He could imagine her sleepy smile. Red hair and freckles, she was a lanky doll stitched together with enthusiasm. She jogged five miles each morning before going to work at a design firm in the valley. One day, she swore, she was going to build the perfect home. She saw him living in it with her. He promised to help her put the pieces together, knowing it would never happen. Sometimes being with her made him think of Amy even more.

Of course, the essence of their relationship would have been obvious to a first-year psychology student. He treated Cindy as Amy had initially treated him. Their bond was a sixties pop song—he kept her hanging on. Amy had not even let him kiss her for several months. When he made out with Cindy, he kept his eyes tightly shut. He knew what he did to her was wrong and he did it anyway.

"I was just thinking of you," she said in a drowsy voice.

"You were asleep."

"Then I was dreaming of you." She yawned. "I'm glad you called. Hey, happy birthday. How does it feel to be thirty?"

"Good." Nothing felt good. "How are you doing?"

"Great. Looking forward to your party tonight. Wish I could fly over to Catalina with you. Why don't you take me?"

"It's better you get to my mom's before me. You can keep her company." He was glad Cindy would be with his mother when she received the news that his plane had gone down. Cindy was strong; she would get his mother through the first dark days.

She groaned. "You're so difficult. Hey, I need that guy's number who taught you how to fly. You said he might want to come with his girlfriend. Was it Clark?"

"Yeah. I can get it for you later." He did not want Clark at the party. He did not want an expert—personally connected to him—going to the Santa Barbara Airport and studying the radar tapes that described the course of his plane before it crashed. Not that Clark should be able spot anything unusual, but one could never be sure.

"When?" she asked.

"I'll call you from the road with it." Another promise he would not keep. He did not want to contact Cindy again. If his cell phone records were later examined, they could show that he had not been in Orange County during the first half of the day.

"Great." Her voice softened. "I miss you. I wish I was there with you now, lying beside you."

They had slept together eight times and not had sex. He told her he opened up slowly—a favorite Amy line. The odd thing was that Cindy was every bit as attractive as Amy. But to lie naked beside her in bed did nothing for him. While the mere thought of being close to Amy filled him with longing.

"You okay?" she asked when he did not respond.

"Yeah. Just thinking about the day."

"Do you miss me?"

"Sure. But I'll see you tonight."

She hesitated. "Can I sleep with you at your mother's house?"

She wanted to make love. Normally, he would have responded with his standard, "We'll see." But now all his promises were moot. There was no reason not to leave her with a dream. Amy had not bothered to do the same for him.

"That would be great," he said.

She sighed. "I think I could love you, Matt."

"I feel the same way," he replied, the worst lie of all. He had to get off the phone before he caused more harm. "I better go."

He sounded too abrupt. He should not appear conflicted.

"Are you sure you're all right, Matt?" she asked.

"I'm fine."

They exchanged goodbyes. Time to start the long day.

■

NOW IT was time to change into his alter ego, Simon Schiller. The transformation took several steps. First, he had to get his other car, an old Honda Civic that he had registered two months ago under that name. The vehicle was parked five blocks from his apartment—at present— although he seldom left it in the same place twice in a row. In the car he kept his disguise: a blond wig, mustache, beard, and green contact lenses. Plus he had a makeup kit. When he walked the world as Simon, he gave his skin a deep tan. It was incredible how powerful the simple disguise was. With sunglasses on, his own mother wouldn't have recognized him.

The morning air was brisk, February's gray hand. He walked the empty streets and tried not to think. Every detail of his plan had been worked out long ago. The only thing that could sabotage it now was a failure of will. However, pain over Amy's betrayal dogged his steps. He did not have to contemplate the actual atrocities she had committed to feel it. He merely had to exist for the pain to exist. In the end that was why he had formulated his plan. He could not go on living without seeking retribution.

But what happened if the pain did not stop when he finally had his revenge?

A question he preferred not to dwell on.

Once at the car, he drove to a deserted supermarket parking lot and applied his disguise. He had bought the stuff at—literally—a disguise shop in Hollywood. The beard adhesive gave him an itch. Later, he would have to grow a full beard to take the place of the disguise. It was the small things that could destroy his plan. But he was practiced at being Simon Schiller. The disguise took him less than fifteen minutes to put on.

His next destination was the marina, a few miles south. The day's schedule was tight. Nevertheless, he swung north toward Brentwood, where Amy and her husband lived. A nice house bought with real money. David had purchased her as well.

Or at least that was Matt's main rationalization for why she had betrayed him.

He parked half a block down the street from their house and turned off the engine. Staring at their dark windows and brick walls, he wondered what they were doing that very second. It was early; they would still be in bed together. The weather was cold but they could be lying naked under the blankets. David would roll over and gently touch her nipples. She would stir and smile and lower her hand to his crotch and the ordeal would start all over. For him . . .

It was a cliché to say it was a nightmare but so it was. He could not wake up from the horror he had fallen into seven months ago when he had caught them together. Kissing on a side street in Westwood after a late movie. He had been out for a snack; he never had food at his apartment. She had said she would be out of town that weekend but she had only gone a few miles from home. To fuck another guy when she wouldn't even fuck him. Not even after a year and a half of dating. Not even after she had performed oral sex on him a hundred times and promised him that soon they would be together forever. His Amy, in the arms of her old boyfriend, a guy she had sworn she hated.

His Amy, not really his at all.

He had cracked then. All that was joyful and worthwhile in life evaporated. He continued to breathe but the air was filled with vapors. Everything hurt, even his hair, and the weird thing was that it had not gotten better with time. He wondered if it was because she was his soul mate. If he hurt her, did he harm his own soul? Whatever—fuck that and fuck her. He hoped when he died it was forever because the thought of seeing her again—even in another body—made him want to vomit.

Yet he still missed her terribly.

He was about to leave when the door opened and out stepped Amy, many months pregnant, in a white bathrobe. The size of her belly startled him. He had known she was expecting but had not seen her in eight weeks. Staking out their house was a habit he was desperately trying to break. Neighbors had eyes and ears. The stalking could destroy his plans. He was not sure how many months she was along. He only knew it could not be his baby because they had never had intercourse. When they had finally talked—after he had caught her with David—she had sworn she had only started to see her ex a month before. But she had lied about so much. What did it matter what she swore?

Whether his or not, Amy was very pretty. Half Colombian, half English, she had long brown hair and doe-like brown eyes large and deep enough to suck the heart out of the unsuspecting. He remembered how when she used to look at him, he had felt like the luckiest man in the world. Her magical gaze, clear windows to a soul just as pure.

Immediately following her betrayal his main emotion had been confusion. Because she could not have done such a thing. She was neither a liar nor a cheat. He knew because he had stared into those eyes. But it had all been fun house mirrors. The love they shared had emanated from him alone.

Freckles sprinkled her light brown skin, particularly around her nose, which was short and cute. Her face was round but exotic. She cloaked herself in a silence that was often mistaken for depth by strangers. In reality, Amy was more shy than himself and did not socialize well. She had difficulty carrying on a conversation until she knew someone well. But alone with him she had been wonderful to talk to.

Her great loves were movies and books. She could dissect and re-create a story from a dozen different angles, each one unique.

Her prize was her mouth; large and full lipped, with teeth so white they could have been bought at Cartiers. When she used to kiss him, he had felt if he died tomorrow he would have already attained everything life had to offer.

"Hey, honey," he whispered as she picked up the paper. On her way inside, she paused and turned in his direction. A picture to cherish: the long fall of her hair; the grace of her movements, mysteriously enhanced by her pregnancy. He remembered what it had been like to hold her, that delicious warmth.

He did not panic. She could not see him through the morning shadows. Besides, he was Simon Schiller, just a guy, no one she knew, sitting in a car.

She stared in his direction a moment, then went inside.

He felt the familiar ache: pain and love, the devil stabbing the angel. But soon he would give her such pain, it made him wonder if he was the demon. Yet he had been through these mental gymnastics before; he would not change his course. Starting his car, he drove toward the freeway.

He had been to the marina before, as Simon Schiller. He had rented the same boat he was renting today, even driven it north to the waters off Ventura. He had secured the rental with cash, as he planned to do this morning. He had a fake credit card he had purchased on the Internet—there was nothing you couldn't get on the Web—but he was reluctant to use it in case it was traced back to him.

The boat was a wide-decked thirty-footer, with twin two-hundred horsepower engines. The width was critical because he planned to parachute onto the deck. Because he intended to return the boat, there should have been nothing worrisome about renting it. Nevertheless, if the police checked on rentals in the harbor and showed his picture around, it was possible he could be identified, even with his disguise. Then people might wonder. For that reason, he wanted to get out of the harbor fast.

It was not a wish he was granted.

There were three unusual items he needed to bring aboard: an inflatable dinghy, signal lights, and an extra anchor. His dinghy was no small, nor was the motor he planned to attach to it to drive him back to shore. A man from Harry's Ocean Rentals came over to give him a hand. Matt waved him away but the guy was probably anxious for a tip. He followed him back to his car after Matt had obtained the keys to the boat. When Matt opened his trunk, the man saw the deflated dinghy, and looked puzzled.

"Are you going diving or what?" the guy asked.

That would be one reason to bring along a dinghy. But Matt could not hide the fact that he had no diving equipment. Then he had an idea.

"Yeah," he replied. "I'm picking up friends on Catalina. We're going to rent our equipment there, then check out the caves on the backside of the island."

"You need diving equipment? We rent that as well. I bet you could get a deal from Chuck since you've already paid for the boat."

"No thanks. My pals have already got their stuff reserved."

"Hey, the name's Timmy." He offered his hand and Matt had to take it. "You sure? Chuck will give you a deal."

"I'm sure."

Timmy was straw-blond with a crooked mouth and sloppy feet. He had bumped Matt twice on the short walk to the car. Now he gave him a peculiar look. "I thought you told Chuck you were heading south to fish?" he asked.

Timmy must have been in the back when Matt had spoken to Chuck.

"Later I'll head that way. I have the boat for two days," Matt said.

He nodded as Matt bent over the trunk. "Let me help you with that motor."

"It's not necessary."

Timmy touched the lights and the supporting car battery. "What are these for?"

"Oh. They're stage lights. Leave them."

"You're not taking them aboard?"

Matt shrugged. "No. What would I need them for?"

Timmy insisted on helping him with the dinghy and the motor. Matt slipped him five bucks and thanked him. But the guy simply refused to go away, and Matt could not leave the harbor without the lights. He needed them shining toward the heavens in order to spot the boat in the middle of the ocean. Good old Timmy, he wanted to talk about the Lakers, and the tits on the chick who worked with him in the store, and how drunk he had been the previous night. Finally, Matt had to get rude and ask to be left alone.

Timmy sulked as he shuffled away.

Timmy would remember him, if someone dropped by to ask.

Matt returned to his car and wrapped the lights in a blanket and finally got them aboard. Thankfully, the anchor and its extra rope were hidden in a large backpack. They were not conspicuous. He stowed the equipment below and motored out of the harbor at a brisk clip.

It was a quiet day on the bay, especially for a Saturday. The morning gloom might have discouraged the rich sailboats and their spoiled masters. The wind and chop picked up as he reached the open sea but his ship—*The Mistress*—handled smoothly. Turning north, he was able to lock the steering wheel and concentrate on the folded dinghy and foot pump. The coast crawled by on his right, desolate in the gray light. He started to work on inflating the dinghy. It took forever. The foot pump had been designed for party balloons.

His work was mechanical, not distracting enough. His mind wandered and there was only one direction for it to go. He could not stop thinking about the day they had met.

He had been out for a walk and had passed the park. Twenty-eight at the time, he'd had his contractor's license for only two years, but already he had more business than he could handle. He specialized in bathrooms; didn't mind the gross wallpaper or moldy plumbing. Some weeks he put in eighty hours and did three bathrooms and cleared four grand. He remembered that morning thinking that maybe one day he would get married, a possibility he had never seriously considered before. He had struggled with so many jobs for so long. Now he had a new car, and a spacious apartment in a rich high-rise. But he had not been in a real relationship in six long years. Talk about someone primed for a fall.

He saw her. Kite and string in hands, four-year-old on her hip, the face of a doll. Sure, he knew skin-deep innocence was a myth, but there was something about her that made him think about the good old days—days he had never actually experienced. He imagined she could stand in the shade and glow. She was a picture of vulnerability, and he found that attractive. He did not understand then that vulnerable people often had horrible self-images, and were capable of horrible deeds.

He stopped to ask what she was up to. She gestured helplessly to the kite.

"We've been trying to get it in the air but there's no wind." Her voice was so soft she was hard to hear. There was no ring on her finger, but he had to wonder if the child was hers. Something in her body language said no.

Matt gestured to the park. "There's too many trees here. You need to go down to the beach."

She nodded. She did not give the impression she wanted him to go away, but she was not exactly comfortable either. He offered to take the kite, surprised at his boldness.

"I can give it a running start. I used to run track in high school. I might be able to get it in the air."

"Could you?" the little girl asked. They were somehow related; the child had the same incredible Latin eyes, lashes long as tears.

"Sure." He glanced at the woman. "If that's okay with you?"

She hesitated. "Fine."

He took the kite and string and searched for a runway. The park was hopelessly choked with trees. Still, he was determined to get the blasted thing in the air. Taking off at a hard clip, he fed string after the kite. To his surprise it caught an invisible current and he was able to slow down. The kite bobbled between the branches and rose into the blue. The two joined him by the swings. Handing the string to the kid, he felt the courage to introduce himself.

"The name's Matt," he said, offering his hand. She touched it briefly.

"Amy." She paused. "This is my niece, Debbie."

"Hi, Debbie."

"Hi! Thanks for getting my kite up!"

"You're welcome." He looked around. "Do you come here often?"

"Sometimes," Amy said.

"I think I've seen you before."

She nodded at the ground. Not big on eye contact.

"It's a nice day," he said.

"Yeah."

"I hope I'm not bothering you." He paused. "Am I?"

She shook her head.

"Hey, can I buy you coffee? There's a Starbucks around the block."

Amy gestured to her niece. "I promised her I would play with her for a while."

"I understand. I'm out for a walk myself. But I'll be back in an hour or so. If you're still here would you like to go then?"

She considered. "Okay."

He was not sure he had heard her. "Sure?"

She nodded. "Yeah."

He smiled. "Okay, Amy. I look forward to it."

He was lousy at asking women out. He did not know what had come over him to press himself on her. He expected her to be long gone when he returned.

Surprise, surprise, she was still there. Her house was not far, she said. They walked her niece home before going to the Starbucks. Along the way the conversation stalled. He did discover, however, that she worked part-time in a lawyer's office and that she lived with her father and sister—Debra's mother. He assumed the kid's father was long gone.

They ordered coffee and pastries and sat in a quiet corner. She continued to have trouble looking at him. He had the opposite problem. Her skin was like the coffee and cream he was drinking. Somewhere along the line he asked if she had a boyfriend and she shook her head. He did not think for a second she was lying. But later he was to come to understand that she still had some contact with a guy named David, who lived on the East Coast. However, the guy was not a part of her life, she made clear. He worked on Wall Street, brokering commodities for his rich father.

By chance Matt mentioned an Alfred Hitchcock film he had seen the night before and her eyes lit up. Sweet, innocent Amy was a hard-core mystery buff, of both books and films. Her tastes belonged to an earlier generation. Besides Hitchcock, she loved Sherlock Holmes, and everything Agatha Christie had written. Suddenly their talk took off, and he had to struggle to keep up. He wished right then that he was a writer. He would have done anything to impress her.

They went on a real date, dinner and a movie. She was a vegetarian. She liked Indian food, so he learned to like it. She did not kiss him on their first date. She did not kiss him on the second either. In fact, he was to date her three months before he was allowed to kiss her good night. The experience was frustrating—very weird, actually—but he felt she was worth the wait. He was not totally naive. He saw an element of manipulation in the way she kept her distance. But he attributed it to her Latin blood. Make the guy beg.

When they finally did make out, the first time, after her family had gone to bed, she burst out crying. Concerned, he begged her to tell him what was wrong. She shook like a wounded child. An old pain had come up, she said. She refused to elaborate. He did not even think of David; she had assured him that was over. But from that night on he got a sick feeling in his gut, a feeling that was never to leave him over the next eighteen months.

Yet she could be so fine. Dozens of times she surprised him at his various jobs with delicious homemade lunches. She just had to flash her killer smile to change his whole day.

Amy took over his books. She managed his money and did a great job. She was good at other things as well. After they had been dating nine months, she began to sleep naked beside him. At first she would only touch him, make him come, but not let herself be touched. Then she began to go down on him, and vice versa, and the sight of her so close to him, so happy with him in her mouth, drove him crazy. He asked her to marry him. She said, sure, soon, you have to get me a ring. But she would never go with him to buy one and it made him wonder.

Then he caught her with David.

Nothing to wonder about anymore.

Matt finished inflating the dinghy and attached the motor. Raising his head, he saw the bare hills of Malibu. He was already north of the stars' homes. Taking the wheel, he veered west. He had to get farther from the shore. The plane had to go down in deep water. There could be no chance of recovery. He also had to be far enough from land so his parachute could not be spotted. But there would be no moon tonight— he had already checked—and he had dyed his parachute pitch black.

Matt carried a global positioning system (GPS), which was accurate to within two hundred feet. This evening, while flying on a line between Catalina and Santa Barbara, it would help guide him back to his boat. The GPS helped him now as he aimed for a point exactly between the two locations. He ended up in an area five miles out—an ideal distance from shore. Farther out might burden the motor on his dinghy. Any closer to shore and he might be spotted.

It was eleven o'clock. The ship was equipped with a depth indicator. He was in four hundred feet of water. He had to move to a shallower spot. They were around; he had found one last time, on his trial run. The anchor attached to the ship could only reach down two hundred feet, and was questionable help. It would create drag against any local current, but it could not stop the boat from drifting. However, the anchor he had brought aboard was attached to a three-hundred-foot rope. After a few minutes of scanning the area, he found a spot where the latter anchor would catch on the sandy bottom.

Matt tossed both anchors overboard.

A minute later the boat came to a firm halt.

He set up his panel of lights. They came equipped with a timer, and would only turn on after dark. Yet he momentarily activated them—using a manual switch—to make sure they were working. They were bright, and blinked red and white—Christmas colors come early this year to call down his doomed sleigh. He hoped there was no fog tonight or low-level clouds. Either could utterly ruin his plans.

Matt took off his disguise and stowed it below.

He shoved the dinghy overboard and climbed in and started the motor. The ocean chop was not bad—he would make good time back to shore. Glancing back at the boat as he sped away, he cursed the fact that he had not brought an inflatable dummy to set up on deck with a fishing line and a hat. Now he was full of great ideas. There was always a chance another ship would cruise by and want to investigate.

He knew the beach where he wanted to come ashore, but he deliberately steered near the mainland far north of the beach—in no man's land—before turning south. He did not want suspicious eyes seeing him arriving on a dinghy from far out at sea. It was his wish to be seen as a simple fisherman. He wanted to be a nobody. He knew that when a nobody died, nobody cared.

He wondered if she would attend his memorial service.

"Amy," he said to himself. "Why?"

The beach landing was uneventful. He dragged his dinghy onto the sand and kept his head down as he stomped the air out of it. There were a handful of people sunning themselves but they would not remember him. He detached the outboard motor and hauled everything to his car.

This was his *real* car, registered to Matt Connor, a two-year-old Toyota truck that he had parked a block from the beach the previous night. He had everything in the back within twenty minutes of coming ashore. Jumping on the freeway, he headed south. But along the way he swung behind a grocery store and dumped his dinghy and motor in a large Dumpster. Stopping at a self-service car wash, he vacuumed the sand out of his truck.

He drove toward the Santa Monica Airport. He was himself again in more ways than one. He was no sailor but he was a superb pilot. He had a Cessna 172 waiting for him. It bothered him that he would not be returning the plane. He had learned to fly on the Cessna and it was as close to an idiotproof plane as had ever been built. That was both good and bad. Tonight, it would be easy to jump from, but people would wonder how such an experienced pilot as himself could have crashed such a simple plane.

At the airport, the guys at the rental agency wanted to shoot the breeze. He forced himself to socialize a few minutes. He even told a dirty joke. Did you hear about the girl who was cheating on her boyfriend and he walks in on her . . . ? They laughed, they liked him. He had worked on their office building in exchange for hours with the plane. He had put in a new bathroom, reconfigured their walls so they had twice as much useful space.

Lack of cash was the biggest weakness in his plan. It was not like he could crash in the ocean with everything in his bank account suddenly withdrawn. Talk about raising a red flag. For the last four months he had been taking cash on most jobs. Building up a nest egg that never saw the inside of a bank. He had forty-five grand saved but that was not going to last. Then again, what kind of time frame was he talking about?

Frankly, he had no idea.

They let him go. Wished him happy birthday and good luck on his scuba lessons. No one worried about him flying from Catalina to Santa Barbara in the dark. But it was not as if he could leave Catalina at night. The runway had no lights. He had to depart at sunset, or immediately after. His plan required the dark. From now until he disappeared, timing was everything.

He forced himself to concentrate as he checked out the plane. Ninety-nine percent of the time the ritual was unnecessary. Study the hull for broken rivets. Test the radio and battery supply. See if the flaps were in sync. Look at the color of the fuel. The latter was a light blue, high octane, but as Matt stared at it he saw red. His heart pounded behind his eyes.

He talked to himself as he circled the plane. He was not bringing the Cessna back. He was ditching it in the dark ocean. Amy was not coming home to him. He was going to ditch her as well—into a bottomless well of agonizing loss. It was only right that they should suffer together.

But there would be a difference in their suffering.

He would know why. She would know nothing.

But when it came down to it, he still did not know why she had left him. She had loved him, he could not have been *that* deceived. So her love had been twisted—it had been real, David's money and his baby aside. The question spun endlessly in his head.

Why?

In a way, Matt wished she could know it was he who was going to destroy her life. At least then she would know how much he still thought of her. He wondered if she ever thought about him—the single most devastating thought of all.

Matt stowed his gear aboard the four-seater plane and climbed into the cockpit. Inside his bag was his black parachute and a lightweight wet suit that covered his torso only. He planned to wear the suit when he jumped from the plane—not during his scuba instructions—in the event he missed the boat and ended up in the sea. February water was ghastly. The suit could keep him from hypothermia, make the difference between life and death.

Using the plane's foot pedals, he crept out to the runway where he was given permission to take off. Getting the Cessna airborne was a snap—student pilots did it on the first day of instruction. He merely had to align the plane with the runway and pull the throttle all the way out. When his speed reached sixty miles an hour, he eased back the yoke and the plane was airborne. Even after so many hours in the air, it always struck him as a miracle when he left the ground.

LAX and its crowded airspace usually dictated his course when he took off from the relatively small Santa Monica Airport. The flight to Catalina should have taken a mere twenty minutes, but he had to steer south of the international airport before he could even turn toward the water. The actual flight to Catalina always took him forty minutes. Greg, his scuba instructor, would be waiting for him.

Soon he was out over the ocean. The plane practically flew itself. He had a visual on Catalina. He stabilized his altitude and speed. Once again, like on the boat, he had too much idle time.

His thoughts returned to the only real vacation they had ever taken together. It had been to Bryce Canyon National Park, where he turned her on to rock climbing. Initially she resisted the sport, but when he finally got her up on a stone wall a deep inhibition broke inside and she began to laugh and couldn't stop. That afternoon they scaled several cliffs; and that night, lying naked beside her in their sleeping bag under the stars, she told him that she had never loved anyone so much as she loved him.

Just one month before he had caught her with David.

Catalina's airport was located on the far side of the island. To an inexperienced pilot the landing strip was scary. Besides being short, it ended at the edge of a cliff that dropped straight down to the water. The area was famous for its dramatic upward and downward drafts. None of that concerned Matt. He could land a plane in a snowstorm. But today he put the Cessna down with a hard thump. He saw Greg waiting for him by the gate and waved. It was past two—he was forty minutes late. Before the sun set he had to complete two dives in order to earn his PADI certificate. It would look odd if he left before he qualified. His birthday party would not be excuse enough.

Greg Pander was twenty years old and more than sure of himself. He had beach-bum good looks and Matt thought it would be safe to say the kid had already had more sex in his short life than he ever would.

But Greg was an excellent instructor. He was patient when necessary and was not easily flustered. Matt had chosen to meet with him privately rather than take a class because it allowed him to dictate their schedule. Without the diving lessons, there would be no reason for him to be on Catalina. Simply flying up the coast to see his mother would not have worked. He needed a good excuse to be far from shore when his plane crashed.

Matt left his gear locked in the plane and walked toward Greg. The hulky blond gave him a casual smile. "I was worried you wouldn't show," he said.

"I was working a job this morning in Orange County. Had to finish it to get paid."

Greg gestured to a bus they could take to the harbor. This was the second time they had met on Catalina. Diving directly off the L.A. coast was miserable. You could see your hand in front of your face and that was it. At least here they had fifty feet of visibility and beautiful kelp forests.

"Our gear is stowed at the old casino," Greg said. "We better get in the water quick. Hey, it's your birthday today, right?"

"Yeah."

"Cool. Having fun?"

"It's been an interesting day," Matt said.

They dove off the shore near the main harbor, beside the huge rocks that circled the old casino. Matt would have preferred diving from a boat but this way was quicker. With all the gear on his back he weighed a ton. Climbing down the slippery rocks was a challenge, but Greg saw it as part of the fun. He laughed when Matt slipped and almost broke his tailbone. They had on full wet suits, plus headcoverings and gloves. The water was only fifty degrees.

Matt was fit. His job kept him limber and he worked out three times a week at a gym. The endurance aspects of the dives did not trouble him. Greg had him ditch his equipment on the surface and climb back into it. They practiced buddy breathing. Greg tore his mask off underwater and had him put it back on and clear it. They went down to sixty feet and Matt had to make a slow ascent on a single breath.

The second dive was more recreational. Greg swam beside him and pointed out a variety of fish and interesting kelp formations. Matt was glad for his mask. It hid his total lack of interest.

They finished at five-fifteen, ten minutes after sunset. Greg presented him with a temporary diving certificate. The real one would come in the mail in two weeks. Matt had posed for the ID's picture on the previous trip. Greg was excited for him and Matt forced a smile and gave his instructor a thank-you hug. But Matt begged off any further celebration. He told Greg he had to get to his party. After a shower and change at the harbor, he took the bus back to the airport.

It was almost dark when he arrived. The guy on duty was already closing up.

Matt ran to the gate. "Hey, my plane's here. I'm leaving tonight."

The guy checked his watch and shook his head. "Sorry, bud. Didn't anyone tell you that this is a day-only airport?"

"I know the rules. I can leave within forty minutes of dusk. You've got to let me go. I fly all the time at night."

The guy continued to lock the gate. "It's not my decision to make."

Matt put his hand in the space between the metal bars. "Listen, it's very important I get to Santa Barbara tonight. My family's having a big party for me."

The dull-headed lug stopped. "What's the party for? Did you win something?"

"The lottery. Hey, why don't I slip you twenty bucks and you let me go and no one will be any wiser? What do you say?"

The guy wasn't a complete fool, he took the money. Climbing into his plane and fastening his seat belts, Matt swung onto the narrow runway. The wind was up—he had not noticed it while in the water. As he pulled back on the throttle and sailed off the edge of the cliff, he felt a sharp downward yank. His nose lowered dangerously and his wheels came within ten feet of skimming the water. It would have been ironic, he thought, after all his preparation, to have crashed and died immediately after leaving the island.

Amy would never have known what she missed.

He gained altitude but kept his speed low. It was not completely dark and the night was his shield. He wished he could circle and stall for time but feared other planes in the area might notice. Low-lying clouds crept in from the west. He could barely see Los Angeles off to his right. Nevertheless, he was familiar with the route and confident in his instruments. He did not have to see the coast to keep on course. Yet he could not jump out of the plane unless he could see the boat. He prayed everything went smoothly and yet he hoped he failed. The truth was, he was a mess. He felt so lonely he wanted to cry.

Like that night, he would never forget that night.

When he saw them kissing on that side street in Westwood, he thought he was mistaken. He drove around the block and parked. He told himself it was not Amy. Yet the girl had looked like Amy and was dressed like Amy. Still, he almost stayed where he was. But of course that wasn't true. He got out and *ran* around the corner.

They were still kissing.

So cold, his guts right then.

He walked up and they parted and looked over. Amy quickly lowered her head while David regarded him quizzically. Matt did not know what to say. But he knew he had finally met the infamous David. The guy was plump, light haired, and well dressed. He looked like a used car salesman. Matt smelled alcohol on both of them.

"Who are you?" David asked. His voice was soft and fruity.

"I'm her boyfriend. Who are you?"

The guy smiled. "I'm her other boyfriend. Who are you, really?"

"I'm her boyfriend." Matt glanced at his girlfriend. "Isn't that right, Amy?"

She would not look at them. David did a double take.

"Are you serious?" he asked.

"Yes. I'm Matt Connor." He turned to Amy. "Tell him who I am."

She turned and ran. She could move when she wanted. He chased after her and it took him half a block to catch her. She shook him off roughly.

"Leave me alone!" she cried.

"Leave you alone? Amy, stop, we have to talk. What is going on here? You have to talk to me!"

She stopped. David walked toward them slowly, still over a hundred yards away. Amy stared at the ground.

"That's David," she whispered.

"What's he doing here? When did he get here?"

She looked like death. "It's sort of a recent development."

"What are you doing with him? Why were you kissing him?"

She shook her head. "It's not like it looks."

"Have you been sleeping with him?"

She would not raise her head. She would not answer.

Matt glared down the block at David. The guy moved like a zombie. "Answer me!" he yelled at her.

No response. He tried to grab her arm again and she shook him off. Taking a step back, he swore at her. "Then I'm going to talk to him. I have to know what's going on here."

She looked at him with such bitterness. "You would do that to me, huh? Now I know what kind of man you are."

He was incredulous. "What kind of man I am? What about you? You're the one who's always talking about honor and honesty. Now I know who you are."

"You're no better. You show up here and say these things and try to hurt me." She wept. "You're hurting me!"

None of it was real. He tried to hold her. He hated her right then but at the same time he had never realized how much he loved her. David was close. She struggled in his embrace.

"Let me go!" she screamed.

"Amy! We have to get out of here! We have to talk!"

She cried as she fought him. "Leave me alone! I want to go home!"

"Amy! Please?"

She broke free and ran away. He chased after her for a moment and then gave up. She went around the block and vanished. David walked up at his side.

"What a bitch," he muttered casually.

Matt staggered to the curb and sat down. He vomited in the gutter.

David stayed with him, he wanted to talk. Matt realized later that he was only interested in gathering information to hold over Amy's head. David was upset but also pleased in a strange way. He wanted to know the details of their relationship. Matt told him the whole story. For being the "other guy," David was remarkably self-assured. He was also a snake. Matt saw that much.

While they spoke, David got three calls on his cell phone. He told Matt they were business related and didn't answer them. Matt was so dazed he did not understand that Amy was calling David because she was worried what the night had done to *their* relationship. She was not worried about her relationship with her boyfriend. She was just trying to arrange a place to meet David afterward.

Finally David left. Matt stood and staggered back to his car. He was in absolute shock but he was aware enough to realize he was looking at a torturous future. Amy was his life. He had thought of little else for the last two years. She could not have done this, it was not happening.

He drove to her house and was surprised to find her car missing. He assumed she'd be home. She had said she wanted to go home. She would not have gone to David's house, for godsakes. He knocked on the door and her father, a retired schoolteacher, answered in his pajamas. Bent with age but nevertheless wise from years of working with rowdy kids, he saw something was wrong and quickly invited Matt inside. They sat on the couch and Matt told him what had happened. Amy's father had always loved Matt deeply, but there was nothing in the universe more precious to him than his daughter. He kept shaking his head as Matt spoke.

"She wouldn't have done this," he said. "She would never have betrayed you this way. I know my daughter, that is not her, no."

Matt shook his head sadly. "None of us knew her."

He waited an hour for Amy to show up but she did not. Finally it sunk in that she was with David. He said good night to her father and went home and lay on the floor and wept. He kept hoping she would knock on the door to beg his forgiveness. His brain had short-circuited on an endlessly repeating loop:

This is not happening. This cannot be happening.

At two in the morning, she called.

"Hello?" he said.

"Hi," she said, cold.

"Where are you?"

"It doesn't matter."

"It does matter. Where are you?"

"I'm not going to tell you," she said.

"I have to see you. We have to talk."

"I'm not going to talk to you."

He could not believe her insolent tone.

"You're not going to talk to me? After what you've done? You should be on your knees begging me to take you back. How dare you! You cheated on me!"

"Look what you did to me! You talked to him because you wanted to hurt me. You wanted to convince him that I was really your girlfriend when I'm not. You were always trying to convince me that he was a jerk and I never believed you."

"Wait a second. What are you saying? You're my girlfriend. You've been my girlfriend for two years."

"I have not! Did I ever have sexual intercourse with you? Did I?"

Matt got a real bad feeling on top of a mountain of bad feelings. "Why are you saying such things? Is he there? Are you trying to get me to say I'm not your boyfriend?"

"He's not here."

"Liar. He's listening right now. Or else you're taping this conversation so you can play it for him later. You're trying to put words in my mouth so you can swear to him you were never in an intimate relationship with me. Where are you?"

She hung up. He hit *69 and got a number in Brentwood. There was no answer. He dialed a dozen times but apparently they had gone to bed.

Them in bed together. The image was a curse he was never to be free of again. How many nights after that night did he want to take a gun and blow that picture right out of his brain?

She did not call the next day. What did it matter? He was never going to see her again as long as he lived. Nevertheless, the day after that, at five in the morning, he drove to her house, saw her car was parked out front. Using a side gate to get in the backyard, he stepped to the sliding glass door attached to her bedroom. Peering inside, he saw her roll over in bed and sit up. She had on the pink pajamas he had bought her the previous Christmas. She let him inside and they sat on her bed together and she wept.

"I'm sorry, Matt. I'm so sorry."

She told him her story. She had been with David six years before she met him and even when it had ended it had not really ended. He knew that, she said. He knew she was still obsessing on the guy. Actually, Matt did not know that but he let it pass.

She had seen David four times in the last two years, for a week each time. Matt remembered the occasions. They were supposed to be the times she had gone to visit her relatives in Colombia. She had called during those trips, every night, to see how he was doing. Matt asked if she had slept with David during each trip. Stupid question. Yes, she said. But each time she had sworn to herself she wasn't going back to David. She had cared for him, Matt. She had wanted to make it work with him.

Had cared. *Had* wanted to make it work.

It was hard to miss her choice of tense.

"How long has he been here this time?" he asked.

"A month. He called—I told him I wouldn't see him. But he kept calling and I finally gave in."

The other trips were a while ago. Maybe he could forget, maybe he could forgive. "Have you slept with him in the last month?" he asked.

She took a long time to answer. "Yes."

His turn to cry. He had never wept in front of someone as an adult. He honestly felt like he would die. She kept squeezing his hand and saying she was sorry but somehow it did not help.

"Are you going to see him again?" he asked pitifully.

She hesitated. "I'm not sure. After what happened the other night, he doesn't trust me anymore."

"So you're over him? It's done?"

She looked away. "I'm still conflicted."

"What does that mean?"

"I feel like I have to get him out of my system if I'm going to be with you." Taking his hands, she stared him straight in the eye. Her sorrow somehow intensified her beauty. But there was something wrong with the picture.

She was not asking him to take her back.

"I really wanted to be with you," she said. "But you know how I've kept my walls up. I think it was because of David. I have to resolve this once and for all if I'm to have any peace."

"But you just said he doesn't want to see you again?"

"I said I wasn't sure."

He pleaded. "But we're happy together. We've had so much love together. You can't throw it all away. Please, Amy."

"I have to get over this. It's tearing me apart."

He was going to be sick. "Do you love him?"

She sighed. "I don't know."

"Do you love me?"

"Yes. I love you a great deal."

"Then how can you do this to me?"

She spoke with feeling. "I wanted to spare you the pain. I knew if you knew he was in town you would never be able to rest. You would always be wondering where I was. I thought that I could finish it with David and come back to you a hundred percent." She ran her hand through his hair. "You're so good. You're so perfect. You've taught me what real love is."

The words sounded good. There was just one problem.

She was choosing David over him.

That night, he sat in his car outside her house for several hours. Until she finally appeared and drove over to David's house. Now Matt knew where the guy lived. David was a swell guy. He had already forgiven her. At least enough that he was able to fuck her again. She spent the night with him, and the next four nights as well. She never did call Matt. She had told him she would only contact him when she was ready to come back a hundred percent.

A month later Matt read about their wedding in the *Los Angeles Times*.

He stalked them and discovered she was pregnant. And from the size of her, he knew she had gotten pregnant while she had been dating him. That same day—it was a very special day in many ways—he began to formulate his plan. The pieces just fell into his head. God could have e-mailed him the blueprint. The plan was intricate but simple. Pain in exchange for pain. And no Matt Connor left alive to take the blame.

Seven months of planning. Now he flew toward his destiny.

Only he could not clearly see where he was going.

The darkness grew swiftly and he no longer felt the need to stall. But the clouds got worse the farther north he went. He decreased his altitude until he was flying a thousand feet above the water. He could not stay at such a height. He had to leap from at least two thousand feet to have any chance of maneuvering toward the boat. He had hoped to be a mile high. But even if he had an hour in the air with a parachute, it would do him no good if there was no boat beneath him.

He forced himself to focus on his GPS. The coordinates could not lie. But not even a zealot such as himself would leap from a plane without seeing the boat lights. He did not want to die. Certainly, he did not want to drown all because of a girl he hated.

He spoke to the Ventura tower, told them everything was A-OK. They asked why he was flying so low, and he explained about the clouds. They wished him Godspeed. But how would the experts explain why he suddenly increased his altitude just before he crashed? They would have their theories. Fortunately, he would not have to be there to answer their questions. Nor would the wreckage of his plane be located in such deep water. The Coast Guard would send out a boat to make official the paperwork, nothing more. No one would expect to find his body.

But he had to increase his height! His instruments told him he should already be able to see the flashing lights. Where was that damn boat? The ocean was a dark gray soup. He scanned with his binoculars and saw nothing. This was insane, the boat could not have drifted from where he had anchored it!

Then he understood. He still had a thin layer of cloud beneath him. What he had thought was water was in reality mist. He had to drop lower, down to five hundred feet. Now he played a dangerous game. If he got confused even slightly, he would crash into the water and die.

At five hundred feet he saw the lights. Two miles directly in front of him. The boat had indeed drifted slightly north. It had probably gotten caught in an exceptionally powerful current, and his spare anchor must have lost its grip on the ocean floor.

Immediately Matt banked upward. He would lose sight of the boat above the clouds. He would have to estimate when to jump. Jesus, he had not put on his wet suit yet! He had forgotten all about it, and now there was no time.

He reached into his bag and pulled out his parachute and put it on, yanking the waist strap tight. From the same bag he took out a steel yardstick. He needed it to prop open the door while he climbed out. His Cessna had not been designed for skydivers. Luckily, the wings were above the cockpit, not below. They would not obstruct his path when he bailed out. He hoped the yardstick didn't snap in his face.

His speed was eighty knots, ninety miles an hour. He pulled back on the throttle, strove for five thousand feet. Yet already he could see he wouldn't reach half that height before he flew over his target. The clouds wiped away his last sight of the boat but he was certain he was directly above it.

Now or never. He could not circle back. No single act would be more suspicious to those in the towers who studied his course on their screens. At least his descending and climbing could be explained away as simple confusion or panic.

He cracked his door and shoved it open with his left hand. The wind slapped his face like a cold fist. Bringing the yardstick out, he wedged it between the top of the door and the side of his seat. The door remained open but the precarious situation could not last.

He had the nose up, now he had to bring it down hard. He wanted to give the impression that he had become completely disorientated—could not tell up from down. That he had fallen into the infamous graveyard spin that was the bane of all inexperienced pilots who had lost all visual clues. The problem with the Cessna 172 was that it naturally resisted such a spin and righted itself. Unless he forced the plane into the water, it would continue happily along for several more miles. It might even veer east and crash on land. Then how would a medical examiner explain his missing body?

Matt thrust the yoke flush with the control board. As the plane sank he pressed the throttle down. His altitude was twenty-two hundred feet and dropping quick. Now, even had he wanted, he could not have saved the plane. He was falling fast into a black cauldron. He had been falling since he had caught Amy with David.

Matt climbed out the door and leapt from the plane.

CHAPTER TWO

Four months before FBI Agent Kelly Fienman was called in on the James Techer case, and thirty-six hours after Matt Connor jumped from his plane, Kelly sat in a parked car in the Hollywood Hills with her partner, FBI Agent Charles Fitzsimmons. For twenty hours they had eaten doughnuts and drank coffee and hardly left the vehicle. They were both giddy with exhaustion and caffeine rushes, but they were having fun. Besides being each other's favorite company, they were hoping for a big reward from their surveillance.

Down the hill from where they sat was four hundred thousand dollars in small bills. It was stuffed in a briefcase in a garbage can, waiting to be picked up by the kidnappers who had swiped ten-year-old Buddy Smith. The money had been dropped the previous day by Buddy's father. Along with a dozen other agents who staked the garbage can, Kelly and Charlie believed that someone would soon show up to claim it.

"Could they wait a week?" Kelly asked as she studied the can through a pair of binoculars. A mile distant, the loot was stashed behind a 7-Eleven that stood on Sunset Boulevard between a strip joint and a pharmacy. "Could they leave it altogether?"

"They could do anything. They could have killed the kid already."

Kelly lowered the binoculars and glanced over. "But you don't think so?"

"No." Charlie straightened his lanky form and sipped his coffee. It was a cool February afternoon but the sun was bright through the windows. Charlie had stripped down to his T-shirt. She wore shorts and a tank top. They both needed showers and deodorant in the worst way. Charlie added, "When Vicki spoke to that bastard last Tuesday, he tried hard to sound like a murderer, but he was a weenie."

Vicki Bane was the head of their L.A. office, bitch and boss in one tight-assed package. Twenty years ago, after a Christmas party, she and Charlie had gotten drunk and slept together. They had been in their thirties, both between marriages. Later, Charlie swore he had been more afraid screwing Vicki than the time she'd shot a bank robber who was holding a gun to his head.

Vicki was a crack shot. She had missed Charlie by two inches and poked out the guy's eye. And she knew how to talk to kidnappers. At that instant she was farther down the hill; it would not have surprised either of them if she was sitting inside the garbage can, chewing tobacco.

"What does a murderer sound like?" Kelly asked.

"They can be anybody."

"But you just said—"

Charlie raised his hand. "The guy was small time, had no idea how to negotiate. He should have asked for at least two million."

Buddy Smith's parents were big-time sitcom producers. They had won six Emmys in ten years. In industry-speak they had so much clout they just had to make a "call." It didn't matter what the call was about, if the person on the other end of the line did not make sure that they got what they wanted, then no one in town would ever call the fool again. And since Buddy was the Smith's only child, if he so much as got scratched, never mind died, then for the next decade, every FBI character on network TV would look like a total asshole.

In other words, it was a high-profile case.

The kid had been snatched while his mother was having her hair done on Melrose Avenue. He had been playing jacks on the sidewalk outside the beauty parlor. Kelly had interviewed the parents and found them to be two of the most despicable people she had ever met. Grief had not softened their hearts. They gave orders; they expected to be obeyed. They did not listen either. While delivering the ransom, the father had insisted on carrying a revolver. Like he was going to shoot whoever came along for the money. However, from his pictures, Buddy looked like a sweetheart. Kelly desperately wanted him back.

"The amount is odd," Kelly agreed.

"They might view it as a down payment."

"You think they'd risk that stupid game?"

"They might." Charlie searched the doughnut box. He liked the chocolate ones. She preferred glazed. Charlie said that was because he was black and she was white. He added, "I don't think they're very bright."

Kelly raised her binoculars again. "I hate waiting."

"Then why did you become an FBI agent?"

"I wanted to be a hero."

A casual comment that said a lot.

How did a woman with a doctorate in mythology become an FBI agent?

Nine years ago she had been a twenty-five-year-old student at Princeton in dire need of a theme for her Ph.D. dissertation. She did not want to go the usual route and write about how one character in a book related to another character, or how when one author said *this* he was subconsciously contradicting another author who believed he was saying *that*. It was all so much academic bullshit.

She did not want to write a thesis at all. She considered them a waste of time. No one ever read them. How did they contribute to society? But she desperately wanted her doctorate because at that time she believed she wanted to teach. She remembered the night she was sitting alone in her apartment—not married at the time, not even looking—and came across a program on David Koresh and Waco.

The documentary was of mediocre quality; she saw it as a piece of poorly edited anti-FBI propaganda. Ironically, she did not focus on the parts on the FBI. It was David Koresh himself that fascinated her and the messiah quality he endeavored to project. She found his blend of sexual manipulation and strict religious persuasion curious. Most of all, she was struck by how he saw himself as a hero. A hero fighting a villainous society that had no regard for a higher truth.

The next day she visited the bookstore and picked up a half dozen tomes on cults and their leaders. Mostly they concentrated on the usual list of suspects: Charles Manson, Jim Jones, and so on. Once again she was impressed by how these people saw themselves as heroes. Not an earthshaking revelation, to be sure, but it piqued her interest. Koresh, Manson, and Jones were never described as serial killers. They had caused pain and death to their victims but they were labeled cult leaders. That was their designated title and no one seemed to want to debate the issue.

But how did they relate to serial killers?

The next day she was back at the bookstore and bought a dozen paperbacks on serial killers. She was a fast reader—it took her three days to devour the material. At the end of that time she was struck by what she considered a revelation. No matter how the FBI or the police sought to describe the motivation of a serial killer, they invariably came back to a single theme: these single white intelligent males committed murder to "get off."

Sexually.

It was admittedly a crude interpretation. The famed FBI profiler, John Douglas, had spent years developing the sacred trinity that described such people: manipulation, domination, control. Yet those qualities—from the killer's point of view—were still ultimately aimed at achieving sexual satisfaction.

But Kelly thought the core assumption too simplistic.

She felt serial killers and cult leaders were directly related.

Most *successful* serial killers were voracious readers. As a prelude to their killing sprees, they almost invariably developed a bizarre sense of what was good, what was evil. Few serial killers, when caught, would acknowledge they had done wrong.

For that reason, Kelly felt it was their distorted outlook of good and evil that gave them the strength to commit their cruel deeds, rather than the need for sexual release.

At the same time, she did not dismiss the system John Douglas and other profilers at Quantico had developed to evaluate killers. She merely thought the messiah component a missing piece of the puzzle. Her theory could be boiled down to a single sentence: serial killers felt they were acting righteously when they murdered.

It was *just* a theory. Maybe she was wrong.

But how to translate the idea into a mythology thesis?

One that her department heads would buy.

She had another insight. It came to her while watching Martin Scorsese's *Taxi Driver*. The main character, played by Robert De Niro, was a veteran living on the edge. After being rebuffed by the woman he loves, he decides to kill the presidential candidate she works for—either to impress her or devastate her. Kelly was never completely sure of his motivation, and it didn't matter anyway. Toward the end of the film, the guy fails to kill the candidate, and out of frustration he goes on a killing spree in a tough part of town, in which he slays a number of pimps and drug dealers. Because he is shot and wounded in the process, in the final scenes he is recognized by New York City as a major hero.

The point? The line between hero and villain was paper thin.

Her thesis? Serial killers were not so different than the major villains in literature that had just missed becoming heroes. Certainly most of these people—real or imagined—started out *wanting* to be heroes. The killers simply made a few wrong turns along the way.

Her theory was outrageous, it had a thousand holes in it, and yet as soon as she started researching and writing it, she saw she could run with it. The examples in mythology were numberless. In fact, it was hard to find a hero who had not almost fucked up his life, or the lives of those close to him. One could go as far back as Homer. The old bard had instinctively understood that Ulysses needed several years to cool off before he could return home. Kelly had great fun writing a section that analyzed his desire to steer his men near the bone-strewn shores of the Sirens' inhospitable island. She posed the simple question in her thesis: what kind of sadistic nut would do such a thing?

She wrote the line half in jest but, hey, she figured, the fossilized academics above her needed a jolt just to know they were still alive. Her dissertation was entitled "Heroes and Villains," and no one was more surprised than she when a mere month after handing in her paper, Princeton granted her a Ph.D.

So the story might have ended there. Three years later she was married, living in New York City with dashing Tony and little Anna, and teaching creative writing and mythology at NYU. She would have liked to say she was happy. On her list of things to accomplish in life, she had already crossed off the top five.

Yet Kelly was bored out of her skull.

She hated teaching: grading papers, the students who didn't care what she talked about, the university politics. Also, although she didn't like to admit it in a room filled with those of a right-wing persuasion, being mom twenty-four hours a day was tedious. A quarter of that time would have been perfect. In reality, she did love her daughter. And Tony was great; she faked her orgasms less than 50 percent of the time, which she knew was a huge positive when it came to most marriages, never mind what Dr. Phil thought.

It was just that she never seemed to have any fun anymore.

That was who and where she was when *the* call came.

John Douglas's offspring had read her thesis. They thought she was loose with her conclusions but they were nevertheless intrigued. Apparently they had been running into a few too many messiah-driven killers lately. The bastards had come out of the woodwork after the millennium. The bright boys at the FBI wanted to know if she would like to be a part-time consultant. Someone they could call when it came to cases where the murderers were fans of Shakespeare, Cervantes, or Socrates. They invited her to Quantico to talk. Kelly said sure, why not. She had only seen the place in the movies.

She left Tony and Anna at home. That in itself might have been a mistake.

They took her into an office buried deep inside the academy and threw a test file at her about a serial killer who was going after handsome males between the ages of twenty and thirty. He was chopping them into tiny pieces and sinking their remains in rivers. He was also leaving behind what looked like Egyptian hieroglyphics written in blood at the places where he cut up his victims. The FBI boys wanted to know where the guy was coming from.

Obviously, she thought, they knew nothing about mythology.

She explained the myths surrounding Isis, her husband Osiris, and their evil half brother Set. The latter had cut Osiris into tiny pieces and taken him to the underworld. The reason the killer dumped the remains in a river, she said, was because it symbolized to him the River Styx, which was associated with the underworld in Egyptian mythology. In other words, she thought the guy saw himself as Set. Plus there were a few Egyptian texts that hinted that Set had a crush on Isis. Chances were that all the victims had known a certain woman that the killer was in turn obsessed with. Find that woman and they would find the killer.

The FBI boys clapped. They had been humoring her. They had solved the case a month earlier by making the same Isis-Osiris-Set connection. But they admitted that it had taken them five months, and she had done it in five minutes.

They made a generous financial offer, considering how few hours they were asking of her. They explained they would call her from time to time and ask her input. Now and then she would have to visit Quantico. Occasionally she might need to travel to the crime scene. However, they added, they had several private jets that would be at her disposal, should the situation arise. They smiled and kept pouring it on. Kelly was so overwhelmed she asked if she could stroll the grounds and consider their offer.

A typical summer Virginia afternoon—high clouds, heavy humidity. The walk around the academy changed her life forever. She saw young men and women working out, shooting guns, practicing karate, apprehending fake bank robbers, and all around having fun. If I'm going to work for the FBI, she thought, I shouldn't be a consultant. I should be *one* of them.

Kelly wanted to carry a badge, a gun, and be tough.

But just on the side, she told herself. She could still be a consultant and get paid the big bucks. When she returned to the profiler's office, she told them she would accept their offer if they would first train her as a field agent.

Her demand did not bother them. They saw the logic in it. She would be better able to advise them if she understood their methods. They threw her into the class that was just starting. NYU and Tony and Anna loved that. Her husband had to stay in New York with his job. At first she tried caring for her daughter in a small apartment outside Quantico, but the hours were brutal. Tony eventually had to take Anna back home. Kelly found the separation devastating, and liberating. She called home twice a day to assuage her guilt. But she did not fool herself. She was being a *bad* mother.

She had always been athletic and enjoyed the physical aspects of the training. The classrooms were a challenge because the material was so different from what she was used to. The legal texts were particularly grueling to memorize. They reminded her of the days she had spent writing her thesis. Nevertheless, Kelly embraced the training and graduated near the top of her class.

The profiler's office waited. Then fate intervened. Her husband got a great job offer. The hottest ad agency in Los Angeles wanted him. Fat salary and stock options. Plus an old college pal to work beside. He told her he could not say no. How could she say no to him? She had put him through hell indulging her own fantasy. She inquired if the FBI would be adverse to her practicing the things they had taught her for a short time. In other words, could she work as a field agent out of the L.A. office?

They said okay, but just for a few months.

Funny how, if one waited, months eventually turned into years. Six to be exact.

Quantico still called from back East, with an occasional consultant question. Yet they did so less frequently. Kelly assumed they had found another expert to replace her.

Now, it was hard to believe, she was thirty-four years old. Her face was pretty but intelligent. She honestly tried her best to put her mind before her looks. Since the day she had graduated from Quantico, she had made a decision to limit her flirting. People often saw her blue-eyed stare as intimidating, which she thought was amazing because she was naturally shy. She only got chatty when she tried to hide the fact.

She wore her blond hair long, with bangs. Her mouth might have been her best feature. It was not large or sensual but she knew how to use it; and let's not be modest, in more ways than one.

Charlie, her first and only partner, said she was a catch. He liked tall, sexy women. A grizzled fifty-six-year-old street-smart veteran, he didn't bother to hide his crush on her. But she never felt uncomfortable around him. He was black as oil but more precious than diamonds.

Charlie's cheeks were rough from adolescent acne, his smile sad from having seen what the real world could dish out. Yet he had learned what was probably the main lesson anyone in life could grasp. He always came back to caring for others when it would have been easy to turn bitter. It was true he had lost the love of his life to drugs several years ago—and had not dated another woman since—and yet, every day, he had a smile for practically everyone.

Thin but wiry, Charlie still played plenty of one-on-one basketball in the toughest neighborhoods. At six-three, he had once bet her a hundred bucks he could still dunk a basketball. And although she'd had to help him with his crutches and a sprained ankle the following month, she'd admired the effort. If she had to sit in a sweaty Camry for days on end, he was the one man she wanted by her side.

They were both having fun. Certainly, she was not bored anymore. Someone approached the trash can.

"Charlie!" she gasped.

Charlie had his own binoculars and was already on the radio to Vicki. He gave a description: thirty-year-old white male, short brown hair, dirty mustache, denim shirt and pants. Oh, and the motherfucker has opened the garbage can and grabbed the cash. Kelly watched as their suspect strolled to the front of the 7-Eleven and climbed in a red Corolla—not exactly a getaway car. Not even pausing to look around, the guy pulled out of the parking lot onto Sunset Boulevard and headed east. Vicki spoke sharply over the radio.

"We follow patiently," she said. "Keller in front, Tavor behind. The rest hang loose, stay back. Charlie, what are you going to do?" She had to ask. Everyone knew Charlie did what he wanted.

"I'm a middle of the road boy," Charlie said as he started the car. "I won't be too close or too far."

"Just don't rear-end the guy," Ms. Bane said. "He's got to be a pigeon."

Kelly agreed. The guy might not even realize what he had retrieved. There was an excellent chance he did not know a kidnapping was involved. The pigeon could be a patsy.

Kelly and Charlie roared down the road toward Sunset. Charlie drove like a fiend. They ran the light at the bottom of the hill, and three minutes later they were only forty yards behind the briefcase. It had a tracking device hidden inside but no one depended on it to remain in place or come near Buddy. Kelly studied their suspect through the traffic.

"He's listening to music," she said.

"What station?" Charlie asked.

"He's not scared. He can't be part of the inner circle."

Charlie nodded, pulled out his 9 mm Sig, cocked it. "It would probably be a mistake to kill him."

Kelly checked her own Glock. "Hope the guy knows where he's going."

"Ten to one he doesn't. They're going to call him."

"Cell?" Kelly asked.

"Even these fools—they're not that dumb. He'll stop somewhere.

They'll have a schedule. They'll ask if he's being followed." Charlie stopped.

"What is it?"

Charlie rubbed his three-day-old growth. He had not slept since Buddy had been kidnapped. An agent who cared, they didn't make enough of them. "You'll see."

"Tell me."

"Patience."

"Fuck you," she said.

Charlie grinned. "It's just an idea. Let's see what happens."

The pigeon took Sunset to Fairfax and turned south. The guy continued to act cool. He must be a complete moron. What else could be in the suitcase except money? But Kelly had yet to see him open it.

The guy stopped at a McDonald's and went inside. He left the briefcase in the car. Kelly assumed Charlie would simply drive by—like the other agents—but he pulled into the parking lot. Their radio beeped and Charlie turned it off.

"What are you doing?" she hissed.

"I'm hungry." Charlie holstered his gun and put on his coat over his T-shirt. He looked more like a poster boy for the homeless than an FBI agent. "Let's get a Big Mac."

She had to scramble to keep up. The pigeon was already in line and ordering. He kept looking at the phone near the restrooms. They got in the adjacent line and Charlie talked about *their* kids. Jesus, she was so nervous and he was trying to bust her up. She had left her gun in the car. Her top would not cover it.

The three of them got burgers and fries at the same time. The guy took a seat close to the phone. They sat next to him. It was a crowded lunch hour, lots of kids. The guy was hungry, Charlie was hungry, she had an ulcer. Charlie nodded to the guy and he grinned back through a mouthful of discount dentistry. Charlie kept talking about their kids: Bart and Penelope. Seemed they were straight-A students and natural born athletes. Only in middle grade school and already Harvard was sending letters.

The phone rang and the guy jumped on it.

"Hi there?" he said, sounding like a hick from a pig farm talking to deaf grandparents. "Yeah, everything's cool. No problem. Yeah, I got it in the car. What? No, the car is locked. Huh, sorry, I won't do that again. What? Yeah, I know where that is. Yeah, okay, got ya."

The guy returned to his burger. Almost done, he turned to Charlie and asked where Century and Sepulveda Boulevard were. Charlie gave him directions.

"You want to go south to the ten and take it west to the four-oh-five. Take that south and after about five miles you'll see Century. Get off and go east."

The guy nodded. "East. That's left, huh?"

"Yeah. Got to meet someone?"

"Yeah. Is there a Denny's there, at that corner?"

"Sure is," Charlie said. "They have great chocolate cake."

The guy was interested. "I'll have to try it."

Shit like this does not happen in real life, Kelly thought.

They let the guy go. They got in their own car and reactivated the radio. Vicki Bane gave them an earful. But she shut up long enough to hear about Denny's.

"You're not going in there, Charlie," she warned.

"The guy won't mind," Charlie protested. "He might need more directions. Look, we already have a bond, he trusts me."

"Kelly?"

She took the radio. "Yes, boss?"

"Your partner is losing it. Keep him in the car."

"Can we watch?" she asked.

"No closer than a block." Vicki cut the connection. Kelly glanced over.

"We would never call our kids Bart and Penelope," she said. Her daughter's full name was Anna Marie. She took after her father with her dark hair and gray eyes. Kelly wondered how they were doing without her.

"We can call them Buckwheat and Audrey if you'd let me bring them to life." He was only teasing. He respected marriage vows; and there was a lot to respect about him.

She laughed. "I've never heard that pickup line used before."

They drove to Century and Sepulveda and waited at a respectable distance. The joint already swarmed with FBI. They could only enjoy the show through binoculars and an occasional remark on the radio. Both of them were annoyed they could not go inside and take the guys down. But she was still high as a kite. She prayed Buddy was all right.

Their hick must have gotten lost. They got there before him. Eventually he showed. He was inside all of five minutes when he was approached by a tree trunk that weighed three hundred pounds. From what they could make out over the radio, the guy looked mean. He had beady eyes, was bull-necked, and even had bad breath.

Fortunately, he was as dumb as his help. His pick-up plan was no plan at all. He just took the briefcase from the hick, and Ms. Bane gave the word. Half the agents in the L.A. office moved in at once. Charlie started the car and raced toward the Denny's. As they got out of the car, Vicki had both guys facedown in the parking lot and cuffed. She read them their rights, but kept her gun to the fat guy's head.

"Where's Buddy?" she asked. Vicki was all skin and bones, a scarecrow on speed; intense eyes, sharp nails, black belt in karate. When the guy did not answer, Vicki cocked her pistol and shoved it in the guy's ear, added in a deadly tone, "I've been on a diet all my life. You have no idea how much I hate fat people. Where's the boy?"

It should not have worked. Nothing they had done that day should have worked. But the walrus sang like a bird. Buddy was at his apartment in Orange County watching TV and eating ice cream. The fat guy would show them the way if his cooperation could get him a deal with the D.A. Sure, Vicki promised him a deal. When the hick from the McDonald's got up he stared at Charlie and Kelly and asked what they were doing there.

Buddy was back home and safe within ninety minutes.

Vicki thanked Charlie and Kelly for a job well done. However, the boy's parents did not call. Casually brushing off the slight, Charlie said, "Assholes cannot help being assholes. It is their nature."

Kelly, Charlie, and several other agents from the L.A. office went to celebrate at the Beverly Hills Hotel bar: margaritas, nuts, and plenty of drunken company. By the time Kelly remembered her family, it was after ten. Charlie offered to give her a ride home—he drove significantly more carefully when he was over the legal limit.

When she walked into the house she knew she was in trouble.

Her husband and daughter would not look at her. They were planted in front of the TV in the family room, and she could not get their attention. Clearly, they had agreed upon the strategy ahead of time. It took a mere two seconds for her soaring spirits to hit the floor. Covering her burning eyes, she headed for the bedroom, took a hot shower, and went straight to bed. To her surprise, she fell right asleep.

When she awoke, Tony was sitting on the edge of the bed. She searched for his hand in the dark and squeezed it. "Sorry," she whispered.

He held her hand but his touch was cold. "Two days, and you didn't call."

"I told you, I was on a stakeout."

"And how was I to know you hadn't died on this stakeout?"

She sat up and hugged him. "I have no excuse. I love you. I won't do it again."

He stared at her in the poor light. His face was more noble than handsome. He kept his dark hair short, his gray eyes focused. His eyes carried so many memories for her. She used to think she could see herself through them. But these days his eyes were often distant and her own sense of self shrunk as the distance between them widened.

Tony was a thin book. He could be found in the reference section of a library, a studious soul, not given to emotional outbursts, yet not blasé about human feelings; just careful with what he said and showed. His angular face never tanned. He was good looking, though, especially when he smiled, which she used to beg him to do more often. Normally he wore thick black glasses that matched his hair color. He was smarter than she. His brains were the reason all the big ad agencies wanted him, and also one of the reasons she had said yes when he popped the big question. Tony was a master at shaping public opinion. He could make O.J. look like a Disney character.

She had met him while jogging in Central Park during the time she was working on her thesis. Talk about heroes and villains. He had run over her on his horse—yes, a real live horse—and she had swooned at his feet like a damsel in distress.

Actually, when he stopped to help her up, she had threatened to sue him. But he somehow managed to buy her a milk shake, and they ended up talking for hours, and three months later they were married. When asked by friends why she got hitched so fast, she just said she was in love. And she thought she was, it was absolutely wonderful to fall asleep every night in Tony's arms.

But he had wed a scholar, or so he thought. He didn't want a wife and the mother of his child out all night chasing bad guys.

His stare disintegrated into a sigh and he turned away.

"I don't want this to happen again. Ever," he said.

"What exactly is *this*?"

He did not hesitate. "I want you to quit."

She was shocked. "Are you crazy? I can't quit."

He let go of her hand. "Then we can't do this."

"This? What the fuck is *this*?"

"Our marriage."

She had not imagined it had gone so far, so low. "I see," she whispered.

Tony stood and went to the window. They had a lovely view of the coast, and presently the early morning gray was turning into what was probably going to be another warm day.

She had studied mythology and not psychology while in school, but she knew enough to understand her fairy tale marriage was groaning under the weight of reality. Perhaps it was her fault. She kept trying to reverse the prime archetype of most myths. She was the *woman* but she wanted to rescue people. Yet he still saw her as the beautiful blond princess he had saved from the monsters who roamed Central Park. He stood with his back to her, as if teetering on a cliff, and she instinctively knew that a burst of honesty right then could be deadly.

"Why is all this so important to you?" he asked.

"We got Buddy back today."

"I saw it on the news. You didn't answer my question."

"Isn't that answer enough?" she demanded.

"No. Someone else could have saved Buddy."

"Maybe. Maybe not. You don't know that."

"I'll tell you what I do know." He turned and gestured to the wall of books that lined their bedroom wall. "This was your love. This was the woman I loved."

"I outgrew it."

"The same way you outgrew me?"

"I didn't say that." She added, "I don't want to quit. Don't force me to. Please?"

"Who is forcing whom here? Tell me, Kelly. I really want to know."

She did not have a good answer, and so she gave none. He took a shower and left the house without breakfast. Kelly waited until her daughter woke up and fed her eggs and toast and drove her to school. Anna had dropped the silent treatment, but they didn't exactly have a lively conversation either.

Kelly was shocked to learn her daughter was going to be in a play that Friday evening. Anna was to play the lead role. Kelly wondered if it was time to stop and reassess. She could not imagine a life without the two of them.

■

THE FOLLOWING morning, at the FBI office in Westwood, Vicki immediately took her into a back room and introduced her to Clay Slate, whom Kelly already knew as the heir apparent to the famed profiler— John Douglas. Slate had been one of the people who called her down to Quantico years ago; though he had been the only one in the room that day who had not clapped when she had solved the Set serial file. A short bald man, he had shifty dark eyes that made him look like a killer. Word had it that he only had patience for people whose IQs exceeded one-fifty. Everyone else had to get to their point within five seconds. He was a power in the FBI, and she could not imagine what he wanted with her.

Vicki left the room. They sat across a wide wooden table from each other. Was she going to be forced to transfer back to Quantico against her wishes? Slate immediately dispelled the idea.

"We want your thoughts on a case that has been developing over the last four months," he said. "It's a private matter. Everything you see and hear in this room is to be kept in the strictest confidence. When you know all the facts, you will understand why."

"Did you fly in specifically to speak to me about this case?"

An arrogant question. He was quick to cut her down to size, but praised her as well. "No." He nodded to the newspaper lying at the end of the table. "That was good work on the Buddy Smith kidnapping. Vicki told me what you and Charlie did in the McDonald's."

"Thank you, sir."

"The family has yet to thank us," he said as he glanced at the large plasma screen at the end of the room. He had a DVD in his hand, and seemed to study her as he held it. Kelly brushed her long hair aside and leaned forward.

"I'd be interested to hear about this case," she said. "Should I take notes?"

"Not yet."

Slate gave her scant warning what to expect, except that the DVD contained a recording of five women being killed. But as he lowered the curtains, he referred to the murderer as the "Acid Man." Uneasiness gripped her chest. The tape obviously disturbed Slate and he was a tough sonofabitch.

What Kelly saw next changed her forever.

The DVD was of surprisingly high quality. The camera had obviously been set up out of sight on a low table. It was aimed at a bedroom, more specifically a bed. The furnishings were expensive but sparse. There was a book and a lamp on a table beside the bed. The lamp was turned on. Kelly figured it was a rental home.

A man and a woman walked in. The video had been edited—the man's face was blocked out but not the woman's. The technique was crude but effective. The man had a percolating oval where his face was supposed to be. The woman had long dark hair and wore a black evening gown. Her diamond necklace glittered. His tux fit like a glove. The audio was clear but low.

The guy was probably British, yet his accent was not as clear as it should have been; it was possibly faked. The woman was from the East Coast; Kelly was thinking Boston. They entered the field of view kissing, and when they parted, they were both panting. The woman especially. She was an exquisitely preserved forty-five, and had been to the finest plastic surgeons.

"I can't stay," she said.

He fingered her necklace. "We don't need long."

"What time is it?"

"Ten."

"Liar. It's close to eleven." She glanced at the bed. "You always so neat?"

"I never make a mess," he said. He chuckled and his accent faltered. He had clearly spent time in England but Kelly doubted he had grown up there. His hand slipped down the front of the woman's dress. He touched her right breast and she moaned.

They kissed more; the seduction swung into high gear. But who seduced whom? Although she could not see his face, Kelly knew the guy must be attractive. The woman sighed as he unzipped her dress and pressed her hand to his bulging crotch. She dropped to her knees and undid his zipper. Huge cock—they would not need too long a lineup to identify him. Now naked, the woman sucked him for a minute while the guy groaned and whispered her name over and over again, "Teri . . . Teri . . . Teri."

She removed the rest of his clothes. She wanted to turn off the light. He liked to watch. They moved onto the bed. It was their first time together. The woman was not certain what he liked. But he knew what she wanted. He was down between her legs so long he had to take a deep breath upon surfacing. She came three or four times, and it was just foreplay. He picked up a condom beside the book, and she helped him put it on.

They had intercourse: above, below, and from behind. The guy never came; the woman never stopped coming. When they were done they lay in bed for several minutes not speaking. Just holding each other—he really did seem to like her. But then he stood and vanished from view, and when he returned he was holding a brown paper bag. The woman watched as he set it on the chest of drawers and removed two pairs of handcuffs and a thick roll of duct tape.

"Would you like a glass of milk?" he asked.

Teri sat up quick. "Mike?"

He slugged her in the jaw. She crumpled like a doll but did not lose consciousness. As she struggled to rise, he sat behind her on the bed and unrolled the tape and encircled her head, closing off her mouth. His technique was practiced; he moved like an actor in a play that was regularly performed. He circled her head three times and dropped the tape on the floor and reached for the cuffs. He still had on his condom and he was still hard.

He cuffed her wrists and ankles before she could recover from the initial blow. There was rope in the brown bag. He threaded it through the cuffs and tied it to the bedposts. Now she began to struggle but she was at a severe disadvantage. Kelly noted the calculated force of his first hit. He had only wanted her dazed. He wanted her awake, to watch, to feel . . .

But what?

He removed a metal vial from the bag and stood at the foot of the bed as if to pronounce judgment over his prey. He had put on black gloves. The vial appeared to be made of an alloy of some type; it held perhaps sixteen ounces. Kelly remembered Slate's earlier comment and shuddered. The man's physique was superb. He stood suddenly tall and victorious. Kelly thought him close to an orgasm. He held onto his accent but it was clearly affected.

"You're a married woman," he said. "You took a vow of fidelity to your husband and you have broken that vow. If he could see you now—and he will see you—it would destroy him." The man touched his chest and there was pain in his voice. "There would be a hole in his heart. A hole that would never heal. And why? Just because you wanted to have sex with another man? Just because you thought he would not find out? You're a temptress and a harlot. The fires of Pompeii could not cleanse your flesh." He raised the vial and slowly unscrewed the cap. "It's right that you should die."

The man—his name could not be Mike—climbed onto the bed and knelt beside her. He had tied her like a pro. She could move an inch, no more. Her eyes bulged as he tilted the vial above her chest. The duct tape muted her screams. But the horror in her face—Kelly could not bear to watch. Nor could she look away. A portion of her felt trapped in the same room as the woman.

The vial held acid.

As it dripped onto Teri's chest, the skin ignited in a frenzy of choking smoke and peeling flesh. But that was only a preview of things to come because it was no ordinary acid and he was no ordinary man. The potency of the liquid must have been formulated to push the upper limits of chemical corrosiveness. With a shallow hole in Teri's breastbone already dug, the man continued pouring, without wasting a drop.

The acid bored deeper. The depth of the expanding hole allowed him to empty the last of the vial. He stood back to admire his handwork, or perhaps to give the camera a better view. Teri could not escape into death or shock. The burning liquid worked swiftly but Kelly felt as if the woman perished over days. As the acid ate through deeper layers of tissue, the smoke transformed into a red-stained mist. It hung over the bed like a Satanic fog pumped from below. Teri lost control of her bladder and urine drenched the sheets. She continued to thrash but she was losing strength. Kelly knew what kind of end was inevitable for the woman, but when it came it was still a shock.

The acid ate into the woman's heart. A thick spurt of blood squeezed from her chest and splattered the bed. Three times her heart beat, three times the sheets were soaked with gore. Finally Teri gave a convulsed heave and lay still.

The man stared down at her for a long time. He must have come; he had lost his erection. Slowly, he turned and reached for the video camera. The picture went dead.

Kelly lowered her head and tried to hide her tears. Slate gave her a break. He turned off the screen. But five murders you say. She had four more to watch.

Kelly sat for a few minutes before she gestured for Slate to continue. The next four murders were almost exact copies of the first. The women were pretty, and every one was rich. They wanted sex and he obliged them with great skill. But the location of each killing varied. Two occurred during the day. Kelly thought she heard the ocean in the background of one. The women called the man different names: Jerry, Frank, Bob, Charles. They loved his cock. They all died with holes in their hearts.

His speeches were almost identical as well. Kelly noted slight differences. She needed to study a transcript of each of his words.

Slate turned off the screen and opened the curtains. Kelly took a few deep breaths and sought to compose herself. Slate left the room for a moment and returned with a pen and notepad for her. He had his own stack of notes. He sat down across from her and his expression was grim.

"Tough way to die," he said.

She shook her head. "Jesus Christ."

"These killings occurred in different parts of the country: California, New York, Florida, Texas. The last in Colorado. The press has reported each murder, but does not know they are the product of a single serial killer. They don't know what links the victims, nor any other specifics. The victims—as you've probably surmised—were the wives of prominent citizens. Two were married to CEOs of major companies. One was the wife of an East Coast judge. In each case the husband was the first to learn about the murder of his wife."

Kelly nodded. "He was sent a DVD."

"Federal Express. It's difficult to imagine anything more cruel. The husbands learned in the space of minutes that their wives were unfaithful, and that they were dead. Here's another twist. We haven't recovered a single body. Furthermore, we have been unable to identify even one murder location. We have assumed the states I just mentioned because the women were from those states. They were not gone long when they were first reported missing."

"How long after they disappeared did the husbands receive the DVDs?"

"Usually only two days."

"Incredible." She paused. "Tell me more."

"That's just it, we have nothing more. We're dealing with a brilliant mind. His level of execution is flawless. He leaves no evidence. Yet he mocks us. He gives us a ringside seat to his dirty work." Slate paused. "There's an irony here."

"He feels he's doing the husbands a favor?"

"Yes. He's on a mission. He knows he's hurting the husbands and at the same time he thinks he's freeing them of these sinful women. He considers the short-term pain he inflicts on them the lesser of two evils."

"So you assume," Kelly said.

"You disagree?"

"No. I just don't want to jump to any conclusions." Kelly paused. "Why is confidentiality so crucial?"

"Because each of the husbands in question has been severely ridiculed."

"And because they are important men and don't like to be ridiculed?"

"Yes."

"What about the FBI's level of embarrassment?"

"We don't need the entire country on our backs." Slate raised his hand when she went to protest. "I understand, we lose an important weapon when we eliminate public input. But we feel this guy is too smart to be caught by a random tip."

Many of the most brilliant killers in history had been caught by such tips.

"Really?" she said, a faint note of sarcasm in her voice.

Slate's tone hardened. "Are you suggesting that I'm lying?"

"I just wonder if you're rationalizing. Or is it politics?"

"All of the above, Agent Fienman. You're bold to ask. Perhaps you've spent too much time in the company of Charles Fitzsimmons and picked up his habits. In either case, the choice is not yours or mine to make."

"Yes, sir. I apologize."

"No problem. You wonder why I want your input?"

"Yes."

"Did you notice the book on the nightstand in two of the videos?"

"Yes."

"An enhanced copy of the DVDs reveals that it is a copy of Joseph Campbell's *The Hero's Journey*. You're familiar with it?"

"I've studied Campbell's work extensively."

"We see it as a lead."

"The book alone? It's not much of one." She paused. "Sorry to be so blunt, sir."

"It appears to be an essential part of your personality. No, we see the book in reference to his other comments. You must have noticed that he speaks like someone with a background in literature."

Kelly frowned. "He did make a few references, but they were rather vague. I would need to study the transcripts of his conversations with the women."

He tossed her a manila envelope. "These are not to leave this office."

"Understood. What's your profile on the man?"

"I won't go into detail. I don't want to overly influence your opinion. He's obviously a white male between the ages of thirty-five and forty-five. He's exceptionally handsome. Because he can travel at ease and rent impressive accommodations, he's independently wealthy. He does not have a nine-to-five job. He was probably married in the past and was betrayed by his wife. The chances are that his wife is dead. He's not from England but he's spent time there. He's extremely intelligent and disciplined. He's not specifically trying to impress us. He's trying to scare all women everywhere. He's probably upset his exploits have not been made public."

"You call him the Acid Man?"

"Yes."

"I take it you have not heard from him?" she asked.

"No. What do you think of our assessment? You may speak frankly."

Kelly shrugged. "It's not very useful. I assume you have more."

Slate stood. "Not much more. I want you to work on this matter all day today. Review the video as many times as you feel necessary. I'll call you at home this evening. Be prepared to share your thoughts with me."

She stood. "I appreciate the chance to help."

Slate nodded and left the room. He had not told her the whole truth. The FBI had interviewed the friends and families of the victims and constructed some kind of pattern in regards to when and where the wives met with the stranger. Five prominent women could not see a mysterious man without somebody noticing. The FBI might also have scraps of his clothes—perhaps a fingernail or skin tissue. Slate did not want to share everything with her because he did not want her to independently solve the case. He had not even told her his theories on the source of the acid. He wanted her input, but in a narrow vein. He did not take her seriously and that annoyed her. Also, he did not fully trust her and that bothered her even more.

"Politics," she muttered.

She had to look on the bright side. It was a hell of an interesting case, and she had her foot in the door. Charlie would have died for a piece of the action. She felt frustrated she couldn't share it with him.

"Tony," she whispered, sitting back down. She realized she did not immediately think of her husband when it came to sharing—the very concept of doing things together. There was truth in what he was trying to tell her. Tonight, she would go home early and make him and Anna a wonderful dinner. Both loved roast turkey and mashed potatoes. She could stop at the grocery store on the way back, pick up a bottle of wine. It had been a long time since they had all sat together and watched TV. Of course, she hated TV but that didn't matter. They could always rent a movie.

Kelly studied the transcripts for each of the five murders and highlighted the Acid Man's remarks that directly or indirectly referenced literature or history. There were only a few. She wrote them down on her notepad. Fuck Slate, she was taking these notes home.

> 1. "You are a temptress and a harlot. The fires of Pompeii could not cleanse your flesh."
> 2. "You are the worst of all traitors, the Judas of females. No amount of suffering would atone for your sins."
> 3. "Juliet accidentally betrayed her husband by stabbing herself in the heart. But your betrayal was deliberate. It is right your heart should burst."
> 4. "You are Guinevere. You don't care that Camelot is ruined."

She was supposed to develop a profile with this? None of his references were obscure. *The Last Days of Pompeii*, the Bible, *Romeo and Juliet*, *King Arthur and the Round Table*—everyone knew these stories. It was not as if the Acid Man pretended to have a Ph.D.

Why did he ask Teri if she wanted a glass of milk?

He had asked two of the others the same thing.

Kelly watched the DVD six more times. Despite their duct-taped mouths, she merely had to close her eyes to imagine the victim's screams. The pain increased with each viewing. It was worse that she could not hear the victim's final cries. They all died without being given a chance to curse their tormentor.

Kelly tried to relate the four books mentioned. Each was filled with heroes and villains. But of what use were her academic theories in the face of such a monster? There was betrayal in each story. Yet the Juliet reference was curious because Juliet was the classic devotee. She had died because she could not bear to live without her husband. True, the Acid Man did not condemn her, but he did mention her name in the context of his rant about betrayal. Kelly found the inconsistency odd, especially considering his high intelligence.

How could the FBI have failed to locate a single murder site? No one was that thorough, and they had the videos to identify the places. But it was possible Slate had not lied on that point. The Acid Man kept the furnishings sparse, the clues to a minimum. He might have changed the furniture completely from when he had rented the houses. Kelly worked on the assumption they were rentals. Except for their austerity, none of the rooms resembled each other.

How would such a monster dispose of the bodies? He clearly did not want them displayed as trophies, which was a major break from most serial killers. She wondered if he was drawn to return to the places of murder. That would be classic behavior, yet she doubted that was the case with him. His mission was what mattered. He had to cleanse the world of cheating wives. Missions were also classic. He was a deviant but he was not off the chart.

Except when it came to his effectiveness.

Kelly checked the time; it was noon. She had struggled for three hours without results. Lunchtime, and no appetite to drive her out of the building. Where was Charlie? Probably checking out the local McDonald's.

She went outside anyway, took a long walk, ended up buying a chicken sandwich and a Coke from a deli. Sitting on a bench not far from the UCLA campus, she picked up a discarded newspaper and noticed an article on a plane crash in the ocean off Ventura. There was a picture of a handsome young man, Matt Connor. No body found, no reason for the accident. She did not bother reading the piece. It would only depress her.

Yet there was something about his face that made her hang on to the paper. Matt was one of those rare people whose gaze was more focused internally than externally. She suspected he had been exceptionally intelligent. There was intensity in his eyes, strength in his brow. He looked both haunted and innocent. Had a part of him known he would die young? He had presence—his ghost seemed to stare out at her through the photograph.

Perhaps a spirit touched her.

An eerie sensation of isolation swept over her, as sudden as it was unexpected. She was not sure what triggered it. Could she be experiencing a delayed reaction to the murders? The whole matter threw her off center. Even before Slate had shown her the videos, she had felt an almost supernatural foreboding. She was not normally keen on New Age intuitions, but this feeling was powerful—overlaid with fear for her family.

Where was the connection? She sought to understand its source.

The loves in her life were definitely in conflict: family and career. But was Tony telling her more than he was saying? Was he about to do something that would destroy their home? Was there another woman?

"No. I'm destroying it," she said aloud. Her passion was her job. Why, already she was obsessed with finding the Acid Man, probably a normal reaction after seeing the pain he had caused. However, focusing on the idea of hunting him brought the same fear of losing Tony and Anna.

"Why?" she asked aloud. How were the two fears connected?

The Acid Man killed women and she was killing her family. If she was to save her family, she had to leave her job. That was obvious. But to get out of her job, she had to find the Acid Man. That was not so obvious. Where did that idea come from? Because he was such a bad guy and she was such a dedicated agent that she could not rest until he was caught? She didn't buy it; the world was filled with murderers, as well as capable FBI agents.

Yet she wanted the asshole. Damnit, she wanted to bring him down!

Did she still have the same passion for Tony? To go after the Acid Man, she would probably have to leave L.A. Then Tony might leave her. She felt so confused.

She heard the screams of the women. Screams they had never uttered.

Once more she stared at Matt Connor's photo. Died on his birthday. His face had started her mind on this bizarre direction. That and the

Acid Man's DVD. She stood and tossed the paper in a garbage can. Her mind was a mess. She probably needed a vacation.

But she had just gotten an idea.

When she got back to the office, she watched the video of the five murders again, the transcript propped up beside her on the table. Just before he killed his fourth victim, the transcript quoted the Acid Man as saying:

"My . . . my . . . not happy with the smell. You are like . . . just wanted to fuck, you stinking whore. You don't care what it would do to your husband."

The audio was weak at that point. With victim number four the room was large and the camera was far from the bed. It might have been laziness on her part but Kelly had not stopped to question the accuracy of the transcripts. It was obvious the Acid Man was about to say something about himself—the *my*—and then had changed his mind. Since he was raving anyway, that was a logical conclusion.

Logical, but not necessarily true. He had brought up smell and had called the woman a "stinking whore." Granted, the sentences were incomplete because of the quality of the sound. Still, his use of the word "smell" did not fit in the context of even the half-completed sentence. Kelly wondered if what he had said was in fact:

"Mai Mai was not happy with the smell. You are like her, you just wanted to fuck . . ."

Mai Mai was a character in an ancient Chinese tale. The story was not known outside of China. The only reason Kelly was familiar with it was because she'd tutored a graduate student from China who'd had the story in an untranslated hardcover she had brought from home. A simple fable, it nevertheless carried a disturbing message.

One that was pertinent to the Acid Man's mission.

Kelly recalled she had tried to convince Karen Min—the graduate student—to translate the myth and post it on the Internet. That way it could receive exposure in the West, even if it was never published in book form. The last time she had talked to Karen, the young woman had been working on the project.

Then she remembered, five years ago, receiving an e-mail with an attachment from Karen. She had filed it away on her home computer without opening it. Her computer at work was able to access her home equipment. A few minutes later she had the file up on her screen. A short story entitled "Mai Mai and the Man" was buried halfway through the attachment. Kelly read it with interest.

■

AT A young age, Mai Mai married Telso, the fisherman. At first she was happy to live with him by the ocean, away from her overbearing family. Telso was often gone for many days in a row on fishing expeditions, and she had freedom to wander the coast and collect flowers, and to work on her paintings and sculptures. Mai Mai was an exceptional artist and her husband encouraged her to develop her talents.

But Mai Mai was restless by nature. She resented the times her husband was away. She would get lonely for him. However, she strongly disliked his smell. She was married to a fisherman, but she hated the odor and taste of fish. After being on the boat for weeks at a time, it was difficult for Telso to get the smell off no matter how much he bathed. A year into the marriage, Mai Mai insisted Telso sleep in a separate room, which hurt her husband very much. As time went on, they grew further apart, and she refused to even cook the fish he caught.

Mai Mai's loneliness deepened. Once, when Telso was gone for a whole month, she worked on a sculpture of a perfect man. A fantasy husband, who never left her and who had nothing to do with the sea. She cast him from clay not far from her bedroom window, and when he was finished she painted and dressed him so that he looked almost alive. That was her secret wish, of course, that a mysterious man would come for her and sweep her into another life filled with excitement and magic.

The night she finished her statue there was a terrible storm, with much lightning and thunder. People in the nearby village said it was the worst storm in the last sixty years. Mai Mai spent the entire night with her heart pounding in her chest, cursing her husband for being away when she was scared. Not once did she stop to worry how his ship was faring on the high seas.

The next morning the sun burst bright and clear. Mai Mai was hurt to discover that the storm had washed away her sculpture. Even the clothes she had draped over her clay-man were gone. Her heart broke;

the statue had been her finest feat. She wondered if she would ever have the strength and vision to create another such work.

That afternoon, while hiking the cliffs that overlooked the sea, she saw a man. As she approached, she noticed he was alone, staring over the water. He looked familiar to her, although she knew they had never met before. He did not speak until she said hello. Then he turned and smiled, a wide white smile, and in that moment she felt her heart swell with love. He was younger and more handsome than her husband. Best of all he did not smell like fish. She asked his name and he laughed softly and said that he was a mystery man and did not have a name. But he called her by her own name and she wondered who had told him about her.

She spent the day with the stranger. They walked along the water, picked flowers, and talked about art and music. The stranger was unlike Telso in every way. He was well educated and sophisticated. He also appeared full of joy and good humor. His voice was a delight. Occasionally, when she closed her eyes to listen to him, she imagined he spoke inside her mind.

As the day drew to a close she realized she was hopelessly in love. Still, she did not know his name. He said goodbye just before the sun set but promised to return the next morning. She watched as he walked along the shore and disappeared behind a cliff.

The following week, he came every day, at dawn, and they spent many enjoyable hours together. But each night he left, and Mai Mai would feel a deep loss. Of course, she was a married woman. She knew she could not possibly make love to the stranger. But there was part of her willing to throw away her marriage—and her family honor—just to be with him. The next evening she vowed she would force him to stay with her. Her husband was not expected back for a week.

Early the next day, she saw him where they had first met, high on the rocky cliff overlooking the sea. Once more they spent the day together. Mai Mai had never felt so much love. Not only did she want to make love to the stranger, she wanted to run away with him. As the day wore on and the sun drew near the horizon, she confided in him her wish, and he saw how serious she was, and for the first time he lost his carefree manner.

"Are you sure of this, Mai Mai? If you come with me there can be no going back."

"I am sure. I want to be with you forever."

"But what of your husband? He is a good man."

She shook her head. "He means nothing to me now."

"But he loves you. He would do anything for you."

"I don't care. I only care about you."

The stranger smiled then, but it was a sad smile. "Then if you wish to stay with me, you have to come down with me to the water. We must swim out away from the shore."

She was confused. "But why?"

"You will see."

The stranger led her to the sand and told her to remove all her clothes. Shy but excited, she stripped down alongside the stranger. His body was so perfect; she did not mind that he insisted they jump into the cold water. Later, she thought, she would warm him beside a roaring fire. The sun touched the horizon as he took her hand and led her into the sea.

They swam out a long way from shore. Eventually Mai Mai began to tire, and she told the stranger she wanted to go back. She was surprised when he shook his head. Night had come, it was dark, and the cold had sunk deep into her flesh.

"But I warned you," he said. "There is no going back."

She felt fear but forced a laugh. "What are you talking about? We can't stay out here all night. We're not fish."

It was then the stranger's face began to melt. His nose and ears fell away, like chunks of unheated clay left to dissolve in water. Even the hand that held her own fingers seemed to disintegrate. But she was able to hear him as he spoke, even though his mouth had vanished and had been replaced by silver scales. At last she understood that he was speaking only in her mind; that he had never really used his mouth to form words.

"But I am a fish. And now you will be a fish too, Mai Mai. Because you have betrayed the love of a good husband, you have become what you hate. For the rest of your life you will swim these cold waters, alone, and never again walk on land."

Mai Mai wept in terror. "How is this possible? Why did you come to me?"

"You brought me here. You created me."

She felt her limbs dissolving, her face changing into a slippery mass.

"But I want to go home! I want to be with my husband!"

"It is too late."

Mai Mai looked over and the stranger was gone. In his place was a huge fish. Her own body felt changed and foreign. She was too scared to look at what she had become.

"But I didn't know!" she cried. "You didn't even smell like a fish!"

"It has always been this way, Mai Mai. In the same way a fish cannot smell itself, a cheating wife never sees herself as unfaithful."

Those were their last words together. A wave came and they were pulled under. And there Mai Mai stayed, cold and lost and alone, for the remainder of her life.

■

"A FISH cannot smell itself," Kelly whispered to herself. Betrayal and revenge, the Acid Man's message—both present in the tale. It could not be a coincidence. The Acid Man must be referring to Mai Mai. But how did he find out about the story? Was he as Slate suspected—a meticulous killer with a vast literary background? To think, just two hours ago she had mocked the Acid Man's quotes as too general. Kelly had to remind herself that Slate was no dummy.

Plus there was another reference the Acid Man had made. It had been right in front of her, and yet she had failed to see it. In each killing, he had spoken of how the women—with their infidelities—were causing holes in their husband's hearts. Then he had turned around and burned a hole in *their* hearts. Why did he choose that particular form of execution? Obviously, there was an excellent chance his heart had been broken by a woman, but he was not fixated on just any kind of hole. For example, he never stabbed a woman in the heart.

No, he used acid to make the holes.

There was an ancient story about that as well. The source was on the tip of her tongue but she could not place it and it frustrated her mightily. But one of her teachers at Princeton, Professor McKinley, would know it. He was the one who had told her about the story, that much she remembered. She had his number at home—she could call him tonight. And later, Slate had said he would call her. Hopefully he would appreciate how important these clues were. The Acid Man almost certainly had an academic background. That fact alone would significantly narrow the FBI's search.

Kelly decided to leave work early. She still wanted to make that special dinner for her family and she was tired. There had been the pressure of the stakeout followed by the emotional strain at home. She needed quiet time to recover. She hoped Tony would give her that. She could not remember the last time they'd had sex. Their first year of marriage it had been every day.

Before going to the market, she swung by home to check on Anna. They had a wonderful nanny from El Salvador who helped care for their daughter. However, Kelly found neither Anna nor her nanny at the house. She assumed they had gone out. Maybe Anna was at a rehearsal for her play. Kelly still could not get over the fact that she had not known about her daughter's upcoming performance.

There was a message from Tony, however. He said he would be working late and would not be home until after ten. So much for the big dinner.

Kelly called Professor McKinley. He was delighted to hear from her, although his hearing was poor. At eighty-four, the university had finally forced him into retirement two years ago. His mind was still as precise as an encyclopedia, though. She went to explain the story she was thinking of and he interrupted her in midsentence.

" 'The Tears of Rati,' " he said. "It's from the Vedas, the Arundha Purana."

"I don't remember that Purana."

"It hasn't been translated into English. But Maya Press prints it, I believe. I doubt there are a thousand copies in all of India. It's one of those ancient texts that's largely a compilation of other works."

"Is 'The Tears of Rati' in any other book?"

"Not that I'm aware of. What's your interest in the story?"

"I need a copy of it. Did it have something in it about a hole in the heart? A burnt hole?"

"Yes. The Purana itself hasn't been translated, but I personally wrote down Rati's tale in English." He paused. "Do you want me to read it to you?"

"It might be better to fax it," she said.

"I'm sorry, I don't keep one of those contraptions at my house."

She hoped she had not offended him. He had used to read to groups of them in class. Grandfather surrounded by his eager grandchildren. It had been a love of his. He was a natural born storyteller.

"I would love for you to read it to me," she said sweetly.

He chuckled. He always had a twinkle in his eye; now she heard it in his voice. "This has something to do with FBI work?" he asked, curious.

"You would be amazed."

He left for a minute to find the story. When he returned he warned that he might have to interrupt and clarify a few parts, but he would try to stay out of the way as much as possible. Not to worry, she told him. Sitting back in her chair, she closed her eyes and listened.

■

"RATI LIVED in ancient India. She was the daughter of a rich nobleman and very pretty. When it was time for her to marry, she had dozens of would-be suitors pining for her love, but there were only two young men that she cared for: Vindhu and Hara.

"Vindhu was educated and kind. His family did not have the riches Rati's clan did, but he came from an honorable line of Brahmins. Hara was a member of the warrior caste, a Keshatria, like Rati. Now you know that ordinarily castes marry within caste but in that age it was not unusual for a Brahmin and Keshatria to wed. Even today a union of those two castes is not that odd.

"Hara was a true warrior in many ways, the opposite of Vindhu. Hot-tempered and passionate, he appealed to the dark side of Rati's nature. Theirs might have been the first love triangle in all of literature. Rati loved Vindhu more but was constantly drawn to Hara. She was not above torturing the two men, pitting one against the other. That was hard on both, and they ended up hating each other, and maybe her a little as well.

"But in the end Rati made a decision, choosing Hara over Vindhu, which broke Vindhu's heart. Because all along she had told Vindhu he was the one she truly loved.

"The wedding day came and Rati and Hara were joined as man and wife. At first they lived happily together and time passed. But fiery by nature, Hara grew impatient with Rati when she did not conceive a child. He began to abuse her, not physically, but emotionally and verbally. Rati was no saint, however; she dished out her own share of insults. The marriage began to crumble, but there was no possibility of divorce. Rati kept thinking of Vindhu, how kind and loving he had always been, and she came to regret her decision. She even went so far as to seek him out, to talk about her problems, and to enjoy a few hours in his company.

"One thing led to another. Even though Vindhu was a highly moral man, he loved Rati too much, and when she offered herself to him, he could not resist, and they became lovers. Not long afterward she discovered she was pregnant. Unfortunately, she had no idea who the child belonged to. For his part, Hara had recently taken a secret lover and she too became pregnant. The triangle took on an added dimension.

"Hara did not suspect the relationship between Rati and Vindhu. In that time, it was unheard of for a wife to cheat on her husband, although the reverse was as common as in any other time. Hara was ecstatic that Rati was going to have a baby. Maybe it would be a male child, he thought, and he would at last have an heir. But he had to worry about his lover's baby. He was not sure what to do about that.

"Close to the time when Rati was supposed to give birth, she went to see Vindhu. Her timing was poor. She thought Hara was going to be out late, but he returned home early and followed her to Vindhu's house. He saw them kissing and came to realize that they had been lovers for some time. But he did not do or say anything right away. First he wanted to see if their child looked like him or Vindhu. He still wanted an heir even though he no longer wanted his wife. He decided to keep his wrath in check until Rati gave birth, but it was a great struggle for him.

"Rati and Hara's mistress had their babies on the same day, two male children. Hara was in a quandary. Rati's child could be his or it could be Vindhu's—he simply could not tell. But his lover's baby was clearly his. He saw this the hour they were born, and he came to a terrible decision. While both women were recovering in nearby parts of the city, he switched the babies in their cribs. Then he smothered Rati's baby in such a way that it looked like the child had died in its sleep. Naturally, his lover was beset with grief when she recovered enough to hold the dead infant. He consoled her as best he could before returning home to his wife. Both labors had been difficult. Neither woman had had a chance to get a good look at their children when they had been born.

"Months passed and Rati took care of her son but she did not feel any love for him. Once again, in her melancholy state, she turned to Vindhu for comfort. By this time Hara was in the habit of stalking her. Seeing them together enraged him and he probably would have killed his wife right then except he needed her to nurse and care for his son. But his rage could not be kept hidden long and one night when he had been drinking, he bragged to her about what he had done. He did not think for a moment she would do anything to harm his son. She had cared for him since he had been born. She acted like she loved him.

"But the moment Hara passed out from drink she took the baby and drowned it in a fountain in back of the house. She left the body floating in the water. Now she was in trouble. There was capital punishment back then, even for a woman. Fleeing to Vindhu's house, she explained what she had done and begged him to help her escape to another part of India. His love for her had blinded him; he agreed to go with her. He wanted to leave immediately, but she insisted on going home—knowing that Hara was unconscious—and collect what gold and jewels she could sell on the road.

"That turned out to be a devastating mistake. Hara had already awakened and found his dead son. When Rati crept inside, he cursed her and reached for his sword. But before he could cut off her head she cursed him in turn. He had killed her child, why should she not kill his? Their marriage had turned into a nightmare. Yet in a sense they still cared for each other. Certainly they were still very attached to each other. In that instant they shared the same pain. Hara felt the sword fall from his hand as he started to cry. Rati wept as well, and to both their surprise, she reached out and gripped his tearstained hands and pressed them to her heart. They had been about to kill each other and now they were embracing.

"But the bitterness had not vanished. The tears had only given them a brief respite. Not even that, because as their tears touched and mingled together, their mutual karma of hatred and betrayal also merged, and the tears began to bite. Because Rati was shorter, and Hara's tears were falling on her, she received the brunt of their sting.

"Something transformed those tears into a deadly poison. They not only stung, they started to burn. Rati was touching her chest when this began and the moisture of the tears stuck on her skin above her heart. She could not get the scalding liquid off, and her flesh began to peel away. She screamed in agony. Hara could do nothing but stare in shock.

"The tears ate into Rati like liquid fire. A hole formed in her chest, so deep her heart ruptured and the blood gushed out and she died. In the space of hours Hara had lost his son and his wife. Out of mind with grief, he picked up his sword and fell on it. Only later that night did Vindhu arrive. He never did figure out what had happened. He died not knowing, many years later. He died still loving Rati. It was said the karma of the three was so entwined that they would have to take a hundred births together to resolve it."

■

PROFESSOR MCKINLEY paused and waited. "Are you there, Kelly?"

"*Her heart ruptured and the blood gushed out and she died.*"

"Yes," she whispered. In that moment she knew for an absolute fact that the Acid Man had read "The Tears of Rati." Even psychopathic serial killers did not come up with such inventive ways to murder people. The specific stories meant everything to him. And clearly he was knowledgeable about mythology.

"Does it help you?" Professor McKinley asked.

She had to take a breath. "Yes. Do you have the number for Maya Press?"

"No. But I can get it for you if it's important."

"Please. Have you heard of the ancient Chinese fable about Mai Mai?"

"No. But Professor Jagger is the expert when it comes to Chinese literature."

"Do you have his number? I would like to call him."

"I'll have to get that for you as well. Can I call you back tomorrow?"

"Yes. Any time is good. If I'm not here, just leave the number."

He wanted to know more but she politely put him off. The story had deeply shaken her. She had to see who had ordered both books in the last ten years. It was possible the Acid Man could be easily caught. Yet she knew India and China—she had visited both countries in her twenties. Chances were the publishers had not kept perfect records. She would have to fly there herself to check their files.

She checked the Internet for "The Tears of Rati." No listing.

Her daughter came home at six and they went out for pizza. Anna acted happy to have her mother all to herself. She talked excitedly about her play: *The Last Survivors*—an end-of-the world scenario where kids ruled.

"Why is it fun to have all the adults gone?" Kelly asked.

"Because then you can do whatever you want," Anna said matter-of-factly. Her daughter was her only oasis in what was turning out to be a barren love life. To hear her voice soothed Kelly. She noticed Anna's long dark hair had begun to lighten. Between the ages of four and five, she had grown six inches straight up—into a stick figure minus a touch of glue. Her wit was a tad sarcastic for her age, but she cried at tender moments in books and movies. Kelly did not have to wonder where she had gotten both qualities.

"But if there were no adults around, there would be anarchy," Kelly said.

"What is *anarchy*?"

"What you see on TV. Tell me more about your role?"

"I'm the tribal slut."

Kelly choked on her pizza. "What?"

"That is what Peter says I am. He's the tribal leader."

"What exactly do you do in this play?"

"I act bitchy and have fun."

Kelly enjoyed the evening with her daughter but she continued to be distracted by thoughts of the Acid Man and Tony's late hours. God, what if he was having an affair? She did not think she could bear that.

When they returned home, there was a message from Slate. He wanted her to call. Best to get it over with. He answered on his cell—sounded like he was at the airport. He wanted to know what she had learned.

"Nothing," she said. The word just popped out of her mouth before she realized what was brewing behind it. The Acid Man had made a mistake. *She* could find him. *She* could bring him down. Why share such a big catch with Slate? He wouldn't understand her insights anyway.

Slate was not disappointed. It was obvious he hadn't hoped for much from her. He let her go with a few general questions and a reminder to keep her mouth shut. "Sorry I couldn't be more helpful," she told him.

Kelly was in bed when Tony came home at two in the morning. He undressed in the dark, thinking she was asleep. She had been staring at the ceiling for hours.

"Were you really at work?" she asked as he slipped under the sheets.

He hesitated. "Does it matter?"

"Where were you?"

"I was not at work."

She felt the pain of a hole in her heart. "Anything else you want to say?"

"No. Is there anything you want to say?"

"About quitting the FBI?"

"Yes."

Her voice betrayed no emotion. Nor was there any room for it inside. Her pain went beyond reason. The hole had drained her dry. She turned away and shut her eyes.

"I'll be flying to the Far East tomorrow," she said. "I'll be gone five days."

"Just like that?"

"Yeah." She bit her lower lip and tasted blood. "What's her name?"

He sighed. "It doesn't matter."

■

THE NEXT morning found Kelly on a Lufthansa flight to Madras via Frankfurt. She sat in business class—she had used Tony's frequent flyer miles to buy the ticket. Phone calls and faxes to Maya Press and Kola Press had not gained her the desired information. But both publishers assured her that they would be happy to receive her. They sounded kind of excited to be getting a visit from an FBI agent.

Kelly slept overnight in Frankfurt, in the Sheraton next to the airport, and boarded an early flight to India. Her loneliness was a weight she could hardly bear. She was losing Tony—she might have already lost him. After what he had said, anyone would know he was having an affair. But it was not like him. He was too honorable; he was still her hero. Of course any other wife would have stayed home and tried to save the marriage. But she was driven by something she could not understand. She worried it was connected to a need to self-destruct. Why else was she going after the Acid Man alone?

Madras stank of burnt cow dung and the cows themselves. She arrived late at night, and a gang of Indians fought to help her with one small bag. The humidity was as thick as molasses.

Fortunately, she found a taxi and she was able to reach an air-conditioned hotel. The first thing she did was call Tony, but he was not answering. Her weight of loneliness slowly transformed into despair. She called her office and told them she was down with a bug.

"I am so fucked," she muttered, sitting on the edge of her bed after a shower, trying to get the knots out of her hair. A Coke bottle stood nearby. From previous trips to Asia, she knew only sealed bottles of liquid were safe. Diarrhea would not improve her situation any. She tried Tony again and ended up throwing the phone across the room.

Early the next morning, she sat on the floor of the basement at Maya Press and searched through all orders from America, Canada, and England—for the last ten years. The publisher did not own a computer. They also did not employ a single person in the entire company with legible handwriting. After ten hours of searching stuffed cardboard boxes, she did not find any westerner who had ordered the Arundha Purana. Back in her hotel room, she called home and spoke to Anna. Daddy was not in. Kelly left a message with Anna for him to call when he came in. She never heard from him.

She was losing her mind.

The next day she returned to Maya Press and searched back twenty years. Again, no luck. Finally, a skinny stock boy with beautiful black eyes told her that the Purana was sometimes called the Samadhi Purana. Thank you very much, that little bit of information sure made a difference. Soon she had found numerous orders for the Purana. When she was finished, she had a list of fifty people in the U.S. alone who had purchased the book.

The next day she flew to Kuala Lumpur, then on to Taipei. Kola Press was located on the outskirts of the latter. She had to take a long taxi ride to get there. The boss—as opposed to the secretary she had spoken to on the phone—turned out to be hostile. He was not impressed with her FBI badge. He didn't like anyone going through his computer records. When she pleaded that she only wanted to find who had ordered a book—and after she had given him a thousand dollar bribe—he relented and searched the database himself with her sitting by his side. It took him a minute to find twelve Americans who had ordered the story of Mai Mai in the last ten years. All Chinese surnames except one. That one happened to be on her Maya Press list.

Michael Grander. 1342 Adams Lane, Teff, Ohio.

"Mike?" Teri had said, as he pulled out the cuffs and duct tape.

"I have him," Kelly told herself as her jet left Taipei for the infinitely long nonstop to Los Angeles. She was going home opposite the direction she had come.

But she was not going home at all. There was no point. She could not face Tony until she brought down the Acid Man. Her rationale was pure emotional bullshit. It went against every aspect of her early training. Get backup, don't be a hero, follow the chain of command.

Yet she felt so twisted inside. She kept fantasizing about walking in on Tony and his lover and throwing a newspaper on his bare chest with her name in the headline, and a picture of her and the Acid Man below it. Then she would scream at her husband. "See! I caught this bastard! I saved at least a dozen lives! This is who I am and what I am is important! How dare you fuck another woman!"

She was behaving like a child. She had to watch that. She had always been impulsive. She promised herself she would not attempt to arrest the serial killer on her own. That did not mean she was ready to go to Slate. She needed to take her theory further. That was not bullshit, but a legitimate excuse to delay contacting Slate.

Kelly had already checked on Michael Grander via her connections at the L.A. office and learned that the guy was a graduate student at Ohio State University. He was getting his Ph.D. in mythology. When she arrived at the campus, she would speak to his professors and learn what she could about him.

Then she would call Slate. He would be annoyed, but impressed.

She did not contact Michael Grander's teachers beforehand. Bored academic staffers—she knew the type. They would start gossiping. It would get to Mr. Grander and he would be on the next plane to Rio. In person, it would be a lot easier to explain the delicate nature of her investigation.

From LAX, she flew to Cincinnati and rented a car and drove to Columbus. Her sleep deficit was a yawning chasm. Coffee fueled her all the way to the capital city. For the time being, she had given up calling home. It was odd, but she felt as if she were in the morally inferior position to her husband. And here he was cheating on her. She felt she had to prove something to him to make them equals again.

"No," she said, struggling to stay awake behind the wheel of her rental. "I just want to hurt him."

Kelly went straight to the English department head—Professor James Shelly. Elderly but impeccably dressed, he reminded her of that old breed of scholars that had vanished with the advent of a middle class and color movies. Definitely very old school, but he had a pleasant smile, and she was not above flirting to get what she wanted.

He was impressed to meet an FBI agent that was as well-educated as himself. They gossiped about her alma maters—Princeton and Yale, lovely campuses he said—before she turned the conversation to business. She explained the FBI was investigating Michael Grander in connection with a crime, but did not say what the crime was. The professor seemed to appreciate the delicate nature of her visit. He suggested she talk to Professor Gene Banks, Michael Grander's faculty adviser.

"That's exactly who I want," she said. "The man closest to him."

"He has office hours now," Professor Shelly said, reaching for the phone. "He's only a five minute walk from here." He dialed the number and Professor Banks appeared to answer. "Yes, Gene, I have a surprise for you. There's an attractive young woman from the FBI here who wants to talk to you. Yes, you lazy goat, your reputation has traveled far. No, I'll let her explain that to you. She wants to know if she could come over now? Fine, I'll draw her a map." He hung up and added, "Gene and I go way back."

Kelly stood. "It sounds like it."

Professor Shelly stood behind his desk. "I can walk you over if you'd like."

"It's not necessary. I've already taken too much of your time. Just point me in the right direction. I have an uncanny sense of direction when it comes to college campuses."

Professor Shelly gave her directions and they exchanged goodbyes. Her fatigue was becoming a major impediment. Before heading to Banks's office, she stopped for a coffee at the campus cafeteria. Charlie was on her mind. She wished he was with her.

Tony haunted her as well, even more than the Acid Man.

Professor Gene Banks's office had a waiting area. A woman near Kelly's age sat with a boy who looked to be her son. The ten-year-old fidgeted impatiently with a laptop. The woman was a delicate beauty, with a long fall of dark hair framing a pale face and piercing gray eyes. Her thinness accentuated her frailty. She nodded as Kelly walked in, just as the little boy scowled.

"Are you waiting for Professor Banks?" Kelly asked, taking a seat.

"Yes. He's with a student now." She added, "I'm his wife."

Kelly offered her hand. "Kelly Fienman. Pleased to meet you."

"Julie Banks." She gestured to the boy. "My son, Robert."

"How are you doing, Robert?" Kelly asked.

The boy sulked. "Doing homework."

"Solving a big math problem?"

"Yeah." The boy added, "I hate math."

"That makes two of us," Kelly muttered.

"Are you a student here?" Mrs. Banks asked. "I only need a couple of minutes with my husband and then he's all yours."

"Take your time, I'm in no hurry." She did not want to answer the woman's question. Hopefully, Banks would not blurt out her identity when he came out of his office.

Professor Gene Banks appeared five minutes later. In his early fifties, he had a closely cropped gray mustache and beard, but still a full head of hair, which he kept on the long and wild side. His rimless glasses were a nice touch. He looked like a man who lived with books during the week, but who knew how to party on the weekends. Although he was just of medium height and build, he nevertheless filled the room. He had a bounce to his step, an energy in his voice. As he escorted his male student to the front door, he was upbeat about how the guy would finish his paper before the coming Monday. The young man seemed to appreciate his confidence. Finally, with the guy gone, he turned to Kelly and offered his hand.

"Sorry to keep you waiting," he said. "If I can have just two minutes with my family, I'll make you wait no more."

"No problem," Kelly said.

He ushered his son and wife into the hallway but left the door open. Kelly could not hear what was being said but they laughed easily together. It made her long for the idyllic days she used to have with Tony. Banks knelt and hugged his son, and the boy brightened. Naturally, it caused her think of her own daughter. She made a mental note to call Anna when she left the building. Tony and she could not divorce; they still had too much good left between them. Maybe they could get counseling. She could work fewer hours. Banks and his wife enjoyed a long lingering kiss.

Two minutes later Kelly sat in his office, which overlooked the center of campus. A herd of students dashed from one class to the next, but she found the view serene. His office had charm: a wall of books, a Matisse print on the door, a plant climbing a wooden statue of a Greek god, just one computer, plenty of pictures of his wife and son. She used to have such an office.

Banks quizzed her briefly about her literature and FBI background before they moved on to the matter at hand. Professor Shelly must have called him again after she had left the department head's office. Banks knew more than he should have. He chewed on a point Professor Shelly had let pass.

"Why would the FBI send an agent all the way from L.A. to investigate someone in Ohio?" he asked. "Why not use a local agent?"

"The case that brought me here concerns a very delicate matter."

He considered for a moment and then smiled. He did not believe her but was too polite to say so. She did not blame him; after all, she was lying. He spread his hands.

"Tell me what I can do for you," he said.

"Professor Banks," she began.

"Gene, please. We have a common background."

"Thanks. You may call me Kelly." She cleared her throat and was surprised at her nervousness. "I'm here in regards to Michael Grander. He's a suspect in a series of murders that have been committed in various parts of the country. He—"

Banks snorted. "I'm sorry, Michael's no murderer. He's one of the most passive people I know. Why do you suspect him?"

She took a pen and notepad from her bag. "I'll get to that in a minute. But first I need to ask a series of questions about Grander. I'll rattle them off, one after another, and you might feel like you're being interrogated. I apologize ahead of time. I know this must be difficult for you. He's obviously an important student to you."

Banks shrugged. "We're not that close, I just know him. But I'm willing to answer your questions if you'll answer mine when you're done. Agreed?"

"I'll tell you what is permissible. First, how long have you known Grander?"

"Five years."

"As a faculty adviser?"

"Yes."

"His specialty is mythology?"

"Eastern mythology, yes."

"How old is he?"

"Forty."

"He's working on his doctorate?"

"Yes. He has been working on it for ten years."

"Why has it taken him so long?"

"He's in no hurry. He enjoys traveling."

Not a small point. "He is wealthy, then?"

"His family is. I don't know his exact finances."

"But he must have access to money to travel so much?"

"I would not disagree with that."

"Has he traveled much in the last few months?"

"He comes and goes."

"So he does not maintain a full class load?"

"No. He's working on his thesis. I don't think he's taking any classes this quarter."

"Is he handsome?"

"What?"

"Is he attractive?"

"Yes. By most standards, one would say he is very handsome."

"Has he studied in England?"

Banks paused. "I don't know. But I know he's been there."

"Do you know if he spent substantial time there?"

"I honestly don't know."

"Is he married?"

"No."

"Was he ever married?"

He hesitated. "Yes."

"What is it?"

"Nothing."

"Please, tell me about this nothing."

Banks shook his head. "He's no longer married."

Kelly considered. "Do you know if his ex-wife is still alive?"

"She died in some kind of accident. They were still married at the time." He added, "I know the loss still haunts Michael to this day."

"What was the accident?"

"I don't know."

She pressed. "You're sure?"

Banks hesitated. "Not exactly. It had something to do with a fire." He looked uncomfortable. "I'd rather you asked him these questions. If you met him, you'd know right away he wasn't a murderer."

"I would like to meet him," Kelly said. The statement was a bold change from her plan. She had promised herself she was merely going to strengthen her case so that when she presented it to Slate, he acted quickly. But now she wanted another notch on her gun. Unknown to Banks, he had just described the Acid Man to the letter. She added, "When do you meet with him next?"

"Thursday afternoon. But I can call and bump up the appointment. I could make it for today. He wanted to see me as early as possible."

"Why?"

"He said he had to go out of town on business."

She closed her notepad. "Go ahead and make the appointment."

The professor made his call to Michael Grander and the guy agreed to meet him in an hour at the professor's home. Kelly had not planned on that wrinkle.

"Won't your family be home?" she asked as Banks set down the phone.

"No. Our meeting place is an apartment I keep near campus. I see most of my graduate students there. My real home is thirty miles from here." He stood and reached for his hat. The Midwest sky was in a foul mood. All she had was a flimsy leather coat. He offered her his down jacket and asked if she would have lunch with him. He assured her that they had time. She accepted both offers.

Her anxiety remained. She was playing with fire.

Lunch was at the student cafeteria where she had grabbed coffee, but the food was decent. Kelly ordered a turkey sandwich and Banks had a bowl of soup. While they ate, he asked what her all-time favorite book was. She answered without hesitation.

"*The Lord of the Rings*. I think it's the greatest work in the last century."

"I would have thought you would have chosen something more romantic."

"There's romance in the story. There's the love between Aragorn and Arwen."

"In the movies, yes. But in the novels, Arwen only comes in at the end, after all the excitement is over. Besides, I think you're more intrigued with Eowen, who had the misfortune of falling in love with Aragorn before the great battle." He added, "Did you know Tolkien only put her in the books because his daughters complained there were no girls in the story?"

"I didn't know that." She paused. "Why do you say I'm intrigued with Eowen?"

He studied her and she was struck then by how penetrating his eyes were. She suspected he was an excellent teacher and had the loyalty of his students.

"Because she was a maverick. She wanted to be a hero in a time when only men were heroes. She also had a broken heart, and wanted to cure it by dying in battle." He added gently, "You look troubled, Kelly."

He knew how to touch a nerve. "Perhaps Eowen and I do have a few things in common," she admitted.

He nodded sympathetically. "It's only a story."

They walked to his apartment. Gray gusts tugged at her coat. It was a relief to get back inside. His place overlooked a wooded stream. The furnishings were rich and tasteful: cedar to clear the nostrils, carpets on the floor, handmade lamps, and another huge case of books. The wall facing the stream was glass—the sky seemed to reach inside the room and chill her. He acted pleased when she complimented him on his fine taste.

"My wife deserves all the credit," he said.

"She's a lovely woman." Kelly stood beside the tall window. The adjoining room was full of exercise equipment. She could hide in there, she thought, while the two talked. Perhaps she could match Michael Grander with the man in Slate's tapes, although faces and bodies did not always fit.

"There are few like her. May I get you a drink?"

"No thanks," she replied.

"Are you sure? I have sherry."

"Sorry. On the job."

"Of course."

There was a black-and-white picture of a man and a boy standing in front of a run-down office building. The man looked gruff, the boy lost. She pointed out the photograph.

"My father and I," Banks said, coming up at her side. "You'd never guess, but I grew up only a few miles from here."

"Was your father a businessman?"

"My father was many things. You could call him that if you want."

"And your mother?"

He shook his head. "A long story."

She glanced at her watch. "It's been an hour. Perhaps we should make a plan?"

"If you like. Michael is always late." Banks headed for the kitchen and she heard cabinets being pulled open. "I think I'll have that drink without you. Do you mind?"

"Not at all. I'm the one who has intruded on your day." She glanced again at the exercise room. He had a treadmill, a stationary bike, and an elaborate weight machine for circuit training. He must be serious about his body. "I was thinking I could stay out of sight in here while you two talked."

Banks reappeared with a bottle. "You don't want to meet him?"

"I don't know what I would say to him."

Banks smiled. "You won't introduce yourself as an FBI agent? I suppose not. Hey, I remember now. I answered all your questions, but you didn't answer any of mine. Why is Michael a murder suspect? What exactly did he do?"

It was warm in the apartment. "I'm sorry. I'm not at liberty to say."

He continued to stand in front of her. "But he's my student. I think I deserve to know at least some reason why you suspect him."

"He left clues pointing to him at the scene of the crime."

"Physical clues?" Banks asked.

"Not exactly."

"Then you have no physical evidence linking him to the crimes?"

"We have evidence." Once more she checked her watch. Sweat gathered around her; she felt *very* hot. Her anxiety mounted. In minutes she would be standing in the same house as the monster. She added, "I'm sorry I can't be more specific."

"They didn't tell you everything about this guy, did they?"

The remark caught her off balance. "Why do you say that?"

"It's obvious, Kelly."

She almost asked him what was his point. But she was his guest. She could not be rude. Just being there, she was out on a limb with Slate. If all this led nowhere and he found out about her trip, she could get fired. Tony would love that. She would be even more at his mercy.

Kelly suddenly felt confused. She sought for its source. Something in her immediate surroundings was giving rise to the sensation. Bottle in hand, Banks continued to stare at her. She saw him and understood him. But she felt as if there were things around her that she was seeing and not understanding. The amount of exercise equipment bothered her—she didn't know why. Then there was the picture of Banks's father—it also troubled her. Even the style of the apartment; it was important in a way she couldn't pinpoint.

Banks took a step closer. "What's wrong?" he asked.

"Nothing." She paused. "I'm sorry I can't tell you everything I know."

"Don't let it bother you. Like I said, I don't think you know that much about this guy."

"Really?"

He nodded gravely. "Yes."

"Why do you say that?"

"It's just an impression I get." He paused. "I'm not trying to be rude."

"You're not being rude." She paused. "Are you sure Grander's on his way?"

"Yes. He'll be here soon."

"But he's always late?"

"Yes."

She turned and stared out at the flowing river, the trees, hoping the natural setting would settle her mind. But her confusion deepened. There was a portion of her mind that refused to quiet; it marched forward in search of significant connections. Why? With her back to Banks, she asked her next question.

"Why did Professor Shelly call you a lazy goat on the phone?"

"I don't remember him saying that."

"He did. I remember."

"I told you, we're old friends. We're always teasing each other."

"Oh."

"Are you sure nothing's bothering you, Kelly?"

"I'm sure." She did not like him calling her by her first name. She had invited him to do so but she wished he would stop. More than anything else, she suddenly wanted to get out of the apartment. She stayed, though; she had come far, and she had a job to do.

Banks moved until he stood a mere arm's length from her back.

"You're very pretty for an FBI agent," he said.

She turned with blood in her cheeks. "Thanks. I work at it." She stopped. "You must work out a lot. You have so much stuff."

He set the bottle down on a ledge and patted his firm stomach. "I gain weight looking at food. My wife likes me fit." He added, "It's important to her that I stay young."

"How much older are you?" A personal question, but it was one of those facts the confused portion of her mind felt might be significant.

"Twenty years. It's not so long for some women, but for others . . ."

He did not finish his sentence, which also added to her confusion.

"My husband is ten years older," she said.

"Do you love him?"

"Yes."

"That's good."

Kelly glanced at the picture of the factory. The hard father and the despondent child. Money and emptiness—no mother, long story.

"Is your father still alive?" she asked.

"No."

"Does your wife work?"

"No."

"It must be nice you can afford this apartment, and a home as well."

"It's nice." He paused. "My father left me a sizable inheritance."

"Lucky you." Yet the word luck felt out of place in the apartment. She moved closer to the window. Gray outside—inside getting dark. Still, she did not understand the change in her mood. Naturally she would be scared to spy on the Acid Man. But he would not know she was present. She was not required to take action against him. She just had to listen and observe.

"Yes," he said softly.

Once more she had her back to him. She spoke over her shoulder.

"It probably gives you the freedom to do what you want."

Banks was near. "Yes. It's a blessing."

It was only God who could bless. She had been taught that as a little girl. She wondered where God had been when the Acid Man had five times uncorked his vial of liquid fire and poured it onto the chests of those women. There should have been at least one religion in the world that demanded God answer that question before he asked to be worshipped.

Here she was a Jew, and she suddenly realized she had the Hail Mary running through her mind.

"Holy Mary, Mother of God, pray for us sinners, now and at the hour of our death, Amen."

"Fuck," she whispered under her breath, too soft for him to hear. Perhaps the prayer was real and brought a blessing, but at that moment she felt cursed beyond belief. Her mind underwent a complete breakdown and restructuring. The many insignificances that had plagued her since entering the apartment were suddenly gathered together in her head into one huge flashing red sign.

Finally, she began to understand . . .

Banks was lazy because he seldom worked. He seldom worked because he frequently traveled. He could travel a lot because he was rich. He was fifty years old but he exercised religiously. From the neck down he looked younger than he actually was. He had been able to get Grander on the phone and change the appointment so easily because he had not spoken to Grander and there was no appointment. He had brought her to this apartment because he wanted to be alone with her. And he wanted that because—

"Kelly?" he said at her back.

"Juliet accidentally betrayed her husband by stabbing herself in the heart."

The Acid Man had cursed the righteous Juliet. For no reason.

Except Professor Gene Banks's wife's name was Julie.

In a single fluid move Kelly reached inside her leather coat and pulled out her 9mm semiautomatic Glock. The weapon was small and efficient and she was not a bad shot. But in whirling she had the gun held low. She was not given a chance to bring it up. Not to heart level, not to where she could get off a fatal shot. Facing Banks, she found herself staring into the barrel of a Colt Python .357 magnum. He had already cocked the trigger; she had not heard.

"Put the gun down slowly," he said.

Kelly considered. He was an established killer. Basic FBI training stated that an agent never surrendered his or her weapon to a known killer. It said so right there in the fucking manual. Because such a murderer would almost invariably kill the said agent.

Banks would probably kill her if she did what he said. He had the drop on her, true; nevertheless, it might be better to risk exchanging shots with him. She probably had more experience with handguns.

He was the goddamn Acid Man! She didn't want to surrender to him!

"You're thinking of trying to get off a shot," he said calmly. "Let me assure you that won't happen. I'm a crack shot, and I'm less than three seconds away from putting a bullet in your brain." He shook his revolver. "Do as I say or die. One . . . Two . . ."

She had to play the unknown odds. She put down her gun.

"Please step away from the window. I'm going to draw the blinds."

She moved beneath the photo of father and son on the wall. Keeping his aim on her chest, he closed the blinds and the room darkened to late evening. The time of day did not matter to her body, though, with all her travels. She was exhausted and soon she would be dead. The fatigue excuse did not stop her from cursing herself for missing the obvious. Banks had played her during the interview on Grander just as he had played the five women he had fucked and killed. He picked up her gun and shoved it in his belt. He studied her in the poor light as if trying to read her mind.

"How did you find me? The truth."

"You made a reference to 'Mai Mai and the man' and 'The Tears of Rati' on your tapes."

"You went to India and China and found out who had ordered both books?"

"Yes."

"You went by yourself?"

"No. My partner Charlie Fitzsimmons accompanied me. He expects a call from me any minute."

"You lie. You're a maverick. You're Eowen. You rushed alone into battle in hope of a proud death."

"As you said, it's only a story."

"But stories are our lives, Kelly. That's how you found me. That's how I figured you out. And I knew it was only a matter of time before you saw through me."

"Why did you put the book orders under Grander's name?"

"A precaution. A poor one."

"What did you do with the women's bodies?"

"Does it matter? I'm sorry, I don't think we have time for a lengthy interrogation. But I understand your curiosity. You may ask one question you really care about."

She paused. "Why?"

He must have expected it but the word deflated him. He sucked in a breath. A shudder went through his body, and he stumbled back and had to steady himself on the nearby wall. "It's difficult to talk about," he mumbled.

She aimed for sympathy. "You haven't been able to talk to anyone about it?"

"No." He blinked and in the dim light she lost the sense of his eyes. Or maybe she lost him altogether. Her terror in that moment was infinite. She was not going to psyche him into sanity. He was intelligent and methodical. He would kill her when it suited him. He straightened and came back a step. "Why do you care?" he asked.

"I want to understand you."

"Tell me, what do they call me at Quantico?"

"The Acid Man."

"I'm not surprised."

"Would you prefer another name?"

"It doesn't matter." He took another ragged breath. "Just before you reached for your gun, you made the connection between Juliet and Julie?"

"Yes." How would he kill her? "What did she do to you?"

Anguish. She saw tragedy in the fact that he had not been able to talk to anyone about what had happened. Sometimes the difference between murder and a dark mood was a sympathetic ear. Yet he was too complex for simple analysis. His efficiency and brutality indicated deep obsessions. Except for a slip of the tongue, he might have killed a hundred women and never been caught. She marveled at how easily he had manipulated her to this point. Yet he had given her a thousand hints. Sincerity was his disguise. When he spoke next it was in a wounded voice. It made her wonder.

"Julie and I met twelve years ago. She was only twenty and I was of course forty. There were many precious details to our meeting, many magical moments to our courtship that I unfortunately cannot share with you. Suffice to say I loved her in a way I had never imagined loving anyone. It was as if her love transformed me into something no longer mortal. She gave me an eternal sense of being that I carried with me always."

He lowered his head and fell silent. All she had was the darkness. A lump in her aching heart. He could do to her what he had done to the others. He could operate and burn out that lump, and everything else that made her Kelly Fienman. She wondered if her daughter was sitting at home, waiting for her to call.

"But something happened?" she said.

"Last year I discovered she was having an affair with a graduate student of mine—Michael Grander. By chance I stopped by his apartment one afternoon and knocked on his door. When he didn't answer, I glanced though the window and saw my wife on her knees sucking his penis." Banks trembled. "I could not have imagined."

He wept without tears. She listened without hope. His suffering did not alter his aim. All she could do was keep him talking—a futile plan.

"Are they still involved?" she asked.

"Yes. She was going to see him this afternoon."

"Why haven't you confronted her?"

"I don't have the strength." He added, "I'm afraid to lose her."

"You cannot bear the pain?"

He shook his head. "You don't understand. It's not a question of what can and cannot be borne. My pain transcended human dimension. It took me to a place where good and evil were irrelevant. It *changed* me. And yet, in time, I began to see it as a gift."

"The pain?"

He nodded. "I saw many things I had never seen before. Julie could not be saved. I could not be healed. What to do? The world is filled with pain and deception. I decided to take what had been given to me and give it back to the whole world." He paused. "Do you understand?"

"No." The rationale was too linear to explain the complexity of his crimes. So was his entire story. She was not sure she believed him. Yet she believed his pain.

"I didn't think that you could." He was weary. "What are we going to do?"

"Put down the gun and surrender. The FBI knows I'm here. Your boss knows I'm here. If I disappear, the Bureau will come after you like a storm."

"True. They will come for me. But I cannot let you go."

"There's no point in killing me. You can't escape. Let this nightmare end, Gene. Give me the gun."

"No. I have prepared for this day. I have a false passport and plenty of cash. I can be in Europe in twelve hours." He paused. "Besides, I cannot surrender to you and go to jail without saying goodbye to Julie."

She caught his hidden meaning. "You always intended to kill her?"

"When I was finished, yes. The two of them together. First him, then her."

"Go ahead, kill them. I'll wait here until you get back."

He smiled. "You have spunk, Kelly Fienman. I like that."

She didn't thank him for the compliment.

He gestured toward the back room. "We should begin."

She could not feel her legs. "You don't want to do this. I've done nothing to you. And I've never cheated on my husband."

"But I need to bring Julie and Michael back here and show them your body. The acid works swiftly. Since he'll go first, he needs to see how horrible his death is going to be."

"What about your son?"

He did not answer. He shook his gun. In the room.

The bedroom was small and austere. It also had a view of the river. He quickly closed the blinds. He turned on a floor lamp with a red shade. The light spilled over the cramped space like a bitter sunset. He ordered her to lie on the bed. She stared at him and shook her head.

He showed another side to his personality, as if she needed to see more. He belted her across the face with his gun. The shock of the blow was disorienting. For a moment she staggered and almost lost consciousness. Blood spurted from her mouth and nose and he forced her down onto the sheets.

It was only then she realized the obvious. She needed to scream—he was going to kill her anyway. But before she could utter a sound duct tape appeared. He closed off her mouth with the same precision he had demonstrated on the DVD—three wraps around the head. Her brain still swimming, she fought to sit up and he struck her with his gun on her jaw. The flesh along her chin tore and blood sprayed everywhere.

His expression was detached. He was not mad at her. She had not cheated on her husband. But he was going to kill her anyway because of

Julie, all because of Julie. Once more he raised the gun as if to strike her and she cringed. It was impossible to think what was going to happen next.

"Don't move," he warned.

She wanted to disobey but could not. Fear had turned her nervous system to jelly. It was only then that she realized how far she was from being hero material. Sick at her inability to resist, she watched as he removed a thin rope from a nearby drawer and began to tie her limbs to the four bedposts. He did not have his handcuffs and he did not need them. In a past life he must have been a Boy Scout. He effortlessly knotted her feet together and drew her arms spread-eagle above her head. He was not interested in rape. He wanted to hurry and finish her so that he could get to Michael Grander's place and catch them in the act. She tried not to imagine how she would look when the three of them returned to his apartment.

When he had her securely tied, he removed her gun from his belt and set it on the table beside the bed. The taunt was deliberate. The Glock was only two feet from her right hand. Taking a step back, he pointed his own gun at her chest. She thought he had changed his mind, that he was going to shoot her and be done with it. But then he set his weapon on top of a chest of drawers. He crouched low and opened a drawer and dug around in the back. When he stood, he had a silver vial in hand. One pint—give or take an ounce of pure hell. She'd never gotten a chance to ask where he got the stuff. Probably he had a chemistry buddy on campus who whipped it up in exchange for rare videos.

Banks put on black gloves and removed the lid from the vial and returned to the side of the bed. He clearly wanted to get it over with, but he stopped to study her. There was nothing in his expression. He could have been daydreaming.

"Would you like a glass of milk?" he asked.

How wide her eyes must have been right then.

He stared at the vial. "I know this is going to hurt. I know you do not deserve it. But in a sense it is all your fault. You came after me alone because you wanted to prove something to yourself. You won't understand this, but I killed those five women for the same reason." His eyes met her eyes and he sighed. "But it's all useless in the end, don't you think? Pain cannot heal pain. No one will remember what happened here today. And Julie will never be mine again."

She shook her head vigorously. No.

Yes. He held the vial above her heart and began to pour.

The acid did not touch her chest. Her body reacted instinctively. With a strength bordering on the supernatural, she jerked back and the entire bed moved a foot. Rather than burn into her breastbone, the acid splashed onto her abdomen. It was like being licked by a blowtorch. As the material of her blouse peeled to ash and steam rose from the ruin of her belly button, she convulsed sideways and threw several fat drops flying in his direction. He also reacted by instinct and took a step back. He seemed surprised by her strength.

A drop of acid hit the length of rope that ran from her feet to the right bedpost, near her head. The rope was thin—it took two seconds for it to sufficiently weaken under the pressure of her writhing. Then it snapped. In an instant her right hand—although still encircled at the wrist—was relatively free.

She was in agony, she was going into shock. She had given up hope and she was definitely no hero. But she saw the opportunity and she seized it before he could respond. As if reaching for a phone that had startled her in the middle of the night, she stretched out her hand and picked up her gun and pointed it at his face. If she had not had duct tape on her mouth, she might have ordered him to drop the vial of acid and put up his hands.

As it was she said nothing.

He stared at her. "Oh my," he whispered.

Banks turned and ran for the door. She followed his movements— the back of his head in particular—and pulled the trigger. A nine millimeter was not a heavy round. The recoil of the Glock did not make her lose control, even given her desperate situation. She could have shot him twice, three times if necessary. But red blossomed at the base of his neck and he went down. She assumed he was dead.

Pain. The acid on her abdomen had not stopped digging. It would not halt until it ate her alive. She did not have time to untie her hands and feet. Taking aim, she blew away the rope on her left and leaned forward over the mass of tissue that had been her guts and yanked both her feet loose. Her ankles were still bound and she could not walk, but that fact would not stop her.

Kelly threw her feet onto the floor and *hopped* toward the bathroom. They had passed the bathroom minutes earlier on the dark road to the bedroom. Going by Banks—facedown and bleeding on the floor—she almost tripped. Her vertical position had given the acid a new direction. She felt it begin to burn into parts she needed to keep in order to live in the world as a woman.

In the shower she looked down and found her entire front soaked red. The liquid flame refused to stop. The acid had already penetrated her abdomen wall. Her intestines were on the move. She feared—when she turned on the water—that they would bulge out and spill onto the tile floor. But the water was her only hope. Tearing apart her fried blouse, she closed her eyes and turned the shower on high. The spray came out cold and hard and hit her belly like baking soda thrown into a vat of vinegar. The pain, which could not have been worse, shot up tenfold.

Kelly fainted. When she came to she was lying in the shower with the water still spraying her abdomen. Her skin had split open, and she saw organs that were never meant to see the light of day. The water chased a red river down the drain. She was bleeding to death, and perhaps it was a blessing.

Life was stubborn, though, she realized then. Using both hands to hold her guts in place, she struggled to her feet and hopped into the living room. There she saw a phone. Tearing the duct tape off her mouth, she dialed 911. A girl who sounded all of sixteen answered and asked her to state the nature of her emergency.

"My name is Kelly Fienman and I'm in the apartment of Professor Gene Banks. It is close to the University of Ohio campus—I don't know the address. He has burnt me with acid and I shot him." She began to weep. "Please hurry, I think I'm dying."

The girl wanted more details. Kelly could not give them to her. Her vision blurred and she slumped to her knees and dropped the phone. She tried desperately to hold onto her intestines but her fingers vanished in a slippery gore. The burning would not stop, the Acid Man was inside her now. Even if he was dead, he lived there. She was his sixth victim, a statistic, and her own husband didn't even love her anymore. But the Acid Man had been right when he had said pain could not heal pain. Even if she did survive, she knew she would never recover.

That was her last thought before she blacked out.

CHAPTER THREE

An itchy right leg woke Matt Connor—four months after he had leapt from the plane and into the ocean. He scratched the scar for a minute before he realized he was back in the real world. The skin on his leg had been tender even after it had healed but he didn't mind. It was a fun itch to scratch—a problem easily solved. And he knew that if the scar was all the damage he had to show for that night, then he had gotten off lucky.

Yet he awoke with many emotions. Since he had killed Matt Connor, he had felt relief. It was as if a portion of his grief had died with the name. The last months in his trailer on the outskirts of Modesto—a boring city if ever there was one—had changed him. In the guise of Simon Schiller, he had picked up odd jobs at local construction sites, working for cash at half his old rate. His routine was simple. He installed an occasional bathroom, went for long walks, and read practically a book a day. He didn't even rent DVDs nor watch TV, nor go out to eat.

His trailer cost two hundred bucks a month and even at that stringent rate, it was no bargain. A twenty foot long box of metal, all it had to recommend it was a working toilet and complete isolation. But it suited his austere state of mind. There was nothing more simple than being dead. He thought of himself that way, and it was not depressing.

He had overstayed his welcome in the twilight zone, though. He had planned to return to L.A. a month earlier and complete his revenge. It was now May, four months since he had leapt from the plane. The faint stirrings of peace had slowed his hand. The idea of seeing her again filled him with dread. It brought him back to the torturous nights he had spent staking out David's home in the days after her betrayal. Often he thought of letting it all go and living forever as a nobody.

Yet there was an element to the path he had chosen that made stopping halfway difficult. He had sacrificed more than the loss of his personal identity when he had leapt from the plane. In a sense, he had put justice on trial that night. He had jumped to correct a wrong. He had to stick with his plan to achieve balance—for himself as well as Amy. Perhaps he was old-fashioned—an eye-for-an-eye misfit—but he truly felt it was immoral that Amy not be paid back for what she had done to him.

Of course, that was all bullshit. He was better but he was not well. He could not think of her without experiencing a sick mixture of love and hate. The former somehow gave the latter strength. When it came down to it, he still wanted to hurt her. And hurt her he would, beyond her wildest imagination.

He got out of bed and showered—cold water, all his trailer had to offer. He put on oatmeal and—while waiting for it to cook—logged onto America Online. He knew his mother's screen name and password. In the last few months he had tapped into her e-mail several times. Two weeks after his plane had gone down, she had received an e-mail from Amy's father. An e-mail he had printed out and read numerous times. He read it once more before he checked for new mail.

Dear Nancy,

I am sorry I did not have a chance to speak to you at your son's memorial. There were so many people around, I hesitated to intrude on your grief. Also, I was not sure if you wanted to talk to me after what Amy did to Matt. It is a grim task to apologize for a daughter but I will try as best I can. Matt was a fine young man: kind and caring, honest and noble. What Amy did was unforgivable. Even after all this time, I have been unable to accept or even understand her actions. But in her defense I must say she struggled with inner demons. When she chose David over Matt, a part of me died inside. I know David and he is no good. But I suppose that's a lesson Amy must learn for herself.

You must have noticed Amy was not present at the memorial. She wanted very much to come, but we both agreed it might agitate you and other close friends of Matt's. When she received the news of your son's death, I can honestly say she was devastated. Perhaps it was not until then she realized how much Matt meant to her. That's another sad testament to my daughter's character, but I think the realization was better late than never. Even though pregnant, she was unable to eat for a week. Many times she told me how perfect Matt had been.

Nancy, what can I say? Your loss is so great and my words are so inadequate. What I wouldn't give to be able to open my front door and see Matt sweep inside like he used to, all smiles and good cheer, his eyes alert for everyone's feelings. That is what I remember most about him—how he cared for all of my family, not just Amy. He was a rare soul, he can never be replaced. But I hope in time you are able to find a measure of peace and reason in this great loss. You deserve that, and so much more.

My daughter hurt your son, but I know she would now do anything to take back that hurt. But that's the trouble with these mortal lives. Seldom are we given a second chance. Please forgive her, if you can, please forgive all of us. We love you and we think about you all the time.

Take care, John

Matt did not know what to make of the letter. John was a great guy, but he was still Amy's father. He would have put the best spin possible on Amy's concern without resorting to overt lies. Matt seriously doubted Amy would have done anything to take back the hurt she had caused. Because the truth of the matter was that she hadn't done anything. His death had just been an excuse for her to act like she was consumed with remorse. Why, she had not even bothered to warn him about her marriage to David. She had just discarded him, forgotten about him, and gotten on with her plush life. She had not come to his memorial because she was probably getting her hair done that afternoon.

Of course it was nice to pretend she had been devastated.

Dangerous to pretend. Today of all days.

His mother had fresh mail. There was another e-mail to his mother from John.

> Dear Nancy,
>
> This is just a quick note to thank you for your kind letter. Yes, I am a grandfather all over again, it is hard to believe. Little Jimmy is such a delight. He almost never cries and he has Amy's incredible eyes. How I wish he belonged to another father, but it is too late for such sentiments. But I know Matt would have made an incredible dad, he was so good with kids.
>
> Ah, Nancy, I should not talk about these things. Amy's marriage to David has gone bad—already the milk has soured. They fight all the time and even though she does not say, I suspect he beats her. Even if he doesn't hit her, his emotional abuse is constant. When I see her eyes heavy with dried tears, I can't help but think back to how happy she was with Matt. I hope my saying so does not hurt you. I still think of your son every day. God bless you for having brought him into the world—so that he could have been in our lives at least for a time. My prayers are with you constantly.
>
> Yours, John

Matt logged off and shut down his computer. For a long time he sat staring at the blank screen. It made no difference, he told himself.

He packed his car and drove toward Los Angeles.

■

WHEN HE jumped from the plane, he estimated his altitude at two thousand feet. In the absence of clouds, the wisest strategy would have dictated that he open his parachute early so that he could leisurely maneuver toward the boat. But more time in the sky was not an advantage when he couldn't see where he was going. It even posed a risk, since he was more likely to drift farther from the boat with his chute open than closed.

Still, as he fell from the plane into the low-lying clouds, he knew all the plans and calculations in the world wouldn't help if he panicked and didn't get the chute open at all. So in the end he let himself fall only a few seconds before he pulled the ripcord.

The parachute expanded and he hovered in a bardos-like realm. He had already lost sight of the plane. For a frantic minute all he could see were his feet. From his brief low skim over the sea, he knew he should come clear of the cloud cover at five hundred feet. That would give him scant time to reach the boat if it was more than two hundred yards away. He wondered how long he could swim in the cold water. Already he was cold. The moist February night sent shivers through to his bones. Damnit, he should have put on that wet suit!

Finally, he got a break. When he emerged from the clouds, the flashing red-and-white lights of the boat were almost directly beneath him. The relief he felt in that instant was immense. For a long time it had seemed as if the universe was bent on screwing him. He hardly had to turn to align himself toward the deck.

The type of parachute he was using was called a Ram-Air-Canopy. It was several generations more advanced than the round parachutes soldiers had used in World War II. Through the use of steering lines and stiff panels on the rear of the parachute, it could be navigated to drop a person on a dime. He had no trouble lining himself up with the boat.

But then he ran into two sets of problems.

One he had control over. The other he didn't.

In training, he had been taught to turn into any kind of wind at five hundred feet. Skydiving facilities usually had a bright red inflatable bag that showed which way the wind was blowing. Turning into the wind gave a natural brake action. Of course he had known ahead of time he would not have the luxury of such a bag while trying to land on the boat. But he had hoped to get some sense of the direction and strength of the wind before he neared the boat.

As he started his final approach, he realized the wind was directly at his back, which was the worst possible scenario. It would force him to compensate for his extra speed by pulling his toggles early. The latter were his steering lines, and to really slow down, he had to yank them as far as thigh level. Ordinarily, without wind at his back, he would only yank them hard just when he was about to touch down. They were designed to flare the chute and bring a person into a full brake position. The toggles were an ingenious invention—they allowed a skydiver to touch down with hardly a bump.

But, once again, because of the wind at his back, he could not just use the toggles briefly, fifteen feet above the ground—or in this case, the water. He had too much damn speed. The boat seemed to rush toward him.

He pulled his toggles hard.

The braking effect momentarily kicked his feet and the rest of his body horizontal to the water. But then he went right back to a vertical position which was good and bad. He wanted to land on his feet, but he immediately saw that he had given in to panic and braked too early. He still had too much speed, and he desperately wanted to gently touch down on the boat. It was not stable like the ground. He would have no room to roll.

So he flared again. He had never done that before in practice, two flares.

If the first flare was too early, his second one was much too late.

Matt jerked into a horizontal position again. Swooping toward the rear deck, his feet were literally pointing toward the horizon. A weird, slow-motion fog filled his brain—probably brought on by terror—and he felt for what seemed a whole minute that the boat had slipped *behind* him. But the truth was his awkward angle had given him the wrong impression. Blinking, he suddenly saw a silver guardrail rush toward him, and he tried to brace for impact, but there was not exactly anything for him to grab hold of. His right leg hit the railing hard, and a raised screw—or perhaps a twisted corner of metal—dug into his flesh and he felt rather than saw himself flip in midair.

In a way, although it was cold, he was lucky to land in the water.

The next thing he knew his soaked parachute was trying to drown him. Ironically, the temperature of the sea did not bother him. Even though he knew there was something seriously wrong with his right leg—it was burning hot when it should have been freezing cold—he felt a large measure of relief. He was out of the sky and the boat was near at hand. After struggling uselessly with the chute for several seconds, he calmed down and dug himself out from beneath it. He had to be careful with the pile of material. He could not simply let it float away. Some genius could find it and put two and two together.

Earlier he had attached a ladder to the rear of the boat. He was able to climb onto the deck without straining. He had to struggle with the parachute for several minutes but then he had it aboard as well. It was only when he sat down to catch his breath that he realized how cold he was; and that the sticky warmth dripping from his leg was colored red. Pulling up his pants leg, he saw that he had a gash in his calf that was at least an inch deep and over a foot long. The deck was already soaked with blood. He wondered how much blood he had left in the water.

There was a first-aid kit inside the cabin. Tearing off his pants, he treated the wound with hydrogen peroxide and two rolls of gauze. The treatment was a joke. He needed a dozen rolls of gauze and thirty stitches. He could not stop the bleeding. He ended up ripping apart a spare sweatshirt he had brought along to keep himself warm and cozy in the event he went in the water. He firmly tied the material directly over the wound and the pressure finally halted the bleeding.

He toweled down and changed into dry clothes. The chill lingered; it followed him all the way down the coast to the marina. He had to wonder if it was more from his brush with death than simply the effect of the cold water. But he counted his blessings. He had come out of the low-lying clouds—his worse fear—directly over his boat and he had not broken his back.

He reached the marina at one in the morning, his disguise in place. He had told the rental firm that he intended to bring the boat back the following afternoon, but with his injured leg he wanted to get off the water and into a hospital. Yet even with the pressure of his injury, he knew he could not go to a clinic in the L.A. area.

There was a fresh water hose at the dock. He washed off the blood as best he could. Fortunately, there was no one around. The harbor guards seemed to be hanging in the coffee shop. Unfortunately, the pain in his leg escalated rapidly. He had a hard time transferring his beacon lights into the trunk of Simon Schiller's car. He suspected he had lost two or three pints of blood. As he worked, dizziness swept over him and there was a ringing in his ears that reminded him of a high school fire alarm.

He got on the freeway and tried to drive using his left leg. He longed for a doctor with a kind bedside manner and a syringe filled with morphine, but had to wonder if he was already too late for stitches. He remembered reading that they were only effective in the first six hours, and it had been longer than that since he had cut himself.

He drove north for a few minutes, then got off the freeway and swung by a 7-Eleven and bought a bottle of Tylenol. He decided to swallow a dozen pills with the help of a tall coffee and try to make it all the way to Modesto without stopping. The idea was patently foolish but he wanted out of L.A. so bad he didn't care.

The sun rose as he reached his trailer in Modesto. He went inside and took off his clothes and plopped down on the bed and slept like a child. Even the pain in his leg did not wake him. He was a dead man. He could sleep forever and no one would care.

■

AS MATT took the Grapevine into the L.A. basin, old demons returned to haunt him. He was plagued by the desire to drive straight to her house and knock on her door. He could pretend he was a ghost and tell her that she had to change her ways or else she was going to die and go to hell. That she had to get away from David and spend the rest of her life mourning the tragic loss of Matt Connor. What was amazing about the fantasy was that he spent an hour trying to figure out how he could pass for a disembodied spirit.

His entry into Santa Monica sobered him. The city looked dirtier than he recalled, more crowded. Modesto was dull but moved at an easy pace. He drove aimlessly and for a time all he saw were the places he used to visit with Amy. The torture was faint but only he knew how quickly it could grow. The smart thing to do was to get a motel and settle in for the night. But he ended up driving to a dead-end street a block over from her house.

A bluff rose behind the neighborhood. Taking a steep dirt path up the hill, he crouched down in a cluster of bushes he knew well from his old stalking days. He had brought a pair of binoculars; he had a small telescope in the car he planned to use later. The vantage point was ideal. He could see all of the backyard, and through most of the windows at the rear of the house.

It was a Monday evening. How did David and Amy spend their free time? In the next few days Matt had to learn the "Techer routine" inside out. He was not sure if David kept regular office hours. Amy could have a live-in nanny. There were so many potential obstacles. But this was one area where he would not rush. He would wait a month, if necessary, for the perfect moment to strike.

"God," he whispered.

He saw her. The sight was not particularly noteworthy but it was enough to tell him that he was not over her at all. Holding her child to her breast, she carried the baby from one room to the other. Dressed in white pants and a yellow blouse—her hair down and her figure already back to its pre-pregnancy form—she looked ravishing. He could see that she sang to the infant as she walked. Amy had always had an enchanting voice. In happier times she used to sing to him as he fell asleep after a hard day's work.

"Darling," he said and set down the binoculars. He had seen enough for the day. But he would return tomorrow, and the day after that, until his opening appeared.

■

BY FRIDAY, Matt felt confident to make his move. The Techer routine was simple. David went to work each day at eight o'clock, although he came home at odd hours. He could be back by six in the evening, or stay out as late as midnight. Had Matt not been so preoccupied, he would have followed David. Probably the creep was banging one of his secretaries. Matt fantasized of taking pictures and mailing them to Amy. It was possible there would be time for that later. Amy's pain need not emanate from one source alone.

The point was that David was gone all day. Amy and the baby's timetable also appeared set. She did indeed have a nanny, but the woman only came in the morning to help with the child. Even then Amy was usually with her son. There was no question she was an excellent mother, that she poured her heart into her baby. The nanny would leave at one sharp and Amy would breast-feed the infant and put him down to rest and then take a nap herself. But as far as Matt could tell, Amy never slept in the same room as her son. For an hour each afternoon they were separated by a distance of two rooms. If she did happen to go out, nap time was always late in the afternoon.

While stalking them before he had jumped out of the plane, Matt had never paid attention to the neighbors behind David and Amy. He had always figured when the big day came he would climb their front gate. But these neighbors were *never* home in the daytime. He decided their front and back walls would be the best point of entry. True, the stone walls were high but the twenty-foot aluminum ladder he had just purchased from Home Depot would take care of that. Of course walking down the street with a ladder under his arm would look suspicious, but a can of paint in the other hand would allay most doubts. Plus, when he left the house, he could leave the ladder. Gloves would take care of any fingerprints.

Friday looked perfect and he was psyched but a team of gardeners showed up and he had to swallow his nerves and wait until Monday. That weekend was one of the longest of his life. When he was not in his motel room, he drove into the Santa Monica Mountains and hiked until his legs crumbled. He kept worrying—what if Amy woke up when he was in the house? What would he do to her?

Monday afternoon, at half past one, he watched through his telescope as Amy put her baby in his crib and then yawned, went into her own bedroom, and laid down. No one knew better than he how deep she slept. He had always found it endearing how such a small woman could snore so loud. She also had a habit of twitching her legs in her sleep like a dreaming dog. He didn't know why such quirks used to mean so much to him.

He gathered together his telescope and half-eaten lunch, swept his bush haven clean, and walked back to his car. Gloves were a constant companion. The FBI might figure out the vantage point he had used to plot his crime but it would tell them nothing. Over the weekend he had stripped the soil in the area and dumped it at the beach. The FBI wouldn't even find an eyelash to trace him with.

At his car he stowed his telescope and took out the ladder and can of paint. In his pocket he carried a ski mask, which he would put on when he was in the neighbor's backyard. For the moment he kept on his painter hat and dark glasses. Even if Amy did awake and spot him, she would not be able to identify him. Naturally, he had on Simon Schiller's beard and mustache. She would not recognize him. If by chance he did confront her, it was important that he not utter a word.

The neighbor's block was deserted. He was pleased to discover that they had left their side gate open. He did not need his ladder until he was climbing into Amy's backyard. By then he had on his ski mask and was feeling powerful. The sensation surprised him. He had assumed he would be a nervous wreck, but an odd calm had settled over his mind. He had planned for this moment for so long it was as if it were happening to someone else.

On top of the wall that separated the neighbors from Amy, he reversed his ladder and climbed down. They had a large pool, a lovely deck area with a marble Jacuzzi, and a waterfall. From peering through his telescope, he knew the back sliding glass door was unlocked. David and Amy were lazy when it came to security. They thought they were untouchable. They could ruin a good man's life and walk away and pretend nothing had happened. They thought, we are rich and well-connected and don't give a fuck. Matt was shocked at the wave of anger he felt but it merely added to his sense of power. Now, finally, after a whole year of planning, they would pay.

In a moment he was inside, and immediately he smelled her. For skin lotion she used a secret homemade recipe that contained a touch of rose oil. To him she had always smelled like a spring bouquet. Nowadays he couldn't see a rose without remembering its thorns. With her scent all around him, he felt his anger and strength drain away. It happened so quickly, he could hardly believe it. What if she were to see him and speak to him? He might break down and surrender. God, he was so pathetic he made himself sick.

He moved upstairs, his tennis shoes light on the wooden steps. He was shaken but still in control. On the second floor were four bedrooms. Jimmy slept in number two on the left. Amy was on the far right, in the master suite. The hallway had deep carpet. He could hear his heart but not his feet. He moved slow and steady, and then, with a start, he saw himself in a mirror at the end of the hall: his frumpy paint clothes, black gloves, black face mask. He looked like a fucking apparition.

The baby's room: blue and cheerful, smiling angels staring down at sleeping Jimmy from all corners, figures Amy had no doubt painted while pregnant. On top of everything else she had been an excellent artist. What a time to remember her talents.

Matt stepped into the room and stared down at the child. He had assumed he would hate the sight of the little tyke but in truth the kid was kind of cute. He looked a lot like Amy, not at all like David. Matt was happy he was well-wrapped. He would be that much easier to carry. He would have been even more relaxed to know the kid had popped a sleeping pill after lunch.

Jimmy's waking and crying was the single biggest uncertainty in his plan.

Matt bent and picked up the child. Jimmy stirred but did not open his eyes. Now was the time to get out of the house quick. Matt had no explanation for why he stopped at Amy's bedroom door. He supposed he was tired of seeing his pain in the mirror. Now he could stare right at the source.

Amy rested on her back with her eyes closed. She wore blue shorts, a white T-shirt, and white socks. Her tan legs were smooth and toned and her breasts full. Her long lashes flickered as if she dreamed. Her dark hair was shorter than he remembered but otherwise she had not changed.

She was all he had thought about for so long that he feared he would long for her even in the grave. Revenge guaranteed him no peace—it might just damn them both. He stared at her for a precious minute, and she did not move once. He could not hear her breathe. In a sense, she was like him, he thought. She could have been dead.

"Love you, honey," he whispered.

A tear crept over his cheek as he turned and left the house.

CHAPTER FOUR

Approximately three hours after the kidnapping of three-month-old James Techer, Kelly Fienman rode in the car with Charles Fitzsimmons toward David and Amy Techer's house. The motion of the car, simple things like taking a corner, made Kelly nauseous and she had to wonder if she had come back to work too early. It had been a month since she'd had her colostomy bag removed and her scar—a minor mark compared to the hideous incisions that had accompanied her first operations—was still tender.

Yet it was not so much her outside that disturbed her as her insides. She did not have a whole lot of intestines left. Her digestion was weaker than an infant's. She could get sick just smelling food, and she had to wonder if she would always be this way.

"How are you doing?" Charlie asked, glancing over.

She nodded. "Great. Good to be out of the house." Not that she had been in her real home in months. Good old Tony had taken it when he had filed for divorce, along with her daughter. He had explained the logic: there were two of them and only one of her. Anna could not leave her neighborhood friends. Lying in a hospital bed at the time of his explanation, the mathematics had not impressed Kelly. She believed there were in reality not *two* of them, but *three*. Tony's new love had already moved in.

"You look like shit," Charlie said.

"Shit is not a word you want to use with me since I just had my shit bag removed a few weeks ago." She shook her head. "I can't get rid of the smell of that thing."

"You smell fine." Charlie paused. "And I'm sorry, I didn't mean it that way. I just don't think you should be trying to save the world before you've got your strength back."

"Did it occur to you that I might never get my strength back?"

"Kelly, you're going to be all right. You just need time is all."

"Do you know what I had for breakfast this morning? White rice, without butter or spices. I had rice for dinner last night. I'll have applesauce for lunch this afternoon, with a glass of water. There are six foods I can eat without getting sick. Did you know the acid ate away a portion of my pancreas? I might never be able to digest anything fun again. No pizza, no ice cream, no steak, no popcorn. What do you think of that? Could you live that way? Would you *want* to live that way?"

"You're alive, and after what you went through, you shouldn't be. You're a lucky lady."

Kelly snorted. "I lost my health. I lost my husband. I lost my daughter. I stopped the most dangerous killer of recent time and I was reprimanded by my superiors. And you say I'm lucky?"

He looked at her with his big wise eyes. "Does it help to feel sorry for yourself?"

"Yes! I want to feel sorry for myself. I fucking feel like I deserve to feel sorry for myself. You got a problem with that?"

"No."

"Then fuck you, what are you saying?"

Charlie got a tear in his eye. "I'm just happy you didn't die."

She patted his arm. "I couldn't have made it through all this without you."

"I didn't do shit . . . I mean, I didn't do anything for you."

"Right. Like you didn't visit every day for hours."

"That was nothing." He added, "I love you."

She smiled weakly. "Do you? Did you love me even when I stank?"

"You didn't stink."

"Yes, I did. Every time you came to the hospital or the apartment, you wrinkled your nose. I didn't blame you. Tony didn't like the smell either. He kept his distance. I guess colostomies aren't sexy. What do you think? Is that why *People* wasn't interested in interviewing me?"

"If *People* knew what you did, they would have put you on the cover."

"That's the rub, though, no one knows."

Charlie was serious. "It doesn't matter. Fame is for phonies. You did the job and you stopped him. No one could ask any more of you."

"I fucked up is what I did."

He nodded. "You did that as well and you paid the price. But you've got to let it go, that's what life is about. Throw the pain in the river and let God take it away."

"Do you believe in God?"

He shrugged. "No one knows if there's a God except God, and He's not talking. But I do know human beings weren't designed just for good times. Happiness can make us feel big and sure of ourselves, but only pain gives us depth."

"You sound like a New Age seminar."

"Whatever. You've got to let it go."

She was suddenly close to tears. "I don't want to let him go. I love him, and he's in love with another woman."

"You don't know that for sure. She might just be temporary."

"Oh, that makes me feel a lot better. He dumped me for someone he doesn't even care about."

"Kelly . . ." he began.

"It's not your fault, it's me, I'm so pathetic. I lie on the couch at night and imagine all these horrible things I want to do to Tony and his chick. At the same time, I'm terrified of seeing them together. I love him more now than I loved him when he was mine." She had to stop herself. "What does it all mean?"

"It means your heart's broken."

"Tell me something I don't know."

"You'll feel better with time. You're strong—you're going to get over this and have a great life."

"I don't want a great life. I just want my family back."

"You still get to see Anna."

"Hardly." She looked out the window. "I wish I had never dialed nine-one-one."

David and Amy Techer's house had no FBI cars parked out front. The Bureau, when possible, tried not to announce to kidnappers that the tough guys had been called in. Charlie had received instructions to park a street over, and come in through a neighbor's backyard. But when they did so they ran into twenty-five-year-old Agent Fred Lentil. He was supervising the dusting of an aluminum ladder they assumed the kidnapper had used to get into the Techer yard. Smart, stealth investigators, Kelly thought sarcastically, coming in the exact same way as the bastard.

"Any prints?" Charlie asked, gesturing to the ladder.

"Looks wiped clean," Agent Lentil replied, staring at Kelly. She was a politically incorrect celebrity nowadays. She was admired by the rank and file, they just didn't want to talk to her. Lentil looked like his name, only undercooked. He had the personality of cardboard. Charlie said he had to snort Viagra just to masturbate.

"We should find out who sells these ladders," Charlie suggested.

"I'm on it," Lentil said, and nodded to Kelly. "Vicki's been looking for you. She wants you to interview the parents."

"How do I fly over this wall?" Kelly asked.

Lentil had a ladder of his own, on the other side. Someone pushed it over and Charlie went to help Kelly up. She brushed his hand away. "I'm not a cripple," she said.

The LAPD was not present. The mother of the missing child, Amy Techer, had originally called the cops but they had handed it over to the FBI because the kidnapping had national potential. The grandfather of the child—Carl Techer of Techer Securities on Wall Street—had recently completed a hostile takeover of a huge office supply company. The deal had added cash to the stock price but had dumped ten thousand employees on the street, while leaving bad blood on the boardroom table. Vicki had already suggested that Carl Techer fly out to L.A. and be questioned. Their boss didn't trust anyone who was worth more than a billion. Carl Techer had many enemies.

Inside, Vicki Bane was directing traffic. The house bustled with activity: flash bulbs popping, trails of tape being strung up, fingerprint dust flying everywhere. Their finest criminologist, Dr. Jerry Sharp, was also monitoring every detail. He had a large skull, and one of those thick black mustaches that looked like an extra mouth. He also had a penchant for standing too close to a person when he spoke. Sharp didn't do it to intimidate; he was just a warm-fuzzy kind of guy, especially considering the fact that he worked with cadavers all day.

Dr. Sharp seldom missed a thing. He was very "hands on." Presently, he was vacuuming the upstairs carpet. Kelly climbed the stairs to get an update. The word was Sharp had already tentatively mapped out the course the kidnapper had taken while inside. The criminologist quickly pointed out something of interest to Kelly.

"Looks like he peeked in the master bedroom after grabbing the kid from the nursery," he said.

"Then he left the house?"

"Yes."

"Why do you think?" Kelly asked.

Sharp shrugged. "He must have wanted to see the mother."

Vicki came and took her by the arm, after sending Charlie off to talk to neighbors. Kidnappings were getting to be big business in L.A.—particularly when it came to the rich and the richer. In the last eight months, there had been six major cases in the county—involving sums in excess of five million dollars. None had been reported in the newspaper. Only one kidnapper had gotten away with the loot.

From the look of things, Carl Techer's son had a few bucks.

Kelly saw Vicki was in her element—her steely eyes focused, her strung-out personality bent toward a solitary goal. She had already wired the phones and organized a network of agents to canvass the area. She was frustrated, though, because she was not getting much out of the parents.

"Talk to them, push them," Vicki said.

"Give me what you got," Kelly said.

"Amy Techer set her baby down and went for a nap and when she woke up it was gone. What does that tell you?"

"Do you really buy the Techer Securities connection?"

"Hey, Carl Techer is not a nice man. Even before this happened, I used to read about him in the papers. He's a total bottom-line kind of guy. I'm not shitting you."

Kelly held her side. "Don't say that word around me."

Vicki waved her hand. "Oh yeah, sorry. Anyway, the son reminds me of the old man. Total asshole . . . I mean, you'll see why in ten seconds. This could be connected to a shady deal back East. David Techer came out here from New York a year ago."

"What about Amy?"

"She's a wallflower. Doesn't say much. But I think she loves her baby."

"Where are they?"

"Downstairs, in the dining room. Tape the interview."

"Of course," Kelly said.

Kelly entered the kitchen—from where she could see into the dining room—and puttered around for several minutes. She wanted to observe them interacting with each other, without them knowing. In any kidnapping case, it was standard FBI procedure to first scope out the parents. Too often it was the mother or father who was guilty.

Her first impression of Amy Techer was poor. The woman sat at the kitchen table clutching a cup of tea so hard she might have been trying to strain the leaves. Her pretty face was flaccid, lost of all willpower— her dark lashes dragged down by dried tears. She seemed lost in a reverie that she dared not solve by action. Under normal circumstances, Kelly suspected Amy did not relate well to others. It was merely an observation.

David Techer was another matter. He couldn't decide whether to sit or stand so he polluted the air with waves of nervous energy. His eyes were a cold blue, his skin red and puffy, probably the result of an overworked liver and too many drinks after twelve-hour days. He was clearly a type-A personality, who carried disdain for every other letter of the alphabet. His flabby gut hung over his belt like a loaf of bread waiting to rise.

When Kelly finally did enter the dining room, David Techer gave her a look that said he didn't like her. Well, she thought, ditto. He especially didn't appreciate the black tape recorder she set in the center of the table. He pointed at it like it might chase him to court.

"We've already told your boss everything we know," he said.

Kelly ignored him and sat across from Amy, spoke in a soothing tone. "My name is Kelly Fienman. I've a lot of experience in cases such as this, and I know this is a terrible time for both of you. I also know our procedures must seem clumsy and ineffective. But there's a reason behind them that usually produces good results. Now I have to question you about a few details, and some of them will appear unrelated to your son's abduction. Please, for the time being, just bear with me."

Her politeness had the desired effect. David settled back into a chair and glanced at his wife. The look said it all. He blamed her for the loss of their son. Amy lowered her head and searched for reassurance in her tea leaves. Clearly a product of European and Latin blood, she had a large sensual mouth and beguiling cheekbones. Kelly addressed her directly.

"May I call you Amy?"

She nodded, spoke in a little girl's voice. "That's fine."

"Were you alone here with your son when he was taken?"

"We've already talked about this with that other woman," David interrupted.

"I need a complete record, from scratch," Kelly said firmly, before turning back to Amy. "Were you alone?"

No energy in the reply. "Yes."

"How long had you been alone?"

"An hour or so. Rita, our nanny, left at one."

"What is Rita's full name?"

"Rita Garcia."

"How long have you known her?"

"She's worked for us since Jimmy was born. I've known her family since I was a kid."

"There's nothing wrong with Rita," David interjected.

"Do you know her address?" Kelly asked Amy.

Amy went to stand. "I can get it for you."

Kelly stopped her. "Later. Let's continue. Rita left at one and then what did you do?"

"Fed Jimmy and put him down." Amy rubbed her eyes, struggling. "That would have been about one-thirty."

"How old is Jimmy?"

"Three months."

"Is he still being breast-fed?"

"Yes."

"What does that have to do with anything?" David asked.

"It's important to know if it will be easy for the kidnapper to care for the child," Kelly explained. "If Jimmy is not used to a bottle, he might have difficulties."

"I sometimes give him a bottle," Amy said. "With water or juice."

"Did you often nap after putting your son down?" Kelly asked.

"Yes."

"Today, did you fall asleep right away?"

"Yes."

"Did you hear anything while you slept?"

Amy hesitated. "No."

"What is it?"

"Nothing."

"Tell her," David ordered.

Amy cast him a look that Kelly had no problem reading. Her husband controlled her, she let him, but she didn't like it. She often thought how she could turn the tables on him. It made Kelly wonder.

"I sensed something," she said.

"While you dozed?" Kelly asked.

"Yes."

"Then you were partially awake?"

"I don't know." Amy was puzzled. "But I felt something . . . familiar."

"Where?"

"Nearby. In the house."

"Could you elaborate, please?"

"I can't."

"Is it possible you smelled something? The scent of the kidnapper?"

David nodded enthusiastically. "Amy has a nose on her like a bloodhound. You must have smelled the guy. What did he smell like?"

Amy shook her head. "I don't know."

"What time did you wake up?" Kelly asked.

"At two-twenty."

"Did you immediately check on your son?"

Amy paused. "No."

"But you said you did," David interrupted. "Why didn't you check on him?"

Amy spoke to her husband, annoyed. "I went to the bathroom. I made a call."

"Who did you call?" David demanded.

"My father." Amy suddenly had tears. "What's wrong with that? Why don't you leave me alone? I didn't do anything wrong."

"You just lost our son is all," David muttered.

They were not a couple who regularly contemplated their wedding vows. As if stabbed in the gut, Amy bent over and wept. Kelly gave her time; indeed, she used the time to fix her gaze on David. The guy stared down at his lap and said nothing. Finally Amy spoke.

"I checked on Jimmy about a quarter to three." She gestured helplessly. "He was gone."

"Was the room disturbed in any way?" Kelly asked.

"No."

"Are you sure?" Kelly asked.

"Yes."

"Our people suspect the kidnapper paused at your bedroom door before leaving the house with Jimmy. Do you have any idea . . . ?"

"How would they know that?" David interrupted.

"The impression of his shoes in the carpet," Kelly explained, before asking Amy, "Do you have any idea why he would have stopped to look at you?"

Amy shrugged. "I guess to see if I was up."

"Any other reason?"

"I don't understand what you're asking," Amy said.

Kelly was thoughtful. Something bothered her. It was there in the air like the scent of acid. Her guts gurgled and she pushed aside a wave of nausea.

"Do you have any enemies, Amy?" she asked.

"Not that I know of."

"How long have you two been married?"

"Ten months."

"Were you pregnant when you got married?"

David was livid. "You have a lot of nerve asking—"

"Please," Kelly interrupted. "We need to know. Were you, Amy?"

"Yes."

"How pregnant were you?"

"Three months. Why?"

"Did you have an old boyfriend?"

Amy hesitated. "I've had other boyfriends."

"Were you seeing anyone else in the year before you got married?"

"No," David said.

Amy looked miserable. "I was seeing this one guy. His name was Matt Connor."

"Did you break up with him long before the marriage?"

Amy was a long time answering. "It was a few months before."

"Was Matt upset about the breakup?"

David snorted. "He was a loser. He was nothing."

"Matt didn't take Jimmy. He died four months ago in an accident," Amy said.

"I see." Kelly continued to feel troubled. "Do you have any other old boyfriends who might be angry at you?"

"No," Amy said.

"How about you, David? Any old girlfriends who might carry a vendetta?"

David shook his head. "No."

"Any business enemies who might bear a grudge?"

He stiffened. "No."

"Your father is a big man on Wall Street. He must have some enemies."

David glared. "My father is a highly respected businessman."

"But he recently completed a hostile takeover of a large corporation. A few people made a lot of money. A lot more lost their jobs. We need to talk about that."

David crossed his arms over his chest. "I never talk about my father's business."

"Then we'll have to talk to him about it."

David didn't budge. "That's your choice."

Kelly turned off the recorder. "I appreciate your time and patience. I must warn you that this is only a preliminary interview. Later, we'll have to go through each of these points in more detail."

"You've got to be shitting me," David said.

Kelly stood and slipped her recorder in her pocket. "I would not do that to you, Mr. Techer."

Amy looked up, her eyes haunted; yet still capable of casting their own spells. Kelly could see how any man—even an insensitive jerk like David Techer—could be bewitched by them. Yet Kelly believed her gaze deceptive. Amy was not innocent. She had lied during the interview. She had lied when her son's life was at stake.

"What will happen next?" Amy asked.

"We suspect we'll hear from the kidnapper and he'll want a ransom."

"How much?" David wanted to know.

"Probably a lot. My boss, Vicki Bane, will discuss the specifics with you."

"What if we don't hear from the kidnapper?" Amy asked.

"We almost always do," Kelly said. "Usually within two or three days."

"But what if we don't?" Amy persisted in her exhausted little girl's voice. "Could he kill Jimmy? Could Jimmy already be dead?"

"I honestly don't think so. To you, this is a devastatingly personal attack. But to the kidnapper, this is just business. He's stolen something you want back and he's going to make you pay to get it back."

Kelly ended on that note, went looking for Vicki, found her outside by the pool. She gave her boss a rundown on the interview. Vicki told her to press Amy more about her old boyfriends. Kelly promised to do her best.

Charlie reappeared fifteen minutes later and asked Kelly to walk with him. They ended up two blocks over in a cul-de-sac that pressed against a hill. Charlie pointed out a dirt trail.

"Feel strong enough to climb?" he asked.

"Don't patronize me."

"Then stop acting like you've got something to prove."

She nodded. "Fair enough. Did the kidnapper take this trail?"

"Oh yeah."

Charlie had been right to ask about her strength. Although not far, the climb was steep and she found herself easily winded. She was relieved when Charlie stopped in a cluster of bushes near the edge of the cliff. The view led straight into the Techer backyard. Kelly knelt and studied the ground.

"He took away the soil," she said.

"True. A smart operator. I doubt we'll even get skin."

Kelly stood. "How long do you think he staked them out?"

"The neighbors saw no one, but I think he's been around. When he struck, he was confident."

"Do you think he knows them?" Kelly asked.

"Maybe. Here's an interesting point. I talked to Lentil. That ladder we saw was not where they found it. Lentil had moved it to get in the Techer backyard."

"*What?*"

"Lentil thought it was *our* ladder. He arrived late and was anxious to get in on the action. He pulled it back over the wall. Vicki gave him an earful, but it was an innocent mistake. The ladder was wiped clean. The point is that the kidnapper did not leave the way he came in. He did not take a route he had already established to be safe." Charlie paused. "Guess."

"He walked out the front door with the baby?"

"Yes."

Kelly considered. "Why would he do that?"

"Because he now had the baby in his hands and he wanted to be careful. He didn't want to risk dropping it while he switched the ladder from one side of the wall to the other."

Kelly nodded. "He cares about the baby."

Charlie nodded. "He peeked at Mom. He might care about her as well."

"Interesting."

"How was your interview?"

"Amy lied to me. She lied about an old boyfriend."

"Do we know the guy's name?" Charlie asked.

"Matt Connor. But he's dead."

"Then why do you care about him?"

"Because I sense she did."

"I don't see the good that does us. How many old boyfriends does she have?"

Kelly shook her head. "Don't know. I need to get her alone and drill her. But not today. She's a mess."

"You don't think she stole the baby?"

"No way."

"What about the husband?"

"A prick."

"Aren't they all," Charlie said.

They returned to the house. Vicki wanted to talk to Charlie. The house was still under siege. Kelly wandered around inside, ended up downstairs in Amy's studio. There were bright watercolors on the walls: landscapes and country villages. The woman had talent. On an easel stood the beginning of a portrait of her son. Kelly felt a sharp pang. She thought of Anna suddenly taken from her.

Through a crack in the top drawer of Amy's desk, Kelly glimpsed a picture in a small frame. She let out a gasp. She recognized the guy—he was the one she had seen in the paper the day Slate had introduced her to the Acid Man. It had been his boyish yet intense face that had got her thinking about "Mai Mai and the Man," and "The Tears of Rati." The photo was the same as the one that had appeared in the paper. What a coincidence.

"May I help you?" Amy asked at her back.

Kelly whirled. "Sorry. I was waiting for my partner and I thought I'd have a look around."

Amy was not bothered. "That's the boyfriend I mentioned, Matt Connor."

"I read about him. He died in a plane crash?"

Amy came farther into the room and took the picture and stared at it a moment. "Yes. He was flying from Catalina to Santa Barbara at night. He had just finished scuba lessons and he was going to his birthday party." Amy sniffed. "He was an excellent pilot. They don't know why his plane crashed."

"Were you two very close?"

"We were not supposed to be." Amy sighed. "You understand."

Kelly nodded. "I didn't mean to plow through your stuff."

Amy opened the drawer and put the picture back. "David doesn't know how I feel about a lot of things."

"I'm very sorry."

Amy studied her. She was quiet but not stupid. "Are you married?"

"Sort of. We're . . . we're going through a transition."

"I hope it works out for you."

"Thanks. Me too."

"What happened to your chin?"

A red scar courtesy of the Acid Man's gun. It was fading, with time. "A customer got rough with me."

"I hope you set him straight."

"He'll never do it again." Her bullet had blown out his seventh cervical vertebrae. Professor Gene Banks was now a quadriplegic, a total cripple. Once again the world was safe for cheating wives. Kelly reached in her pocket for her card and added, "Let me give you my office and home numbers. Call me any time of the day, even if it's just to talk. I promise you, Jimmy will receive the highest priority."

"Thank you." Amy started to lose it again. Kelly had to reach out a supporting arm. "Who could do such a terrible thing?" Amy asked, weeping.

"It's hard to imagine," Kelly said.

Charlie finished with Vicki and offered to take Kelly home. He had picked her up that morning. On the drive home, she debated asking him to shoot Tony. It was dark by the time they reached her apartment building. Funny how she didn't have a view or decent furniture anymore. Charlie offered to come in and have sex with her. Kelly laughed sadly.

"God knows I have an extra place to put it," she said.

"Not anymore. I think you're ready for action, girl."

"Not tonight, Charlie."

"Okay. But any time you feel lonely, call. I don't care what time it is."

"Thanks. I might call." She hesitated. "But all we talk about nowadays is me and Tony and Anna. I never ask how you're doing. That's not fair."

"There's nothing to say. I'm doing fine."

"You live alone. You've been alone since I've known you."

"Your fault. I pine away for you."

"Bullshit. Did Margaret make you lose all interest in women?"

Charlie was quiet. "I lost a lot with Margaret."

Margaret had been his second wife and the love of his life. But in the sixth year of their marriage she developed a bad habit—heroin. He did not see the signs, and Charlie saw everything. But when it came to his wife, the addiction made no sense, at least on the surface. She was an RN three nights a week, and the rest of the time she took care of him and did volunteer work at her church. She appeared as far removed from temptation as a nun.

In retrospect, Charlie understood that was Margaret's problem. She was only so perfect because she lived in such perfect denial. She always smiled, had a kind word for everyone. But something inexplicable tore at her emotional center and she slipped into the habit of dulling the pain with Vicoden she swiped from the hospital. In time, she went on to something stronger, oxycodone; and then, finally, heroin and the needle.

He only discovered her habit the first time she overdosed. He found her in the garage, not breathing. It was then he knew why she would only make love to him with the lights out. She had not wanted him to see her tracks. But he never got a chance to talk her into rehab. The paramedics came quick, but they had their red lights off on the drive back to the hospital.

Charlie didn't like to talk about it. A boring story, he said. Kelly could respect that. Sitting in the car beside him, she wished she had not brought up Margaret's name.

"I'm sorry," she said.

"It was years ago." He ran his hands over the steering wheel. "It doesn't matter."

"How did you ever get over it?"

He stared down the street. "Who says I did?"

"You can't tell me that. Not now."

It was his turn to be sorry. "You can't compare my situation to yours. Tony and Anna are alive. Where there's life, there's hope."

"I don't have any hope," she whispered.

"Then let me come in. We can talk about it."

"No. I hate talking about it. I hate thinking about it."

"When did you talk to him last?"

"Last week."

"What did he say?"

"Nothing. He told me when he was going to drop Anna off. Did you know he is suing for full custody? My lawyer tells me he'll probably win. I mean, I'm her mother for godsakes."

"What's his argument?"

"I'm never home. I'm physically ill. Emotionally, I'm too reckless."

"Is there any way I can help?"

"Yeah. Kill him. Kill his girlfriend too."

"I can do it tonight if you want. Make it look like an accident."

Kelly smiled. "Yeah. They were both cleaning *our* guns at the same time and accidentally shot each other."

Charlie shrugged. "O.J. had less going for him and he walked."

Kelly considered. "You can help me. I want you to get me a number."

"Whose?"

She told him and he shook his head. No fucking way. But she persisted; by the time she left his car he promised to have it for her by that night. She did not know how he would get it. Charlie had his ways. If only she had called him on the flight to Ohio.

Kelly went inside her apartment and immediately felt worse. Emptiness waited in every room like an open grave. She did not know whether to bury the past or pray for tomorrow. Of course it was the present moment that really sucked. There was nothing to do with her loneliness. She could not call Anna because Tony would answer and the sound of his voice would make her go mental. She was the outsider now. There was nothing she could do to get back on the inside. And she had always been a person of action.

She made herself a bowl of white rice and had a glass of warm water. There was a whey protein drink she was able to swallow without barfing but she was not in the mood. She didn't even have a TV. Worse, she had no real friends. For the last six years, her family and job had been her life.

The phone mocked her. She could call Charlie but he must be sick of her by now. How many times could she keep asking the same question?

"Why did he leave me?"

"Because he doesn't care anymore," she mumbled.

When she had awakened in the hospital, she had thought the doctors had amputated her lower body. She remembered looking down and seeing a mass of oozing tubes and bloody bandages. The pain was a crawling insect the morphine drip was unable to crush. It was only when she shot herself into a stupor that she had been able to bear it.

A group of doctors came to talk to her. They brought colored diagrams of her intestinal tract and pointed with a pen to the parts they had cut out. She was not exactly sure but it looked as if they had left her with drastically stripped-down equipment. One surgeon joked that at least she didn't have to worry about appendicitis anymore. Banks's acid had melted away the pesky thing.

What the doctors did not tell her at the time was that they thought she was going to die. The waste in her lower bowels had spread throughout her abdominal cavity and she was a cesspool of bacteria. The antibiotics they pumped into her veins were losing the war. Her fever bordered on 105 degrees—brain damage zone. Tony, Anna, and Charlie came to visit and she remembered talking to them but she could not have said about what. There were whole days when she was only conscious of the morphine drip, the fire in her head and guts, and the blank expression of the Acid Man as he had poured his cocktail onto her belly. For the longest time she did not even remember to ask if she had killed him or not.

Then, by some miracle, the infection retreated and her fever went down and she began to gain strength. Charlie explained the Acid Man was in the same hospital, alive but paralyzed from the neck down. That made her feel *real* safe. Tony visited and said that nothing mattered except her health. Then she asked about his girlfriend and somehow the conversation turned to divorce and suddenly her injuries were not so important as the question of when she could move out.

No, that was not fair. Tony had not wanted to discuss their relationship until she was feeling better. She was the one who had insisted on laying it out on the table. If only she had waited until she was home, maybe they would have had time to patch it up. Hey, maybe he would have fallen in love with her again. She was a nice girl; she had a lot going for her. So she had a shit bag attached to her belly. It wasn't a permanent fixture.

Unfortunately, the day she left the hospital was the day she was told she was not allowed back inside her own home. The girlfriend had already moved in. Her name was Claire. She taught grade school, had a B.A. in art from Long Beach State, and was always available by three o'clock to watch after Anna.

Slate visited her that first night in her apartment. Charlie was staying over to help take care of her but Slate sent him out for a long walk. Slate sat on a chair near the couch where she rested on her back. It would be another two months before her colon would knit together enough that the doctors could sew the last stage of her colostomy. Slate was sympathetic to her condition but still a hard man. He did not mind bringing bad news.

"Agent Fienman," he said. "Professor Banks has pleaded guilty to five counts of murder one. There's not going to be a trial. He's unable to move from the neck down. He's no longer a threat to society. He'll remain under house arrest for the remainder of his life."

She could not comprehend what he was saying. "Why house arrest?"

"He's too expensive to take care of. He's personally wealthy. He can afford around-the-clock care. The state of Ohio does not want to foot the bill."

"But he's a serial killer. He has to go to jail."

"He's already in jail in his own body. He cannot be punished any more."

"He can be executed."

"This isn't going to trial," Slate repeated.

Then she understood. The Bureau did not want the case publicized. "You're still protecting the husbands of the victims. They don't want anyone to know what their wives did."

"What's wrong with that? What purpose does it serve to ridicule the men, and yes, their wives? The women are dead, let them rest in peace. Let's leave the husbands alone too. They have suffered enough."

"It's not a question of purpose. Professor Gene Banks is a serial killer. He must be found publicly guilty. That is protocol. Anything less than that is unacceptable."

Slate was annoyed. "You have the nerve to lecture me on protocol? From the moment I brought you in on this case you violated the trust I placed in you. You lied to me about what you learned from the videos. You took an unauthorized trip to India and China and sought out information on a suspect, which you subsequently withheld. You ignored the chain of command of your home office, and pursued on your own a man of unquestionable ferocity. All because you wanted to be the big shot. And you still have the same motive and you won't admit it. You want a trial because you want to be publicly acknowledged as the one who stopped the infamous Acid Man. Say it, Agent Fienman, you don't want justice, you want personal acknowledgment."

His verbal attack took its toll on her. Much of what he said was true. "I didn't think I would meet him face-to-face," she muttered.

Slate softened. "You made a mistake in judgment. I don't condemn you for that. No one is asking you to leave the FBI."

"I seriously doubt I'll be of any use to the FBI in this condition."

"That's a question you need to discuss with your doctors. At present—when and if you do feel better—you may return to your job. You'll receive a reprimand that will go on your record. But I have two of those and they haven't hindered me in my career."

"Has he told you what he did with the bodies?"

"No. He refuses."

"You made such an extravagant deal with him and he still refuses?"

"The matter is closed." Slate stood and offered his hand. "You behaved like a fool, but at least you were a brave fool. Best wishes on a speedy recovery, Kelly."

She gave him a feeble shake. "But you don't want me signing any book deals in the near future?"

His tone hardened. "The Acid Man is history. Understood?"

"Yes, sir," she said, and she understood that she was history as well.

"But I did stop him," she said aloud, back in the present, as she stretched out on the couch. It was easier on her guts to lie down, especially after she ate. But there was not much she could do on the couch except read. When she was completely bored, she sometimes went online. But talking in chat rooms was like masturbation. She always felt empty afterward.

Her new screen name was AcidQueen666.

Maybe she *was* losing her mind.

"Call me," she told the phone. "Please call me."

He did not hear. The phone did not ring.

Kelly stood and grabbed her keys and went out.

There was only one destination. It was sad how sick she felt driving up the street to her old place. The feeling of being the outsider returned stronger than ever. Parking a hundred yards down the block, she stared at her house and wondered if the Accord out front belonged to Claire. Maybe Tony had bought it for her; it looked new. It was half past nine—they should not be in bed already. She felt she could stand talking to Tony if he wasn't just coming from the warm clutches of her arms.

"This is a mistake," Kelly muttered as she got out of the car and slowly walked toward the house. Tony was the source of her pain and he was the only one who could ease her pain. But intruding on him like this without warning would lead to more harm than good. Yet she kept walking—her loneliness would not let her stop. Knocking on the door and waiting for him to answer, she felt like an ant staring up at a shoe.

He opened the door and peeked outside. Not yet ten o'clock and he was in his bathrobe—looked like it was all he was wearing. "I didn't know you were coming," he said.

"I was in the neighborhood."

"Kelly," he began.

"May I come in?"

He glanced over his shoulder. "Now is not a good time."

"Oh." There were not a lot of places to go after that. She tried to go there anyway. "Can't Claire wait in the other room while we talk?"

"I don't think that would be fair to her."

Kelly swallowed. "What about what's fair to me? I was your wife, you know, the mother of your child. I still am in case you've forgotten. Can't you spare a minute?"

"It won't be a minute."

"Damnit, Tony!"

He paused. "Wait here." He closed the door on her face.

Kelly sat on the porch and quietly wept. He was gone five minutes, and when he returned he was fully dressed. It didn't look like she was going to be invited inside. He offered to walk with her.

"I was hoping to see Anna," she said.

"She's already in bed."

"Claire keeps an early schedule?"

Tony nodded down the block. "Let's walk. You'll feel better."

"Okay."

Her old block, her old love. How easy it would be to slip into the fantasy that they were back together. Yet she did not let herself fall far in that direction. But he looked so good, her Tony, that she reached out and took his hand. It meant a lot to her that he didn't resist.

"What do you want to talk about?" he asked.

"I miss you."

"I miss you." But he had to add, "I've missed you for a long time now."

She strove to keep her voice even. "I want to come back. I want to work it out. We were happy together, we can be happy again." She added, "I'm willing to give up my job and work in a library if you want."

"You only say that now because you're depressed."

She stopped. "I say it because I love you. Because I can't live like this. Do you know what it's like for me alone in that apartment? I'm dying, Tony, I'm really dying."

He didn't want to hear. "How's your health?"

"It sucks. Going to tell that to your lawyer?"

"You were the first one to hire a lawyer."

She spoke with emotion. "You were the one who filed for divorce. Look, I'm begging you, tell that girl to go away and leave us alone. Tell her it was a mistake. Tell her anything you want but please get rid of her."

He looked away. "You act like you're the one who got dumped. That's not true—you dumped us both years ago. I don't know how long I pleaded with you to be my wife, to be a mother to our child. Do you know when the last time was that we made love? Ten months ago."

"That's not true."

"It is true. I remember the day."

He was not lying, he had never been a liar.

"I can change," she said. "I'm willing to do whatever it takes."

"It's too late, Kelly."

Tears. God how she hated to show how desperate she was. "Why is it too late? You don't love her, do you?" she asked.

"I don't know."

She was aghast. "But you just met her!"

"Kelly," he began.

"What about me? Do you still love me?"

"Of course I still love you."

She sobbed. "Then take me back! I want to come back!"

He hugged her, held her, comforted her. But he wasn't going to tell her what she wanted to hear. When his arms tired of her quivering form, he walked her back to her car. His eyes drifted toward the house.

She could see he was anxious to get inside to Claire. Didn't want to anger the new and improved screw. No way did he want to wait another ten months to get laid. Kelly got in the car and slammed the door. But she was a wimp. She rolled down the window so he could say a final word. But they were empty words.

"I'll bring Anna by, Friday evening at six," he said.

She put her keys in the ignition. "Fine. Just don't bring Claire."

"You're going to have to meet her sometime."

"Fuck you."

He was not impressed. "You brought this on yourself."

"Yeah? Maybe I did. But you're my husband. When I fall, you're supposed to stop and pick me up. You're not supposed to kick me when I'm down."

Distracted, Tony did not react. "A friend of yours called today."

"Who?"

"Agent Slate. He said he was calling from Quantico. You know him?"

"Yes. What did he say?"

Tony looked at her. "That you were a hero. That society owed you a debt of gratitude it was never going to be able to repay."

She was stunned. "What do you think of that?"

He was thoughtful. "I don't know what to think."

Her apartment was no less empty for her conversation with her ex-husband. She had a bottle of wine in the cupboard. Taking it out and opening it, she wondered what it would do to her guts if she drank the whole thing. Since her liver was having trouble with dry toast, she supposed the alcohol could kill her outright—not an unattractive idea. In the end she poured the wine down the drain.

The phone rang. She skipped across the room. Maybe it was Tony. Maybe he had gotten in a fight with Claire. Maybe he wanted her back.

"Hello?" she said.

"Agent Fienman?" a small voice asked.

"Yes?"

"It's Amy Techer. I don't know why I'm calling."

"Oh, Amy. No, I'm happy you called. How are you feeling?"

She sounded so sad. "Not good."

Kelly sat down. "Tell me."

Amy talked, wept, fell silent. What was there to say? Her world had come to a halt. There had been no word from the kidnapper. Kelly hoped they heard something in the next three days. Otherwise, they would probably hear nothing after that, and the child would almost certainly be dead. A fact she did not share with Amy.

Toward the end of the conversation, Amy asked a strange question. "Do you believe in sin?"

Kelly had to think no further than vials of sulfuric acid. "I do."

"I have sinned. Do you think that's why God took my baby?"

"God didn't take your baby. A madman did."

"No," Amy replied. "God took him."

Eventually Amy said goodbye. Kelly wanted to remain with her longer but knew there were places a person had to go alone. It was then she noticed the light blinking on her answering machine. Charlie had called, with a number. Kelly wrote it down on the back of an envelope and then threw it away and got ready for bed.

But as she turned out the lights, she dialed from memory. In the dark she entered darkness and embraced it, for a short time. She was not surprised he was able to answer. She had heard he had faint feeling in his right hand.

"Hello?" he said, a dry rasp.

"It's me," she said softly.

Silence, breath, wonder, and fear. But was that him or her?

"Hello, Kelly," he said. "I pray you're well."

"Getting there. How are you feeling?"

A chuckle, not bitter. "You know I feel nothing. Thanks to you."

"I want to ask a question. I want you to answer it. I feel you owe me that."

"All right."

"Why didn't you just kill me? Why did you have to mutilate me?"

"I told you why."

"But you lied. I was innocent. Why did you use the acid on me?"

"That is why I used it on you. You only thought you were innocent."

"And no one is?"

"That's it. No one at all."

"You're sick," she swore.

"No. I'm numb. You're sick."

"Is Julie there with you?"

Bitter now. "You wish to hurt me."

"True." She paused. "Julie is gone. Your son is gone. They left with Michael Grander. And you are all alone in the world."

He was still dangerous, she should never have called.

"You sound as alone as me," he replied.

She hung up the phone and laid back in her bed.

That night, she never did fall asleep.

CHAPTER FIVE

There were more e-mails from Amy's father to his mother, back and forth. Matt Connor had made a file of them. They helped pass the time late at night, when the baby was asleep. It was a perverse pleasure. Normal people had sex and money, love and companionship. He had a child that was not his own. The son of the man and woman he hated more than anything on the planet. Yet, after only a month, he cared for Jimmy with a depth of affection he found inexplicable. He had not disposed of the child in some third-world country as he had planned.

That said something. But what?

His deepest fears and hopes had not materialized. His revenge had brought no final peace, but it had not hurt, either. On a hypothetical scale of joy and sorrow, he was happier now than before he had wounded Amy. The righteous were mistaken—if revenge was not sweet, it at least had flavor.

However, when he thought of Amy crying at night because of her lost child, he wept with her. He could feel the walls closing in on her as the days passed. She would think the worst; her baby dead and buried. She could not imagine that the shadow she had cast over Matt Connor's life had returned as an avenging angel.

Yet, sometimes, late at night, when he stood over Jimmy, he felt like he would give his life to protect the child. He imagined he was a much better father than David.

The e-mails were interesting. While Jimmy slept peacefully not four feet from his desk, Matt flipped through his favorites. It was thirty-three days since he had taken the child.

> Dear Nancy,
>
> Thank you for staying on the phone with me so long the other night. I'm sorry I broke down and wept like a fool, somehow I couldn't help myself. The nights are the worst. Often, I swear, I hear my grandson crying outside my door. Several times I have gotten up from bed to check—the sound is so real. But, alas, Jimmy is never there.
>
> Amy has been destroyed. Nothing I say can console her. She has this idea in her head that God is punishing her for what she did to Matt. I tell her that is nonsense, that this tragedy would have been the last thing Matt would have wished upon her. But she's in a dark place and there's no reaching her.
>
> Her husband is no help. The looks he gives her—I think he believes she took Jimmy and buried him somewhere. David is a sick man. I wish he'd get out of our lives.
>
> Nancy, how can we live? You lost a son and I lost a grandson. Such a cruel world, this one we are cursed to live in. It is only the love of people like you—and the memory of men like Matt—that make it bearable. My prayers are with you, and I hope yours remain with me.
>
> Yours, John

The next one had come the previous week.

> Dear Nancy,
>
> Hope fades. It sounds as if the FBI no longer believes we'll be contacted by the kidnappers. Amy and David spoke to them yesterday and the woman in charge of the investigation, Agent Bane, said it was unlikely to receive a ransom demand after

such a long lapse of time. I think the FBI has known this for a while, but to have it confirmed is devastating. Amy has turned into a wraith. You know, she used to weigh only a hundred and five pounds. Well, she has lost fifteen of that. If this keeps up she'll have to be put in a hospital.

What can I say? I miss my grandson. I miss my daughter. I miss Matt. I cannot be free of the idea that if your son had not died, all this pain would have been avoided. I think of myself as a religious man, but I catch myself cursing God. There is no justice in this world. David should have gone in that water. Matt should be with us now.

Sorry, Nancy, I rave. I better go.

Yours, John

Matt found it interesting how Amy's father made a connection between his death and the kidnapping. The man had always been sensitive. It was as if Amy's dad had a psychic antenna for the good and evil in people. Matt felt awful about the pain the man was going through. The guilt was not erased by the agony Amy was experiencing. However, there was only so much guilt he could allow himself to feel and stay sane.

There was good news. Cindy had a new boyfriend. His ex-girlfriend had written his mother yesterday about the guy. He was a handsome lawyer from a rich Southern family. Matt honestly wished her the best. He had not missed her as much as he imagined he would. In fact, he had not missed her at all. That was the problem with obsession. It lumped every small good in life into one indistinguishable mass of nothing.

There was a knock on his trailer door. Matt looked up and saw Lupe Chavez outside the window, Jimmy's eighteen-year-old nanny. He had found her in a coffee shop with a girlfriend two days after he had taken Jimmy. Both girls were from Guatemala, and desperate for jobs. When it came to finding employment, Lupe had distinct advantages over her friend. Her English was excellent and she projected a competence beyond her years. He occasionally worried about her sharp mind. A simple girl from a remote village would have been a better choice to care for a kidnapped child. But he liked Lupe, and he worried about leaving Jimmy in the hands of a simpleton.

"You're early," Matt said as he opened the door. There was no mistaking Lupe's resemblance to Amy, another fact that made him wonder about his state of mind. They were about the same size, five foot tall and slim. Lupe had the same large Latin eyes he seemed unable to get enough of. Her face was more alert than Amy's; however, she was not nearly as pretty. It occurred to him then how easy it had been for Amy to hide her real intentions. She showed so little of her internal state that one was constantly filling in the blanks.

"I went shopping for the baby and finished faster than I expected," she said as she held up a bag of diapers and formula. Matt remembered the day he had swiped the child. A hundred miles north of L.A., in the middle of nowhere, Jimmy had awakened hungry and upset. He had wanted his mother's breast, and his frantic efforts with a formula bottle had not been appreciated. Naturally, Matt had considered beforehand how difficult it might be to feed Jimmy. In his telescope, he had seen Amy occasionally giving her son a bottle, and he had hoped for the best. But he had never imagined Jimmy's crying could shake him so deeply. For two hours he had seriously considered the impossible—dropping the whole scheme and returning the child to Amy.

But then Jimmy had fallen asleep and the next time he awoke he had taken the bottle happily. The kid must have been starving. His huge eyes had stared up at him with such trust that it had touched him deeply. Matt had been surprised that the routine tasks of caring for the boy did not bother him. Even changing Jimmy's diapers when Lupe was gone was no hassle.

"Great, come in," Matt said, opening the door wider. "I've errands I have to get done anyway. The sooner I start on them the better." It was a Saturday, he did not have to work. He had not planned to work as long as he had the child, anyway. But now that Jimmy had become a permanent member of his household, that was impractical.

Matt needed to get out in either case.

Playing father was fun but not twenty-four hours a day.

Besides, he had a new girlfriend, twenty-five-year-old Debra Marsh. That was his supposed chore, to go over and have lunch and sex with her. She was good for him in a lot of ways. She talked a lot and didn't mind if he listened. He had met her at a bar. In Modesto, drinking was as obligatory as wiping the dust from one's eyes. She worked in an office somewhere downtown. There was only one problem with the relationship. He could not come during sex unless he pretended she was Amy. It was not as disgusting as it sounded. He suspected the technique kept a lot of couples together.

But he did not *love* Debra any more than he had *loved* Cindy.

Yet he liked her; there was a lot to be said for just liking someone.

"What are you reading?" Lupe asked as she checked on sleeping Jimmy. Matt hastily put away the copies of the e-mails. He was a fool to keep them. Lupe could read them when he was out and put two and two together. He reassured himself she was not a snoop, but the truth was, everyone was.

"Just some old letters from online friends," he said.

"Girlfriends?" Lupe only appeared conservative—one of those staunch Roman Catholics who carried a condom in her purse. She had come on to him several times, but he knew it would be a mistake to mix business with pleasure. Jimmy was used to her. It was odd, but in this matter, he had no trouble putting Jimmy first. Lupe added, "You need to get out more."

"You don't like Debra?" he asked.

"I like her. I like watermelons too. But it doesn't mean I would sleep with one."

"She's not that stupid."

"She's not smart." Lupe moved closer to Jimmy. She loved him as if he was her own. He had told her that Jimmy's mother had died in a car accident not long after giving birth. He had said it with such feeling, they had both ended up crying. Lupe gently poked Jimmy. "I think he's waking up."

Jimmy had one eye open, and was yawning. He looked unbearably cute. How could anyone think of the long term in the face of such innocence? Yet, Matt knew that one day he would have to decide what he was going to do with the child. Only, it would be tomorrow, always tomorrow.

"He only took a little formula before his nap," Matt said. "He's probably still hungry."

Lupe brushed aside a wisp of Jimmy's hair. "He looks more and more like you each day."

Matt shrugged. "I don't know."

Lupe shook her head. "He has your eyes, exactly, and the same shape of face. Get some of your own baby pictures and compare them. You'll be stunned."

Matt stared down at Jimmy and a sensation both hot and ice-cold swept over him. The baby had opened both his eyes and was smiling up at him.

"I'll do that," he muttered.

■

THERE WAS an obvious detail that did not have to be considered because it was . . . well, so obvious, besides being indisputable. Jimmy couldn't be his kid because he had never had sex with Amy. Yet, once out of the trailer and on the road toward Debra's house, Matt did consider the idea.

He was in a unique position to evaluate impossibilities. After all, as far as the cops knew, he could not have been the one who had kidnapped Jimmy because he was dead. And look how well that logic worked for the authorities.

He had not had actual intercourse with Amy, but they had fooled around mightily. One of her favorite tricks when they were hot and heavy and naked in bed together was to grab his dick and rub it against her clitoris. She really got off on it, and he had to admit he had almost come at such times.

The key here was, he had *almost* come.

Matt knew enough about physiology and pleasant tingling sensations to realize he could have had a significant amount of sperm at the tip of his penis when she had stroked him close to climaxing. He also knew that sperm trained for the hundred-meter butterfly from the moment they were born. And it wasn't a far swim from the surface of her vagina up to her tubes. Indeed, he had actually read about such cases.

He might have impregnated her and not known it.

But had she known it? A disturbing question, to be sure, but then everything about Amy was disturbing. If she had indeed gotten pregnant with his baby and had still chosen David over him then that made her out to be worse than a whore.

An interesting idea . . . to no longer be dead. His prefabricated nonexistence was liberating and stifling at the same time. He missed his mom. He missed Los Angeles. He still missed Amy . . . No, it was better not to go there. No *fucking* way should he go there. Yet if Jimmy was his child and she did *not* know it, and he was able to prove it, then how long would David hang around?

"I'm not going back to her!" Matt screamed inside his car.

Even he was not that crazy. She wouldn't come back anyway. She was a slut and he didn't have any money. That was all she had wanted. Besides, babies looked like a lot of people when they were Jimmy's age.

Still, the possibilities were interesting.

Matt did not go to Debra's house. He swung by the library instead, found a book on DNA testing and paternity cases. He didn't have to read long to learn what he needed. It took only a week to determine who the father of a child was. In the back of the book was a list of laboratories that performed the test. Matt used the library pay phone to call a lab in San Francisco. The woman who answered was informative. All they needed was a cheek swab of the child and the suspected father—plus five hundred dollars. Matt had feared it would cost a lot more.

"Do these tests hold up in court?" he asked.

"Absolutely," the woman said.

Matt reached for a pen. "Tell me exactly how I should send the swabs."

CHAPTER SIX

When the call came, Kelly Fienman was at her desk and contemplating quitting the FBI. Five months had elapsed since the Acid Man had wrecked her life. Six weeks had gone by since Amy Techer's baby had been kidnapped. Now it was mid-June, and summer already looked like it was going to be hot and miserable.

What did the passage of time mean anyway without love? The days just made her older. It was bullshit that time healed all wounds. It merely buried them, she thought, and not that deeply. She still went to sleep and woke up thinking about Anna and Tony. They called so seldom.

But Amy's call, that got her attention. Kelly had an apple in her mouth when the phone rang. She could eat them, along with other fruit, if she chewed slowly. But she still could not digest much else. She was twenty pounds lighter than when she had gone to see Professor Gene Banks.

Charlie sat across from her at his desk, devouring a romance novel. He moved his thick dark lips as he read, intent on every comma and orgasm. Go figure—he said he had bought a box of the books for two bucks at a yard sale and he was determined to get his money's worth. He did not look up at the ringing phone. They were both bored with their jobs. If she quit, he said he was quitting too.

"Hello?" she said, swallowing carefully. Her esophagus hurt on top of everything. Her stomach acid preferred to travel up rather than go down because her guts were still so messed up.

"Agent Fienman?" Small voice, big expectations.

"Amy? How are you?"

The words burst. "I got a letter from *him!*"

Kelly dropped her apple and it rolled over and bumped Charlie's foot. He looked up and stared into her wide eyes and motioned for her to put it on the speakerphone. But she shook her head.

"The kidnapper?" she asked.

"Yes. It's him, I know it's him. He sent a tape of Jimmy talking and crying and a few of his hairs. Jimmy's alive!"

"That's great news. What else did he send?"

"A note. He sent a note. He wants money."

"Good. Now you need to listen to me, Amy. Listen closely. I don't want you to handle what he sent anymore. Just leave it where it is. Don't even pick it up to put it in a safe place. Agent Fitzsimmons and I are going to come over right now. We'll be there in less than half an hour."

Amy was ecstatic. "I'm going to get my baby back!"

"We'll get him back," Kelly said. She set down the phone and stared at Charlie. He picked up the apple and wiped it off and took a bite. He liked to share food with her. He told her it brought him as close to her mouth as he was likely to get.

"Techer?" he said.

"The kidnapper contacted her. A letter filled with goodies."

Charlie reached for the phone. "I'll get Dr. Sharp. We'll try for prints, material."

"He sent hair, and a tape of the baby's voice."

Charlie nodded. "I'll have Sharp find his samples, try for a match."

"Have him bring his microscope to the house. I want to know when we're there."

Charlie dialed. "Sharp will know."

She stood. "You're the one who said how smart this bastard was. There won't be any prints or skin."

"Does he want money?"

"She says he does."

Charlie took another bite of the apple. "When he tries to collect it we'll see how smart he is."

■

DR. SHARP reached the Techer house the same time as they did. Kelly sat with Amy while the criminologist completed a preliminary examination of the hair fibers, the note, and the tape. David Techer was nowhere around. Amy had not called him, not yet—that said something about the nature of their relationship. But Amy said her father was on his way over. Kelly had met him two months ago. A nice man, loved his daughter, hated his son-in-law.

Amy looked like she had been on the Acid Man fitness program as well. They had lost the same amount of weight, but on five-foot Amy it was even more devastating. Her left eye twitched; she had developed a tremor in her hands. Kelly regretted the promise she had made to her on the phone. This kidnapper followed no pattern. The unexpected was always dangerous.

Sharp had good news, though. The hairs matched the boy, and the baby sounds on the tape were the same as those on videos Amy had made of Jimmy. As the four sat at the kitchen table, Sharp played the tape the kidnapper had sent: a baby's cooing and giggling, mixed in with a radio broadcast of a Lakers game.

"They played San Antonio two nights ago at the Staples Center," Charlie said. "That's the same game. He wanted to date it for us."

"What does that mean?" Amy asked. On the whole she was still subdued, but the threads of the cocoon had cracked, the butterfly stirred. Or was she a moth? Kelly was not yet sure if she liked or even trusted the woman. Amy's eyes darted over the three of them, wanting to hear only good news.

"He wants us to know Jimmy was alive as recently as two days ago," Kelly said. "He wants his money. If we give him what he wants, he's saying he will give us what we want."

Amy closed her eyes. "Thank God."

Kelly turned to Sharp. "Find anything interesting?"

Sharp shook his head. "No. I'll go over it again at the lab but he wiped everything clean with acid. Even the paper."

Kelly winced. "Not strong acid?"

"No. Of course not. But I'm already sure his formula destroyed any microscopic evidence." Sharp nodded. "He knows our procedures."

"Maybe he's a cop," Kelly suggested.

Charlie snorted. "Only in the movies."

"I'm not so sure," Kelly said.

"He reads a lot of thrillers is all," Charlie said. "Let's focus on what we've got." He gestured for Sharp to put the plastic-sealed note on the table so that they could all read it. The demand was printed on plain white paper, eight and a half by eleven, the words formed by a laser printer. Sharp wasn't going to get anything off it. But the note itself— here there was a chest of psychological riches yet to be explored.

Dear Amy and David,

    I have your son, he is doing well. If you would like to see him again, you will have to cooperate. I want a million dollars in unmarked, unsequenced, one hundred dollar bills; along with two million dollars worth of round diamonds—the cut and color of the highest quality—ranging in size from one to three carats. I know you have already spoken to the FBI, but if you call them on this matter you will regret it. They cannot help you anyway. In the next few days you will be contacted as to how and where the ransom is to be delivered. I have selected David to do the honors. Afraid, Mr. Techer?

Once again, the money, the diamonds, and the bag the valuables are to be delivered in are not to be tampered with. If I see any FBI the day of the delivery, Jimmy will lose a father.

Yours, Falling

Amy was worried. "He says I shouldn't have called you guys."

"He would say that as a matter of course," Charlie replied in a reassuring tone.

"He expects us to be here," Kelly added.

"How can you be sure?" Amy asked.

"Because he's smart," Kelly said.

"Why does he call himself Falling?" Amy asked.

"An interesting question," Kelly said, looking to Sharp and her partner.

Charlie spoke. "It's more interesting that he threatens David, and not the child."

Sharp nodded. "I've never seen that in a ransom note before. It's almost as if he's protective of the child."

"He's had him a while, he might have become attached." Charlie was thoughtful. "He was very careful when he carried the boy out of here. Remember?"

Kelly sure did. She turned to Amy. "I know Agent Bane spoke with your husband about the ransom money two months ago. Does he still have the cash handy?"

"Yes. But didn't you guys mark it?"

Charlie spoke. "No. We just recorded the numbers on twenty percent of the bills."

"Why didn't you record all the numbers?" Amy asked, her tone slightly demanding.

"This guy is too careful to use the money himself," Kelly explained. "He'll shop it to a third party—drug dealers most likely—probably out of the country, and accept, say, sixty bucks on each hundred." Kelly paused. "It's the diamonds he really wants."

"Why?" Amy asked.

"It's very hard to trace them," Kelly said.

"Why do they have to be between one and three carats?" Amy asked.

"Four-carat diamonds and larger call attention to themselves," Charlie replied. "Smaller than a carat wouldn't be worth his time to dispose of." Charlie nodded. "The guy is thinking."

Amy stared down at the note, quoted, " 'They cannot help you anyway.' Why is he so confident he's going to get away with it?"

To that question, none of them had a good answer.

■

FALLING, AS he liked to be addressed, called three days after the delivery of his letter. He rang the Techer's directly, on their home line, on a Saturday morning at ten o'clock. He stayed on the line only fifteen seconds, his words distorted through a voice modulator. There was no chance to trace the call. In those few seconds he directed David to a phone booth at the corner of Chapman and City Drive in Orange County, on the other side of town. Falling wanted him there by two. He told David to go ahead and enjoy his lunch. Cool customer.

Kelly listened in on the call. She had been staying at the Techers' residence since the letter had arrived, sleeping in a downstairs bedroom. Amy was lousy company, a waif on Valium. David at least tried to make her as comfortable as possible. The two nights she was there, Kelly heard them going at it in the bedroom.

Carl Techer, David's father, had not flown in for the excitement.

They had gotten nothing out of him when they had questioned him about the kidnapping. The man had had too many lawyers in the room. Yet everything said the Techer Securities link was a dead end.

When Falling called, Kelly and her people were ready. The team—Vicki and Charlie included—arrived at the house within twenty minutes. They had already prepped David on the equipment he was to use. Kelly personally wired David. The microphone—a button on his shirt—was so sensitive it could pick up a voice on a pay phone. He stood nervously in the kitchen as she fixed his shirt and reviewed the features on the large black case he would carry the cash and diamonds in. For the moment the others were in the living room. Vicki saw that Kelly had an established relationship with the Techers and let her act as the FBI's primary liaison.

"We've sewn a tracking chip into the top," she said. "It's virtually undetectable. He'd have to rip the thing to pieces to find it. And we've left the money and diamonds unmarked. But we have a chip in your car. If he instructs you to lose us, you won't be able to. Do you have any questions so far?"

David sweated. He had read the ransom note; he was scared. Amy stood nearby and showed not an ounce of sympathy. She just wanted her baby back, and God help her husband if he failed to bring the child home. Kelly heard Charlie arguing with Vicki in the other room, something about helicopters and visibility. Kelly planned to follow David in her own car with Charlie. The high stakes had the air charged with tension; excitement as well. Kelly felt nervous but alive—more alive than since the Acid Man had baptized her with his unholy waters.

"But when he gets the case he'll examine it," David said. "He'll know we called the FBI. He might kill Jimmy."

"Once again, he'll have a hard time finding the chip," Kelly said. "But it's not our plan to let whoever picks up the money just walk. This person has had your son too long. We cannot simply cooperate, we might never hear from him again."

Amy did not like that. "But you said we were going to cooperate?"

Kelly shook her head. "I told you it had not been decided. But yesterday, Agent Bane—in conjunction with our top people back East—decided that the long lag between the kidnapping and the ransom means this person is unusually unpredictable—even when it comes to kidnappers. And I'm forced to agree with them. Whoever picks up the money, we have to nab him."

"But he could just be a stooge," David said.

Kelly hesitated. "True."

"What's a stooge?" Amy asked.

"Someone who does the dirty work, not knowing it's a kidnapping," David explained, and then glared at Kelly. "I don't like taking orders from you people. I have the final say here and I want to cooperate with this guy. He says he'll give Jimmy back once he has the cash and diamonds and I believe him. What would he want with a baby anyway?"

Kelly spoke carefully; she had expected the outburst. "Of course as the parents you have the final say. But you're inexperienced in these matters. You cannot believe a word this guy says. He could keep your child and demand another ransom, and still another. Then you would be his stooge."

David grumbled. "If this doesn't work you're responsible."

"No," Kelly said. "If we fail to get Jimmy back, the kidnapper will be responsible. We can only do the best we can with what we know, and everything this guy has done so far tells us that he's exceptionally clever. We must stick with our plan. Whatever he tells you to do, do it, don't argue with him. We'll be close by."

"But what if he sees you?" Amy asked.

"He won't see us," Kelly said. "That I can guarantee."

Time to rock. They went out to the driveway. They had the block covered and knew for a fact the kidnapper was nowhere near. Kelly continued to puzzle over why Falling had threatened David and not the baby. Could this be a crime of revenge after all? Before David left the house with the cash and diamonds, he demanded a gun.

"What do you want a gun for?" Vicki asked. "You're not going to shoot anyone." She had a short fuse when dealing with David. She had confided in Kelly that she was often tempted to kick him in the balls.

David was annoyed. "The guy implied he would kill me if I brought the FBI into this. Well, you guys are spread all over the goddamn city. I want a gun."

Charlie spoke. "Have you ever fired a gun before, Mr. Techer?"

David hesitated. "No."

"Then it's too late to learn how to use one," Charlie said, glancing at his watch. "Get in your car and get going. You don't want to be late."

Charlie had that kind of authority. He stared at him and David got in a white BMW. Kelly loaded the bulky case in the backseat. Weird to think a million bucks in hundreds weighed over twenty pounds. The diamonds were lighter. Amy leaned through the car window and hugged her husband goodbye.

"Be careful," she said.

David spoke with feeling. "I'll bring Jimmy home, honey."

Kelly felt touched, despite herself.

The show was finally on the road. Kelly and Charlie picked up David ten minutes later, on the freeway, heading toward Orange County. As usual, Charlie drove like a fiend, even following someone who didn't.

They could communicate with David directly via his microphone, and the implant in his ear. Kelly did a trial test and David complained about the weather. He was a piece of work.

"Think she married him for love?" Charlie asked after she broke the connection.

"Love of money. The real question is, why did he marry her?"

"She's a fox," Charlie said.

"She's strange. She has no personality. She stares too much."

"She's probably a great fuck. The weird ones always are."

"The voice of experience?"

"Damn right. Let's talk about the case. Does this guy have a partner or not?"

"I don't know. What do you think?"

"No way. His connection to David and Amy is personal."

Kelly followed his leap in logic. "I've been thinking the same. So you agree with Vicki that we hammer whoever grabs the money? You think it will be him?"

Charlie paused. "This guy is not going to let us see him."

"Then how is he going to get the money?"

"I don't know."

"Be vague why don't you."

Charlie smiled. "We're in for an interesting day."

It was a lazy Saturday afternoon: overcast but still sticky; L.A.'s infamous June gloom. David drove the speed limit all the way to Orange County, worried the legion of surrounding FBI agents would give him a ticket. He waved to her and Charlie once and she was on the line in an instant, yelling at him not to do that.

"Why are the children of the rich always so stupid?" she wondered aloud.

They had not cased the phone booth, although they had plenty of time. There was an excellent chance the kidnapper could be in visual range of the booth. But they had the corner videotaped in four different directions in case he drove by. Because if he did it once—and he directed David to another location—then he might drive by a second time. Then, later, they could compare tapes and identify his car, if not his face. But Charlie did not think Falling would make such an elementary mistake.

They parked around the corner from the phone booth. They had others to watch David; it was more important for them to listen. The time was ten minutes to two. Vicki came over the line. Kelly was not sure where she was, only that she was close. Their helicopter was five miles south, invisible, carrying a high-powered telescope and a sharpshooter.

"He stands, waiting for the call," Vicki said. "At least he does that well."

"Does he look nervous?" Kelly asked.

"He has his hands in his pockets. I think he's masturbating."

"Crude," Kelly said.

"Hey. I'll blow the bastard if he gets the kid back," Vicki said.

The seconds ticked. Their brains played like accordions. Time compressed and then dragged by. David remained silent, as per instructions. Finally, the phone rang. He picked it up.

"Hello?"

A modulated voice. "Look under the phone, follow the instructions."

The guy hung up. Kelly heard unfolding paper. She spoke into the mike.

"Read it aloud like you're reading it to yourself," she said.

He paused, then read. " 'David, at the corner of Harbor and Chapman, in Santa Ana, you'll see an old two-story office building. Go to the back, suite one-oh-nine. Go inside, and you'll receive further instructions. Hurry.' "

"Do it," Kelly said.

"But . . ." David began.

"You don't need to talk, do it," Kelly snapped. They had supplied him with a map. He could not get lost. Nevertheless, Charlie looked over at her as she cut David off.

"I know, I need to keep him calm," she apologized.

"No, you were fine," Charlie said. "He has to be strong, not calm."

They followed David to Santa Ana. Pulling into a Burger King parking lot across the street from the drab olive office building—which looked like it had been pissed on by the Jolly Green Giant—they were able to watch as David parked and climbed out of his car. Kelly wanted to sit and observe but Charlie was wary.

"Let's go inside and watch from there," he said.

She spoke into the mike. "If there's another note, David, read it aloud."

The interior of the Burger King was deserted. Charlie stepped to the counter to order, either hungry or acting like it. Kelly took a seat by the window and watched David knock on suite 109. He got no answer, so he went inside. Kelly waited for a gunshot, a scream, blood on the window and subsequently on her hands.

But nothing that dramatic happened.

"A video camera," David muttered.

Kelly reacted quickly. "If there's a camera, don't talk. Look for another note and speak only when you have it in your hands. All your speech has to appear natural."

She heard David's steps. Paper crackled in his hands. He read aloud.

" 'David, as long as you're in this room, I can see you. Keep that in mind at all times and don't deviate from my instructions. Take the cash and diamonds and put them in the washing machine and turn it on. Be sure to use the soap I've left you. Don't worry about drying the goodies. When you're finished, put the cash and diamonds in the large canvas bag lying on top of the washing machine. In the meantime, strip off everything you are wearing and put on the hospital grubs you see in front of you. When I say everything, I mean everything—including the microphone in your ear. When you're done, take the bag and yourself to the phone booth at the corner of Adams and Magnolia. I'll call with further instructions.' "

"Do as he says and talk no more," Kelly said quickly. "Don't worry that we're out of touch, we're not far."

David came outside, got the cash and diamonds, and went back inside the suite. Charlie returned with two cheeseburgers, fries, and Cokes. Kelly waved away the food—like she could even eat it. Charlie sat down and proceeded to enjoy his lunch as if nothing was happening. Kelly could only stare.

"Do you think the video camera is live?" she asked.

"No. But we have to treat it like it is."

"Why wash the money?" she asked.

"He worries we've added 'funny money' to the million. We used the stuff in the old days. It explodes with bright colored ink if not handled carefully. He's also worried about a tracking device attached to the dough. Washing the ransom is a smart move from his point of view."

"And he gets rid of our case," Kelly muttered.

"Sure. He gets rid of our wire. But these things we expected."

"What will he do next?"

"Lead us all over town. Kill time until dark."

"Then?"

"The unexpected," he said.

"I think you admire this guy."

Charlie chewed his food. "Not enough to stop me from blowing his head off."

Nothing happened for the next thirty minutes. When David finally emerged he was dressed like an ER doctor and carrying a heavy brown sack. By then Charlie had finished both burgers and they were in their car and on their way to Adams and Magnolia. Kelly speculated on the location of the action.

"He must have the kid in Orange County," she said.

"No. It's a ruse. At the last second, he's going to direct David far from here."

"How come you're so smart?"

Charlie burped. "Because I'm black and beautiful."

It was frustrating to have lost David's microphone. When David went into the next phone booth, Charlie parked around the block. They had to rely on Vicki for input. But there was not much to say. David was in and out of the thing, and then back on the road to another phone booth.

The pattern continued for the next four hours. David went phone booth to phone booth. Charlie was a prophet—by then it was dark and clear to everyone that Falling was merely getting warmed up. David had to stop once to get gas. They filled up as well, at a station down the block. Their helicopter also had to land to refuel.

At a phone booth deep in Irvine—at half past eight—Falling left a cell phone for David. The kidnapper wanted more direct communication.

The move opened up a window of opportunity. Kelly wondered if the guy had finally made a mistake. They could triangulate on the cell and locate its source. So far, they had come up empty trying to trace the calls to the various phone booths. Falling was using public phones—a different one each time—sprinkled across Orange County. But Charlie was not that excited about the cell phone.

"He'll barely use it," he said. "He won't give us a chance to eavesdrop."

Kelly continued to puzzle over Falling's tactics as they stayed a quarter of a mile behind David, heading south on the San Diego Freeway, about to leave Orange County. Luckily, her guts were not acting up. She wondered if they were healing. For the day, she had eaten two apples and one banana, and drank eight ounces of aloe vera juice.

"I'm surprised he hasn't had David switch cars," she said. "He must know we have it bugged."

"He knows and he doesn't care," Charlie said.

"What does that mean?"

"The unexpected."

"Stop that. Could today be a sham?" she asked.

"No. He's spent too much time setting it up. He wants the goodies. He thinks he's figured out a way to get them without us catching him."

David got on the Santa Ana Freeway heading south and took an exit at Mission Viejo. He then got back on the freeway and headed north. Charlie let him slip out of sight and used the next exit to turn around. It took them fifteen minutes to catch up. By then David was on the San Diego Freeway and heading north. Vicki came over the line.

"Falling called David on the cell phone," she said. "We didn't get much, a word or two, useless. What do you have to say, Charlie?"

"I think he's ready to make his move."

"I agree. Oh, we have another helicopter on its way."

"Hopefully we won't need it," Charlie said, glancing out the window at the dark sky. Vicki's chopper was three miles to their left, a mile behind. Vicki signed off.

"Why do you want another chopper?" Kelly asked.

"Gut feeling," Charlie said.

David exited the freeway forty-five minutes later and headed toward the marina. The direction immediately set off an alarm. Vicki came back on the line. Could Falling be planning to take David onto a boat? Charlie was worried that was the case.

"Get a boat right away," he said. "Have it hang a mile off the coast."

"That will take time. Fifteen minutes," Vicki said.

"Bullshit. Make it ten," Charlie snapped.

Kelly glanced over at him. "We in trouble?"

Charlie sighed. "Depends how quickly we get the boat."

David parked at the marina, picked up another note beneath a garbage can, and then headed for the boats. He showed some smarts—he left the note where he found it. Their people recovered it right away—a risky move but a necessity. Before Charlie and Kelly could reach the parking lot, Vicki informed them that Falling had directed David to a ship called *Scallop*.

"He told David to steer the boat toward Catalina," Vicki said. "Even gave him a compass reading to follow."

"Can David read a compass?" Charlie muttered.

"He has a yacht," Kelly said. David had talked about his boat while she had stayed at his house.

"Got an agent in the water yet?" Charlie demanded.

"Almost," Vicki said. "We can't get too close. The helicopters are more important."

"Send a boat from Catalina this way," Charlie ordered.

Vicki considered. "Do you think Falling's aboard this boat?"

"It's possible," Charlie said. "Do we have a line of sight on David right now?"

"Yeah," Vicki said. "He's already aboard the boat and winding slowly through the harbor. He seems to know what he's doing."

"Does the *Scallop* have a cabin?" Charlie asked.

"Yes," Vicki said.

"Falling could be hidden below," Charlie told Vicki.

"Yeah. David didn't check inside the cabin," Vicki replied.

"That's bad. Falling specifically threatened David," Charlie reminded their boss.

But Vicki was in no mood to alter their plan. "We've already done enough to scare the bastard away. We keep our distance."

Vicki signed off. Charlie drove into the marina lot. They searched for a parking place near the boats. It was a crowded Saturday night—they ended up a quarter mile from David's car. Hurrying on foot toward the water, Charlie made an astute comment.

"An island's the last place in the world Falling would want to pick up money."

"It would be so easy to trap him there," Kelly agreed. "So why Catalina?"

"He has no intention of letting David get that far."

"He's aboard? He'll kill him?"

"No. That wouldn't help him either."

"But it could all be for revenge. The Techer Securities connection?"

"I don't know," Charlie said.

"Maybe he's going to take him hostage?"

Charlie snorted. "If he knows the family personally, then he knows David would make a terrible hostage. His own wife would just as soon shoot him."

Charlie joked, or so Kelly thought. But it was a fact they could not shoot Falling until they had the baby in their hands. Left alone in an apartment or house, Jimmy would die within two days.

At the harbor, they met Vicki and the other agents. Vicki had already dispatched a boat after David, but had given the agents aboard instructions to stay back a mile. Charlie grumbled—they could not offer David protection at such a distance. Vicki did not care.

"We can't protect him anyway, if he's on the boat with the fucker," Vicki said.

Charlie didn't agree but held it inside. She had never seen him so tense. Her own nerves were frayed. With David out on the water, she felt helpless.

The second helicopter appeared, landing in the marina parking lot. Vicki climbed aboard and Charlie insisted on coming along. They were at each other's throats but Vicki knew Charlie was shrewd and wanted his support. Kelly followed Charlie into the craft without asking permission. The chopper was jet powered, capable of carrying six people at high speeds. They were airborne before Vicki noticed her. Vicki said nothing—she had other things on her mind.

The overcast hung low. At three hundred feet they ran into fog. The pilot had to bring them down to two hundred feet. Vicki cursed the lousy conditions and the creator of the universe. Even if they stayed far north of David's boat—the direction Charlie had advised—they were plenty visible at such a low altitude.

Less than three minutes after lifting off, they were far out over the water. Below Kelly's feet the ocean looked like a dark desert, sullen and silent. Beside her on the left a guy with a high-powered rifle and night goggles scanned the area outside the harbor. Vicki snapped at him.

"Don't lose him," she said.

"I have him," the guy said.

"Is he alone?" Charlie asked.

"Can't tell," the guy replied.

"We have to move in closer," Charlie told Vicki.

"No," she said flatly.

They waited, as if they had all day. Kelly marveled at the feelings Falling invoked in her. Anger and frustration, fear and admiration. Where the latter came from she had no idea. A leap of inexplicable intuition made her shudder. She sensed Falling was trying to tell them something about himself, but they were not listening. Did he want his motives understood? She did not know, but she felt him near.

The blades of the chopper whirled. With the naked eye they could barely see David's boat. He could be dead already. For all they knew Falling was at the helm of the ship. Kelly realized she knew nothing about their foe. The painful seconds built into agonizing minutes. The boat moved a mile from the shore, two miles. Their main agent in the other helicopter—south of the boat, hidden in the mucky sky—came over the line. He had a better line of sight, and he had bizarre news.

"He's loading the money into some kind of receptacle," he said.

Vicki sat frozen, then turned to Charlie. "What the fuck?"

"Is it metal?" Charlie asked the other helicopter.

"It might be. Can't be sure at this distance."

"Are there any other boats in the area?" Vicki asked.

"No. That I am sure of."

Vicki kept her eye on Charlie. "What's he doing?"

Charlie frowned. "What was David doing before he began to load the ransom?"

The other chopper dude heard the question. "Talking on his cell."

"What does it mean?" Vicki asked.

Charlie frowned. "Maybe he plans to have David sink the goods. But—"

"But what?" Vicki demanded.

"The water's deep this far out. He wouldn't be able to retrieve it."

"Could Falling be riding alongside the boat?" Kelly suggested. "Attached to it in some way? Out of sight?"

Vicki was interested in the theory. "He could be hanging on, ready to lasso the money," she suggested.

But Charlie shook his head. "The boat's moving too fast. The pressure from the water would knock him off."

"You don't know that for sure." Vicki ran her hands through her hair. "Jesus!"

"We have to move in closer," Charlie insisted.

"And do what?" Vicki demanded.

Their man in the other helicopter spoke. "He's lifting the container onto the side of the rail. It looks like he's going to dump it overboard."

"Do you see anything in the water?" Vicki asked. "Anything at all?"

"There's nothing and no one in the vicinity of the boat."

"He's too far away to be positive," Charlie said with passion. He grabbed Vicki's arm. "We follow the money, and the money is going in the water. David's not important. Falling only threatened him to mislead us. He doesn't give a damn about the guy. Catalina is meaningless. Listen to me, Vicki! Move both choppers above that boat right now."

"He just threw the container overboard," the guy reported.

"Did it sink?" Vicki demanded.

"Oh, yeah."

Vicki snapped at the pilot. "Move in!"

The helicopter banked sharply. Kelly felt her guts sink along with her heart. She realized they had been out-foxed, although she had no idea how. Falling would not try to retrieve the money later. He knew they would never leave the area unwatched. He must already have the money.

Yet he could not have it. Unless . . . the unexpected.

They raced low over the ocean. Charlie told the pilot to head for the spot where the ransom had been dumped, and ignore David's boat.

A window was rifled back and Kelly felt a blast of cold air. The sharpshooter was moving into position, shouldering his rifle. The helicopter searchlight flashed on. The white beam stabbed the gray surface. A moment later the light from the second helicopter joined them, searching.

There were no other boats in the vicinity.

There was no one in the water. That they could see.

David continued on his merry way to Catalina.

"What just happened?" Vicki demanded. They were fifty feet above the surface. The wind from the rotary blades fanned the water. Furious ripples pressed against small swells. There was no container, no cash, no diamonds. Vicki turned on Charlie, wanting an answer.

Charlie put his hand to his head to ease the pressure. "Get people in scuba gear."

"You think he's below us?" Vicki asked.

"Yeah," Charlie said, uncertain.

"But you said the water is too deep here."

"It is, it should be. But—"

"What?" Vicki asked.

"Something's wrong."

"If he's down there, we've got him. He can't get away," Vicki said.

"Really? How long before our scuba team can get here?" Shaking his head, Charlie added, "We're missing something."

"Should I call for scuba divers or not?" Vicki demanded.

Charlie shrugged. "Do it. But he'll be long gone before they get here."

"He can't go that far," Vicki said. "We'll catch him when he comes up."

Charlie spoke softly. "No. He's thought of that. He's thought of everything. We won't stop him, not tonight. He has the cash and the diamonds, and he's already gone."

Kelly saw his pain, his certainty. "Will he give us the child back?"

Charlie sighed. "I don't think so."

CHAPTER SEVEN

As David Techer drove north on the San Diego Freeway back into Los Angeles County after being led all over Orange County, Matt Connor was already in the water two miles out from the Marina Del Rey harbor. The exact distance was important to Matt, and he helped establish his position with the help of a waterproof GPS device he carried along with his other equipment: a plastic-enclosed cell and tape recorder, scuba gear, binoculars, and two Farallon underwater propulsion devices.

The average ocean depth between the harbor and Catalina was in excess of five hundred feet. But two miles off shore there was an underwater plateau—where the depth was only a hundred feet. Matt had discovered it in the last month while studying underwater maps supplied by the Coast Guard's office.

The two miles served another purpose. Once he had the loot in his hands, he would need room to disappear into. The two Farallons gave him options. Each had a range of two and a half miles. They could travel five miles an hour underwater. But he had already used up most of the battery on the first one getting into position, hence the need for the backup. It was his intent to run the first Farallon into the ground. Then he would discard it, never mind the three thousand apiece cost. The FBI might find it later but that did not matter. Later, too late, they would figure out how he had fooled them.

It had been a busy week for Matt, and an exciting one. When the lab in San Francisco had confirmed Jimmy was his son, he had been overjoyed. It was odd but at that instant he had felt such love for Amy that he wanted to call and tell her the news.

He barely restrained himself. He wrote her a letter instead—the ransom note. He enjoyed composing it. To him it was like a love letter. He only wanted the money and the diamonds so he could take care of their son.

Well, maybe not. He figured that if he had such wealth—and their son to boot—then she might come back to him. A disturbing thought, to be sure. At times he surprised even himself.

He did not understand his own mind. He had hated her for so long he practically had a dagger dripping with her blood etched in his brain. Yet when he had received the letter from the lab and held Jimmy in his arms for the first time with the knowledge the kid was his own, he could think about nothing but how happy the three of them could be together. He felt what he had thought was dead inside him: hope.

Hope was a two-edged blade, though. Despair brought its own perverse relief. Now that he was excited at the prospect of seeing her again, he was sick with worry. She could turn against him again. Worse, she could put him in jail.

His fantasies were all hypothetical.

He had to get the loot first. He had to stay alive.

He had enjoyed setting up the ransom, however; attending to the many details. He had done the bulk of the work over the phone, and used cash to secure the office suite and the required boats. But the camera in the washing machine suite had not even been wired into the wall. He had not seen David the whole day.

He had taken fanatical precautions when it came to choosing the phone booths he called from. Each time he stepped into one he wore throwaway hospital scrubs. The FBI could trace such calls, and all they needed was a single hair, a crumb of skin, that matched hair or skin found at another booth he had used.

Naturally, he knew the FBI would be all over David. From a distance Matt had seen their helicopter. That was fair; it was expected. He had played his game and they had played theirs. Now it was time for hardball, and although they had yet to realize it, they were not pitching. He was.

Nothing he had done so far was innovative. The FBI had decades of experience dealing with kidnappers who tried to collect ransoms. In virtually all cases the kidnappers failed because the Bureau had set plans to deal with every contingency. Even if a child snatcher used a stooge and threatened to kill the child if the stooge was not released with the money, the Bureau did not care. They invariably tracked the stooge to the real villain. The difficult point in all ransom schemes was the money pickup.

Yet Matt had figured out a way to negate that difficulty.

Right in front of their eyes. The poor bastards.

Matt had last communicated with David while standing on land. Now—two miles from shore and treading water—he had to guess how close David was to the marina. He figured the guy must be near the parking lot. He turned on his phone—he had purchased both cells *hot*, south of the border—and dialed the phone he had given David. The guy answered quick.

"Hello?"

Matt spoke through the voice modulator enclosed in the plastic bag. "There's a note under the garbage can in front of Keel Restaurant. Read it, follow the instructions."

"You listen to me, buddy. I'm sick and tired of following your—"

Matt hung up. David had complained several times during the day. He was that kind of guy—probably liked to hear himself fart. Matt knew David would obey—he was afraid not to. In minutes he would be even more fearful. In the recorder Matt carried was a tape of Jimmy screaming. Matt had recorded it when Jimmy had been suffering an innocent case of gas, but David would not know that. David would recognize the sound of his son in pain, and at the crucial moment, the asshole would dance like a puppet.

Matt waited. He had on a full-body wet suit and a slightly overfilled air tank. He had rented the gear south of the border. The FBI would never catch him by backtracking his preparations.

Raising his binoculars, Matt watched as David steered the boat away from the harbor. Matt knew from comments Amy had made long ago that David was a skilled sailor. The compass reading he had given David in the note would cause David to pass two hundred yards north of his present position. Matt wanted the distance—close but not too close. He would complete the last leg to the loot underwater.

Matt raised the phone and modulator to his mouth and called again. David was annoyed. "Do you have my son on Catalina?" he demanded.

"Yes. He's here beside me. But right now you're going to load the cash and diamonds into the container at the rear of the boat. When you're done, you're going to shut the lid tightly. I'll call you back in three minutes. Keep the cell handy." He added, "Hurry or I cut your son right now."

"Don't you dare, you sonofabitch!"

"Then hurry!" Matt played the tape of Jimmy screaming. "Do it!"

Matt cut the line and reached for the binoculars, watched as David rushed to the rear of the boat and began to load the ten-gallon container. It was actually an old metal milk receptacle that he had found in the garbage at the back of a warehouse in Modesto. The container was heavy; it would sink. But it had another feature that was crucial to his plan. He had equipped the lid with a waterproof light that was rigged to go on five minutes after the top was shut.

Matt had experimented in this very water to figure out how bright the light had to be in order to be seen at night from a distance of fifty feet—but not a hundred feet. He needed the light to help him find the container in the dark, but it was essential that not a glimmer of the light reached the surface. He trusted the people at the FBI to figure these details out later, but in the heat of the moment, both the agents in the helicopters and the boats should not know what he was up to.

When they saw David drop the precious cargo overboard, they would simply think he had lost his mind. But it would be David who had lost millions.

Matt reached for the phone again. David had finished loading the money into the container. The boat was near, almost directly north of him. Timing was everything. Right now he needed David's cooperation more than ever. Money was the center of the guy's life. Matt knew it would be hard for him to throw the goods overboard.

"Hello?" David answered.

"Do you have the lid securely shut?"

"I think so. What . . . ?"

"Don't think. Do you have it securely shut?"

"Yeah, yeah."

"Good. Throw the container overboard."

"What?"

"You heard me! Throw it overboard!"

"I'm not going to toss millions of bucks in the water. Are you nuts?"

The boat was directly across from Matt. Now, with each passing second, it was pulling farther away from him, toward Catalina. Matt dared not order David to turn and circle around. Nothing would alert the FBI to his plan more clearly. Indeed, as it was, the helicopter south of him had just pulled closer. Plus, there appeared to be another chopper farther north.

"If you don't do what I say, I will hurt your son."

"Fuck you! You're bluffing!"

Matt wished he could add a dangerous note to his voice. The modulator erased all sense of emotion. He regretted that he had already used the tape of Jimmy crying. Heard a second time around, it would not be nearly as effective. Matt struggled with what to do next. The boat had already moved an additional fifty yards away. If it went much farther, he would have to approach the container partway on the surface, a risky move. He knew the instant the ransom went overboard, the helicopters would come roaring.

"Listen to me bluff," Matt said. "I'm taking a lighted match. I'm touching it to your son's arm. Listen to him scream." Matt turned the volume way up and played the tape again, pressing the player against his cell. Jimmy sounded in agony. Matt heard David's shouts on the line. He put the phone back to his ear.

"You fucking asshole! All right, all right, I'll do it!"

"Throw the ransom overboard and continue on to Catalina to pick up your son."

Matt hung up and watched. He still needed his binoculars. He had purposely killed all the lights aboard the rental boat. Of course, the FBI would have night goggles, and would still be able to see everything.

David struggled to lift the container onto the rail. He almost dropped the blasted thing and Matt silently swore at him. In that moment his hatred for David crystallized into a black needle that he wished to stab into the guy's eye. The power of the emotion shook him to the core. He knew it had been Amy who had betrayed him—that David had known nothing of his involvement with her—but he still wanted the guy dead. The rage was primitive, the stuff of caveman brawls. This was the guy who was fucking his girl. Matt had to console himself with the knowledge that David was a victim as well. The jerk was going to all this trouble to save a child that was not his own.

The container fell into the water and disappeared. Matt was grateful the light had not gone on. But he worried it might remain off, although it had worked well in practice. Without the light it would take him time he did not have to locate the goods. Already the helicopter on the north side had turned and was coming their way at high speed.

Matt took a compass reading on the spot where the money had sunk and did his best to estimate the distance—three hundred yards, more than he would have preferred. Yet the added distance gave him an edge when it came to staying hidden. He seriously doubted anyone in the helicopters had spotted him floating all alone in the water.

He let the air out of his buoyancy control device (BC) and sank below the surface. He dragged both the Farallons with him, as well as his other equipment. The underwater propulsion devices had a slight negative buoyancy. They were a blast to ride—he would get to straddle them like a torpedo—but a diver had to be careful when ascending to the surface. Rising too quickly was a great way to blow out the lungs with an air embolism.

The descent reminded Matt of his leap from the plane five months earlier. He could not turn on his own flashlight until he reached the bottom—another signal to the FBI that had to be avoided. The black was absolute, the chill like the frost of a distant moon. He felt as if he were falling into a forsaken abyss. A part of him truly *was* Falling—the role he had chosen to play.

Matt felt a comfort in the dark plunge. He was in his element when he was hidden. He shared that with Amy—she had hidden so much. The image of her face flashed before his unseeing eyes and he thought he saw her smile. Of course she would weep that very night when David failed to bring her son home to her.

Odd, but he could not stop thinking what it would be like to kiss her again.

After what seemed an eternity he touched bottom. He had been fortunate his ears had cleared all the way down; he had a slight cold. Immediately, he reached for the light tucked in the pocket of his BC. The beam came out through a haze of dust. The visibility was seven feet, but it should be at least three times that when he got near the light on the container. Still, to pass within twenty feet of the container, he would need as much luck as skill. It would be tragic to have come this far and fail.

Matt consulted his compass and powered up his Farallon, staying five feet off the floor of the ocean. He started slow but quickly felt the danger of caution. The FBI would airlift divers out soon. He upped the device's power and felt the pressure of the water on his face mask. Once again the sensation was exquisite; it was like flying through a dream above a nightmarish range that could not harm him. However, he did not relax so much that he took his eye off the compass. The needle was his only link to the ransom.

He almost missed the container. Just when he began to feel he had overshot the spot, he saw out the corner of his eye a feeble image that looked like a ghost. The light was so faint that if he had blinked he would have missed it. In a tight arc, he smoothly changed direction and flew toward his reward. The light grew swiftly, and as he parked beside the container and touched it with trembling hands, he smiled. Indeed, he would have laughed out loud if the act wouldn't have caused him to drown.

He had a canvas bag similar to the one he had told David to transfer the goods into. As he opened the top lid of the container the light went off, but he had his flashlight held ready. He stared at the cash and the bags of diamonds as he used to stare at Amy's naked body.

They reminded him of each other. Naturally, he thought, one could buy the other. Matt figured everything in life has its price. Except for the love he felt in the company of his son.

Matt did not mind that the bills were soaked. He had purposely pierced the sides of the container so that it would immediately fill and sink. But beyond that the pressure of over a hundred feet of seawater on the goodies would disable any tracking device the FBI might still have managed to plant on the ransom. Matt did not fully trust that simply using the washing machine had wiped out any such device. The FBI was pretty high-tech these days.

Matt loaded the cash and diamonds into his bag. A few dollars tried to float away but he grabbed them before they went far. He was in a hurry but he was greedy to escape with exactly a million. He worked without gloves in the cold water. The feel of the damp cash and the hard diamonds in his half numb fingers was like rare tenderloin in a starving man's hands.

When he was ready to leave, he discovered he had a problem. His bag was bulky and heavy, doubly so because it was filled with water. He had to discard the first Farallon, and his binoculars, in order to deal with the burden, leaving them in the exact spot the FBI would search. But there was no helping it.

Taking a compass reading on the shore, he aimed for thirty degrees south of the harbor. He planned to travel along the ocean floor a quarter of a mile away from the drop spot before rising to a depth of fifty feet. After another quarter of a mile, he would move to twenty feet—a depth that should still hide the glow of his flashlight from someone on the surface. The longer he stayed deep, the quicker he used up his air. Already, with all the excitement, and struggle with the bag, he had consumed a third of his air tank.

But the fresh battery in the second Farallon was a lifesaver. He had power and speed. He took off like a rocket, and the water swam by him like a river flowing into the underworld. Nevertheless, riding the back of his torpedo, he *ascended* slowly. The trip gave him time to contemplate all the obstacles the FBI would have to overcome to catch him. They would not have been prepared for an ocean scenario. They would not have divers suited up and standing by. They could not know he had the world's top-of-the-line underwater propulsion device at his disposal, or that he was even beneath the water with the ransom already in hand. All they could see was the huge black ocean, and David in his boat, riding to Catalina and waiting for a call that would never come.

Yet Matt knew they were not stupid. He had taken them by surprise, true, but they would brainstorm and figure out a few details of his plan. If they were smart they would decide that he did indeed have the ransom, and that he was heading back to shore. They would flood the harbor with agents. That was the reason he was not heading to the harbor, but to a spot two miles south of the marina, where earlier he had parked a fast powerboat. The latter was anchored over a mile offshore. He was not foolish enough to try to exit the harbor—later, on foot—with the FBI virtually setting up camp there. He would ride his boat south to Newport Harbor—where he had originally rented the craft—and go ashore in that marina. Even if one among them was brilliant and grasped the general design of his plan, he or she could not read his mind and anticipate his every move.

Matt wondered if he should write thrillers for a living.

Not that he needed the money. Anymore.

He steered underwater and blind until he estimated he was within a quarter of a mile of his boat. Only then did he allow himself to surface and take a peek. His turn to be surprised. He was shocked to see that his boat was still a half mile away—not a small problem, given that he was practically out of air.

Fortunately the battery in the Farallon was still strong. But he feared spending time on the surface. Behind him was a mass of activity. Three boats and two helicopters and their search beams raked the spot where David had dumped the container. But soon—perhaps too soon—those lights would begin to search elsewhere.

Matt finally decided to stay on the surface and race for his boat. He did not want to turn his flashlight back on and his air tank was gasping. The stealth of being submerged and having a compass were nice, but there was no substitute for seeing exactly where he was going. Keeping his head low and the Farallon at full speed, he covered the distance to the boat in a matter of minutes.

He had placed a ladder off the side of the boat. Throwing the container aboard, he climbed up and removed his flippers and air tank before hauling the Farallon on deck. He did not bother taking off his wet suit before reaching for the ignition. The big engines kicked to life with a low but meaty roar. He drew in the anchor and eased away from his position at reduced speed. Still, the searchlights remained on the drop spot. To them he was just another boat on a vast area of sea that presently contained at least two dozen ships.

From the harbor he saw another two helicopters approach the FBI party. He wondered what Amy was doing right then, if she was being fed regular updates. He felt bad for her, but happy for himself. Every rose had a thorn, he reflected. But for once, it was nice to have a grip on the petals.

CHAPTER EIGHT

Picking up the pieces.

Monday afternoon, two days after losing the kidnapper and the rich ransom. The pieces, lots of them, were all over the place. But a few were beginning to fit into a coherent picture. Unfortunately, the picture kept telling them the same thing. Falling was smarter than they were.

Kelly and Charlie stood outside a rental shop in Newport Beach— and inside the harbor—not far from the jetty. Another overcast day, white winged sailboats drifting into an ocean of gray. From conversations on the phone, they were already ninety percent sure Falling had rented *two* boats from this place—Kamin's Rentals. One boat they knew—the *Scallop*, the one David had taken to Catalina. The other one they didn't know, not its name, and yet they were fairly certain the kidnapper had used this latter ship to escape into an early retirement. They had driven down to Orange County to verify these facts, and to get away from Vicki, who was kicking wastepaper baskets, and any agent foolish enough to cross her path.

They were all crushed, perhaps no one more than Charlie. He had not slept the last two days, pushing himself relentlessly to figure out where they had gone wrong. The sad thing was, they already knew. Yet, they still did not know the identity of Falling. He was not big on leaving behind clues.

The owner of the shop came out to talk. A big brawny guy aged by sun and surf, he looked like he wrestled lobsters in his sleep. His story sounded familiar. Sure, he had rented two boats to a guy on the phone. Said his name was John Smith. It seemed John had sent him a cash deposit and told him to leave the keys to the twin boats in an envelope beneath the mat. He said he would pick them up sometime late Friday night. The owner had never met John. He couldn't even remember what he sounded like. Charlie asked the man about the second, mysterious boat, and the guy pointed it out. The ship was docked nearby, looked like it had plenty of horsepower.

"Was he a criminal or something?" the guy asked as he led them onto the dock.

"He was something," Charlie said. "We're going to have to impound this boat. Do you mind?"

"You'll have to pay me for it," the guy replied.

"No, we won't," Charlie assured him with a hard look.

Charlie could be scary when he wanted. The guy immediately backed down.

Charlie called Sharp and arranged for the powerboat to be examined. In the car on the way back to the office, Kelly called Agent Lentil, asked about the Farallon propulsion device they had found. Lentil had more depressing news.

"He must have bought it through a private party," Lentil said. "The Farallon people say they haven't sold any of their devices to anyone in California in the last ten weeks."

They knew Falling must have had at least two of the devices, not one.

"Ten weeks back is nothing," Kelly snapped. "For all we know, he could have bought them a year ago. Get a copy of all their records for the last twelve months. No, go back two years. Look for anyone who bought two or more of the devices anywhere in the country. And Lentil, the purchases do not have to be at the same time. Understand?"

"I know that," he said, insulted.

"While you're at it, check all dive magazines for the last year. Look at the ads in the back for anyone selling Farallons. I want all those people contacted, even if they were only selling one."

"That will take time," Lentil said.

"Take as long as it takes." Kelly broke the connection and turned to Charlie. "How did Lentil become an FBI agent? Is his dad a senator or a congressman or what?"

"He's not so bad. You just intimidate him."

"Why? Because I'm a woman?"

Charlie nodded. "A woman with a dick."

"He said that?"

"He meant it as a compliment." Charlie paused. "I want Lentil to organize our south-of-the-border canvassing. He speaks Spanish."

"You really think Falling will dump the child in Mexico?"

"Somewhere down there. I don't think he'll kill him."

"Could he make a second run at more money?"

Charlie shook his head. "He knows he was lucky to trick us the first time. And he knows we know he won't return the child."

Kelly snorted. "Why doesn't he just give us Jimmy? If he is such a swell guy."

Charlie looked weary. "I don't know."

Kelly regretted her outburst. "You blame yourself too much."

Charlie gestured. "We should have seen what he was going to do once he put David on the boat. We talked about it. Catalina was not an option for him. David was lousy hostage material. The water and the ransom were what mattered. He needed us to put the ransom in the water. That meant he must be in the water—waiting. The formula was simple and we failed to solve it."

"No one could have anticipated the water was shallow there."

"We should have figured that he would have found just such a spot."

"You feel *you* should have figured it all out, in a split second. That's asking too much of yourself. You didn't fuck up, we all did."

Charlie shook his head. "None of that matters. Only the kid does. At the end of the day excuses are for losers."

Kelly wanted to argue the point but realized he spoke the truth. A child did not care about strategy. The kid only knew love and comfort. He just wanted to be home with his mom and dad.

Like Charlie, she did not believe the guy would kill Jimmy. Dumping the child south of the border was the logical step for a compassionate kidnapper—and he had shown definite signs of affection for the boy. Kelly made a mental note to tell Lentil to push their canvassing as far south as Brazil. Rio had a big market for white male infants. Falling might try to sell the kid, not that he needed the extra cash.

Kelly had heard a legitimate rumor that Carl Techer, the grandfather, was filing a lawsuit against the FBI for "gross negligence." He had already hired a team of lawyers, Vicki said, obviously wanting to cash in on the loss of his flesh and blood. Kelly asked herself—if she ended up in court—would she admit that excuses were for losers?

When they got back to the L.A. office, Kelly did not hang around long. Charlie got yanked into a private meeting with Vicki, and Lentil was not around to go over the strategy on Latin America. The time was half past three and Kelly was already tired. Fatigue came quickly and without warning these days. Even protein powder mixed with juice did little to revive her flagging reserves. She suspected she would have had more energy if Jimmy was safe at home. Which reminded her, she had an unpleasant task she was avoiding. She had to talk to Amy and gently explain that their chances of getting Jimmy back were now dismal.

Kelly found Amy at the side of her house, working in the garden. Staying with the Techers, Kelly had been amazed how much time Amy spent on her flowers and plants. Amy said the feel of the soil calmed her. But as Kelly walked up, she looked far beyond calm—somewhere south of the valley of Valiums. Amy raised her head in greeting, but her gaze lingered too long without recognition. Then she shook herself and coughed.

"I was just thinking of you," she said.

"I'm sorry, Amy. I'm so sorry."

Amy stood and pulled off her plastic gloves and dropped them on the ground. "Everyone's sorry," she whispered.

Kelly put a hand on her arm. "How are you doing?"

Amy lowered her head and rocked unsteadily on her feet. It was as if she tried to recall something she had striven to forget. "I used to love to smell Jimmy when I picked him up," she said. "It was one of the things I loved most about him. But just now, out here with the flowers, I realized that I've forgotten that smell. I try to remember it and all I see is his face. But his smell, the feel of his skin, the sound of his voice—they're all leaving me. Why do you think that is?"

"You must miss him an awful lot."

Amy raised her head and looked nowhere. "Yeah. That must be it."

"Amy . . ." Kelly began.

She suddenly turned on her. "Or is it because he's dead?"

"I don't think he's dead."

"But will I ever see him again?"

Kelly could not lie. "I don't know. We lost our best chance on Saturday."

Amy stood staring for a minute. She never did respond, though, merely walked away, into the house. Kelly could only follow, not sure she had fulfilled the reason for her visit, or even if her visit served a legitimate purpose. Amy had been depressed and now she was more depressed.

Yet as Kelly entered the house a part of her felt as if it searched for a clue that had been overlooked. A silly thought but one that persisted despite her best efforts to dismiss it. The FBI had turned the house upside down. What clue could the kidnapper have left that they could have missed?

Then it hit her. Not all clues could be touched. Words for example, they came and went like ghosts. The image of a young man's dead face in the newspaper haunted her. Why? Because she had seen his face in this house. Amy had even spoken to her about the guy.

"He was flying from Catalina to Santa Barbara at night. He had just finished scuba lessons and he was going to his birthday party. He was an excellent pilot. They don't know why his plane crashed."

Catalina and scuba lessons. Falling had directed David toward Catalina. Falling had been an experienced scuba diver. The coincidence was not overwhelming but it was real. Not to mention the fact that Matt Connor had been *that* mysterious ex in Amy's past, the one she refused to discuss.

Had she hurt him? Had he wanted to hurt her?

Kelly wondered if it was another coincidence when she followed Amy into the house and Amy headed straight for the studio where Kelly had accidentally discovered Matt's picture. Amy was still lost in a fog, moving without purpose, touching unfinished paintings, shifting used brushes from one jar to the next. Without asking permission, Kelly stepped to Amy's desk and opened the drawer and took out Matt's picture. Handsome guy, dark hair, powerful eyes. Had the picture been taken before he met Amy or after? Amy might have read her mind.

"I took that picture exactly a year before he died," she said, coming up at her side. "On his twenty-ninth birthday."

"He was a real boyfriend?"

"Yes." Amy took the picture and stared at it with affection. "Greatest guy I ever knew. Matt was . . . he was perfect."

"Why did you two break up?"

Amy sighed. "I married David."

"May I ask a personal question?"

Amy continued to look at Matt but her toned hardened. "Was Jimmy Matt's child? No, he wasn't. Any other questions?"

"Did Matt love you?"

"Yes."

"Did you love him?"

Amy put away the picture. "Yes."

"You miss him?" Kelly asked.

"What do you think?"

"When his plane went in the ocean, did they recover his body?"

"No. They said the water was too deep."

The other night, when the ransom had been dumped, every agent on the case had thought the water was too deep for the cash and diamonds to be recovered.

"I see," Kelly said.

■

THE NEXT morning Kelly headed to Ventura, along the coast, to the airport. The sky was a brilliant blue. She drove with the windows down and the music up loud. Since living alone she had started to play the piano again. As a child she had been considered a prodigy on the in- strument, and she had been happy to discover she could still play with feeling. But nothing sounded as sad as a lonely piano late at night. Tony never called, he never would.

Before leaving for Ventura she had contacted the airport tower and spoken to the air traffic controller who had been on duty the night Matt Connor's plane had gone down. The guy happened to be work- ing that afternoon. He said he would be happy to meet with her. But he sounded puzzled with her request for information on Matt's flight. The feeling was somewhat mutual. She was not sure what she was looking for.

Ventura Airport was modest. She met Gabe Adams in a small office adjacent to the radar room. A small man with the squarest head she had ever seen on a human being—outside of someone who had been pur- posely tortured by the Mafia with a vise—he looked like a robot who could be plugged directly into his equipment. Across a wooden desk, he pushed a file that contained the records of Matt's last flight. There was a DVD enclosed—a copy of the radar path his plane had taken, Gabe explained.

"We automatically record the flight path of every plane that enters our airspace," he said. "If later there's a problem with a plane, that record is transferred to a permanent disc."

Kelly glanced at the disc. Gabe had already informed her that Matt's crash had been investigated by the National Transportation and Safety Board (NTSB), and ruled an accident caused by pilot error. She planned to contact the federal agency later but felt she could get information out of Gabe more quickly.

"I'll study this file later," she said. "But I'd like you to tell me as best you can what happened the night Matt Connor's plane crashed."

"He came on our radar thirty miles south of here, which is normal. His altitude was relatively low—a thousand feet—and I contacted him personally to ask how he was doing. He explained about the low overcast. I asked if he was instrument trained and he reminded me that he was not, but that he was comfortable with the conditions. We had spoken before over the radio. He was an experienced pilot. He was flying low so he could keep a visual on the water."

"Could he see the coast at that point?"

"I doubt it. It was a lousy night to fly. I wished him good luck and he thanked me."

"What happened next?"

"His altitude dropped to five hundred feet. I assumed he was still troubled by the overcast. I knew his destination was Santa Barbara and I considered calling to tell him to move closer inland since we had better visibility here. But I never got to it."

"Why not?"

"He suddenly climbed in altitude, to near three thousand feet. But he was hardly at that height when he started to dive. He went almost straight down into the water."

"Did you try to contact him during this time?"

"Yes. He did not respond."

"What do you think caused him to dive?"

"He got disoriented. He lost sight of the water and the sky and couldn't tell up from down. In such a situation it's easy to overcompensate and send the plane into what's called a graveyard spin. Before he could pull out of it, he hit the water." Gabe paused. "That was the NTSB's conclusion as well."

"If Matt was struggling with overcast and was flying low to avoid it, then why did he suddenly climb so high?"

"I'm not sure. The overcast might have suddenly opened up and he felt confident to go higher."

"Is that likely?"

"No. Five hundred feet would have been low to fly in poor conditions at night. But he did not need to climb to three thousand to get comfortable—especially with the threat of the overcast so near. Also, his climb was bizarre. It was as if he pulled back hard on the wheel. He shot almost straight up."

"How do you explain that?"

"The same way the NTSB did—total disorientation and panic."

"Yet you say Matt was an experienced pilot?"

"He was—he had logged over a thousand flight hours. He often flew to Santa Barbara to see his mother and I had spoken to him many times. But I must stress again that he was not instrument trained. Once he lost all visual clues, his experience did not count for much."

"Was it totally dark when he crashed?"

"Yes."

"You say he regularly flew to Santa Barbara to see his mother. That means he was flying a familiar route?"

"Not exactly. He was not coming from Santa Monica Airport—as he usually did—but from Catalina. That's why he was so far over the water."

"How far out?"

"Five miles."

"When his plane went down, what did you do?"

"I notified the Coast Guard and the NTSB. Also, I contacted the Santa Barbara tower and the Santa Barbara police. I wanted the latter to get ahold of his mother."

"Did the Coast Guard find his plane?"

"They found nothing that night. In the dark—even with our best estimate as to where he went down—it was hard to see much. But in the morning they saw scattered wreckage from his plane."

"Was this a rescue attempt? Did the Coast Guard think he could be found alive?"

"No. At the speed he was traveling when he hit the water, it would have been like hitting a stone wall. He couldn't have survived the crash."

"I assume the bulk of the plane sank. Did it show up on the Coast Guard's sonar?"

"Yes."

"Were divers sent down?"

"No. The water in that area is over five hundred feet."

"How long did it take the Coast Guard to send a ship to the area?"

"I'm not sure. About an hour."

"That doesn't sound like a speedy response."

"I wouldn't know about that."

"Did the Coast Guard see any other boats in the area?"

"You would have to ask them." Gabe paused and looked uncomfortable. Perhaps he feared his own performance that night was being questioned. "May I ask a question?"

"Sure," Kelly said.

"What is the FBI's purpose in investigating this crash?"

"It might have bearing on another case that I'm not at liberty to discuss. Tell me, Gabe, can you think of another reason why Matt's plane behaved the way it did besides pilot disorientation and panic?"

He hesitated. "Yes."

"Tell me."

Again he paused. "Suicide."

"Come again?"

"He might have been trying to kill himself."

"Why would he want to do that?"

"I don't know. I didn't really know him."

Kelly thought of Amy. "I suppose he might have had his reasons."

■

KELLY CONTINUED north to Santa Barbara, to see Nancy Connor. This time she did not call ahead and she had to question her reasons. She had already pulled the record on Mrs. Connor from the computer in her office. The woman was seventy, lived alone, and had no family now that Matt was dead. She apparently subsisted on a small pension her husband had willed to her. To receive an unexpected visit from a stranger—even one with a badge—might intimidate the woman. But Kelly suspected she did not call ahead because she had no idea what excuse to give for her interest in Matt. She just hoped one came to her when the time arrived.

Mrs. Connor lived in a small apartment not far from downtown. Kelly had to ring a few times before she answered. The sight of the old woman took Kelly back a step. She looked like her dead son: with the same intense eyes, the kind mouth, the handsome face that conveyed both strength and fragility at the same time. Kelly immediately glimpsed the woman's intelligence. She would not be easy to snow.

Did that mean Matt had also been bright?

"Can I help you?" Mrs. Connor asked.

Kelly showed her badge. "Kelly Fienman, FBI. Are you Mrs. Connor?"

"Yes."

"I've been working with the kidnapping of Amy Techer's child. I was told you know about it?"

"Yes. I'm friends with Amy's father. What can I do for you?"

"May I come in? I would like to ask you a few questions."

She hesitated, then nodded. "Would you like some coffee? I just made a fresh pot."

Kelly would have *loved* coffee. "I wouldn't mind a glass of water," she said as she stepped inside and cursed her medical condition. Yet with each day she felt stronger. The doctors had said the liver was a forgiving organ. Portions of it might be growing back. A shame her intestines couldn't do likewise.

The apartment was small but neatly furnished. Pictures of a dead husband and a dead son on the wall. Nice one of Matt standing beside a Cessna 172. No pictures of Amy and Matt together. Kelly sat on the edge of a sofa as Mrs. Connor returned with water and coffee. Kelly gestured to the photographs of Matt.

"I understand you lost your son a year ago," she said.

Nancy's lips quivered. A long year it had been. "Yes. He died in a plane crash."

"Amy told me. I'm so sorry, it must have been devastating."

Nancy tried to smile, failed. "He was such a dear boy."

Kelly suddenly seized on a strategy. "I'm not here to question you about Matt. But with this kidnapping, to solve it, we feel we have to get a better grasp on Amy. For that reason, I'd like to ask about your son's relationship with her. All we know is they had one, but that it ended suddenly. But we don't understand why. Whenever I broach the subject with Amy, she gets evasive."

Nancy scowled and set down her cup. "That girl isn't who she pretends to be." Then she stopped and shook her head. "But to lose a child—no one deserves that."

"Amy hurt Matt?"

Nancy stared at her. "Oh yes. She hurt him badly."

"Tell me."

And so Kelly heard the full story of Amy Techer's betrayal. It would have made her angry anyway, but given her experience with Tony—and ironically, the Acid Man—it made her feel sick. Because it was obvious from the start that Matt was an innocent, one of those rare creatures the Acid Man said did not exist. Innocence and insanity were often close friends, however. Amy's cheating had given Matt the perfect motive to seek out revenge, and consequently made him the perfect suspect in the kidnapping.

Except Matt was supposed to be dead.

"It amazes me Amy tried to convince David she had hardly known Matt," Kelly said when Nancy finished speaking. "That must have been quite a task when your son and Amy had been together so long."

"I don't think it was as hard as you think for Amy," Nancy said. "Matt was cut off completely. He wasn't allowed to speak to David. He wasn't allowed to speak to Amy. He was discarded like garbage."

"There's no worse feeling," Kelly said quietly.

Nancy gave her a penetrating look. "Yes, you know that. But I think you knew how to deal with it when it happened to you. Matt didn't, he bottled up the pain inside. He would hardly talk to me about it."

"What about his friends? Couldn't he talk to them?"

"Matt lost most of his friends while he dated Amy. She consumed his whole life. She took everything from him, she demanded it. But she gave him so little in return."

"Do you hate her?"

Nancy was reflective. "I did hate her. How could I not when I saw what she had done to my son? But when she lost her own son. . . . I don't know. I pitied her as well. I'm sure it was the last thing Matt would have wanted to happen to her."

"Are you sure?" Kelly asked, the question popping out before she could stop it. Above all else she did not want to give Nancy a clue as to her purpose in visiting. Nancy might have caught her drift, it was hard to be sure. She did not answer directly.

"Matt was a very kind man," she said.

Kelly spoke carefully. "But he was depressed. I hate to ask this, Mrs. Connor, but is it possible he crashed his plane on purpose?"

She shook her head. "No."

They spoke a few minutes more but the conversation was essentially over. Kelly decided she had gotten what she had come for—an insight into the dark side of Amy. Her vague theory took on greater clarity. Yet it almost crumbled as she went to leave. It was then Nancy brought up Cindy Firestone, Matt's girlfriend at the time of his death. The fact that there was another woman threw Kelly off balance. If he had been seeing someone else, maybe all her ideas were wrong.

"Why didn't you mention her earlier?" Kelly asked, standing at the door.

"I didn't think Cindy had anything to do with Amy." The reply held a taunt. Isn't that why you are here in the first place? Or do you have another reason?

"How long were they involved?" Kelly asked.

"For two or three months before he died. Why?"

"Just curious. Do you have Cindy's number?"

This time Nancy wasn't buying. "What exactly is it you want, Mrs. Fienman?"

"I told you. An insight into Amy's character."

"Cindy never met Amy."

"Yes. But I'm sure Matt told Cindy things about Amy that he told no one else."

"Hardly. Cindy said Matt never spoke about Amy."

Kelly acted casual. "If you don't have the number, that's okay."

Nancy's eyes never left her face. "It's okay because you can get the number in five minutes. I may as well give it to you myself, and at least warn Cindy that you'll be calling. Wait here a moment."

"Thank you," Kelly said, feeling like a fool.

Nancy returned with the number and they exchanged strained good-byes. Driving back to Los Angeles, Kelly regretted the poor ending. Because she knew if her wild idea possessed substance she might need to return to Nancy for things the woman would not want to give.

Kelly called Cindy from the road and they spoke. Nancy had already talked to Matt's old girlfriend. Cindy sounded cautious but unafraid. She agreed to be at home in ninety minutes, the time Kelly told her it would take to get there.

■

CINDY FIRESTONE appeared younger than Kelly would have expected. Kelly was surprised to learn she was twenty-six. Tall and lanky, with long red hair and a thousand freckles, she was built from the stuff of endless youth. Kelly tried to remember an old redhead and could not. Did they all die young? Cindy invited her inside and Kelly had to refuse another offer of fresh coffee.

Cindy had none of Nancy's walls up. They quickly got down to business.

"How upset was Matt about the way Amy dumped him?" Kelly asked.

"It tormented him. He tried to hide it from me but I could see."

"How did he show it?"

"We dated three months and never had sex. We would sleep together naked, but when I'd try to initiate something, he would flinch. He would deny it, but I knew he was thinking of her."

"How could you stand that?"

"I really cared for him. He was an extraordinary guy, funny and brilliant. There was almost nothing he wouldn't do for me. I thought I could help him get over her. But I couldn't, I don't think anyone could." Cindy paused. "I sometimes think he died thinking about her."

"Do you think he committed suicide?"

"Is that why you're here?"

"Please just answer the question."

Cindy hesitated. "No."

"But you think he was obsessed with her?"

"I don't like to use that word. But yes."

"How did he show his obsession with her?"

"Once I stopped by unexpectedly. I caught him as he was leaving, but he didn't see me. I followed him. I wasn't trying to pry, I was just curious where he was going."

Cindy *was* prying. "And he drove to Amy's house?"

"Yes."

"How did you know it was her house?"

"He had told me about where she lived."

"What did he do? Park in front of her house?"

"Just down the street from where she lived, yes."

"Did she come outside? Did you see her?"

"No."

"He just sat in his car and stared at her house?"

"Yes."

"For how long?"

"An hour."

"An *hour*?"

"Yes."

"At any time did he go behind her house and hike up to a bluff that overlooks her backyard?"

Cindy was uncomfortable. "He was obsessed with her but he wasn't a pervert. I hope I haven't given you that impression."

"Did he ever talk about wanting to hurt her?"

"Of course not! Matt wouldn't have hurt a fly."

Kelly raised her hand. "I'm sorry, I have to ask. It's part of the job."

"I don't understand, he's dead. And this child was kidnapped after he died. How can it be part of the job?"

The job is often more about the dead than the living, Kelly thought, although she did not say it aloud. She chose to ignore the question.

"Why did you say Matt was brilliant?" she asked.

"He could do anything he put his mind to."

"Was he an exceptional student while in school?"

"He was above average, although he never finished college. I remember this one time there was an online IQ test, we both took it for fun. I missed half the questions but he got a perfect score. The explanation at the end of the test said that meant he was one in a million."

Kelly thought of hovering in a helicopter over a black ocean.

So close and yet so far. He had just slipped away.

"I can believe it," she said.

■

KELLY DID not get back to her office until late. Charlie was already gone for the day, which made her both sad and relieved. Already she could see she was repeating the pattern she had displayed while pursuing the Acid Man. She had the same rationalization for her secrecy—she was chasing a wild lead, nothing more. Yet she was finally able to admit to herself that she was emotionally ill-equipped to be an FBI agent. She resented the chain of command. She wanted to be the boss. Worse, she wanted to be the hero.

She read over the NTSB report and uncovered a couple of facts Gabe Adams had not mentioned. Matt had been flying a Cessna 172 when he had gone down. The NTSB investigators noted that plane did not easily slip into a graveyard spin. Indeed, the plane was designed so that when one released the controls it spontaneously righted itself. Yet Matt had plunged into the sea as if his plane had been slapped from the sky.

Another point she found interesting was that although Matt was not technically instrument certified, he had completed most of the course requirements and should have been able to fly in zero visibility. Gabe had not fully grasped Matt's skill level. The poor conditions would not have intimidated Matt.

What exactly did she have? She took out a piece of paper and made a list.

1. Matt had been infatuated with Amy and she had devastated him when she had dumped him for David.
2. Matt's obsession had continued long after the relationship ended.
3. Matt's plane had behaved suspiciously before it had crashed.

4. Matt's body had never been found.
5. Jimmy had probably been kidnapped by someone who knew the family.
6. Matt had died after learning to scuba dive, while flying from Catalina.
7. The kidnapper had known how to scuba dive and had tied Catalina to his ransom scheme.

The points were intriguing, but they proved nothing. She had to think backward. She had to assume that Matt had in fact plotted to fake his death and then kidnap Amy's baby. She had to figure out how he could have done it.

How does one crash a plane in the ocean in the middle of the night and survive? Obviously he couldn't have been in the plane when it hit the water. The tape of the radar confirmed that his plane had been traveling in excess of a hundred and fifty miles an hour when it crashed. Therefore, he must have parachuted out of the plane into a waiting boat.

He must have learned to parachute ahead of time.

He must have planted a boat off the Ventura coast ahead of time.

Kelly called Cindy. Did Matt know how to parachute? The answer was a definite no. Cindy wanted to know why she asked. Just wondering, Kelly replied. She told Cindy to keep the call private and rang off.

What Cindy said did not dissuade her. If Matt had intended to fake his death, he wouldn't have advertised the fact that he was learning to parachute. Kelly called the local skydiving school in Perris and asked them to check their records for a Matt Connor. Did he take any classes? The answer was another no.

Still, Kelly did not feel put off. If Matt had wanted to be careful, he would have learned to parachute in another city. He flew regularly—besides Santa Barbara, what was his favorite destination spot? The NTSB report contained a phone number of the agency where Matt had rented his plane. Kelly called and learned that Matt often went up to Fresno. By chance there was a large skydiving facility there. She rang and asked them to check their files for a Matt Connor. But again she came up with nothing.

Nevertheless, Kelly felt she was onto something. Falling had been fanatical in his attention to detail. He had probably not only learned to skydive in another city, he had undoubtedly used a false identity. Before leaving Cindy's apartment, she had asked for a picture of Matt, which was different than the one Amy had taken. There was a chance if she took that picture to the Fresno skydiving facility, she might strike gold.

Too bad she herself did not fly. It would be a long drive tomorrow, by herself.

■

NO POT of gold waited for her at the end of the road. No one in Fresno recognized Matt's picture. At first she felt disappointed but then it struck her how strange that was. Matt had flown into the small airport regularly. She spoke to over two dozen locals. Someone should have recognized him. Then it occurred to her that besides having false ID, he might have used a disguise as well.

But what kind of disguise?

Kelly returned to Los Angeles. The next day she set to work on the other half of her basic assumption—the boat. A call to Cindy confirmed that Matt did not own one. Therefore, he must have rented it, probably on the same day he vanished. Ventura was the easiest place for Matt to have borrowed a boat and placed it in the path of his flight plan. Santa Barbara was also a possibility, not to mention all the harbors in Los Angeles.

Kelly spent the morning on the phone, a stack of yellow pages by her arm. From the start her efforts were handicapped. She was asking the rental agencies to help her identify someone who did not have a name. A person who did not even resemble her suspect. The best she was able to do was to get them to pull their records for the date of February 12th. She realized soon enough that she would have to visit each harbor and feel her way around. Charlie would have been a big help right about now.

Still, she avoided him at the office and let him focus with Lentil on the south-of-the-border connection. Preoccupied, he did not press her about what she was up to. Vicki was also heavily burdened. The lawsuit from Amy's father-in-law looked real. There had been an article in the *Los Angeles Times* about the botched ransom delivery. The mayor had called, complaining. Kelly was able to continue her research without having to answer too many questions.

Checking out the rental places at the harbors proved exhausting. She spent two full days at Ventura alone and came up with squat. Santa Barbara was another dead end. After both experiences, however, she realized she was complicating the situation. Matt had lived in Santa Monica. Although the harbors up north were closer to the spot where the plane had crashed, Marina Del Rey had been closer to him. When she arrived at the marina, she cautioned herself to take her time and examine every rental record personally. She had been to see Cindy once more and had obtained a sample of Matt's handwriting.

She was at the marina ten minutes when she walked into Harry's Ocean Rentals.

Of course she had called ahead of time and the owner—Chuck—had already pulled his records for last February. Studying them she noticed nothing unusual. None of the signatures on the credit card receipts resembled Matt's handwriting. But there was one rental, to a certain Simon Schiller, that had no credit card receipt. She asked Chuck about it and the guy said the customer must have paid in cash.

Falling had paid in cash for his Newport boats.

"Do you remember this guy, Schiller?" she asked.

Chuck himself was memorable. An ex-marine who still favored battle fatigues, he had a four-inch scar down the right side of his face that looked as if it had been treated by a bottle of whiskey the night it had been inflicted. He rubbed his scar as he considered.

"Yeah. That day was not the first time he had rented a boat from us."

"He was a regular?"

"No. But he had been in a week or two before that."

"Has he been in since?"

"Not that I know of."

She took out Matt's photograph. "Is this him?"

Chuck studied the picture and shook his head. "No. Schiller was blond. He had a beard and mustache. I remember that much."

She glanced at the rental agreement. "He took the boat for two days?"

"Yes."

"And he returned it in fine shape?"

"He must have or I would have charged him more."

"Do you remember exactly when he returned it?"

"No. That was four months ago. What did this guy do?"

"I don't know if he did anything. Did anyone else speak to Schiller when he was here?"

Chuck shook his head but then caught himself. "You know, I think Timmy spoke to him. Yeah, I remember now because Timmy said the guy loaded a dinghy onto the boat."

"What's so strange about that?"

"When he came in to rent the boat he said he was going fishing. But then he told Timmy he was going diving with some buddies on the far side of Catalina."

"So this Timmy talked to him some?"

"Yeah."

A dinghy, Kelly thought, and felt a thrill. Matt would have needed one to get back to shore if he parked a boat in the middle of the sea.

Timmy was out back, filling scuba tanks. He had straw blond hair and a goofy smile, a cartoon character who had been exposed to drugs at an early age. He must have liked the look of her—he leapt up and offered his hand and told her his full name. Asking about Schiller and last February, she was disappointed when he drew a blank. But the mention of the dinghy stirred his memory.

"Oh, yeah, I remember him," he said. "He was kind of rude. I tried to help him but he kept trying to shoo me away."

"What kind of dinghy did he load onto the boat?"

"Can't tell you the brand, but it was the inflatable kind. It came with a heavy duty motor. That's what I helped him carry to the boat."

"Did he tip you?"

"What?"

"Did he tip you for helping him?"

"Yeah. I think he did."

"Then he wasn't so rude, was he?"

Timmy looked mildly insulted. "Well, he did lie to me."

"About what?"

"His lights. He had these lights in his trunk, and he said he wasn't taking them with him. But then later, I saw him sneak them aboard."

Kelly's heart pounded furiously. Matt would have needed lights to spot the boat in the dark from the plane. "Tell me more about these lights," she said.

Timmy scratched his head. "It was just a row of lights set in a metal bracket. I think there were four of them."

"Were the lights larger than what a boat would normally be equipped with?"

"Yeah. I imagine they would have been pretty bright at night."

"Did you ask him what he was doing with these lights?"

"At first, yeah, when we were hanging out by his car. He said they were stage lights. But like I said, he told me he wasn't taking them with him, then he did." Timmy shook his head. "He was acting real weird. Chuck and I talked about him afterward. We thought he might be picking up drugs or something out at sea." Timmy acted hopeful. "Was he a drug dealer?"

Kelly took out the photograph. "Was this him?"

Timmy's whole face screwed up in concentration. Kelly had to give him a full minute before he responded. "No. That guy had blond hair."

"Did he have a beard and mustache as well?"

"Oh yeah. This guy doesn't."

Kelly could see that. "How long was his hair?" she asked patiently.

"Pretty long."

"Down to his collar? Way over his collar?"

"Way over his collar."

"How long was his beard?"

"Long. Six inches, maybe more."

"What color were his eyes?"

"I don't know."

"How tall was he?"

"I'm not sure. Tall as me, I think."

Timmy was six foot. Matt had been six foot.

"Is there anything else you remember about Schiller?" Kelly asked.

"Yeah. He looked haunted."

■

KELLY RETURNED to the office and scanned Matt's photograph into the computer. The FBI had a program that helped them build up composite sketches. Ordinarily she would have sought out assistance but the program was not difficult to work and she was in a hurry. It took her awhile but she managed to add a variety of blond wigs and beards to Matt's picture. She also played with his eye color. When she was done she had a dozen different takes of Matt in disguise. Printing them out, she called Chuck and Timmy and told them to remain at the marina until she returned.

She separated them before showing them the pictures. Picture number six—they both agreed, that was Simon Schiller. Neither of the guys even realized they were looking at a modified version of the same picture they had seen hours earlier. Kelly thanked them for their time and returned to her car and let out a scream.

"You sonofabitch!" she cried.

Yet it proved nothing. She could not take what she had discovered to her superiors and say she had solved the case. Her proof needed more layers—or so she told herself as she subconsciously rubbed her scarred abdomen. Falling was not the Acid Man. He was not a murderer. She could proceed alone with her investigation. She was not in danger.

Kelly drove toward Fresno. The next morning she checked the skydiving school for records of a Simon Schiller. Several people at the airport recognized the photograph. He had learned to skydive in the last six months. One instructor said Simon had been an excellent student.

"He could land on a dime," the guy told her.

Back at the office, the same day, she contacted the lawyer who had handled Matt's affairs at the time of his death. Matt had left his mother a meager five thousand dollars in cash and a rundown truck. But Cindy had said Matt had worked almost nonstop the last few months of his life, even though his bank statements showed he had made few deposits. Kelly suspected he had started to work for cash. That he had tried to save up enough money to survive a year or more without taking any jobs.

Was it proof?

"Oh yeah," she said to herself as she lay in bed late at night, unable to sleep. She could not get the name Falling out of her mind, and all that it meant. Had she needed one last stroke of proof, he had given it to her on a platter. Matt must have fallen far the night he had leapt from his doomed plane. He must have fallen into an even deeper darkness when he had caught Amy with David. Sure, she would collect more data and analyze all the facts but in her heart she knew already that she had her man.

Matt was alive. He had Jimmy. He had the money.

But where would an obsessed young man who'd plotted such an elaborate revenge go? To locate him she would have to think like him. More, she would have to duplicate his mental processes from beginning to end. But was that really possible? She had been betrayed herself but she was neither obsessive nor a genius.

Yet she knew such a person.

One who could help.

One who could hurt.

CHAPTER NINE

Matt Connor sat in his car and watched as Amy Techer entered the park where they had met over two years ago. She sagged onto a bench and started to cry. Her grief wounded him, and yet it gave him confidence as well. Her pain only enhanced her beauty in his eyes. The rose that had fallen to the ground. He could bend and rescue her. Once, he had sworn, he would do anything for her. But that had been before she had destroyed him. And now she could destroy him again, with just a look.

Just a phone call to the police.

Two weeks had passed since he had transformed his financial status into that of a millionaire. After seven days in Modesto counting his cash and marveling over the many diamonds—which were all real, and of high quality—he had returned to L.A. to indulge an old habit. But stalking was such a crude term to apply to what he was doing now. He honestly felt as if he was interviewing her for a position that he intended to last a lifetime. That she would be a great mother to his son he had no doubt. But could he trust her to love him through thick and thin? To forgive him for kidnapping her son?

Could he even trust her not to kill him?

Painful questions to be sure, but her obvious pain made him think the answers would be *yes*. The fact that she had chosen here of all places to have a nervous breakdown reassured him. The bench where she wept was ten feet from where they had first talked. Surely, she must be thinking of him right now.

From intercepting his mother's e-mails he knew a few things. David's abuse had reached new heights. He had hit her last week and she had hit back. Divorce was in the air. The names of lawyers were being bandied about. Anger was as much a part of the Techer daily routine as despair. Matt realized he could remove the latter while using the former.

She wiped at her damp eyes. So beautiful.

Still, she could hurt him, in so many ways.

Matt got out of his car and walked into the park. Her head was up now but she was looking the other way. Simon Schiller was a ghost. He had set aside his disguise for the day—by shaving off his beard and mustache, by fixing his hair color, by removing his contacts.

She was dressed in blue jeans and a white sweater. Her thinness accentuated the dark fall of her brown hair. She looked fragile; it struck him with amazement that such a small creature could cause him such huge pain. As he approached, he felt as if he walked toward his grave. Yet his heart pounded with love and joy. God, how he had missed her! Even if she turned and screamed it would be worth it to see her up close.

He sat on the bench beside her. Still, she did not see him.

"Amy," he said finally.

She turned and stared for an eternity. It was as if her face froze and thawed over an eon of both ice and sunshine. But in the end it was her smile—dawning like a candle lit in a dark cave—that told him he had made the right decision. She loved him, he could feel her love, and he had never cared for her more than he did in that instant. She reached out her hand and he took it.

"I knew," she said, and a tear ran over her cheek.

He shook his head. "You didn't know."

She nodded to herself and her single tear burst into a river of weeping. "No, I knew you couldn't be dead. All this time I told myself, 'He was too smart to die. He had too much magic.'" She wiped her damp face and sniffled. "Oh, Matt, why didn't you call me?"

He shrugged. "You're a married woman."

She was in shock, he could tell. She spoke like someone dreaming. "Is that why you had to go away?" she asked.

"Yes. I'm sorry."

She moved close and rubbed his arm. "It's all right, you're here now. I'm glad you're here."

He put his arm around her and the sensation of holding her was another type of falling. Into perfumed clouds of opium, where the warmth and haze were an addiction to die for. He had not planned what he would say to her.

"I missed you," he said.

"I missed you." She placed her palm on his heart and leaned deeper into his side. "I'm sorry about what happened. I'm so sorry."

"It's all right, it's over."

She looked up into his face. He remembered the power in her eyes then, the spell they could cast. The knowledge did nothing to save him. She leaned forward and their lips met and he lost his parachute and forgot all reason.

"I love you," she said.

"I love you," he replied. "I've always loved you."

She sat up and leaned back slightly and stared some more. Then she shook her head and cried a little more. "Are you really here?"

He smiled. "Yeah, it's real. I'm still alive."

Her shock was wearing off. "Can you tell me what happened?"

He had to look away. "I was mad at you. I was in horrible pain. I wanted to hurt you. I wanted to die."

"And you decided to do both?"

He nodded to the ground. "Yes."

"You faked your own death?"

"Yes."

"So you could hurt me?" she asked.

"Yes." He felt the sweat between their hands. "I hurt you, Amy."

She did not understand. "You have no idea. When I heard you'd died, I wanted to die. At night I would go out in my car for hours and search for a cliff to drive off."

"But you didn't," he said, and felt a pang.

"Didn't what?"

"Kill yourself."

She laughed softly and looked uneasy. "But I thought about it. The only problem was you wouldn't be there to read my suicide note. You wouldn't know how bad I felt about what happened. My death would be wasted."

He searched her eyes. "And you were pregnant."

She nodded, her grief near. "Yeah. I didn't want to kill my baby."

"Amy," he began.

"They took him, you know. My Jimmy, he's gone. You must have read about it in the papers."

He sighed. "I read about it."

She went on in her little girl's voice. "I wanted to take a nap. I put him down for a few minutes. And when I woke up he was gone and there was nothing I could do. I called the cops and the FBI came, but they didn't know what they were doing. We never heard from the kidnapper until a couple of weeks ago. He wanted money and diamonds. We gave it to him, but he didn't give us Jimmy back. Oh, God, Matt."

More tears, he had to hold her to keep her from shaking. Time went by but there was not enough of it to bring healing or illumination. Her tears began to dry and he knew it was time to face the monster in the mirror. But he did not want the finger to point at him alone. He continued to feel so much love for her he thought he would burst. And yet he hated her in that moment as well.

"I wanted to hurt you," he repeated.

"Matt?" She raised her dazed head. "What are you saying?"

"Did you know Jimmy was mine?"

Her eyes blinked, the spell faltered. "What are you talking about?"

"Did you know Jimmy was my son?"

The realization dawned in an instant. "You. It was you."

"Yes. It was me. Did you know?"

Suddenly there was something wrong with the picture. She should have stood and screamed. She should have run from the park crying for help. He had kidnapped her son. He was the target behind one of the most massive FBI manhunts in history. But she was an emotional smoothie: ice and sweetness.

He saw why. Because she was herself a master of schemes, she understood his plan and all its implications in a moment. She understood *him*—a subtle distinction. That was the one advantage to having a corrupt girlfriend. His depraved deed did not deeply shake her. To her, there was no conflict in him being both villain and savior. It was all there in her flawless face. She accepted his confession as something normal, when Matt knew even a priest would have had a breakdown if he had told him the truth.

Still, it was weird, too weird.

She should have screamed at him.

He noticed she had not answered his question.

"You have Jimmy?" she demanded.

"Yes."

"Is he all right?"

"Yes."

"Do you have the cash? The diamonds?"

He wanted to laugh but did not. "Sure."

His answers went into her like some sort of key. She laughed to herself but it was as if she dragged the mirth from a place unconnected to reality. "You bastard," she said.

"Me?" He let the question hang. "Did you know he was mine?"

"No."

"You're lying."

"How could he be yours? We never even had sex."

He let out his bitterness. "Yeah, don't remind me. I wasn't good enough for you. David was, though. He shows up in town and you jump in bed and fuck his brains out."

"That's not what happened."

"That is what happened!"

"Matt. I'm sorry." In her small voice. "I didn't know."

"You're lying. We were close enough for you to get pregnant. You knew he was mine the day you learned you were knocked up. Certainly you knew when he was born. He looks just like me. Plus, you're at least as smart as me. Had you any doubt, you would have had him tested." He paused. "Did you?"

She was a long time answering. "Yes."

"So you did know the truth!"

"Yes."

"And you didn't tell David?"

"How could I tell him?"

"Wasn't he suspicious? No, he wouldn't have been because I was just some guy you met and dated a few times. I wasn't your boyfriend for a year and a half."

"Where is Jimmy? I want to see him."

"No," he said flatly.

She feared him then. "You won't let me see him?"

He did not know what he felt. Minutes ago—love. Seconds ago—hate. And now his old friend—confusion. He didn't want to just give her Jimmy back. He wanted what had been taken from him back. But where was love sent for repair when it was torn to pieces? He knew his problem. He still wanted her to heal him when she was the one holding the scapel.

"You don't care if I die on the table," he muttered.

"What?"

He studied her face. She had tried to hide it with makeup, but one eye was bruised. "He hits you."

She nodded. "I must have been out of my mind to leave you for him."

That helped. He had imagined her saying the identical words for over a year. But she probably knew that. She was no fool. The fact he had gone to all this trouble to hurt her told her that he was still obsessed with her. Yet he could not move slowly with her and get to where he wanted to be. They couldn't leave the park until they reached an understanding.

"Leave him," he said suddenly.

She did not hesitate. "I'm going to leave him."

"No. Leave him now, today. I have our son. I have the money."

"But everyone thinks you're dead."

"It doesn't matter. We can go away together."

"Where?" she asked.

"Anywhere. An island in the Caribbean."

She considered. "I need to get a divorce first. David has to be dealt with. If I disappear, he'll suspect something. His father's a powerful man. He'll hunt me down. If he finds me, he'll find you, and you'll go to jail."

"For what?"

"The obvious. Kidnapping. Extortion."

"Jimmy is my son."

Her turn to study him. "You didn't know that when you took him."

His turn to lie, he owed her that. "Yes, I did know."

"How?"

"Never mind. Right now I have to know if you're serious. Do you still love me?"

"Yes. I never stopped loving you, Matt. What I did . . . I can't ask you to forgive me or to even understand why I did it. When you caught me with David I lost my mind. I felt so ashamed and disgusted with myself. I felt the need to run away and hide. Plus, on top of everything else, I knew I was pregnant."

"With my kid."

"I didn't know whose kid it was. Not then."

"These are lousy excuses, Amy."

She nodded. "I've wanted to talk to you about this for so long. Even after I was married to David, I would carry on these imaginary discussions in my head where I tried to make you understand why I did it. It's hard for someone like you who's so strong to comprehend, but I've lived in fear of David ever since I met him. I lost myself in him and I didn't even really like him. I felt I had to obey him and keep him happy. Even when he was living on the East Coast he would call me every few days and demand to know who I was talking to, who I was seeing. I had to report in all the time. I knew it was insane, but I felt too scared not to."

"This went on the whole time we dated?"

She hesitated. "Yes."

"Then you lied to him as well. You never told him about me."

"I couldn't tell him about you. He would have screamed at me. Don't you see, I was afraid of him."

"But he was three thousand miles away. You weren't going out with him. You were going out with me. You saw me every day, for godsakes!"

She shook her head. "I felt I owed him. He made me feel that way. It was as if he had a psychic hold over me. I know that's a poor excuse. But it was my life, my reality, and try as I might I couldn't break it."

"Why did you go out with me at all?"

"Because I adored you. You were the opposite of David. You cared about me in a healthy way. You wanted what was best for me. You wanted me to grow as a person—you helped me grow. You didn't feel you had to possess me. You trusted me, and yes, I know I betrayed that trust. But please believe me, Matt, that was the last thing I wanted to do. When David returned to live here, I was terrified. I made a vow to myself not to see him. But he kept calling—he wore me down—and finally I felt I had to face him to free myself of him."

"Amy, you didn't just face him. You fucked him."

"It wasn't that way. I felt I had to get free of him if I was to be with you."

"But we were so close. We shared everything. You could have told me."

"I wanted to spare you the pain. I told you that before. What if you knew he was in town? What if you knew I was seeing him? You would never have been able to rest. I thought that I could see him a few times and get over him and put it all behind me."

"You didn't want me to know because you knew I'd dump you."

"True! What's wrong with being afraid of that? I know you'll never believe this after what I did to you, but I was in love with you. I didn't want to lose you. The thought terrified me."

"But if I was the one you loved—and you were simply trying to get over David—why was I the one you dumped when I caught you with him?"

"How could I go back to you after what I had done to you?"

"But I would have taken you back. I told you that two days after I caught you with him."

She lowered her head. "I had to free myself of the hold he had on me. I couldn't be with you until I was free."

"Free yourself? Christ, you married him."

"I was pregnant!"

"With my kid!"

"I didn't know that at that time! I thought it was his!"

"No. You suspected it was mine."

"Gimme a break. Who the hell gets pregnant fooling around the way we did? I was sure it was his. Only when Jimmy was born did I begin to think he was yours."

"It's no excuse. You didn't have to marry him. But you did and you still won't admit why. The reason is so old it's boring. He was rich and I wasn't. You married him for his money, nothing else."

Amy was silent a long time. When she finally spoke, it was not in her little girl's voice or even in any other voice he recognized. It was almost as if he heard her for the first time, and he knew she was telling him the truth. More truth than she had ever told him before. Yet her sincerity did not entirely soothe him. The devil knew when it was wise to tell the truth. Amy was honest when she was forced to be, or when it suited her.

"I made a mistake," she said. "I admit it. And I'm sorry."

"That's it? You made a mistake? You're sorry?"

She leveled her gaze on him. "What do you want me to say?"

He wanted to laugh. He came close to crying. "That what you did was horrible. That you're a liar. That you love me. That you'll come back to me."

"Yes."

He was startled. "What?"

"Yes. I'm more sorry than you can imagine. I'm all those horrible things you say. But I love you and I want to come back to you." She paused. "Will you take me back?"

"Will you really leave him?"

"Yes."

"When?"

"Soon."

He heard her but did not understand her. He did not recognize the *later* in the reply—her favorite word from earlier times. Or perhaps he heard and understood it all and simply chose to ignore the fact that she was who she had always been. The devil and her special reasons why. He ached to kiss her again. Leaning forward, their mouths met for a long time and when they were done she sat back on the bench and smiled at him and he decided that yes he would dance one more time with her.

Dance or die.

It was not like he felt he had a choice.

CHAPTER TEN

The Acid Man had a sailor for a nurse. The guy looked like Popeye: tattooed arms, muscles as large as cantaloupes, sloppy white uniform, twisted grin. He reeked of cigarettes and cheap pot. Kelly Fienman had not called to say she was stopping by. But with a flash of her badge, the guy let her in to see Professor Gene Banks. The latter raised his head from a book as she stepped into the living room. He told Popeye to go work out in the next room. Kelly remembered the ton of exercise equipment. Good to know it was not being wasted. Popeye closed the door as he left. She was alone with her assailant in the same apartment where he had attacked her.

"You look well, Kelly," Banks said.

"Thank you. How are you feeling?"

He moved his head. Not much else to move. "I'm fine. It's good to see you again. But I suppose you cannot say the same for me. What can I do for you?"

"I need your help," Kelly replied, and she shivered. The apartment windows were wide open and it was a chilly Midwestern day. Outside the nearby stream gurgled. She remembered how she had initially been taken by the serenity of the view. Green meadows gliding into silent woods. As before, the apartment was neat and tasteful. The only major addition was a large white hospital bed tucked in the corner of the living room. So Banks no longer slept in the place where he had poured the acid onto her abdomen. Did the room give him nightmares? She wanted to ask but would not.

Banks had shrunk. Propped straight in his motorized wheelchair, he looked like a mannequin in need of a new suit. Gone was his long hair and closely cropped beard. He was shaved clean—perhaps to facilitate his care. He had lost weight; his spotted skin hung on his face like dried bark on a dead tree. A spork was attached to his right hand with Velcro. His left arm looked worse than useless. Ironically, he smelled nice—he wore the same cologne Tony favored, Bvlgari pour Homme. Coincidence—or had Banks done research? It begged another question.

Had he known she would appear at his doorstep?

The biggest change was in his eyes. Whereas before they had sparkled—even if with insanity—now they were soaked marbles. He was pleased to see her but seemed unable to summon the energy to focus his penetrating mind on her. She wondered if the decline in his physical appearance was deceptive. He was never who he appeared to be. Even the pajamas he wore—elves playing in the snow with reindeer—mocked his murderous nature. When she had first met him, she had thought of him as a department store Santa Claus. Now she knew the type of toys he carried in his bag.

There was a dark stain on the tan carpet near the phone. Standing in that exact spot, her intestines in hand, she had dialed 911, and then fainted into a nightmare. Banks might have read her mind; the dullness in his blue eyes momentarily lifted. He nodded as if to say they shared the same dreams. Still, they were not the same. He had not replaced the carpet because he wanted to remember her. And more than anything else in the world she wanted to forget him.

Yet, here she was, asking his help.

"I'm honored," he replied. "A case?"

"Yes. A kidnapping." Kelly reached for the briefcase at her feet. She had a gun in it, another in her coat—the one she had paralyzed him with. Both semiautomatics had a bullet cocked into their respective chambers. "I brought the FBI file. I'm willing to leave it with you if you promise to keep it confidential."

He was not interested in her papers. "Why don't you tell me about it."

"Fine." She stared at him. Suddenly it was hard not to. He was the crystal ball she gazed into when she went to sleep at night. He was her scarred and weakened guts. Tony's new and improved screw. Video-taped women screaming for mercy. Her daughter wondering aloud why she never saw her mother. He was so many things to her she could have given birth to him, or vice versa. He waited for her to speak and she could not.

"You don't have to be afraid," he said quietly.

"You said that to one of the women you murdered. I remember."

He moistened his dry lips. "Her name was Sheila. I remember."

"Where is Sheila now?" she asked carefully.

"Dead." He did not elaborate. Pushing him could backfire.

"How do you feel about her now?" she asked.

He wanted to shrug. His right hand bumped a small metal stick on his wheelchair and the motor hummed briefly and he was jerked slightly to the left. The sudden motion startled her. She sucked in a breath and realized how scared she was.

"I didn't know her," he said.

Kelly fought to remain calm. "You knew her. You knew them all."

"The only one I felt I really knew was you."

She forced a sneer. "What do you know?"

"It's not the case that has brought you here, Kelly."

"You don't even know what it's about."

"True."

"I get bored," she said. "Do you want to help me or not?"

"Tell me about it. I'm all ears." His tongue touched his lips again and she saw that they had bled and dried. "My ears are practically all I have left."

She explained her involvement in the case: the initial call, Amy's dead boyfriend and asshole husband, the foiled ransom, her research on Matt Connor. When she was finished she stated her dilemma. She knew Matt was alive and had the kid and the money, she just didn't know where he was. She had to wait for Banks to respond. He appeared to be thinking deeply. He was so smart, the fucking psychopath. But his initial comment threw her off balance.

"I see you're up to your old tricks," he said.

"What do you mean?"

"You're tracking Matt Connor by yourself. What is it about you? You stopped me—the infamous Acid Man. You must be a hero at the Bureau. What do you have left to prove?"

She wanted to lie to him, felt its uselessness. "I just want to get the kid back to his mother."

"No."

"Fuck you." She stood and reached for her bag.

"Sit down, relax." He nodded for her to obey. "You are here. No reason to rush off so quickly."

She sat back down, blood in her cheeks. "Do you want the case file or not?"

"You may leave it if you wish but I don't need it."

"You have solved the case already? Just like that?"

He ignored her. "I'm not Hannibal Lecter, and you haven't come here to play twenty questions with a serial killer. That would be too trite, and we both know you are anything but. No, you came here for closure. Unfortunately, that's not easy for you to achieve for two reasons. One, you won't admit it to yourself. Two, you do not live in the real world. You use this case as an excuse to confront me. But this afternoon is wasted on you because you're a product of your upbringing. You're still living in your books, in your fantasies. It almost killed you to go after me alone and you repeat the same mistake with this guy." He added, "All heroes have a death wish."

"It's you who's mistaken," she replied. "I'm no hero at the Bureau. They think I screwed up, nothing more."

"I doubt that. But let us leave that aside for the moment. Like I said, you came here for closure. But how is such a thing achieved in the fantasy world? You cannot go to a psychotherapist. They do not have them. You cannot take a pill. They do not sell them. No, you can only go after the dragon. And go after him you did, and defeat him you did as well—in a manner of speaking. Yet you did not slay the dragon. He still lives, and while he does you cannot rest."

She was not impressed. "I didn't come here to kill you."

"You are wrong. That is precisely why you are here."

She snorted. "I kill you and I go to jail. Anyway, you are an excellent literature professor and a superb killer, but you're a lousy psychotherapist. You don't know me. I prefer you alive and crippled. That chair is better than any jail. It pleases me to know you suffer constantly for the pain you caused me."

"How do you sleep at night?"

"What?"

"How do you sleep? Never mind, I know the answer. You hardly rest at all. It is not because of your injuries or the loss of your family. Yes, I know your husband has left you for another woman. All these things are secondary. They do not address the core of your wound. I can help you with that if you help me." He paused. "You said once that I owed you."

She wanted to plug her ears, but he sang the Sirens' song. She had to listen, even though she knew she risked being eaten alive. The allure of his words was their truth. It was hard, though, to accept that he knew her better than she knew herself. Perhaps when he had peeled away her flesh with his acid he had seen more than was humanly possible. He did not appear human in that moment. More a demon dug from a crypt in a stinking bog. Suddenly, the cold breeze coming through the open windows carried the stench of their last encounter. Nausea swelled in her dissected stomach. He was right, she wanted to reach for her gun and put a bullet in his brain. He nodded as she shook before him.

"We owe each other," he said.

"I owe you nothing!"

"Had you aimed a fraction of an inch higher my pain would have stopped that afternoon. Had you put a second bullet in me it would have ended forever." He added sadly, "But you chose not to."

Suddenly she understood what he was asking of her. In return.

"I had other things on my mind. Like saving my internal organs. We waste time with your psycho babble. You want to die and you need someone to help you along, then write Popeye into your will and have him shoot air into your veins."

"I asked. But he's a born-again Christian."

"He looks like a Satan worshipper."

"He reads the Bible three hours a day."

"There must be someone else you can find to help you commit suicide."

"There isn't."

"Well, I'm sorry but I'm not going to volunteer my services."

"But you have to. You need my help and I need yours."

"I don't need you that desperately. I'll solve the case on my own."

"The case is immaterial. You need me dead. You won't rest until I am."

She started to respond and stopped. Again, the truth of his words clawed at her. Too many times, late at night, she would imagine him here in this room thinking about her. His memory would overlap with her own. She would hear those five women on the video screaming and the noise would sometimes actually sound exciting. He was a dragon—his breath blistered her life. She could not bite into a red apple without seeing dripping blood. How had he known of Tony's betrayal?

"You want to make a deal with me," she whispered. "What is it?"

"You kill me. But before you do, in exchange, I'll give you the location of Matt Connor. And after you kill me, you get peace of mind."

"In jail. I'll be the first person they come looking for."

"You're clever. You'll figure out a way not to go to jail."

"Where's Matt?"

"Do you agree to my terms?"

"How do you know I'll keep my side of the bargain?"

"You have honor. All heroes do. If you lie you'll lose it, and that's something you cannot do and remain you."

Kelly snickered. "So you imagine. Where's Matt?"

"Do you agree to my terms?"

She hesitated. "Yes."

"Matt is with Amy."

"What? That's ridiculous. Matt hates Amy. He has devoted the last year of his life to hurting her. He would never go back to Amy."

"You say that without thinking. Matt loves Amy. You can only truly hate what you love. All other hate is mere annoyance. You would go back to your husband if he would take you, and you despise him."

"I would never go back."

"You lie to yourself. I don't lie to you. Watch Amy and you will find Matt. He is obsessed with her." He added, "Remember, I know something about obsession."

It took her a moment to digest his insight. Of course he was right, damn him. She asked her next question carefully. She supposed a part of her did feel she owed him after what he had just told her.

"How's your son?" she asked.

He gazed out the window. "I'm not allowed to see him."

"Any phone calls?"

"No one calls."

She reached for her briefcase and stood. "I'll call you if you're right."

He looked up at her. "Then you'll come back for me?"

"I'll come back," she promised.

She was at the door when she turned.

It took a killer to know another killer.

"Is he dangerous?" she asked.

"They are both dangerous," he replied.

CHAPTER ELEVEN

Matt Connor—once more in his disguise as Simon Schiller—was cleaning his newly rented apartment in anticipation of a visit from Amy Techer when he first saw the neighbor who was soon to introduce herself as Kathy Mantein. She was sunning herself by the pool. It was a warm day and a dozen tenants were working on their tans, but she was the only female wearing a one-piece suit.

He noticed her because she was exceptionally thin and pale. She might have been pretty as well, but she sat in the corner of the deck behind a magazine and wore a wide-brimmed hat and thick sunglasses. She seemed to study the small gathering as she relaxed. Always on guard himself, he had a sense for people who kept secrets.

But he did not give her much thought. Amy was coming.

A month had passed since he had met Amy in the park and forged an agreement that on the surface constituted one of the strangest love affairs in history. From the start, Amy had taken charge. If they were going to resume their relationship, she said, he had to get a place nearby where she could sneak out for a few hours and see him and their son. She insisted on an expensive apartment—four thousand a month, he was lucky he was a millionaire—near the beach in Malibu. The apartment did have one major advantage: he could pay month-to-month. He did not intend the current situation to last. Only until Amy was divorced and they could move away. That would be soon, she promised.

In most ways it was wonderful to be back with Amy. He had dwelled on her so long he had begun to think he had created a mirage of how she really was, good or bad. But the truth was that the two of them got along well, as they always had before the dark days. It was a weird observation to make about someone he had plotted to hurt for so long. It was also accurate. They seldom fought, and took pleasure in the simplest things: going for a walk with Jimmy, watching a DVD, making lunch. He had forgotten what an excellent cook Amy was. He had put on several pounds in the last four weeks.

It was a miracle for him to hold her in his arms again. Especially in bed, where she would love him with a fever she had always promised would happen one day. Touching her naked skin went beyond sex—it was a form of worship for him. No matter how much he kissed her breasts or ran his hands through her hair he could not get enough of her.

Yet, when she left to return home to David, he went through withdrawals. But then she would return—virtually every day—and the miracle would happen again. They made love every time Jimmy napped. It was as if the agony he had gone through had been worth it for the joy of seeing her again.

Plus, she was the best mother. Her patience with Jimmy was unlimited. To watch the two of them play together invoked feelings in him he had never experienced before: a feverish desire to protect and nourish; a pride that seemed to arise from the cellular level. He had been a father before Amy had returned to their life, but he had not had a family. The difference was greater than that of a straight line and a triangle. He contemplated the balance of the triangle as he sat near his child and girlfriend.

He contemplated it and he wondered.

Because he was not stupid. They lived in a dream world. Reality waited like a ticking clock beside both their heads. He was an outlaw. He may have been Jimmy's biological father but society did not recognize his role. The money they spent was stolen. They could not simply *move away* after Amy got a divorce. David would keep tabs on her, he was that kind of guy. He would eventually learn Amy had a sweet little boy, not to mention a not-so-sweet boyfriend. It might take a few months, maybe a few years. But the truth would eventually emerge.

What was the truth anyway?

There was only one question that mattered.

Did she really love him?

She said she did, and she did everything she could to prove it. Soft words at passionate moments—they flowed like iced pearls through his heated veins. On the surface he was inclined to believe her. But when his contemplation reached even a minor depth, he ran into what she had done to him in the past. Their history was not merely a shadow—it was a pit. Occasionally, when he dozed naked in her arms on the rare night she was able to stay over, he felt himself falling. No parachute above, no boat below. In darkness he fell and the sound of her breathing was a howling wind in his head, capable of sweeping away all he sought to possess. He would awake soaked in sweat and she would kiss him and tell him to go back to sleep.

Don't worry, baby. Everything will be all right.

All he had wanted to do was love her. In the beginning he had been innocent. Only in the middle had he transformed into a master schemer. Now he just wanted Matt Connor back. He hated the disguise he had to wear to walk outside. He hated many parts of his life; he felt it belonged to him no longer. He was so attached to her she owned him. She promised that everything would be fine, but promises existed in the future. His fears came in the present. He would think of her kissing David and he would feel sick, and the thought of them having sex made him swoon. But then she would notice his silence. She had the antenna of a Martian lander. She swore that she was no longer intimate with her husband, that they hardly even talked. And he wanted to believe her.

Ah, trust; even millions of dollars could not buy it back.

Amy came to the door. Jimmy was still asleep, swinging near the TV in a rocker his mother had bought for him the previous week. It pained Amy that she was no longer capable of breast-feeding their son. Too much time had elapsed, too much grief. One thing that always amazed him about her was that—except for her initial outburst—she did not bring up the kidnapping. She was more forgiving than he, perhaps too much so.

Simon Schiller answered the door. Malibu was a cousin of Santa Monica. Matt was dead, and could not risk running into old friends and being recognized. Yet Amy always acted annoyed when he put on his wig. She had spoken of taking a walk down to the water. He felt he could not be too careful.

"Hi, honey," he said and gave her a hug as she stepped inside. No girl fit so well in his arms as his Amy—she was a regular Lego. There was a red rose in her hair, and her kiss tasted like vanilla. He quickly got an erection and she pulled back and grinned.

"Donate blood and the guy who gets it will never need Viagra," she said.

"The same guy will probably come looking for you. You're early."

"Wanted to see if I'd catch you with your girlfriend."

"She just left, out the back door."

"There is no back door."

They kissed some more and she moved on to Jimmy. He never felt jealous of the time she spent with him. To her credit, she was good at balancing her attention between them. She had picked up bad habits married to wealth, though. When they went out, she spent money. He had never seen that side of her before. Isn't this pretty, Matt? She obsessed over clothes and jewelry. Because she and David were on bad terms, she said she did not like to use his credit cards. Something about how it would look in court when they finally settled. The other day Matt had reluctantly bought her a diamond bracelet that cost six thousand. That was nothing next to what he had, yet it was not as if he had a way of replenishing the dough.

Amy was on him about that. She wanted him to invest the cash and make it grow. She did not accept the reality of their situation. The old adage was true—the FBI caught virtually every thief by following the money. Before renting their apartment, he had driven to Miami and laundered seventy grand through low-level drug dealers. He had met a pal of the dealers while slumming in Modesto. He got only seventy cents on the dollar. At least he was confident the guys had nothing to do with the authorities. They treated their Uzis like pets. They dabbed their runny noses and offered him white sugar that could not be used in mother's cookie recipe. But they liked him, they thought he was a cool guy.

He did not like dealing with such lowlives. He needed to find a connection to unload the whole sum—the diamonds and the cash. But Mexico was hot with FBI, and the guys he would meet farther south would be too scary. He thought of going to Europe. Amy understood none of these things, or if she did she didn't care. He had to watch his own back around her. It was not a good feeling.

Jimmy woke up. Amy fed him, they went for a walk, Jimmy slept some more, they made love. Another idyllic afternoon until she dressed to leave. It was then Matt asked about the divorce, and Amy casually dropped a bombshell.

"David said he'll see me dead before he divorces me," she said.

Matt sat up sharply. "I thought you said he couldn't stand the sight of you?"

"I guess he changed his mind."

"Did you do anything to make him change his mind?"

That annoyed her. "You mean, did I fuck him?"

"Yeah. Did you?"

She turned away, hurt. "You're never going to forgive me."

They'd had this discussion before. He always ended up explaining there was a difference between forgiveness and forgetting. The trouble was, he wasn't sure what it was. He got to his feet and embraced her from behind.

"I'm sorry," he said. One day she would cut off his dick and he would apologize. She used guilt as easily as she breathed. But it was not as if he was whipped. At least, that's what he told himself. She turned and buried her face in his chest.

"He'll never leave us in peace," she said.

Matt sighed. "I'm beginning to think that."

She looked up at him. "You never told me why you decided to kidnap Jimmy to get back at me. Why didn't you just kill me?"

"Killing someone is not the worst revenge. They're simply dead, they don't feel anything."

"But you must have thought of killing me?"

He hesitated. "True."

"How would you have done it?"

"Is this what they call a hypothetical question?"

"Tell me, how did you think of doing it?"

"Are you thinking of killing David?"

"No! We're talking about me."

He sat on the edge of the bed. She was still naked from the waist down and it was not a bad view. "The two best ways to murder someone—if you want to get away with it—are to either push them off a cliff, or drown them in the ocean."

"Why?"

"Unless someone sees you push your victim off the cliff, you can always argue in court that they jumped or slipped. It's similar with drowning in the sea, particularly if you can get enough alcohol in your intended victim. You can argue that the person simply fell off the boat and you didn't know it. That works especially well if you're in the middle of the sea. In both cases there's plenty of room for reasonable doubt."

Amy was interested. "How do you know all this?"

"I'm smart."

"No, really. How did you know how to fake out the FBI when you collected the ransom?"

"I gave it a lot of thought. I had plenty of time."

"You didn't read it in a book or something?"

"No."

She was impressed. "You should have been someone famous."

"Thank you, darling."

"Were you scared you would get caught?"

"Of course. But I was confident as well. Where is this conversation going?"

She smiled to herself. "You're amazing. You do what you want."

He felt uneasy. The observation more accurately applied to her.

"Violence is for the impatient," he said.

She continued to dress. "I'll talk to David again tonight."

"Have you brought up the idea that you might be leaving the state?"

"Yes. He just gets furious."

"Has he given up hope of finding Jimmy?"

"He'll never give up hope."

Matt felt a stab of guilt. "He loves him that much?"

Amy shook her head as she pulled on her jeans. "I don't know if David knows what love is. But he misses Jimmy, he'll never stop looking for him."

Again, the threat. "We should leave now," he muttered.

"No. It'll look suspicious. Besides, we need the money."

"You won't get that much. You weren't married long."

"He'll pay me to keep my mouth shut."

"About what?"

"How he messed up the ransom exchange, for one thing."

"He didn't mess it up. He never stood a chance to begin with."

"It doesn't matter. David is sensitive to criticism. He can't stand people knowing what a prick he is. You know he's hit me. So far, I haven't talked about it, but he knows I might."

He did not like the way her mind worked—so calculated. "This is California. He has to grant you a divorce. You don't need to threaten him."

She was annoyed again. "You talk to me about threats?"

"My situation with you was different. Besides, the longer this thing drags on the more vulnerable we are. I wear this beard and long hair but we live openly here. I don't like it."

"Then move back to Modesto, I don't care."

"Where I go, Jimmy goes."

She was instantly apologetic. She came and pressed his head to her chest. "I'm sorry, that was thoughtless. I know you're under a lot of pressure. I'll do everything I can to get David to listen to reason. All I'm saying is that at one point we might have to take matters into our own hands."

Her chest took the sting out of his anxiety. He spoke in a muffled voice.

"Which means?" he asked.

"Nothing. We just have to keep our options open."

"Okay," he said, not sure what he was agreeing to. "Did the FBI call again?"

Amy began to put on her makeup. She never used to wear it. "Yes. This black guy, Agent Fitzsimmons, Charlie, called. Our main contact person, Kelly, took a leave of absence. Can you believe that? Jimmy is God knows where and she takes a vacation."

"God's not the only one who knows where your son is."

"That's not my point. Kelly doesn't know that and she takes off. To think I really believed she cared about me. She was probably just trying to further her career. When the ransom went south, she split." Amy added, "I hate people like that."

"She might not be gone for good."

Amy shook her head. "I don't care what she does."

"How long ago did she take her leave?"

"Two weeks ago."

Matt was curious. "Was Kelly in charge of the case?"

"Not technically. Agent Bane, the head of the L.A. office, was the top boss. Kelly was our personal liaison."

"Did you ever tell her about me?"

"Why?"

"Because I'm the one who kidnapped your son and if she's real smart it's always possible she could figure that out. Did you tell her about me or not?"

"I told her you were dead."

"Did you tell her how I died?"

"Yes."

"How did she take it?"

"I don't know. She believed me. Why wouldn't she believe me?"

"What I mean is, did she persist in questioning you about me?"

Amy was in front of the mirror, lipstick in hand. She stopped and stared at him in the glass. "She was curious about you. She wanted to know if I cared about you."

"What did you tell her?"

"That I loved you, of course."

"Did she wonder why you married David?"

"I think everyone who meets David wonders why I married him."

"Amy. Tell me everything she asked."

"I don't remember everything. But I know she never considered you a suspect. You don't have to worry about that."

Somehow he still managed to worry. "Where was Kelly the day of the ransom?"

"She was out stalking David with Charlie."

"What is this Charlie like?"

"Nice guy, smart. David hates him."

"Does he ever question you about me?"

"Never."

"When he called last did you act suitably depressed?"

"Oh yeah. I shed a few tears. Don't worry."

"When you leave your house from now on, I want you to check in your rearview mirror and see if you're being followed."

"I told you, they suspect nothing."

"Smart FBI agents suspect everything."

Amy finished dressing and left. Matt felt restless in the apartment. There were only so many books he could read, so many movies to watch. At least in Modesto he'd had his work and Lupe to help with Jimmy. He had given the girl a nice parting bonus. He continued to keep in loose contact. She already had a new job at the supermarket. He was never sure when he might need her again.

Jimmy awoke shortly afterward. Matt took him down to the pool to splash. With his disguise, he didn't swim himself. He sat on the steps with Jimmy and hoped the little guy didn't empty his bladder in the chlorinated water. Jimmy loved the pool and he was so cute, he was always attracting attention. Matt usually explained that Jimmy's mother worked during the day, that he was a house dad.

Once again he noticed the pale skinny woman sitting in the corner of the deck behind her magazine. Her hair was long, blond, her face not merely pretty but intelligent. She had a distinct bone structure, but appeared fragile. Even before she stood and came over and put her feet in the water, he noticed her eyes on him. He sensed she wanted to talk to him.

"How old is he?" she asked as she sat on the deck and gestured to Jimmy. Her one-piece swimsuit was yellow, cut wide, her body well covered. As she spoke, she removed her sunglasses and he saw her eyes were a clear blue. She could have been a model, she was that pretty.

"Eight months," he said. "He's almost talking already." Why did everyone always brag about their kid?

"He's beautiful. He has your eyes."

Lupe had said the same thing.

"I just hope he doesn't have my brain," Matt replied.

"Why is that?"

He chuckled. "I would prefer he had an easier life than mine."

"Is his mother around?"

"Oh yes. She just left a few minutes ago."

"I saw her, I think. Long dark hair? Looks Hispanic?"

"That's her."

"Pretty girl."

"I like to think so." Matt almost added that she didn't look so bad herself. She carried a book along with her magazine—Shelly's *Franken-stein*. He nodded to the title. "Reading it for the first time?"

"No. Read it in college. Just had the yen for something scary and classic at the same time. But I read all the time."

"Me too. I'm addicted to books. Right now I'm reading Dante's *Inferno* for the third time. The imagery is disturbing. You feel like the guy really went to hell."

"He says he did. He says it was a vision." She offered her hand. "I'm Kathy Mantein by the way. I just moved in five days ago."

They shook. "Simon Schiller. How do you like it here so far?"

"Nice." She added, "But I don't know if it's worth four thousand a month."

She must be paying month-to-month as well, he thought. The rent was less if one took a long-term lease. "I hear you," he said.

"So it's just you and your wife and this little guy?"

"Yeah. Well, we're not exactly married. How about you?"

"Oh. I'm separated. I have a daughter but she's with her father right now."

"Do they live around here?"

"Not far." Her eyes seemed to dim and she glanced at the book in her lap. "We'll probably end up getting divorced."

"Sorry to hear that."

She looked up and smiled quickly. "So what do you do for a living, Simon?"

"I was a building contractor for a few years. But right now, I'm taking a break. How about you?"

"Taking a break myself. I'm a psychologist—I have a Ph.D. in the field." She added, "If you need help with that brain of yours, let me know."

The comment was suggestive, and he had already made it clear he had a serious girlfriend. But he was not put off by the remark—she seemed genuinely friendly. He didn't get the impression she wanted anything from him.

"I don't think it's a problem that's easily fixed," he said.

She nodded. "I feel the same way about my life. Wish I could send it back to the factory and get it repaired. Does your girlfriend work during the day?"

"Yeah. She's in real estate."

Kathy glanced at the sun. "I shouldn't be out here too long without sunblock. I need to buy some."

He had noticed she had been in the shade earlier. "I have some up in my apartment. I could get it for you."

"Could you?" she asked.

"Yeah. I can't stay here too long with my son anyway." He lifted Jimmy from the water and his son immediately started kicking. He wanted back in, but Matt stood and wrapped him in a towel. He added, "I'll bring it down to you in a few minutes."

Kathy stood. "Don't bother. I'll save you the trip. I'll come up with you."

"Okay." His apartment was on the fourth floor, facing the beach, with a view up the coast. She pointed out her place—on the second floor—as they went up the steps. Matt had never lived in an apartment that didn't face a wall or a trailer park. Now he understood why people paid for views. The wide open vista was expansive—it made staying home a lot more bearable. Kathy brought a blue towel with her as they walked, wearing it like a cape. Again, he was taken by her beauty and friendliness. Amy seldom talked to strangers.

Inside his place, he left Jimmy with Kathy for a minute and went in the bathroom for the sunblock. She seemed happy to take the child. When he returned they were engaged in an animated discussion about a box of colored blocks Amy had bought for Jimmy. Like his mother, Jimmy was normally guarded with people but such was not the case today.

"Thanks," she said as she took the lotion and studied the label. "Wow, SPF sixty. I can lay out all day with this stuff on."

"I read somewhere that above fifteen, sunblock doesn't get any stronger."

"If you read it then it must be true," she quipped.

"You sound like me. A born believer."

"Or at least we started out that way."

He nodded. "Yeah. I suppose I've lost a little faith along the way."

"Easy to do these days." She set Jimmy down on the floor and messed up his hair. "Take care of yourself, big fella. You too, Simon, hope to see you around. We can share books during our self-imposed sabbaticals."

"I would like that."

She moved toward the door and then paused and glanced back. Her blue eyes pierced the apartment shadows. He thought she would speak again but she only smiled. Then she was gone, and he thought how easy and natural it was to talk to her. He decided right then he would try to bump into her again.

■

MATT GOT together with Kathy two days later, by the pool. They talked about books and politics and she invited him back to her apartment for tea. He had met a teenage girl in the complex who was anxious to make a few bucks babysitting. He left Jimmy with her right then—a risk but one he felt he had to take. He was a good father but not superdad. He had to start getting out more or he would go crazy.

Kathy's home was sparsely furnished. She had hardly moved in at all. He had rented his apartment furnished. It looked as if neither of them knew where they were headed next. She apologized for the lack of places to sit.

"I'm not in the mood to collect stuff these days," she said as she put on the teakettle. He sat at her kitchen counter.

"Same here. I go to stores these days and can't find a thing I want to buy."

"Does that mean we should become monks and renounce the world?"

"Funny you should say that. I was watching a program last night on Tibetan monks and it stirred a deep longing in me. That kind of lifestyle, so simple and pure." He added, "But I have a few attachments that I'm not ready to give up yet."

"Amy?"

"Yeah. Amy."

"You know, whenever you say her name, you lower your voice. Why is that?"

"Probably for the same reason you frown whenever you mention your husband."

"I don't do that. Do I?"

"Yes." Matt hesitated. "Did he hurt you?"

She paused. "I guess you could say that." There was an awkward moment, then she turned toward the door. "I have to use the bathroom. Be back in a minute."

She was gone a few minutes. When she returned, she checked on the water on the stove. She still had on her bathing suit, her legs less pale than the other day. She talked as if they had not been interrupted, a note of pain in her voice.

"There was another woman. There still is."

"Did you know?" he asked.

"I did and I didn't."

"That's rough," he said.

"Do you mind herb teas? It's all I drink these days."

"Not at all. Give me whatever you're having."

She prepared the beverages with her back to him and continued in a soft voice. "I'm partly to blame. He kept telling me I wasn't giving him the attention he needed. That I was ignoring our daughter. But he never told me he didn't love me anymore. Because of that, I think, I never heard him. I just kept doing what I was doing. My career was important to me."

"Were you working long hours?"

"Yes. I was away from home a lot." She returned to the counter with the mugs of tea. "Do you want honey? Milk? Sugar?"

"Honey is fine. I wouldn't have imagined a psychologist would travel much."

"I lectured a lot." She sat and sampled her tea. "Tell me about your relationship with Amy."

"We're attached to each other. But, like all couples, we have our problems."

"Tell me about them."

Matt laughed easily. "You're taking a break from counseling, remember?"

"Forgive me, I'm just curious about you two. I just want to understand."

He shrugged. "There's nothing to understand. We're like everyone else."

She sipped her tea. "Somehow, I doubt that."

The next day he got into another fight with Amy about the divorce. He felt she was stalling and told her so. He believed she was still afraid of David, and she did admit that he could still intimidate her. Of course that set him off. He hated the guy so much for the pain he had caused him. Even though David had known nothing about him the whole time he had dated Amy. They fought for an hour and he ended up apologizing for God knows what.

He was a master at bad timing. He had told Amy about Kathy and when he was walking her down to her car after their battle he decided to introduce them. Not that Amy was ever jealous of him talking to other women. It was like she felt absolutely confident he could never find another woman attractive next to her. The trouble was she was right.

He had seen Kathy enter her apartment only moments before but when he knocked there was no answer. Amy waited with all the enthusiasm of a rock.

"Maybe she's in the bathroom," she suggested.

"Maybe." Matt had Jimmy in his arms. "Too bad, I think you'd really like her."

"I'm sure I would." Amy yawned. "I can meet her another time."

In the basement of the complex, where they parked, Amy brought up the idea of taking Jimmy by herself on Friday. She had brought up the possibility before, but he had always vetoed it. She just had to run into one person she knew and it would all be over. He repeated his concerns but she remained adamant.

"I'll take him down to Orange County," she said. "I don't know any-one there. I want to do some shopping for him. He needs new clothes."

"He has plenty of clothes."

"You don't trust me, do you? You worry I'll run off with him."

The thought had crossed his mind. "It's an unnecessary risk. When we're out of California, you can take him all you want."

"I deserve to spend time alone with my son. Who knows how long it will take to get away from David?"

"Ain't that the truth," he muttered.

"That isn't fair. You want him out of the way so badly, get rid of him."

"How?"

"Kill him."

"I'll buy a gun today."

"Why the sarcasm? You kidnapped a kid. I would think killing an asshole like him would be a snap for you."

He studied her. "You're serious, aren't you?"

"You keep putting all this on me. Why don't you do something for a change?"

"Amy. In case you didn't know, I'm not a murderer."

She glowered. "Sorry, I didn't know that."

That Friday afternoon—when Amy was away with Jimmy in Orange County—Matt had an early dinner with Kathy. He wasn't sure who in-vited whom but he drove them both to the restaurant. It was a pleasure to be in the car with a woman who liked the music real loud. Particu-larly, the rock stations—Kathy had tastes similar to his own.

"Do you notice how lousy music is these days compared to twenty or thirty years ago?" she said. "All that rap shit. If you say you hate it you get accused of being racist. But I don't think anyone with a brain likes it. Give me Led Zeppelin or The Who or The Rolling Stones any day."

"Real cerebral music," Matt remarked.

"Hey, at least they have rhythm. I listen to rap and I feel like I have to load my piece or abuse my woman."

"Do you have a piece?" he asked.

She gave him a look. "What if I told you I did?"

"I'd be careful not to abuse you."

They went to Gladstones, at the end of Sunset by the beach. Got a booth by the window. The sea was gray, the blue sky partly cloudy. Kathy wore tight black pants, a white blouse, a red scarf around her neck. She'd put on makeup; her lips were as red as her scarf. He ordered swordfish and Kathy asked for the same. He dug into the bread and salad while they waited for their meals, but Kathy begged off the preliminaries.

"Don't be offended if I eat only a tiny bit of fish," she said. "My digestion is lousy. I have to watch my diet carefully."

"Has it always been that way?"

She hesitated. "No. Just in the last year."

"What brought on the problem? Stress?"

"Yes."

When their fish arrived, he realized she had not been kidding. She ate very slowly, chewed every bite as if it was her last. Along with her fish and rice, she had water and a handful of pills she described as digestive enzymes. She saw his concern but brushed it off.

"This way I don't have to diet," she said.

"Have you seen a doctor about it?"

"Yeah. Lots of doctors."

"What did they say?"

"That I'm a very lucky woman."

"Kathy?"

She smiled. "Let's not talk about me. Let's talk about you. Where is Amy today?"

"Amy is me?" he asked, teasing.

Kathy spoke seriously. "Is she?"

Matt chewed on his bread. "Sometimes I have to wonder."

But he didn't tell her much. And she didn't tell him that much about Tony.

They stayed out past dark. Matt called the apartment from the restaurant. Amy was already back with Jimmy. David was out of town—Amy said she could stay over. He thought it was a perfect time for Kathy to meet her. But Kathy begged off when they reached the complex.

"I'm feeling tired," she said. "I can meet her another time."

"That's fine. Since you're so curious about the two of us, I just thought that you'd want to come up."

Kathy patted her stomach. "Believe it or not, that was a big meal for me. I have to lie down and concentrate on my digestion." She gave him a quick hug and a peck on the cheek. "I had a fabulous time. You're a neat guy, Simon."

Her tone was sad and it made him wonder. "Thanks. I had a great time as well. Will you be around tomorrow?"

She glanced up in the direction of his apartment. "No. But the day after that, let's get together. Give Amy my regards."

"I will," he promised.

Two days later Kathy was not answering her door. For some reason he sensed something was wrong, and when she finally did respond—long after sunset—she looked terrible. Her face was streaked with tears and she held her right side.

"Kathy! What is it?" he cried.

She was having trouble breathing. Her bathrobe was soaked in sweat. He struck out a hand to support her as she bent over.

"I'm pretty sure I'm passing a gallstone," she whispered. "This has happened to me before after . . . after my injury. But it has never gone on so long."

"How long have you been in pain?"

"Six hours."

"Kathy! You have to go to the hospital."

Her head shot up. "No. If I go to the hospital, they'll take out my gallbladder."

"But if that's what it takes to get better . . ."

She shook her head and tears crept from the corners of her eyes. "No. You don't understand. I can't have another operation. I can't let them take any more out. This stone will pass, it has to pass. It's just stuck. Please, just come in and help me. But don't make me go to the hospital."

"I'll help you," he promised. "Give me a minute to take Jimmy to Barbara. She can watch him tonight. But Kathy, why didn't you call me earlier?"

She closed her eyes and grimaced. "I didn't want to bother you."

"How could you ever think you were bothering me?"

Matt hurried and turned his son over to the babysitter. Jimmy was comfortable with Barbara; the girl had a good head on her shoulders. As he rushed back downstairs, he was determined to talk Kathy into going to the hospital. But once inside her place he realized there was no chance. She would rather die first than go under the knife again, she said.

"What was this injury you mentioned?" He sat beside her on the couch and held her hand. There could be few things in life that could inspire greater helplessness than to sit beside a friend in agony and not be able to stop it. She gulped the air, when she could. Her whole abdomen was one massive cramp.

"I got hurt. It's a long story."

"The injury involved your gallbladder?"

"All my guts were hurt. Please, I don't want to talk about it. Just stay here with me." She winced and bent into a ball. "I'm so scared."

He put his free hand on the side of her cheek. "I'm only asking so I can figure out what to do for you. Do you have pain medication?"

"Yes. Percocet. I tried to take some at the beginning of the attack but I vomited it up. It makes you nauseous if your stomach's empty. But I haven't been able to eat. And when I threw up it hurt so bad, I'm afraid to take it again."

"Maybe you took too much at once. Let me cut the pills into quarters. You can take one with a sip of water, and if it stays down, you can take another quarter. You have to stop this pain, you can't go on like this."

She nodded weakly. "I'll try that."

He found the bottle of pills spilt over the bathroom counter. He took a knife from her kitchen and diced a pill. When he returned to her side, she was crying into her pillow.

"This is so humiliating," she said.

He handed her a glass of water. "Pain makes a coward of us all. Come, swallow a piece and we'll see how it goes. My mother used to have gallstone attacks but they would pass."

She raised her head and looked at him like a wounded child. "What if this stone is really stuck?"

Then she had to go to the hospital. But she did not want to hear that.

Kathy got a quarter of a pill down. A few minutes later she managed to swallow another piece. An hour after entering her apartment, he had coaxed two ten-milligram Percocets into her belly without her throwing up. The medication slowly took effect and her breathing eased. She was able to sit up, although she remained in considerable pain.

"What does it feel like?" he asked as he brought her a second glass of water. He suspected she was dehydrated on top of everything else.

"Pressure. Like something is seriously blocked."

He nodded. "It's the common bile duct. I studied the anatomy when my mother got sick."

She rolled her head in his direction. "How's your mother now, Simon?"

He hesitated. "She's fine."

Kathy was mildly stoned. "She must love you very much."

He nodded past his own pain. "Yeah. She kind of likes me."

Kathy stared at him. "You haven't seen her in a long time."

"Why do you say that?"

"Because it's true."

"Hey, I was waiting until your pain decreased to suggest this. Have you ever heard of something called a gallbladder flush?"

"No. Tell me about it."

"It's used to flush a huge amount of bile through your gallbladder and the duct so that if there are stones in the way, they're pushed into the colon. The way it works, you drink an entire cup of olive oil along with a cup of freshly squeezed lemon juice."

"Yuck!"

"The olive oil causes your liver to produce a ton of bile. Oil is fat—the body digests fat with bile. The lemon juice causes the gallbladder to contract and squeeze out whatever stones are there. Basically what you're doing is putting a rushing river behind the stuck stone. Now that will increase the pressure in the area, but that should only be for a short time. The stone should be shoved out of the way. But there are risks. If the stone is so big it can't be pushed out of the way, the pressure will intensify. Also, there's always the slight chance that the stone will get stuck in your pancreas on the way to your intestines. Then you can get pancreatitis. That's when the pancreas starts to digest itself. If that happens you have to get to the hospital or you'll die." He added, "But the chances of that happening are less than one in a thousand."

She stared at him stupidly. "Are you a doctor or what?"

"I told you, I've been through it with my mom. She used to do flushes. Most of the time they go well. Even a big, hard stone can be pushed out safely. But you have to understand there is a slight risk."

She considered. "I have trouble digesting fat these days. When I was injured, my liver was damaged."

"You know your body better than me."

"How many times did your mother flush out stones?"

"Six times that I know of."

"And it worked all six times?"

"Yes. You have to drink the oil and lemon juice and lie on your right side and try to fall asleep. If all goes well, the pain will stop after a few hours, and then you'll have to rush to the bathroom with the worst case of diarrhea imaginable. You might even find the stones in the toilet bowl."

"Sounds romantic. I have no olive oil or lemons."

"I can get the stuff for you at the store down the street."

She grabbed his hand. "I don't want you to leave."

He patted her arm. "I'll be back in twenty minutes. You're still in pain but we have it under control. But it's up to you. What do you want to do?"

"I have to do something." She groaned and looked at him with her blue eyes. Although bloodshot, they were still beautiful, and a little dopey. "I'm a hero, did you know that?"

He smiled. "I couldn't tell by looking at you."

"All heroes are gamblers. But they're not all good gamblers. I found that out big time when I got hurt." She sighed. "I know, you have no idea what I'm talking about. It doesn't matter. I'll try it, what the hell."

He leaned over and kissed her forehead. "I'll be back soon."

The market was within walking distance but he drove to save the extra minutes. He was reluctant to prescribe a home remedy to someone in so much pain. But he knew what Kathy meant—the hospital would just cut out her gallbladder. Using this technique, his mother had avoided surgery for twenty years.

But the flush worked best if one prepared for it in advance. The malic acid in apples was effective at softening the stones. That way they moved through the bile duct easier—like marshmallows as opposed to rocks. His mother would drink a gallon of apple juice every day for two weeks before a flush. Matt vowed that if her stones didn't move within a few hours of ingesting the lemon juice and oil, he was taking Kathy to the hospital, even if he had to drag her.

He wondered how she had been injured, and why she called herself a hero. She was drugged, though; he couldn't take her seriously.

There was plenty of olive oil and lemons at the market. He was back in her apartment in less than twenty minutes. She had turned on the TV but did not seem to be watching it. The Percocet still percolated in her bloodstream. She seemed to be having trouble focusing. He juiced the lemons and put the olive oil in a glass. He had bought the extra-light virgin kind. He hoped she could keep it all down. When he returned to the living room, she had a worried look on her face.

"What if my guts explode?" she asked.

"I'll clean up the mess." He sat beside her on the couch. "It might be better if you go to the bedroom. Once you drink this stuff, you won't be able to get up and walk around without feeling nauseous."

She took his hand. "I don't want to go in there. It's dark in there."

"I can turn on the light."

"I want to stay out here with you. I can lie down on the couch."

"Okay." He handed her the glass of oil with a straw. He also had an open bottle of Coke handy. "Drink it quick, and try not to let it touch your lips. If you get nauseous, sip some Coke. It will take the taste of the oil away. Plus Coke has something in it that suppresses nausea."

She sniffed the oil. "Will this turn me into an Italian?"

"A pizza. Drink it, don't think."

She drank it down in several tortured gulps. She kept signaling for the Coke. His mother had used to do the same thing. Kathy gagged when she gave him the empty glass back. "That was awful," she swore.

"The lemon juice goes down much easier." He handed her the glass. "Just get it over with."

She made another face and swallowed the bitter drink. "Jesus Christ!" she said, and winced like, well, she had just drank a pint of lemon juice. "Did you just make up this formula or what?"

"I give it to all my girls. It makes them horny." He took away the glasses—put them in the kitchen—then eased her onto her right side. "Now try to sleep. I'll lower the light."

"Don't turn it off." She refused to let go of his hand. "Don't leave me."

"I won't leave you. I'll stay here all night if you want."

"Good." She closed her eyes. "This stuff feels weird in my stomach."

"Do you need another pill?"

"I don't know what I need," she mumbled.

She began to doze. He sat on the floor near her head and continued to hold her hand. There was an interesting program on TV—a *CSI* rerun—about a murderer who pretended to be a judge during the day. It was informative, all the new high-tech methods criminologists had at their disposal to catch killers. Matt wished to God Amy would stop talking about whacking David.

Kathy fell into a deep sleep and he turned off the TV and the light. He sat in a chair by the couch, and the darkness enveloped him with strange warmth. The sound of her breathing was a lullaby in the night. It struck him then how much he cared for Kathy, and how different the feeling was from his love for Amy. The truth of the matter was his attachment and love for Amy were so intertwined, it was hard to tell if the former was not merely giving rise to the latter. The question was old—what was love? Whatever it was, he suspected obsession had nothing to do with it. Yet the realization did nothing to blunt his fixation. Even now, concerned for Kathy, he was still haunted by Amy.

What was she doing right now with David?

Kathy awoke four hours later in horrible pain.

She sat up suddenly in the dark. He almost knocked over the lamp reaching for the switch. The light washed over her like radiation. She was ashen—her face twisted in a mask of torture. Her breath came in sharp stabs.

"It hurts!" she cried.

He leapt to her side. "The pain is worse?"

She nodded, tears squeezing from her eyes. "I can't stand it!"

"This is how the flush works. It puts pressure on the stone to move."

She doubled up and shook her head violently. "It hurts too much!"

"We have to go to the hospital then."

On her knees, she buried her face into the end of the couch. "I don't want to go. Please don't make me go."

He spoke firmly. "The flush will still probably work but we can't risk your life. At least at the hospital they can monitor your condition and give you something stronger for the pain."

She protested some more but he was not listening. He went into her bedroom and found a long coat. Somehow he managed to get her into it and out the door. She almost fainted in the elevator that led to the parking structure. He held her and whispered soothing words in her ear. At the same time he cursed himself for trying a flush when he did not know the extent of her internal injuries. These days it seemed he was always cursing something.

"How are you doing?" he asked as they pulled onto the Pacific Coast Highway. Middle of the night in Malibu—the road was deserted. He was not sure where he was going. There was St. John's in Santa Monica—an excellent hospital, he had heard—but it was fifteen miles away. At the same time he didn't want to search for another. Kathy was in no shape to help with directions.

"I feel like I'm going to die," she whispered.

"I have a cell phone. Is there anyone you want me to call? Your husband?"

She rolled back into a ball. "No. Not him."

He reached over and stroked her shoulder. "You're going to be all right."

She gave him a desperate look. "Promise?"

He nodded. "Absolutely."

"Look at you. You're God, and you're acting like a doctor."

He had to laugh. What a girl, even when she was dying she didn't lose her sense of humor. Amy never made him laugh.

They reached St. John's fifteen minutes later. He'd run a few lights. He headed for the emergency entrance. But as he went to stop the car, Kathy grabbed his arm.

"The pain stopped," she said.

"Kathy, that isn't going to work with me. They can help you inside."

She sat up straight. "I swear it just stopped." She shook her head in amazement. "It's like someone threw a switch."

He saw she was serious. "The stone must have moved out of the duct."

She smiled. "Cool." Then she lost her smile. "Stop the car!"

"What?"

"That worst case of diarrhea imaginable that you talked about is about to arrive. Let me out!"

She didn't even wait for him to stop. She leapt out of the car and vanished inside. He parked beside a stretch limousine where a local newscaster was getting drunk with his driver and probably waiting for his girlfriend to recover from her latest overdose. He was hardly out of his own car when Kathy reappeared looking exhausted but relieved.

"They asked if I had insurance when I asked where the toilet was," she said.

"Feel better?"

She nodded but grimaced as she touched her side. "The scary pain is gone but I'm sore. What time is it?"

He checked. "Five thirty. Want to go for bacon and eggs?"

"And you call yourself a doctor? No, I think I need to go to bed. Sorry I kept you up all night. I feel so stupid."

"You should. You're in agony and you have the nerve to mess up my evening."

They drove back to Malibu. A hint of light appeared in the east. On their left, the ocean was as flat as a lake and the air felt unusually serene.

"What a night, huh?" Kathy remarked.

"I'm sure we'll both remember it for a long time."

She yawned. "Did I say anything embarrassing while I was on the couch?"

"You asked me to marry you."

"Really? Did you say yes?"

"I can't remember."

She gave him a serious look. "How am I ever going to thank you for what you did for me tonight?"

He shrugged. "You would have done the same for me."

"But I owe you now."

"Yeah? How are you going to pay me back then?"

She continued to stare. "I could pay you back."

"Kathy?"

She shook her head and did not explain.

Back at her apartment, the residual soreness in her side continued to bother her, enough that she worried she would not be able to sleep. He talked her into taking another pill. She swallowed it and changed into her pajamas and climbed into bed. Still, she feared to let him go. He could see the trauma of the night reminded her too much of a previous ordeal. As the birds began to sing outside the window, he sat beside her on the bed and gently rubbed her abdomen through her pajama top. The massage seemed to soothe her, and she began to babble as the drug slowly took hold.

"So discarded," she mumbled. "When Tony said he was sleeping with her, I felt like I wanted to die. I felt like garbage, like something that had been dumped. You know what I mean?"

"Yeah." There was something wrong with the skin on her stomach and abdomen. It was hard and lumpy in places. She laid on her back with her eyes closed. There was now enough light in the room to see what was the matter in that area, but he did not wish to invade her privacy by lifting up her shirt.

"That word—*dumped*," she said dreamily. "I hate that word but it is so apt. You feel like you've been dropped, but you never reach the ground. You just keep falling and falling. You feel you'll never stop." She added softly, "I know you know how that feels."

"How do you know that?"

"I see it when you talk about Amy. She hurt you bad. She dumped you, and no matter how hard you try to pretend she loves you, you can never forget that."

He was shocked. "You see all that?"

"Yes. I have thought about it a lot. I have a similar situation with Tony. It's not exactly the same—he's still fucking that cunt—but I wonder, maybe he'll want to come back to me. Then I say to myself, I can't take him back. He betrayed me. I could never trust him again because he might betray me again. I had so much pain. How could I face it again? But two minutes later I think the opposite. How much I love him. How much I miss him. I think that he's basically a good person. That I have to give us both another chance."

"Maybe you will have that second chance."

She opened her sleepy eyes. "But what is true of us is not necessarily true of you two. Maybe Amy is not a good person. Maybe she will betray you again no matter what she promises. Have you thought of that?"

Her question cut to his core. She was the sick one and yet he was the one who suddenly felt weak. A door opened with her question. He wanted desperately to talk to her about what he had gone through. Perhaps if there had been someone there to begin with—to listen to him— it would never have gone this far.

Then again, he would never have known about Jimmy.

He missed his son right then so much.

They would take him away if they caught him.

"I have thought of that," he said.

"Please don't trust her," she blurted out.

"What? Why?"

"She's dangerous."

"Who?"

"Amy."

"Kathy. You haven't even met her."

"It doesn't matter. I know her." She gestured weakly. "Trust is like glass. You think you can see through it, that you know what's on the other side of it. You pretend you know your partner and that he knows you. But it's all an illusion. One day you bump against it and it cracks and you cut yourself and you bleed." She noticed his hand on her abdomen. "You can see how much I bled. Go ahead, I don't care, look at my scars."

He lifted her shirt, gasped. It was as if her entire abdomen had been scissored opened and hastily reclosed. "What happened?" he whispered.

"I ran into a bad man."

"Who?"

"It doesn't matter. I fixed him. But what about you? How do I fix you?"

"What do you mean?"

"Simon." She reached up and brushed his hair. "Your mother must miss you."

"I told you, my mother's fine."

Her arm dropped. She closed her eyes and began to doze.

"The dragon lives," she mumbled.

She was asleep before he could ask what she meant.

CHAPTER TWELVE

Kelly Fienman did not awake that same day until well past noon: sore, relieved, and confused. Grateful as well; and what a curious feeling to have for the subject of one of the biggest manhunts in FBI history. For she cared about Matt Connor, even though she didn't completely understand him. But most of all she worried about him, as he had worried for her all night.

It was not a small problem.

She had accepted the Acid Man's advice and stalked Amy. It had taken a mere two days for Amy to lead her to Matt and Jimmy and the apartment by the sea. That had been quite a moment—seeing the couple embrace by the swimming pool, Jimmy laughing in his stroller.

Right then, Kelly had thought it over. The mystery finally solved, justice ready to be served. But as she stared at Matt—still handsome in his fake beard and wig—she felt inexplicable sorrow. His own mother had explained Amy's betrayal, and no single talk could have moved Kelly more.

She knew she would have to turn Matt in. She was a law enforcement officer and she got paid to catch bad guys. But she did not know *him*, and felt she could not destroy the unknown, when the reverse should have been true. She remembered the first time she had seen his picture in the paper. A haunted stranger who was supposed to be dead. His face had stirred something deep inside that had set her on a collision course with her own nightmare. But when she finally saw Matt in person, she felt she came face-to-face with the ghost who walked beside her in her dreams of the Acid Man. Only he was a friendly ghost, who kept telling her not to be afraid.

A major dilemma gripped her.

Was Matt Connor really a bad guy?

She had taken the apartment in his complex because she wanted to answer that question. But doing so compromised her relationship with the Bureau. She could get in serious trouble withholding information on such a sensitive case. Especially in light of her handling of the Acid Man. But her feeling on the matter was . . . fuck them, she owed her conscience greater allegiance.

Still, Matt had kidnapped someone else's kid. He probably was psycho. Moving into the apartment two stories below, she figured she could spend time with him, confirm her worst fears, and then call in Charlie and Vicki, no harm done. They would privately chew her out but cover for her officially. Once more she could be the hero, and perhaps this time her efforts would be acknowledged.

Yet, from the moment she met Matt her fears grew.

For reasons she had not anticipated.

First, there was the obvious physical similarity between Jimmy and Matt. That resemblance had not been apparent in the pictures Amy had shown them of the infant Jimmy. When she saw the two together by the swimming pool, she knew Matt was the father. Talk about throwing a wrench in the works. Kidnapping one's own kid was still illegal, but it radically altered the complexity of the crime.

Then there was the way in which they related to each other. Matt was not merely a good father, he was a goddamn saint when it came to his son. Jimmy was clearly happy in his arms. It made her shudder to think of sending the kid back to an asshole like David.

Nevertheless, these were secondary matters to Kelly. She still would have turned Matt in if she had not slowly begun to understand that he was the main victim in the whole goddamn scenario. Sure, she had known since her visit to Santa Barbara that Amy had screwed another guy behind his back and then dumped him like garbage. But talking to him over several days, Kelly had come to grasp the depth of Amy's manipulation. It went beyond mere lying and cheating. Because Matt was not blind to Amy's lies. He was too smart to be fooled, and he had been more than warned. Nevertheless, he chose to ignore her contradictions. The distinction was subtle but disturbing. Amy had not conquered his head, but had somehow managed to destroy his heart.

She was a psychic surgeon. She was a fucking vampire.

Whenever Kelly talked to Matt right after Amy left, he was always down. It was as if Amy hooked him up to an IV line that dripped toilet water into his veins. But Kelly could see he was not normally depressed. She would chat with him a few minutes about books or movies and he would perk right up. But she suspected that unless he had that outside infusion of friendliness and simple decency, he would remain in a dark state. She wondered what it had been like to live alone in his mind after Amy had betrayed him. No wonder the scope of his revenge had grown so intricate.

That was something else she spotted about Matt. He was truly brilliant; in his own way, as unpredictable as the Acid Man.

The comparison worried her. The day after her gallstone attack—lying flat on her back in bed while the sun painted the ceiling—Kelly reflected on the matter. Her initial question had been answered. She should have been satisfied. He had taken care of her as if she were the only thing in the world that mattered. His compassion had touched her deeply, and perhaps saved her life. He was definitely one of the good guys.

Here was the rub, though. Not only did bad things happen to good guys, good guys occasionally did bad things. Matt was too smart for his own good, and he was acting out of a compromised state. Kelly preferred to think of him that way as opposed to disturbed. But the point raised another question that she felt she had to answer before she made her next move. Despite all of Matt's quality, was he still a danger to society?

Or was the Acid Man right?

Were they both dangerous?

Amy was driving Matt toward a goal. That was her nature—she used people. Kelly had spotted the quality during the time she had spent at the Techer house. What was it Amy wanted? Money, of course—she had dumped Matt to get to David's wealth. But that answer was too pat. Shallow people were not necessarily easy to predict. Often they acted more erratically than people with high IQs. Amy wanted the cash but how far was she willing to go to get it? The more Kelly thought about it, the more she worried.

Perhaps Amy was the main question mark. Not Matt.

One thing for sure, Kelly was not going to let the bitch get off free. Amy lied to all who loved her. Let her try lying to an impartial jury.

Kelly decided to bug their apartment.

The decision pained her, though, made her feel guilty.

It had felt good to have Matt massage her belly. Simply having him near all night had been comforting. Beyond that, he'd felt *familiar*. Stars from the same constellation, perhaps, she thought, falling from the same sky. She wondered if she had a crush on him.

"I know how to pick them, that's for sure," Kelly said as she got out of bed. Her side ached but it was not a sick pain. In fact, she felt as if the flush had cleared a chronic block from her digestive system. After what she had gone through the previous night, she felt surprisingly energetic. Maybe there were no more stones in her gallbladder. Maybe she was going to stop hurting, in a lot of ways.

She checked her voice mail and there was a message from Tony.

"I miss you, Kelly. Can we have lunch today?"

The two sentences annoyed and thrilled her. They blew her apart from the inside out. She sagged onto the bed and trembled. What nerve, for him to think she would eat with him after what he had done to her. That would be a cold day in hell.

Then again, she thought if she called she would not have the strength to say no. Five months of healing had not made her any less pathetic. She looked at the phone and wept. And here she had thought she was over him, when only the Acid Man could have burned her longing for Tony out of her heart.

She called him and said okay. Lunch in one hour.

Ironically, they met in the same restaurant where she had gone with Matt. That seafood place by the beach. They got a booth outside and the summer sun was as delicious as the menu. She loved fish and was relieved she was now able to eat it again, if only in small bites. She let Tony order for her, he knew what she liked.

"So how have you been?" he asked. It was of course a law of nature that the person who did the dumping always looked great, even though the person who had been dumped had just gone through months of hell. Tony had bulked up—in a good way—and had on a new sports coat. At that moment she wouldn't have traded him for the world.

Not that she was in a position to trade. That required a relationship. And they didn't have one of those and could never have one because he had betrayed her and that she could never forgive.

Still, she wanted him so bad.

"I'm fine. How are you? How's Claire?"

She had not intended to ask that question.

"I'm not sure. I haven't talked to her in a month," he said.

"*What?*" she gasped. Naturally Kelly had seen Anna plenty in the last month, and during the daughter-parent trade-offs, had seen Tony as well—if only for a few awkward minutes. But neither one had said a word about Claire's departure. Kelly was thrilled and disgusted at the same time. Tony looked out over the ocean.

"I'm not sure what happened," he said. "We were doing so well. She and Anna got along beautifully. And she was always there when I came home. Dinner was always cooked. We seldom argued, and we shared a lot of common interests."

He was cruel, he stopped. She had to say it. "But?"

He looked at her. "I have thought about this a lot, especially knowing I was going to see you. What it all boils down to is that I didn't love her."

"Did she love you?"

He shrugged. "She said she did."

"That's no answer."

"True. But it doesn't matter if she did or not. What I'm trying to say is I love you." He paused. "I want you to come back."

Kelly almost threw up. Her body went into a weird kind of shock. Her heart pounded and seemed to sink into her solar plexus. She had to strain to form words.

"Are you crazy?" she mumbled.

"I'm serious. I know you're still living alone. I know you miss me. I miss you terribly. I do the simplest things with Anna—go to the movies, walk the dog—and I think how much more fun it used to be with you."

"We don't have a dog."

He was embarrassed. "We do now. We have a collie. His name is Faith. You would like him."

"Would I? Is he loyal?"

"What I did was wrong. I made a mistake. My timing was terrible—you were so sick. But you have to admit, the decisions you made forced me to leave you."

"Funny, I don't feel the need to admit that at all. From where I sit you just wanted to fuck Claire instead of me." She paused. "When was the last time you fucked her?"

"I told you, a month ago." He paused. "Two weeks ago."

"I understand. The lights were out. You didn't actually see her when you stuck your dick in her pussy that last time."

"You don't need to get crude."

"That is another statement I disagree with. I feel a great need to get crude. And an even greater need to get even. You know I miss you? You know I am alone? You don't know shit. You dumped me for your new girlfriend. You can't just sit here and ask me to come back and expect me to jump at the offer. How could I sleep beside you again when you've been sleeping beside her all this time? I would just end up vomiting on you in the middle of the night."

"I'm sorry, I thought we could be mature about this."

She was outraged. "When it comes to betrayal there's no such thing as maturity. It's too basic a violation. You hurt me as bad as a human being can be hurt. At least the Acid Man was honest with me when he poured that stuff on my belly. He just wanted to torture me to death. There was a beginning and an end to his crime. But what you did to me has no end. It eats at me night and day. You talk about how much happier you were when I was in your life. I have been left to live the dark side of that equation. I can only think back to when I wasn't in pain all the time. I can't think about happiness, not at all. That's a luxury you stole from me."

Tony leaned forward. "Then let me give it back to you."

She sat back. "No."

"Kelly?"

"No!"

He got annoyed. "You're acting like a child. You would rather hold on to your bitterness than have happiness. We were both hurt by what happened. We can go on being hurt or we can try to make a life together again. I admit I made a terrible mistake. Why can't you do the same?"

She hated her tears. "Because I didn't do anything wrong. You did it all. You *hurt* me."

He stopped. "I know I hurt you."

She shook her head. "You cannot imagine. You just think you can."

He spread his hands. "What do you want me to do? Beg?"

She pounded the table. "Yes! I begged two months ago and you turned me down. You had it all, you were in total control. You had our daughter, your new-and-improved screw, our home. What did I have? A tiny apartment filled with nothing. Guts that didn't work. A heart that was broken. You broke my heart, Tony. I used to think that was such a cliché expression. I don't any longer. When it gets broken, really broken, it can't be fixed."

They sat in silence. How strange, she thought, to fight so hard to destroy the very thing she had prayed for so long to get back. Finally he spoke.

"Are you saying it's hopeless?" he asked.

"Yes."

"You don't want to think about it?"

"No."

"Is there someone else?"

The feel of Matt's hands on her body returned to mind. So strong his touch, for such a vulnerable soul. He was the Acid Man's cousin, but also his opposite. Matt had magic but the wrong spells. What could she teach him?

"There might be someone else," she said.

The news shook Tony. "Charlie?"

She shook her head, bitter. "You never understood our relationship."

"Who is it then?"

"Some guy." She shook her head. "You don't know him."

What was there left to talk about? Their food came but Kelly had lost her appetite. Begging to be excused, she left the restaurant. There was much she had to absorb. In her car, driving down the coast toward Charlie's house, her emotions made her wonder. The chance to return to her family thrilled her. But she had striven so long to convince herself that she didn't care that it terrified her as well. It some ways it was easier to concentrate on kidnappers and murderers and worry about it later. Work gave her peace of mind.

But Matt did not. With him it was personal now, not professional.

Charlie lived in a cheap apartment in Compton, home to gangbangs and drive-in funerals. He had grown up in the neighborhood—he saw no reason to leave. Parking on a block that had graffiti for street signs, she strode briskly toward his door. She felt plenty of eyes on her ass, on her gun as well. She let her coat open, let the locals see her Glock. They all knew Charlie was FBI and left him alone.

He was watching baseball when she knocked. He was a fanatical baseball and basketball fan. He had season tickets for the Lakers and the Dodgers. He also collected Persian rugs and violins—they were all over his apartment. If he ever got broken into he would have a long talk with his insurance agent. He was an accomplished musician. They had played together a few times, with her on the piano: mostly jazz and classical. But his real joy was to rework the violins and sell them for a profit. He had a few dollars socked away. Charlie wouldn't have to beg in his old age.

What she had told Matt was partially true. She was on a leave of absence from her job. She'd told Vicki it was because of her health and no one at the Bureau had questioned her excuse. Charlie was not so easily fooled; he thought she was up to something. When he had her comfortable on the sofa with a glass of apple juice, he studied her.

"You gonna tell me or is it a secret?" he asked.

"Good to see you, too, babe."

"Jesus. You disappear on me for a month."

"I'm on vacation," she said.

"So you have a tan. You're not on vacation."

"How's the Techer case going?"

"Nowhere. We'll never find that kid."

"Sorry," she said.

"Yeah? I thought we agreed to work on it together until we did find him. Why did you bail on me without talking to me about it?"

"I told you," she said.

"Yeah. During the ten minutes you were cleaning out your desk."

"Charlie, please, don't be mad. I needed to get away from the office for a while and sort things out." She paused. "I just had lunch with Tony. He wants me back."

"Is that good news?"

"I don't know. How are you doing?"

"Horrible. I miss you. Why don't you come back to me instead of Tony?"

She sipped her apple juice. "Fine. But first you have to do me a favor. I need to eavesdrop on an apartment. I need three bugs, and a transmitter with enough power to go through lots of walls. A recorder with high storage would be a plus. The equipment has to be top-notch. Not that shit you see on the Internet."

"Why don't you request it through the usual channels?"

"This isn't for official business."

"You mean it's for illegal business?"

"Sort of. But the end result could be legal."

"Does this have anything to do with Tony?"

"Maybe."

Charlie snorted. "That's a great way to restart a relationship."

"A girl's got to do what she's got to do."

He gave her an eye. "You saw Banks."

She was staggered. "How did you know?"

"I have my ways. Don't worry, I'm the only one at the office who knows." He paused. "Why?"

"Haven't you heard of the therapeutic value of confronting old demons?"

"Talking to that monster is not therapy. It's sick. What were you trying to do?"

"I don't want the bugs for Banks. This is another matter."

"You didn't answer my question."

"I've had nightmares. I was hoping if I saw him they would go away."

"Did they?"

"No. Can you get me the equipment without going through the usual channels?"

"Sure. But I have to know what you want it for."

"I can't tell you. I need you to trust me."

"Trust you? I don't even know where you live these days."

"I don't want you to know. Don't follow me or try to find out through any other means. I want to be left alone for two more weeks. Then I will tell you the whole story. That's a promise. How long will it take you to get the equipment?"

"Is this what they call an 'assumed close?' Three days."

She stood and set down her juice. "I've missed you too. Let me tie up a few loose ends and I'll be back to work."

He was concerned. "Just don't hang yourself with those loose ends."

He didn't add: *again*. She was grateful.

Later that day—late that night actually, when everyone was gone— Kelly drove to the office and went to her desk. Charlie had exaggerated. She had grabbed her tampons and chewing gum when she had split. She had not emptied her desk. Vicki expected her back soon, and maybe that would happen.

But right now Kelly heard the hiss of the dragon. The bodies had never been located. Banks still refused to say what he had done with his victims. There was no negotiating with him. A guy without a body had nothing to lose. But for the families of the victims, the lack of closure was painful. Beyond that, Kelly felt an unsolved mystery in those remains. The bodies might tell her what he would not.

Like who the hell he was. Or *what* he was.

Kelly got on her computer and called up the Acid Man's file. She wasn't the only one connected to the case. An agent out of the Ohio office had made additions to her notes. The woman—Special Agent Dana Richards—had interviewed Julie Banks in the hope of finding out what made her husband tick, and where he had gotten the acid. Dana had struck out. Julie said she had never suspected a thing.

"Sure, you didn't," Kelly said. She noted Julie's current address. The woman had not moved from her old house. It was impossible to imagine she remained so close to him after all that had happened. Especially since Banks was not allowed to see his son.

Kelly decided to book another flight to Ohio.

■

MICHAEL GRANDER answered the door—the guy she had originally thought had ordered the books from China and India, Julie's boyfriend. He had classic good looks: tall and dark, thick eyebrows and heavy lips—someone to eat, not marry. He regarded her through the screen door with a mixture of innocence and confusion. She already had her badge out and was feeling official.

"Kelly Fienman, FBI. Julie around?"

A kid squealed at his back and he glanced over his shoulder.

"She's on the phone, long distance. Was she expecting you?"

"No. But I was in the neighborhood."

Recognition flashed in his eyes. He opened the door and stepped onto the porch. The house was a wooden castle with a green lawn in place of a moat. He had on a white T-shirt and blue shorts—sexy legs. In a way she was pleased to meet him first. He had always been an enigma to her. He was Banks's imaginary pawn.

It was a hot Ohio afternoon. She was dehydrated and not particularly lucid. The air conditioner in her rental was broken and the drive from the airport had been a swamp. A barbecue simmered off the side of the house—tender meat and mystery sauce. She needed a cold drink in the worst way.

"It's you," he said, impressed.

"Yeah. I'm the one."

He was instantly sympathetic. "How's your health?"

"Getting there."

"Happy to hear that. You don't know how much Julie and I talk about you."

"Yeah?" Julie had not even sent her a card at the hospital. "How's Julie these days?"

Another glance in the house. "As well as can be expected. You can imagine what a shock this was. I don't think it's something one ever gets over."

"It must have been a shock for you as well."

"That's putting it mildly."

"Mr. Grander, may I ask a few questions?"

"Michael, please, you may ask what you want. I don't forget that it was you who saved my life and Julie's." He stepped off the porch and headed for the barbecue. "But let me check the food. First I was watching it, then Julie was—now I think it's burning. Can I offer you something to drink?"

"Do you have Sprite?" She could manage soda these days, but not her favorite, Coke.

"Plenty of Sprites in here." He stooped beside an ice chest and tossed her a cold can. They had a couple of burgers on the grill, plenty of chicken. She wondered if she could eat the latter, if she chewed slowly and didn't have sauce. She had not eaten on the flight. She was experimenting with her diet these days. But she still never went anywhere without her digestive enzymes. She watched as Michael picked up his utensils and flipped the burgers. The Sprite tasted like heaven in her dry throat.

"We've been trying to build up a background on Professor Gene Banks," she said. "The Bureau is interested in the psychology of all serial killers. But Banks is particularly interesting because he has never revealed what he did with the bodies of his victims. You were a student of his for several years, and were obviously close to the family during that time. I'd like you to tell me what you can about him."

"You're too polite. You know I wasn't merely close to the family. I was sleeping with his wife, and still am."

"When did the affair begin?" Kelly asked.

"Two years ago. It's not something I like to brag about. I've never been involved with a married woman before. In my defense I can say that I love Julie. She feels the same about me. It was as if we were thrust together." He added, "We never imagined our involvement could have led to such catastrophic results."

"Do you believe it was your affair that sent Banks off?"

He was surprised. "We were told your version of what he said when he was alone with you. Didn't he blame us?"

"Yes. But I have thought about what he said for the last few months and I find the motivation rather simplistic for such a complex character. Don't get me wrong, a feeling of betrayal is a powerful thing. But I think it's only part of the equation. Banks—Gene—was obviously deeply disturbed before you started sleeping with his wife."

"I thank you for saying so, Kelly. But it's hard not to blame oneself."

"As a student of Gene's, did he ever give signs of being nuts?"

"I'm sure you'll ask Julie the same question. She'll say she never noticed a thing. Hard to believe, but I assure you she'll be telling the truth. But there were a few times that struck me as odd, especially when I was alone with Gene and he was describing to me the underlying symbolism of certain villains in literature. For example, when he talked of the Medusa in Greek mythology, he saw the creature as a master manipulator. To him the capacity to transform a foe into stone represented the ability to dominate another's will."

"So?" she said.

"The interpretation was insightful, but that's not what bothered me. It was Gene's admiration of the Medusa. If he could have been a character in mythology, he told me he would have chosen that creature." Michael paused. "That's just one example. He almost always related to the villain more than the hero."

"I have a background in literature as well. That's not unusual."

Michael stared at her. "How many people identify with a monster with crawling snakes for hair?"

"Point taken. What else struck you as odd?"

"The last year we were together he was always taking off. He would never say where he was going. But there's no mystery there." He sighed. "To tell you the truth I didn't mind when he left."

"Because you could be alone with Julie?"

"Yes."

"Do you know anything about his childhood?"

"Julie might. He never spoke about it to me."

"Where did he get his acid?" Kelly asked.

"He's resourceful. Maybe he manufactured it himself."

"Any idea where he might have put the bodies?"

Michael gestured to a lush vegetable garden that ran alongside the property. The lot was over fifty acres—they had plenty of privacy. "Julie says Gene loved to come out here and take care of his tomatoes and carrots and broccoli. He was out here at all hours of the day and night. Maybe he buried the bodies here. It's a sobering thought." He pointed to the slices of tomato waiting on a nearby table. "We get most of our vegetables from the garden."

"I doubt he would have been so obvious," she replied, knowing the FBI had thoroughly examined Banks's garden.

"Are you going to visit him while you're here?" he asked.

"I might."

"You have nerve."

"Have you seen him since last February?"

"No. Don't want to either."

"Has Julie?" Kelly asked.

"No. She hasn't even spoken to him."

Julie appeared a minute later, her son Robert by her side. She had gained weight since the last time they had met—which suited her. Her face was still pale, though, and she continued to wear her hair long and straight down her back.

But her eyes had changed. The warm ease was gone, replaced by the shadow of the dragon. Standing on the green lawn, the hot Ohio sun shining down, Kelly was struck by how all four of them had been stained by Gene Banks. Even the little boy looked troubled, holding his mother's hand tightly, and staring at Kelly as if she had killed a family member. Kelly wondered what he had been told. Julie whispered in his ear and the boy ran inside the house.

"I didn't know you were coming," Julie said as she approached. She did not offer her hand and Kelly did not make the effort.

"I should have called," Kelly admitted.

"But you were afraid I wouldn't see you," Julie said.

Kelly nodded. "Can we walk a few minutes?"

Julie glanced at Michael. "It's all right," he said.

Julie nodded. "Very well. But I have nothing to add beyond what I told that last agent who was here."

They strolled away from the house in the direction of a large pond that separated the house from an enchanted forest. The air buzzed with insects and the smell of daisies, and moist grass saturated the air. It was difficult for Kelly to envision Banks living in such a serene environment. Julie seemed to read her mind.

"He had it all," she said.

Kelly eyed her. "Are you serious?"

"You refer to my infidelity? My marriage was over long before

I met Michael. Gene and I were together for Robert, no other reason."

"That's not the impression he gave me."

"Then he lied to you. He's a skillful liar, isn't he?"

"I don't know what he is. That's the reason I'm here. I have to be blunt with you, Julie. You were married to a monster and yet you say you had no idea there was anything wrong. A lot of people would find that hard to believe."

"Why? If I had caught him brewing acid in our basement, of course that would have set off warning bells. But I'm being honest when I say he showed no outward signs of instability."

"Michael disagrees."

"Michael knew him in a different context. Gene and I were like any other married couple that had left the good times behind. He was often distant but he continued to act as if he cared for me."

"Did you have a sexual relationship during the last two years?"

"Why is that any business of yours?"

"It's FBI business. We still don't know what he did with the bodies."

"If I was having sex with him in the last two years, will it help you find them? Yes, we had a sexual relationship after I started sleeping with Michael. I know that's what you are asking."

"Was it a normal relationship?"

Julie hesitated. "Yes."

"You don't sound certain."

"He liked to do unusual things. Many men do. I didn't mind."

"What sort of things?"

"I don't think you have the right to ask that question."

"Okay. Tell me about his childhood?"

"Gene seldom talked about his family. I know his mother died when he was ten and that he was raised by his father. I know he revered the man."

"Is the father still alive?"

"Yes. He lives in Trenton. That's twenty miles south of here."

The Acid Man had said his father was dead. "Does he know the details of Gene's crime?"

"Of course."

"How old is the father?"

"Eighty-one. But he's sharp. He used to be a doctor."

"How did Gene's father feel about you?"

"Why do you ask?"

"Please don't ask me to explain each of my questions."

"Gene's father was very happy when we married. When Robert was born it was hard to imagine a prouder grandfather."

"Do you know how the mother died?"

"Gene said she fell down a flight of stairs."

"Did Gene witness this event?"

"I don't think so."

"What sort of romantic relationships did Gene have before you two met?"

"I don't know. He never talked about other women."

"Didn't you find that odd?"

"I considered it a blessing. I don't like men who gossip about past affairs."

"But do you know if he was with someone before you? In a serious relationship?"

"I told you, I don't know."

Kelly was annoyed. "Why the hostility? If it wasn't for me, you would probably be dead."

"He wouldn't have killed me."

"He would definitely have killed you."

Julie was certain. "Not until he was done."

"Done murdering? It wouldn't have lasted forever."

"How do you know?"

"Julie?" Kelly said, shocked. The woman almost sounded disappointed.

Julie stopped walking and gave her an odd look. It was as if she weighed her in terms of competition. She glanced toward Michael, then turned toward the pond. Black blue water, calm as the floor of a deep well. A swarm of mosquitoes hovered near like a cloud of bad thoughts.

A sudden change came over the woman. Her self-righteousness was replaced by an uncivilized veneer. Her breathing deepened and seemed to expand. She rested her hands on her hips and kicked off her shoes. Stepping forward, she touched a toe in the water. It was as if the liquid hissed. Perhaps it was the mosquitoes.

Kelly felt confused. Julie's next question did not help it.

"Did he kiss you before he poured the acid on you?" she asked.

"No," Kelly replied.

"Did he touch you?"

"No. All he did was tell me I was very pretty."

"You liked him, didn't you? Before he attacked you."

"I found him charming. What's your point?"

Julie glanced over and smiled—a twisted affair, equal measures of longing and loathing. "I think of him sometimes with those women he killed. I never saw the videos he made but I heard about them. I was always curious to . . . to see them." She paused. "Did you see them?"

"Yes. They were horrible."

"I can imagine."

Kelly felt cold. "What else can you imagine?"

Julie's smile widened, changed. Her bare foot rested in the mud. The allure of the snuff film, even the wife was not immune. "I can imagine him doing it to me," she said.

Kelly moved close. "And?"

Julie just stared. "You asked me why I'm hostile toward you."

Kelly was suddenly sick of her sick attitude. "You play a dangerous game, girl. He's still alive. His body may be crippled but his mind isn't. No one knows what that mind is capable of. You and Michael don't realize it, but you're in danger here. So is your son. You should move from this place, go far away." Kelly stopped. "But you stay here on purpose."

"This is my son's home."

Kelly felt disgust. "You like to be close. It turns you on."

"I have Michael now. He turns me on. He doesn't want to leave here."

"Do you ever visit Gene?"

"No."

Kelly nodded. "But you drive by the apartment. You park across the street and stare at the windows. You hope for a glimpse. You wonder if he's thinking of you."

Julie's chuckle surprised her. "You wonder the same thing."

Kelly felt bitter. "You're disgusting. Where did he bury the bodies?"

"I don't know." Julie picked up her shoe and stepped past her. "You can leave now."

Kelly grabbed her arm. "When he went off for weeks at a time, did you ever ask why?"

"He said he had to lecture."

"But you didn't believe him."

"I didn't care. I wanted to be with Michael."

Kelly was not sure what made her ask her next question.

"Did you ever want to be with the two of them at the same time?"

"Ask him." Julie brushed off Kelly's hand and walked away.

■

A HOT summer evening. The Acid Man's father and Kelly sat on his porch and sipped lemonade. A draped insect screen surrounded them like a layer of illusion. The houses beyond the porch appeared blurred and unreal through the cloudy material. Dr. Fred Banks looked like a creature dug from the past. He wore his age like a scar. He'd had a hard life, Kelly had no doubt. The last five months must have been particularly rough. When he'd answered the door ten minutes ago, he had stared at her a minute before saying, "You the one who shot him?"

Yes, she replied. I shot your son.

He asked if she would like some lemonade.

Dr. Banks had rotten lungs. Sitting nearby, his wheezing sounded like a death rattle fed through an amplifier. He had tossed out something about emphysema, before lighting up a cigarette and blowing smoke toward a yellow overhead light that flickered with annoying regularity. His wrinkled skin appeared pulled apart from the inside out. He was more than old, he was worn out. He was going to die soon with the knowledge that his son was a murderer.

"Why did you come?" he asked in a surprisingly smooth voice. His stained teeth were false and smelled. There was a spark in his eyes, however. He was no fool.

"I want to understand your son better."

"For personal or professional reasons?" he asked.

"You know what Gene did to me?"

"Yes. How are you feeling?"

"Physically, I improve each month. I'm able to eat somewhat normally now. But emotionally I still bear the scars."

"I'm sorry." He considered the ash at the end of his cigarette. "I wasn't surprised when the call came—what he had done."

"Did you see it coming?"

"It wasn't like that. Gene never displayed violent behavior, as a child or as an adult." He paused. "But something was wrong."

"When did it start?" she asked.

The question stirred the old man's deepest burden. It was as if he shrunk farther into his wicker chair. At the same time he struggled against the past. He wanted to talk to her—she could tell—but was ashamed to. She gave another word of encouragement.

"How did his mother die?" she asked.

He looked up. "Who told you?"

"Julie. But she didn't say much. Could you?"

"It's not a pleasant story."

"Please, it's important for me to understand."

He appeared to grasp the need. He took a drink of his lemonade and cleared his throat.

"Gene was shy as a child. He was born in this house and grew up on this block. But he was a loner. He had hobbies. He used to like to collect bugs and he loved astronomy. He would stay out half the night with a small telescope I bought him. But he wasn't into sports. He never played baseball or football. I used to worry he spent too much time at the library. That was his true love—reading. He was especially fond of fantasy. When he went off to college, I was not surprised he majored in literature. I wanted him to be a doctor but I didn't push him to change. People like what they like. Gene kept his own counsel." Dr. Fred Banks paused. "That was later, of course. His mother died when he was ten. That was a bad time. But before I continue, may I ask that what I have to say be kept off the record?"

"No problem," Kelly said.

"I haven't told a soul what I'm about to tell you."

Kelly paused. "Why tell me at all? A complete stranger."

He coughed and shook his head. "I suppose because I'm old. There's little the law can do to me. My life is finished. I suppose if anyone should know the truth it should be you—who was hurt so badly by my son."

"What you tell me now will remain between the two of us," she promised.

He returned to his cigarette, seemed to search the cobwebs of his life.

"I killed her," he said suddenly.

She jumped in her seat. "Pardon?"

"I was responsible for her death. Not intentionally, of course, but I killed her nevertheless. I kept the truth hidden from the police. I had my children to raise. When Maggie died I saw no point in going to jail."

"Gene wasn't an only child?"

"No. He has a younger brother."

"Please continue."

"Maggie was my childhood sweetheart. We met in high school. She was the only girl I ever kissed. I should show you a picture. She was the cutest thing—long brown hair, brown eyes large as God made them, such a laugh. We used to laugh a lot together in the early days. After the war, when I returned from Europe, we married and moved into this house. I remember it cost five thousand dollars. That seemed like an impossible sum to me. But not to Maggie, she always felt we could do anything.

"I should rephrase that. She was the one who felt she could do any-thing. Maggie was wild and full of energy. She had a reckless side, an impatience with life itself. It was part of her charm but it was a curse as well. Tonight, you see Trenton all around you. The population is ten thousand. It was half that in those days. I was the town doctor. I had a busy schedule. Time didn't weigh on my hands. But when Gene was ten, I think the endless succession of bridge on Tuesdays and bowling on Saturdays began to wear on her. We'd recently had a new child, Scott, but it was just another burden to her. She would tell me she wasn't happy. I heard her but I didn't really. I should have seen the warning signs. I would come home from the office unexpectedly in the middle of the day and she wouldn't be here. It got so we never made love. She be-gan to act distracted and withdrawn. I was such a fool."

"She was having an affair," Kelly said.

"Yes. Such an obvious thing but it never occurred to me she would do it. Not my wife, not to me. I wasn't the last person in town to find out, but I wasn't the first either. My patients began to treat me differently. It was like I was the one who was sick. They would come to my office and try to comfort me. But for what I didn't understand. Until one evening Maggie said she was going out to visit a girlfriend. She left Scott and Gene home with me. I remember that night well. Scott was asleep upstairs in his crib. He was maybe a year old, no longer breast-feeding. Gene was building a model plane out of balsa wood on the kitchen table. I was in the living room reading a medical article about the spread of venereal disease in society as a result of all the soldiers coming back home infected. It was a warm night like tonight and I had the windows open. Then it occurred to me that I had to find Maggie. That something was wrong. But I can't say I thought she was with another man."

"You just felt sick in your stomach?" Kelly said.

"Exactly. I told Gene to keep an eye on Scott, that I would be back in a few minutes. That might seem a strange thing to do—to leave a ten-year-old with an infant. But Trenton was safe in those days. No one ever locked their doors. I planned to hop over to her girlfriend's house and come right back. It was only two blocks away. But when I got there, Elaine said she hadn't seen Maggie. She hadn't spoken to her all day."

Dr. Banks took a drag on his cigarette. He continued to stare at the night. "My guts turned to ice. It was as if everything unusual about her behavior crystallized right then. I knew she was lying to me. I knew she was with someone else. There was this man, a contractor named Bob Mortega. He had done some work for us on the garage a few months before and I remembered how uncomfortable I had felt while he was in the house. The way he and Maggie would look at each other when they didn't think I was watching. He was handsome, Italian—one of those guys who flirt with every pretty woman. But he was so crude I didn't know what she saw in him. But obviously he did something for her that I could not. That night, when I reached his house, I peeked in the side window and saw them kissing on the living room floor. He was in the middle of undressing her. His hand . . . his hairy hand, was on her breast."

Dr. Banks stopped. They sat in silence. His wheezing grew worse and he stopped smoking. The ash gathered at the end of his cigarette.

"What did you do?" she asked finally.

"I went home."

"You didn't stop them?"

"No."

"Did you speak to her when she came home?"

"No. Not right away."

"But you have not confronted her?"

"No. I don't have the strength. I'm afraid to lose her."

"You were afraid to lose her," Kelly said.

He nodded sadly. "I was so weak. Here I had been humiliated in the worst possible way and I lacked the nerve to confront her. You must think I was a spineless toad."

"No. I understand exactly how you felt."

He glanced over and raised a hairless eyebrow. "I suppose it's an old story."

"Unfortunately. Please continue."

He gestured weakly. "The next week, being in the same house as she, was a living hell. When I was at work it was even worse. I kept imagining them together. I would sit alone in my office and cry. Maggie and the kids were my life. I thought if I confronted her she wouldn't be able to face the shame. She would take the kids and leave town. But I thought if I didn't stop her, I'd go insane. I didn't know what to do.

"But the pressure kept building. In the end I don't think it would have mattered what I decided. The pain had a mind of its own. One night—it was about ten days later—I caught her alone in the upstairs bedroom, laughing on the phone. The look she gave me when I barged in the room—I knew she was talking to him. She had Scott in her arms but I didn't care because obviously she didn't care—about either of our sons, about me. I rushed in and slammed down the phone and screamed at her about what I had seen. I'll always remember her expression right then. She didn't say a word in her defense. It was almost as if a peace settled over her face. Maybe it was a relief for her to have the secret out in the open. I kept yelling and threatening her and she hardly responded at all. But at one point she stood and walked out of the room and stopped at the top of the stairs. She still had Scott in her arms. He was crying; she was rocking him to get him to stop. But I was shouting so loud there was no way he was going to stop. I was half out of my mind. The neighbors could hear everything I was saying. If there was anyone in town who didn't know my wife was having an affair, they would surely know by morning.

"Her silence drove me to the brink. I went after her in the hall and demanded she tell me why she had done it. Still, she said nothing, just kept rocking Scott and staring at me. I didn't know what to say. The strength went out of me. My voice fell to a whisper. I asked what she planned to do. I asked if she was going to take my children and leave. Finally she said something. A simple sentence, really—who would have guessed it had the strength to change so much? She said, " 'This one isn't yours.' "

"Jesus," Kelly whispered. "What did you do?"

"I pushed her."

"Down the stairs?"

"Not intentionally. I pushed her away from me. I barely shoved her. But it was enough, she fell down the stairs. All the way to the bottom. All the time holding Scott, protecting his little head from damage. Leaving her own body open to the worst the fall could do. When they came to rest, they were on the floor of the living room. Maggie lay unconscious on her back, her eyes wide open. Scott was on her chest. He had stopped crying but he appeared unhurt. Gene stood by their side, and he stared up the stairs at me. His little face looked so sad right then. I'll always remember what he said."

"What?"

" 'May I have a glass of milk?' "

Kelly almost choked. "Why did he say that?"

"I don't know why."

"Was Maggie dead?"

"No. She was seriously injured but she was still alive. I called for an ambulance. She was taken to a hospital in Grant, twenty miles from here. She had suffered trauma to the brain. She was in a coma. Neurology was a primitive field fifty years ago. I brought in the best specialist but there was nothing they could do for her. After a month I checked her out of the hospital and took her home to care for her."

"The police talked to you about the accident?"

"Yes. Like I told you, I lied. I said she slipped and fell. With all the shouting and carrying on, the neighbors knew different. But people minded their own business in those days. They realized whatever I had done to Maggie, I had not meant to do it. They knew me, I was the one they always called when they were sick. Also, they could see that I was already paying for what had happened. Maggie was a complete vegetable. She needed around-the-clock attention. She could do nothing for herself. I fed her through a gastric tube, but it was not long before she turned to skin and bones. I could never get her eyes to stay shut. I taped them closed but they'd pop back open. Talk about having a ghost in the house."

"Scott was all right?"

"He was fine."

"Gene?"

"He was not fine. He wouldn't go anywhere near his mother. I tried to talk to him about what happened but it was useless. He didn't want to hear. At the same time, he didn't blame me, which I found surprising. He seemed to understand what his mother had been doing with Bob Mortega."

"You're saying he blamed his mother for what had happened to her?"

"Yes."

"At that young an age, that's unusual."

"I thought so. I wish now I had forced him to discuss it with me. But a part of me was concerned that he would talk about it at school, then I would end up in prison. I'm not a coward, Ms. Fienman, but I saw no point in leaving my children to the care of the state. Or, to a family who cared nothing for them."

"How did you feel about Scott? After the revelation?"

"What could I do? He was only a baby. He'd been my son for a year and he wasn't going to stop being my son overnight. But as he grew older and began to look more and more like Bob Mortega, it wasn't easy. But I'm getting ahead of myself. After a few months in a coma, Maggie developed an irregular heartbeat. She had trouble breathing. I often had to suck mucus from her lungs. She was prone to respiratory infection. That put an even greater strain on her heart. One night her heart just stopped. By chance I was by her side. I had to inject epinephrine directly into her cardiac muscle to revive her."

Kelly had to breathe. "You stuck a needle in her heart?"

"Yes. A large needle."

"But Gene was not in the room?"

"He was in the room. It was one of the few times he was there."

"A hole in the heart," she whispered.

"Pardon?"

"How did he react to all this?"

"Fine. He displayed neither relief nor disappointment when she started to breathe again. He was alert the whole time. He helped me prepare the shot. He was a smart kid. He didn't panic in an emergency."

"How was he the day after Maggie's attack?"

"He went off by himself. More quiet than usual."

"But he must have said something about how he felt?"

"Not a word. It was like he just accepted it."

"He did not accept it. He internalized it. Changed it into something it was not, until it changed him."

Dr. Banks nodded. "You're perceptive. Of course I knew what was going on inside Gene could not be good. But I didn't know how to address the problem. I had my hands full with Maggie and Scott. She continued to deteriorate. A month after her first attack, she had another one. I remember, it was the Fourth of July. Fireworks were going off outside. I gave her another shot, but her heart did not restart. She was dead." He closed his eyes and put a hand to his head. "She was thirty years old."

Kelly gave him a minute of silence.

"Was Gene in the room when she died?" she asked.

"No."

"He didn't assist you with the shot when she died?"

"No. But he came in a few minutes later and closed her eyes. They stayed closed this time."

"I'm so sorry."

He nodded sadly. "So you see why I'm to blame for what my son became. Those women he murdered, what he did to you . . . It was all my fault."

"You mustn't think that way."

"It's all I think about."

She was not going to salvage his conscience with a pep talk.

"How was Gene after his mother's death?" she asked.

"You're asking if he was better. I'm not sure. He started to talk more."

"This all happened when he was young. How was he in high school?"

"Shy. He kept to himself. He never dated."

"Do you think he hated girls?"

"He never displayed any hatred."

"Was he gay?" Kelly asked.

"No."

"You sound so sure?"

"I can't be sure of anything these days. He never showed an attraction to guys."

"Did he have relationships with any women before he met Julie?"

"He met Julie when he was forty. He was involved with several women before then."

"Did he have any long-term relationships?"

Dr. Banks hesitated. "No."

"Did that concern you?"

"Sure. I wanted him to find someone that could make him happy. When he finally met Julie, I was relieved. They seemed the perfect couple."

"You've heard the story of her infidelity. Do you think that set him off?"

"Yes. Don't you?"

"It's the obvious answer. But your son is anything but obvious."

Dr. Banks shook his head. "Does it really matter, one way or the other?"

"Perhaps not. Where is Scott these days?"

"Forgive me. When he learned what happened, he asked that he not be brought into the matter. He has ____ job and a well-adjusted lifestyle. For his sake, I'd prefer ____ that."

She persisted anyway. "____ anything to do with his brother?"

"No. They haven't spoke____

"Why did Scott avoid Gene before all this happened?"

"I don't think he trusted him."

"Interesting. Did Gene ever display a fascination with acid?"

"No."

"He used acid to torture and kill his victims. Where do you think he got it?"

Dr. Banks coughed hard. "I have no idea."

"Perhaps you should have a drink."

He reached for his cigarette instead. "This goddamn emphysema."

"Clearly Gene was exceptionally intelligent from an early age. Do you think—as an adult—he had the know-how to manufacture the acid by himself?"

"Yes. If he wanted to learn something, he reached for a book. No one had to teach him a thing."

"What do you think he did with the bodies?"

"He hasn't told you?"

"No. He's stubborn on that point."

"Then the bodies probably no longer exist. He reduced them to ash with his acid."

An insightful comment. It would take a tremendous amount of acid to accomplish such a feat, though, many gallons.

"What was it like to live here after your wife died?"

"We didn't stay. A month after Maggie's funeral we moved to Chicago. I ceased practicing medicine."

"What did you do?"

"I started a pharmaceutical company."

"What was it called?"

"Banks Pharmaceuticals. We were best known as the inventors of Ribzor—that's a diabetes drug. It controls blood sugar levels. It's still used today. We were bought out by Merck in the mid-nineties."

"For what amount?"

"A decent amount."

"You must be rich."

"I'm not hurting."

Yet he lived in this old house. "Did you share this wealth with Gene?"

"I shared it with both my sons."

"When did you return to Trenton?"

"A year and a half ago."

"That was about the time when Gene started to kill."

"Was it?"

"This house was left empty all this time?"

"No. I rented it. I just never sold it."

"Why did you come back to Trenton?"

"To be near my son and grandchild."

"Did you see much of Gene during the period he was killing?"

"No. He was often away. But I saw plenty of Robert and Julie."

"What do you think of the man she's with now?"

"I don't know him."

"You haven't seen her in the last five months?"

He hesitated. "No."

"Do you blame her for what happened?"

Dr. Banks gave her a cold look. "Do I blame Maggie for what happened? A part of me blames them all."

Not both. All. And she had asked about Julie, not Maggie.

"Have you seen Gene in the last five months?" she asked.

"He's not allowed to have visitors."

"I know. But that isn't my question, is it?"

He sucked on his cigarette. "I haven't seen him."

CHAPTER THIRTEEN

The day started out good for Matt Connor. The one thing he loved was to hike in the Malibu Hills with his son strapped on his back. And on this particular hike, on a path he came across by chance, they stumbled into a running stream and a low waterfall, which to Jimmy turned out to be pure heaven. There was also a small natural pond, and Matt was able to go for a swim, while his son played in the mud on the shore. It was simply one of those mornings where everything seemed perfect with the world.

Back at the complex, Matt stopped at Kathy's door and knocked. She had called the evening after her gallbladder attack. She had sounded like she was at the airport, but she had not let on that she was leaving town. That had been four days ago and he had not seen her since. Once again there was no answer at her door. He missed Kathy; he hoped she returned soon.

Amy showed up shortly afterward. After so much fun in the hills, Jimmy was exhausted and fell quickly asleep. Then they made love and it was terrible. The perfect day was about to go to hell in a handbasket. For the last week, Amy had slipped back into her distant state. A state he was familiar with from the old days. When they were in bed together, she touched and kissed him with all the enthusiasm of a corpse. While she dressed to go, he asked if anything was wrong.

She shook her head. No.

He persisted. She got annoyed. He dropped it.

What a relationship. She kissed him goodbye and left.

Hours went by, it got late. Time for a bad day to change to horrible. He didn't know that of course—not for sure—when eleven o'clock came around and he suddenly felt the need to drive to Amy and David's house. To hike up to the bluff that overlooked their backyard—and more importantly their upstairs bedroom window—and spy on what they were doing. The urge came like a raging infection. He felt as if someone had lit a wick in the center of his brain. He suspected it was because for a long time he had repressed the desire to spy on them. He had told himself that there was no need—Amy loved him. But if the truth be known, he had not wanted to know. Now all he could think about was the need to know for sure. Amy had become particularly distant just before he had caught her with David.

His babysitter was still awake. He offered her twenty dollars if she would stay in his apartment and take care of Jimmy for an hour. No problem, Barbara said. She could watch TV as easily at his place. As he went out the door, she asked if he was okay. He must have looked strung out.

"Just got some business to take care of," he said.

He drove to the Techer residence in a dream. He did not park on their street but one over. The moon was full; his shadow chased him up the dusty hill. He had brought binoculars. As he nestled on his belly in his old spot, he thought of those dark days a year ago when he used to spy on Amy and her new husband.

He remembered that pain.

Especially as he focused his binoculars on their bedroom.

They were in bed together watching TV. Amy had sworn she no longer slept in the same room as David. Lie number one—did he need to hang around and count to ten? Matt could hear his heart pound into the ground as he watched. He felt close to the earth right then. He understood that it was right and proper that human life should end six feet under. He wished he could die but he had a problem. His heart kept beating and he had to keep watching.

They turned off the TV and the lights. The moon was the brightest he had ever seen it. God in His infinite wisdom had decided to shine a spotlight into their bedroom. Good old God and His sense of humor. Matt burst out laughing when David rolled over and started kissing Amy. It took them an entire minute to get their pajamas off. Then they . . . well, they . . . they just started to have sex. Her on top, her legs spread, rolling her vagina on his penis, probably breathing heavily and making all kinds of other sounds. Yeah, Matt could see that, he could understand that.

His Amy still liked to fuck David.

He did not remember standing up and walking down the hill. The next thing he knew he was outside the gate of the neighbor who lived behind David and Amy. He was familiar with the wall. He had scaled it when he had come for Jimmy. He looked down at his hands and realized he had left his binoculars up on the hill. He stared at his hands and imagined what they could do to David and Amy. He felt a moment of clarity and strength. He would break into their house and kill them. Ted Bundy had nothing on him right then because nothing else mattered.

He flew over the neighbor's wall, then the wall that led into David and Amy's backyard. He moved with the silence of a panther, but if anyone had looked out their window they would have seen him. Not that he cared. Creeping onto the porch beneath their bedroom balcony, he was treated to the sound of Amy's orgasm. It did not help that she made more noise with David. She even had to shout out his name.

"Cool," Matt whispered. He continued to chuckle softly to himself. All he needed now was a plan. He tried the back door and it was locked—not a major obstacle. Their bedroom screen door led onto a balcony and it was wide open. He would have preferred to enter through the kitchen and get a knife. But it looked as if he would have to scale the dangling ivy and come in through the bedroom. Still no problem. He would take them by surprise; he was twice the man David was. He would kill him first, then Amy. He would use his bare hands if he had to. He would stare into her eyes as she choked. It would be interesting to hear what sounds she made then.

Would she try to say his name?

"Matt," he said aloud. The word just burst out. He gasped at his carelessness and put his hand over his mouth. Twelve feet overhead, the heavy breathing stopped but after ten tense seconds of waiting no one reacted to his blunder. Yet the sound of his name had a profound effect on him. It reminded him who he was—Matt Connor, a fool in love, but not a fool when it came to revenge. A stab of sanity seared him. If he killed now he'd be killing himself. He'd go to jail and Jimmy would grow up with no one. It was the thought of his son more than anything that brought him to his senses. Slipping to the ground, he buried his head between his knees and quietly wept.

"Jesus," he whispered. How could she have done this to him?

No. The question was: how could she have done it to him again?

Matt sat for several minutes in his misery before realizing his vulnerability. Neither David nor Amy could be asleep yet, and there were always the neighbor's rear windows. He had to get out of there! But the stretch of backyard that had not bothered him minutes before suddenly looked like a shooting range. He did not want to retrace his steps. He decided to do what he had done before with Jimmy. Go out the front.

David had not installed a new security system. Useless after the fact, the bastard probably thought. Matt climbed the side gate and seconds later was just another guy out for a late-night walk. He retrieved his binoculars from the hill and got back in his car and drove home.

Kathy was entering her apartment as he hiked up the stairs.

"Simon!" she called and waved.

He did not want her to see him in this condition. But he did not see how he could escape her. Already she was coming up the stairs to meet him. Wearing torn blue jeans and a gray sweater, her blond hair loose down her back, she looked like the summer sun. He wiped at his face and felt half-dried tears. He was having trouble breathing. He was back in the place where he had been when he had first caught Amy with David. In a place where only bad things were possible. Kathy smiled at him but then lost it as she came near. He tried to put on a brave front but she saw right through it.

"What's wrong?" she asked when she reached him.

"Nothing. Had a rough night. Did you just get back?"

"Fuck that. What's wrong?"

"Nothing. Where did you go?"

Kathy took him by the arm. "You're coming to my place. We have to talk."

"I have to pick up Jimmy from Barbara."

"I'll call her. She can watch Jimmy a little longer."

Minutes later he sat on her couch beside her. He didn't know what to say. He could not tell her the truth, yet he hated to lie. She was a good person, she cared about him—without wanting anything in return. He was so tired of all the lies and cheating in the world. He wished he could open his heart to her completely. She had already called Barbara. The girl said she would be happy to watch Jimmy all night, at twenty an hour.

"Something happened with Amy," Kathy said.

Matt nodded reluctantly. "You could say that."

Kathy took his hand and squeezed it. "Did you two have a fight?"

He shook his head. "Not exactly."

She stared for the longest time. "You caught her with someone else."

He desperately wanted to deny it. He feared if he opened up even slightly he would crack all the way. He would burst out crying, and that was one thing he had never done in front of anyone since the nightmare had started over a year ago. But Kathy's eyes were such a deep blue—twin seas he wished he could dive into and disappear. He did not answer right away and then he did not have to because she already understood.

"That whore!" Kathy swore.

"It's not the way you think."

"It is! The details don't matter. I see it in your face. She betrayed you before and she's betrayed you again."

He tried to stand. "I'm tired. I better go."

She grabbed his arm and pulled him down. Kissing his hand, she pressed it to the side of her face. Her cheek was damp—tears shed for him, he could not believe anyone would bother.

"Simon," she said, almost pleading. "Let her go. Take Jimmy and leave. She's not worth it."

All he knew was agony. Why had he stayed to watch? The image of them fucking would haunt him the rest of his life. Death would not erase it. The galaxy would collapse into a massive black hole and it would remain. His Amy on top of that asshole. Kathy waited for him to respond.

"I don't know," he whispered.

"That's not true. You do know what you have to do. But you're afraid to do it because you're afraid of losing her. Let me tell you something, you have already lost her. In fact, you never had her to begin with. She's an obsession, she's not a love. Simon, there's a difference. Love brings happiness. She just brings pain."

He struggled. "If I didn't love her, it wouldn't hurt."

"All right, say you're right. What difference does it make? Stay with her and you'll suffer. She wants you to suffer. She's a small person. It makes her feel big to see a great man like you weep."

"You haven't even met her."

"I don't need to meet her! I just have to look at you. She's killing you. What happened tonight?"

He shook his head. "I can't talk about it."

Kathy stood and paced. "Then fuck you both. You want to throw away your life on a little shit like her, you go ahead and do it."

He looked at her in wonder. "Why do you care so much?"

"I don't care, that's my point. You want to behave like an idiot, you do it on your own time. I don't need this shit."

He stood. "I have to deal with it in my own way."

She stopped him again. "No. You can't go. You can't be alone tonight."

"But Jimmy . . ."

"Barbara will take care of Jimmy." She hugged him and buried her face in his chest. "Stay here tonight."

"Kathy?"

She looked up at him. "You can sleep in my bed beside me. I won't touch you, I swear. You take the Percocet this time. The pain will recede, believe me. It won't vanish but it will feel like it's happening to someone else. It will help you fall asleep. Then, in the morning, you can figure out what to do."

"I don't like to take drugs."

"You don't like to get fucked in the ass either. But it's already happened. Take two pills if you need them to sleep." She reached up and kissed him on the lips. "Whatever gets you through the night."

It was good to hold her. He kissed her back.

"Thank you," he said.

■

THE EFFECT of the pills could not last forever, though. The morning sun came and with it his memory of the night's events. Kathy said she wished she could stay with him but she had business to attend to. She left early and he picked up Jimmy and returned to his apartment, which now felt like a prison he had taken a lifetime lease on. There was only one solution to his dilemma. Kathy had said it. He had to take Jimmy and leave. Not even say goodbye to Amy. There was no other course and there was no point in delaying.

Yet he waited for her. She was supposed to come at twelve.

For once Amy arrived early. Perhaps she sensed something was wrong. Then again, she didn't need to be psychic to know she was in trouble when she entered the apartment. He looked at her a long time and said nothing.

"What is it?" she asked.

He kept his voice low. Jimmy was asleep in the next room.

"I drove by your house last night. Saw you fucking David."

She did not respond. Time took on an added dimension right then. It was as if he stared at her through a warped looking glass that distorted as well as revealed her. He did not recognize her—she looked like a witch. That was the point, though, he was finally seeing her as she really was. Amy died a little before him while the witch grew more substantial.

"I can explain," she said.

He raised a hand. He was seated on his favorite chair, where they often snuggled.

"No. Don't bother. I just wanted you to know that I know."

"Matt."

"I don't want to hear your lies. It's over between us."

She came and knelt by his side. Already her eyes were damp. She tried to take his hand but he wouldn't let her. "I'm so sorry," she whispered.

"Right."

"I do love you. I know you can't believe that right now but it's true. I know I lied to you when I said I wasn't having sex with David. What happened between us last night was rare, but I admit it's not the only time it's happened since you came back into my life. But you have to understand why I lied to you. Why I am still sleeping with him. It's not because I wanted to."

"I heard your orgasm. It sounded like you enjoyed it."

"You're wrong. I faked that orgasm. I hate having sex with David. I hate him. But I'm still afraid of him. He still intimidates me. Yes, it's my old lousy excuse but it's still the truth. I've told you how horrible it is to live with him and you don't listen. I'm a captive in that house. I don't have my own free will."

"You're lying."

"No. Since Jimmy disappeared from his life, he's become a tyrant. He blames me every day for what happened. I don't have a moment of peace. He controls everything I do. It's easy for you to sit here with no one to answer to and judge me."

"You're right. I had an easy night."

She grabbed his hand. "Matt, don't hate me. Things are not the way they appear. You're in my heart. I don't want to be with David. But until this divorce is over, I'm under his thumb."

"We could leave here tomorrow if you wanted."

"Don't be naive. We can't leave with David still in the picture. We've discussed this. He and his father will find us. They'll find Jimmy, and you'll go to jail. You won't believe this but the main reason I stay with David right now is to protect you."

He snorted. "I can do without your protection."

"You think you can. You're in constant danger. We both are as long as David is alive."

"Is that what they call a hint?"

She sat on her knees and stared up at him like a little girl. Even in his pain, he had to marvel at how innocent she looked. His angel, talking about murder. He had no illusion about what she would say next.

"I've thought about this a long time," she said. "If I'm lucky and I finally get a divorce, David will still know where I am. But if I try to disappear, he'll get suspicious. The FBI would probably do the same. Either way it's hopeless. But if David dies in an accident then all our problems are solved. I no longer have to be with him behind your back, and you no longer have to keep looking over your shoulder."

"And you get his money."

"The money isn't as important as our peace of mind."

"You can have peace of mind with his blood on your hands?"

"Yes. He's a horrible person. He doesn't deserve to live. If he ever finds Jimmy again, he'll raise him to be a monster. You don't want that any more than I do."

"He won't want Jimmy once he discovers he's mine."

"Do you want to take that chance? Or an even worse chance? That Jimmy grows up with no father at all."

Matt waved his hand. "You mention the FBI. If David should suddenly die after all this kidnapping business, you can be sure they'd be all over you."

"No."

"Don't *no* me. I know what I'm talking about."

"That's right. You understand the FBI. You outwitted them like no one ever has. You can do it again. I have faith in you. You can figure out a way to get rid of David so that they'll suspect nothing."

Matt had to chuckle. "I would rather kill you first."

Amy's face was still damp. "Kill me then. I would rather die than live like this."

"Famous last words."

Amy stood and grabbed her purse from the coffee table where she had put it when she entered. Returning to his side, she removed two prescription bottles and handed them to him. Both were made out to Amy Techer: Seconal and Phenobarbital.

"I got these on the Internet with a phony prescription," she said. "It's a well-known combo in certain circles. Take twenty of each and you go to sleep and don't wake up."

He was unmoved. "So?"

"I carry them with me all the time. It's only you and Jimmy that keep me from doing it."

He tossed the pills back at her. "Take them and save us both the trouble."

She looked so frail. "Are you serious?"

"Yes."

Amy went into the kitchen and returned with a glass of water. Sitting at the table, she opened the bottles and poured out a handful of red and yellow pills. She tossed a half dozen in her mouth and used the water to swallow them.

"You're bluffing," he said.

She did not respond. She swallowed another half dozen.

"Amy," he said.

"What?"

"Stop it."

"No." She grabbed more pills.

"I mean it, stop it."

"No." Another ten down the chute.

He stood. "You're not going to kill yourself in front of me."

She looked up at him; her lower lip trembled. "Would you prefer I wait until I get home?"

He grabbed the bottles from her hands and studied the labels more closely. The prescriptions had been filled by drugstore.com—biggest online pharmacy in the world.

"Christ," he swore. "These are real."

"I love you, Matt."

"Shit!" He grabbed her by the arm. "Come, you're going to throw up in the toilet before they dissolve in your stomach."

She shook him off. "No."

He yanked her to her feet. "This isn't funny anymore. You have to throw them up immediately."

She went limp in his hands. To his surprise, she smiled and leaned forward and kissed him on the lips. "I love you. Do you love me?"

He was exasperated. "How can I love you after what you've done to me?"

"You don't know me. Everything I do, I do it for you. Now I'll die for you."

He dragged her toward the bathroom. "You're not going to do this." Moments later he had her above the toilet. "Stick your finger down your throat."

She looked dazed. "No."

"If you don't, I'll have to call an ambulance."

"Call one then."

"You know I can't do that. It would bring too much attention."

"Then I guess I'll just have to die."

He shook his head. "You're bluffing."

She lost her smile. "I know your torture but you don't know mine. Let me die, Matt. If you like, I can walk across the street and pass out in the park. It will be over before help can reach me. It'll be better that way for both of us."

He saw she was serious. He tried to force his own finger down her throat but she bit him. "You cannot do this!" he shouted.

A wave of fatigue swept over her and she sagged against the wall. He shot out a supporting hand and she rested the back of her head on the blue wallpaper with the white angels. Once again he was struck by how beautiful she looked. The thought of her laid out in a coffin smothered him with grief. And ten minutes ago he had wanted to kill her.

"I feel funny," she whispered.

He grabbed her by her hair and forced her face toward the toilet. "Stick your finger down your throat this instant!"

She did not resist him but she did not cooperate either. On her knees, she muttered under her breath. "How can we be happy while he lives?"

The question weakened him as much as her suicide stunt. Because it was so true. He could never relax while David was in the world. He would never be free of the fear that she would go back to him. That did not say much for his trust in her—it was just reality. David and Amy were connected in the same way he and Amy were connected. The triangle felt ancient to Matt. Amy understood the strength of the button she pushed in him. Slumping beside the toilet bowl, she reached up and took his hand and kissed it.

"I will live if he dies," she said. "It's the only way."

"We will never get away with it."

"You will never get caught."

Matt sighed. "All right. He dies."

CHAPTER FOURTEEN

Kelly had no trouble planting her bugs in Matt's apartment. The day after his discovery of Amy's infidelity, she took him out for dinner at the Beverly Hills Hotel. She intended to pay but figured he could afford it if he insisted on being a gentleman, which he did. As they were being seated, she acted chilled and rushed to get her coat. The valet had seen them together seconds before and did not hesitate to give her Matt's keys. Once in his car, in the parking lot, she made an impression of his apartment key. The following morning, she flashed her badge at a locksmith in Santa Monica and got two copies made.

It was Matt's custom to go for a walk with his son along the beach after lunch. While he was gone, she was in and out of his place in fifteen minutes. Charlie had gotten her the good stuff. When Matt returned home, she listened with 100 percent clarity as he watched two *Star Trek* reruns and the news.

Amy arrived at four in the afternoon. What timing.

They immediately began to plan David's murder.

"Fuck me, O.J.," Kelly whispered as she listened.

"You said the two best ways to kill someone are to either push them off a cliff or drown them in the ocean," Amy said. "David's father is coming out in a couple of days and staying two weeks. Carl and David will be taking the boat out plenty. Can we get David then?"

"How large is the boat and where will they take it?"

"It's huge, an eighty footer. Fast too. That sucker can get to Catalina in an hour."

"Can you all go over to Catalina for the night? Then change your plans at the last minute and come back late?"

"Sure," Amy said. "Why do we need the change of plans?"

"We need to strike late at night. We need David drunk. It's better to keep the plan simple. When the boat's coming back in the middle of the night, lure him onto the deck and push him overboard."

"*You'll* have to push him overboard," Amy said quickly.

"I understand. But you'll have to get him drunk first, stoned if possible. Does David do drugs?"

"Pot occasionally. But he takes Valium and Xanax. He's been taking a lot since Jimmy disappeared."

"Good. He'll have a residue in his system. But while you're on Catalina, it will help if you can spike his drinks with more of the drugs."

"Why are the drugs so important?"

"You're trying to build up the case that he simply fell overboard in the middle of the night without your knowledge. His body could be found."

"Do bodies sink or float?"

"They can do either. A lot depends on how much water goes into the lungs. That's something out of our control. Besides, the more intoxicated David is, the easier he will be to push overboard."

"You'll have to be aboard to do that."

"Obviously. But I don't want to come aboard here. I'll board on Catalina while you guys are off drinking and dancing."

"There's this club on Catalina that David and I both love—Rosie's. Carl will probably have one of his underaged bimbos with him. The four of us can go there and get wasted."

"No. Not the four of you. *All* of you must leave the boat. How much crew does David usually take with him when he goes out?"

"Two. Gilbert and Mark. Gilbert's a captain, Mark's a friend of his. Sometimes we go without Mark. Lately, David's preferred to handle the boat as much as possible. I might be able to stop him from taking the guys. David's pretty competent on the water."

"No," Matt said. "We need at least Gilbert present. Remember, you're going to lure David onto the deck in the middle of the night in the middle of the ocean. You want to get David out of bed if possible. The more disoriented he is the better. Someone else must be piloting the boat back to L.A."

"But Gilbert will see us."

"Gilbert might see you and that's a problem. How many levels is this boat?"

"There are three levels on top, two below."

"Gilbert steers from the top level?"

"Yes."

"Good. It won't take long to get David in the water. The best place to push him overboard is at the rear. The roar of the engines should drown out his cries, particularly if he's drunk and stoned. He might just go under and not come up."

"But where will you be when I get David on deck?"

"Around. I'll have to examine this boat ahead of time. When can I do that?"

"Tomorrow. We can go to the marina together."

"We will not go together. You'll go ahead of me and unlock everything. I'll sneak aboard later. What's the name?"

"The *Stardust*. I'll find out exactly where it's docked."

"Do that. But be careful how you ask the question. Be casual."

"Don't worry about that. I like this plan."

"This plan is far from perfect. It needs work. If Gilbert even sees you on deck with David, and David's later found missing, it will look suspicious. Before you bring David on deck, you have to check and make sure Gilbert is concentrating on what he's doing. He must have his eyes on L.A."

"He usually does. He's a no-nonsense kind of guy."

Matt continued. "Let's back up a second. We need to get Gilbert off the boat on Catalina while I sneak onto it. Is it possible he would accompany you and David and Carl to the club?"

"No. Carl and David are real class conscious. They like Gilbert but he's still a hired hand. They would never go drinking and dancing with him. But I can figure out a way to get Gilbert off the boat."

"How?"

"I can send him on an errand. Don't worry, I'll take care of it."

"I do worry. The way to make this work is to worry about every detail. I can't just turn over a part of the plan to you."

"You don't have to get snotty."

"Listen to me, Amy. We can't bring personalities into this. We're talking about drowning your husband and making it look like an accident. You can think about how you're going to get Gilbert off the boat. But before we do anything, you're going to have to tell me exactly how it's going to be done."

"Okay. We're going to be in touch during this time, aren't we? I can call you on my cell?"

"You can call me but not on your cell. If someone dies in this manner, the police will check the phone records of everyone involved. I'll give you a cell to use that can't be traced."

"Where will you get it?"

"I have places. I'll get two of them, one for each of us."

"Are you saying the police will automatically suspect murder?" Amy asked.

"No. But they'll want to cover their bases. David and Carl are rich. Suspicion will turn toward you, especially since you recently lost your son. You have to be ready for that."

"Don't worry, I can lie with a straight face."

"I know."

"Matt!"

"Sorry. What excuse will you give to get them to leave Catalina in the middle of the night?" Matt asked.

"I can say I just remembered that I have a doctor's appointment in the morning."

"You'll have to set a doctor's appointment for the next morning."

"The police will check that?"

"They might. Why would you go to the doctor?"

"For a regular checkup."

"Would a checkup be enough reason for David and his father to disrupt their plans and come home?"

"Sure. When they get back to the marina, they won't even get off the boat. They'll sleep there all night, if it's late enough."

"David won't. David will be dead, remember?"

"I know," Amy said.

"Can I hide on the lower level of the boat?"

"Yes. We have the perfect place. A storage room. No one ever goes in there."

"Gilbert could check it out before leaving Catalina."

"No. At best he will make sure we have all our life rafts and stuff before we leave the marina. You'll be safe there. This is an incredible plan, Matt."

"Don't get excited. The part where we push David overboard is the most critical. Gilbert must not see or hear us. He can't see David either."

"Can't we hit David over the head with something before pushing him overboard?"

"No. Like I said, his body might be found. How would you explain the blow to his skull? Also, he could bleed on deck. The police would never let up if they find blood. The simpler the plan the better. Fewer things can go wrong that way."

"Gotcha."

"We have another major problem. I have to figure out a way to get off the boat before you dock in L.A."

"Why?"

"What do you mean, why? I can't be hiding aboard when it's discovered David is missing."

"Why don't you jump overboard when we're creeping through the harbor?"

"That's what I'll probably have to do. But I don't like it."

"Why not?"

"The longer I'm on board after David goes in the water, the more vulnerable I am. I need to think about this."

"No one will know you're on board," Amy said.

"We'll see. You should discover that David is gone the moment Gilbert docks."

"Not before?"

"No. You only wake up when he docks. You discover David is missing. You have no idea what happened to him. Don't suggest he fell overboard. Let the others do that. Carl will call the police and the Coast

Guard. The cops will question you at length. Does anyone know you and David have marital difficulties?"

"I'm sure his dad knows."

"How does he feel about you?"

"Carl likes me. He loved Jimmy. He feels terrible about what happened with the kidnapping."

"He won't suspect you?"

"No. Impossible."

"I wouldn't count on that. David is his only son. When he's dead, you'll see a whole new side of Carl."

"You're wrong. Carl will never accuse me."

Matt took a long time responding.

"Exactly how well do you know Carl?" he asked.

"What is that supposed to mean?"

"Nothing."

"That is such a shitty comment. You owe me an apology."

"I owe you nothing after what you did the other night."

"We have been over that. Why do you have to bring it up?"

"It's not like you were ten minutes late to a dentist appointment. I'll bring it up whenever I wish."

"Look, you're the one who said what we're trying to do is critical. We have to trust each other or this is not going to work."

"Trust is built up between two people over time. When I came back to you, you promised to be straight with me. Well, you lied to me again. How am I supposed to trust you now?"

"If you don't trust me, then how can we do this together?"

"I have asked myself the same question," Matt said.

"Are you backing out?"

"No. But I'm keeping my options open."

"Which means what? You might run off with Jimmy when my back is turned?"

"I'm not saying that. But you sleep with David again and I swear to you I'm out of here with Jimmy."

"I don't want to sleep with David! I want to kill him!"

"Shhh. Keep your voice down. Someone might hear."

"No one can hear us," Amy said.

Matt said something about needing time to work out the details. They tentatively planned to kill David the following Friday, in five days. It seemed David was out of town until the end of the week. They talked about seeing a movie that night. Kelly had to turn off the sound for a few minutes. She felt sick to her stomach.

Worse, she felt betrayed.

It was only then she realized how much Matt meant to her. Her remark to Tony had been largely vindictive—she had wanted to push his buttons. But now she saw that having Matt in her life had made it easier for her to play hardball with Tony. Romantic fantasies about a proven criminal were of course absurd. To hear Matt calmly discuss murder with that bitch shook her to the core. What had Amy done to him that he would even consider this?

Kelly knew. Matt had caught Amy and David screwing. Then Amy had promised to stop if Matt would just screw David big time. When Kelly had run into Matt the other night, he had been out of his mind. Amy had probably been able to flip his insanity so that she came across in his mind like a sweet-natured nun with guy problems. I'm the victim. David is the bad guy. All we have to do is get rid of David. Then we can be happy together . . .

Matt had fallen for it. How could he be so naive?

Kelly had not failed to notice Amy's disinterest in whether Matt got off the boat or not. It was obvious Amy was ready to play both ends of the equation. If things went bad, she could always point the finger at Matt. He killed my husband. He is supposed to be dead. He has my baby. Either way Amy was going to win. She would dispose of David, inherit the money, and have her son back. Matt was so smart, why couldn't he see that?

"He might see it. He might just need time," Kelly said to herself as she paced her apartment. Should she give him that time? It was the scariest decision she'd ever had to make. David could die. Matt could be locked up for murder. But to intervene now would destroy all she was attempting to do. She could not arrest Matt and she could not warn him away. Then she would never know if he would have gone through with it. She would never know if she should care.

That is why she felt sick.

She wanted to care. He cared for her.

The next day Kelly went for a walk with Matt. He appeared to have a lot on his mind—big surprise. The temptation to warn him away from Amy was overwhelming, but Matt had to sink or swim on the strength of his own basic integrity. Kelly had to admit his plan to murder David was clever. Assuming Gilbert did not see them, it would be difficult to prove that David had been a victim of foul play. Yet the scheme was almost too simple for someone as subtle as Matt. Once again, in her mind, she compared him to the Acid Man. She wondered what he thought about as they walked.

She wondered about Professor Gene Banks.

She had not gone to see him after interviewing the father. The tale of the tragedy of their lives had deepened the spell the Acid Man had cast over her own life. She could not be free of certain images: the boy looking at his comatose mother lying at the bottom of the stairs, the night Maggie died—the long needle sliding into her heart. Kelly felt sure Dr. Fred Banks had left something out about how Mrs. Banks left this world. Gene would have been there, she was sure of it, close at hand.

She had not met with Gene Banks, but she had driven to his place and parked across the street. In the same manner she had accused Julie, she tried to glimpse him through the window. She felt sure he knew she was there. But she saw nothing, only shadows, flickering lights, ghost images of the TV perhaps, or else the shifting auras of the spirits that haunted their mutual dreams. What was that quote from the Bible about the sins of the father? Flying home, she had thought that a person who could start a pharmaceutical company would have to have a knowledge of chemistry.

The Acid Man called on her cell when she returned from her walk with Matt.

"How did you get this number?" she demanded.

"Does it matter?"

"Yes."

"It's listed. The FBI has a list."

A curious comment. Did he have an ally in the FBI?

"What do you want?" she asked.

"How are Matt and Amy?"

"They couldn't be happier."

"Matt will not be happy long. He knows."

"You've never even met him."

"Does it matter?" he repeated. "We have a bargain. Independence Day is a week away. I'd like to celebrate my freedom then. Close all the files so to speak. I'm sure you understand why."

He said a lot with few words. He wanted her to kill him on the same day his mother had died. He knew she had been snooping on him. She forced herself to focus. He was clever but perhaps she could get him to reveal a few secrets.

"Do you really want to die?" she asked.

"The instinct to survive is not as strong as people think. Pain is more daunting than life. The sick and depressed crave extinction. Even content souls wonder about death."

"Do you think the women you killed wanted to die?"

"They did when the acid began to eat into their hearts."

"Where are they now?" she asked.

"Don't you know?"

Such a simple question. He was telling her she should know. That meant she had learned more on her last trip than she realized. Or else he was playing with her. Always a possibility.

"No," she answered.

"Don't worry, I'm not disappointed in you. But Amy will disappoint Matt. Have you tried to talk him into killing me?"

"I don't know him that well."

"Are you sure? Have you slept with him yet?"

"Why did you call?"

"I told you. July fourth. A hero's day. Will I be seeing you?"

"I'm not sure I'll be finished with my business by then."

"You'll be finished. Neither you nor Matt will disappoint me."

"Why did you say he was dangerous?"

"I didn't say that. I said they were both dangerous."

"The combination?"

"Yes. When combined with the other. The triangle, you know."

" 'The Tears of Rati'?" she asked.

"Yes. You wonder why I'm so interested in Matt?"

"You feel he's a kindred soul?"

"Perhaps. But my disposition might lie elsewhere."

Was he sympathetic to Amy? "Where?"

He yawned. "I'm tired. It's time for my nap. Come after the fireworks. I'll be sure to be alone. We will talk."

He hung up. Setting down the phone, she felt as if she had just been asked what size coffin she wanted. And this burial plot over here, Kelly Fienman, we have plenty of room left if you're in the spirit. He did not threaten her—he could not—yet she felt as if she was walking into a trap.

Her vow to kill him was bullshit. She could ignore him for the rest of her life. But who was she fooling? He had her number—she would have no rest if she did not destroy him. He would keep calling or, worse, she would continue to park across his street and gaze at his window. Searching for that Ghost of Christmas Past. There was a surprise buried at the bottom of the stocking he'd made for her.

Her talk with Gene Banks had stirred a strange question inside her.

How had Charlie known she'd visited the Acid Man?

Kelly suddenly noticed that there was something wrong with her apartment. The observation was disturbing because she could not pinpoint its source. Nothing appeared out of place. Yet it was as if the entire environment had been lifted up and set down again. Quickly she checked her gun in the closet. It was where she had left it, but had she placed it with the butt pointed up?

"I'm losing it," Kelly muttered to herself as she went through her apartment. She had few possessions, there was little to search. She remembered the key she had made of Matt's apartment. On impulse she checked her own lock. The handle looked fine but the dead bolt was faintly scratched. Of course it probably had always been scratched. But had someone picked her lock?

"How does he do this to me!" she yelled at the ceiling.

Did she ask about the Acid Man or Matt?

The next day Kelly went for another walk with Matt, along the water. Jimmy was left with the babysitter, Barbara. The air was hot and stagnant. Even so close to the sea, she felt as if the sun ate at her flesh like hungry insects.

Matt wore shorts and nothing else. His well-defined muscles shone with a faint layer of sweat. If he had reached for her hand, she would have accepted. It was possible Matt was already beyond her reach. He said little—she sensed his mind churn: three days until David was supposed to die. Amy had not been back to Matt's apartment since the planning session.

"So what's new?" she asked after a long pause.

"Nothing."

"How's Amy?"

"She's fine," Matt replied.

She was casual. "I sometimes worry if I have another gallstone attack I won't be able to reach you. The other day I tried to call on your cell and couldn't get you."

"Really?" He was surprised. Why not, she was lying.

"Do you have another cell phone that you use?"

He paused. "Yeah. I can give you the number."

"Thanks."

"How are you feeling in that area?"

"Fine," she said.

We are all fine. Me, you, Amy, Jimmy, and the Acid Man. The latter acted like they were all invited to the same party. Tony was not so fine, though. The lonely boy had called her machine a few times. She replayed the messages endlessly. He begged her to come back. Good for him.

The next day, Wednesday, she talked to Matt on the phone but did not see him. Amy had yet to return to his apartment, although Kelly knew from eavesdropping that they were having lunch meetings. Kelly wished she had been able to place a bug inside Matt's skull.

Thursday evening Matt disappeared and Kelly panicked.

Kelly spoke to Barbara and learned Matt was to be away for two days, and that Barbara was taking care of Jimmy for that time. That did not mean they intended to kill David Thursday instead of Friday. Matt might be using Thursday to prepare. Yet Kelly had a sinking feeling. She had been lucky to hear of their plan, but luck was a pendulum that always swung the other way. She cursed herself for not having checked on Matt earlier. It was already after six.

Playing FBI, she called the Marina Del Rey harbor and told them to check on the status of the *Stardust*. Her guts felt like bleeding ice when they told her the ship had set sail early that morning. That meant the Techers were already on Catalina. Matt would be nearby. Not sure what she was doing, Kelly tried both his cell numbers. No answer.

"Oh shit," she whispered.

She had to get to Catalina. A frantic five minutes of research told her that she'd missed the last ferry and helicopter ride over. A blessing in disguise perhaps. The more she thought about it, the more she wanted her own boat. Her dad had taught her how to sail as a teenager. A trip to Catalina was nothing to her—just eighteen miles across the open water.

Kelly was not ready to give up on Matt. She suspected that crazy part of her which had driven her to confront the Acid Man and the mysterious kidnapper of Amy's baby would allow the drama to play out until the last instant. If she had a boat, she could always rescue David from the water.

"No, you're not doing that," she swore as she drove toward the harbor. She had already called Harry's Ocean Rentals and spoken to scarecrow Timmy, the guy who had helped Matt load his boat on D-Day. Timmy complained that he was about to leave for the day. She said if he did not have a boat ready for her when she reached the harbor she would arrest him for crimes he had not committed. Torturing him gave her pleasure. He promised her their fastest powerboat. Then he asked her out on a date. She would think about it, she said.

The sun had settled into the underworld by the time she reached the dock. Timmy handed her a set of keys and helped her load three extra drums of fuel onto what looked like a twenty-foot jet. He wanted to flirt but she cut him short. Once on the open water, she revved the engine and was shaken as the nose popped up and the roar deafened her ears. It was fortunate the ocean was flat and visibility was near perfect. The *Capricorn* was full-throttle testosterone. The bow shredded the water. She had to strain to hang onto the wheel. A salty breeze stung her eyes and her hair flapped like torn wings. The faint lights of the islands shone across the dark water. She would reach Catalina in under an hour.

But then what?

CHAPTER FIFTEEN

Matt stood beside the slippery rocks and cold water where he had completed his scuba lessons. The spot was next to an old casino that had been famous in the twenties and thirties as one of the West Coast's hot celebrity clubs. In those good old days—that had probably been more intolerable than history remembered—the casino had offered a sampling of vices society had voted to forbid: gambling, wine, women.

But now the casino was shut, and lay as dark and silent as the surrounding night. He was thankful for the solitude the place had to offer. Catalina's main harbor lay off to his right—its dozens of boats gathered like so many white whales peering through the dark—and distant sounds of partying echoed over the black water.

The *Stardust* itself was anchored more than a quarter of a mile offshore, almost lost in the night. But he had binoculars, and he knew that Captain Gilbert had departed for shore less than fifteen minutes ago. The *Stardust* was a powerful and well-maintained ship. Empty now, though, it was as vulnerable as the rest of them. He planned to board her soon.

But not for the purpose Amy imagined.

The time was close to midnight. A fitting moment to start on a course of action that would affect him and Jimmy for the rest of their lives. Yet his torment was less than he would have imagined. He had come to a painful decision, but pain was always relative and any decision was better than the wasteland he had lived in since he had reunited with Amy. He had refined his murderous plan with her over the last few days, while he had privately devised a more profound scheme. One that would prove to him once and for all if she loved him. A plan that both solved their dilemma and gave them a reason to solve it. Everything was set—she only had to choose.

He honestly didn't know what she would do.

It didn't matter. Either way there would be relief.

At exactly midnight, Amy called.

"Where are you?" she asked.

"Near the harbor. Where are you?"

"In a stall in the restroom at Rosie's."

"That's the club?" he asked.

"Yeah. I'm alone. Can you see the boat? Did Gilbert leave?"

"He left a few minutes ago. How long will he be gone?"

"Until I go fetch him. He should be in a bar down the street. By chance, I met a few friends of his and I called him to come over and see them."

"That wasn't part of our plan."

"I can improvise, Matt. The excuse was better than the one we had. Don't jump all over me."

"I'm not."

Amy chuckled. "You'll be happy to know David's been drinking all night. The bartender commented on it. I slipped two Valium in his liquor. He can hardly stand up." She added, "Carl's here with his girlfriend."

"Good," he said without enthusiasm.

"What is it?"

"Nothing. How's Carl?" Why did she call him by his first name?

"Loaded. Too bad you can't meet his new babe. She's two years younger than me and has tits out to the moon. I already told them I have to get back for a doctor's appointment in the morning and they're cool. We'll leave in the next hour or two."

"Did you actually set the doctor's appointment?"

"I told you I did. What's wrong with you?"

"Nothing. I'm going out to the boat now."

"Great. What are you going to do with the boat you use to get to David's boat?"

"Set it adrift. Let me worry about it."

"You don't sound happy," she said.

"I have a lot on my mind."

She lowered her voice and spoke with love. "It'll all be over tonight, Matt. Then we can be together forever."

"That's what I want." His heart ached. "When you're aboard and David's asleep, come down to the storage room. I want to talk."

"Why?"

"Just do it."

She hesitated. "Okay," she said.

They exchanged goodbyes. His boat was tied around the bend. He had already loaded his equipment: a Farallon propulsion device, two wet suits, a waterproof bag with a strap, a GPS device, a diver's flashlight. He had rented the boat on Catalina earlier that day. Not being able to return it made him feel guilty, but he hoped to steer it back toward its rightful owners. He had leased the boat under the name Maxwell Adams.

The boat was equipped with a feeble twenty-five horsepower motor. He crept toward the *Stardust* at arthritic speed. The night was remarkably warm and still. Every sound was amplified. He could not have approached the ship with Gilbert aboard. Even a quarter of a mile from shore, he could distinguish the actual sentences of people talking in the restaurants. To be safe, he closed on the *Stardust* in a long arcing curve, coming at it from the seaside. It was almost as if his pounding heart echoed over the black water. He dismissed what he had felt minutes before. His torment was swiftly increasing.

Boarding proved easy. Gilbert had left down the ladder. Matt merely had to tie on for a moment, carry his stuff onto the deck, and then aim his own boat in the direction of the harbor. The small outboard spurted away as if personally rejected. It did not have the speed or bulk to damage whatever it hit. But it was a loose end, and those were not good when it came to a police investigation.

He was familiar with the layout of the ship from an inspection he had made the previous day. The storage room Amy had described made an excellent hiding place. Besides being tucked in the bowels of ship, it was stacked to the ceiling with yachting shit and was L-shaped. He imagined he could remain out of sight even if Gilbert had the urge to grab an extra life jacket or a spare wrench. There was a great corner to disappear into. It was here he stacked his equipment and lay down to wait on top of a partially inflated raft.

The room was hot and stuffy and he was exhausted. He yawned and closed his eyes but did not worry he would sleep. He had not slept well since he had caught Amy with David. His frantic heartbeat settled into a silent throb. A secret pain—he felt so alone in his distress. God had no interest in his dilemma. Matt did not believe in the power of divine grace, anyway. Matt had prayed for peace when he had first caught Amy with David. Now he just blotted things out.

There was a lot to be said for denial.

Until it blew up in your face.

Ninety minutes went by. Finally he heard sounds coming from above. The happy party returning from another night of selfless service and deep meditation. There was plenty of giggling and cursing. He thought he heard David grope Amy. No, that would not have been possible. But Matt had to ask himself if she would fuck David before he fell asleep. One last screw before the grave. Matt regretted that he had not checked out their private cabin. It would have been a pleasure to rub super glue on their condoms. Or acid on her lipstick. Bring out the blowtorch, baby.

Kathy had muttered a lot about acid when they had slept together.

Matt realized how much he missed her. Her simple honesty.

The ship got underway. Matt estimated that Gilbert had the engines at half throttle. They could take two hours to return to the mainland. The length of time should not have bothered Matt and yet it did. He had told Amy the truth when he had said how vulnerable he would be while he was on the ship. Perhaps that had been a mistake. She knew how to take advantage of weakness. God, he could not stop thinking how much he hated her. And here she was the love of his life. It made him wonder if he had gotten the definition of the words mixed up in first grade.

"The opposite of love is not hate," he muttered. "It's sex."

Amy appeared a half hour later.

She had on teddy bear pajamas, no makeup. She must have washed her face before going to bed; if she had gotten that far. Her big brown eyes were a mystery. He had expected to find her either scared or excited or a combination of both. But there was sorrow in her face, coupled with a peculiar detachment. That was his Amy—a complex nothing. He had known her almost three years and he hadn't the faintest idea what went on in her head.

"David's asleep," she said.

"Good." He sat up and reached for his GPS.

She nodded to the Farallon. "What's that for?"

"Our escape."

"What?"

"I'll explain."

"You'd better hurry. David could wake up any second. Why did you want me to come down here?"

"We need to talk."

"About what? You're not changing the plan again."

"I am. We're not going to kill David."

"*What?*"

"Shh. Gilbert will hear you."

Amy was livid. So much for the mystery. She practically hissed as she spoke.

"Are you out of your goddamn mind? After all the trouble I've gone through to set this up? You're chickening out?"

He spoke in a calm voice. "I've come up with an alternative plan. It'll solve all our problems if you've the guts to follow it." He tapped the GPS. "This is what is called a global positioning device. It'll tell me when we near a boat I've anchored in the middle of the ocean. Our course will pass near it. I doubt the boat will be more than a quarter of a mile away when we leave the *Stardust*."

"Leave the *Stardust*? Make sense, Matt."

"You know I have to leave here before we dock. Well, I'm leaving earlier than you expected. The two big changes I'm making to our plan are that you can leave with me, and still leave your husband alive."

Amy shook her head. "That's crazy."

"No. It's sane. What we were plotting was crazy. Don't you see the beauty of what I'm proposing? Before we were going to have David disappear into the ocean. But we can achieve the same effect by having *you* disappear. You can be the one the whole world thinks fell overboard and drowned. Only you will live. We will jump overboard together and ride this Farallon to the boat I've set in place. I've brought wet suits for both of us. At this time of the year the water isn't that cold, anyway. We can get to my boat in a few minutes. I have clean towels and a change of clothes waiting for you. We might reach the marina before the *Stardust*. David probably won't wake until then. Either way, it doesn't matter, we'll be long gone before then. Jimmy included." He added, "Plus we'll have the money."

She stared. "You have lost your mind."

He met her gaze. "You keep saying you love me. Yet you keep doing stuff that would convince any reasonable person that you're a liar. Here's your chance to finally prove your love. You have to follow in my steps. You have to pretend to die like I did. You have to vanish from normal society. To be with us, you have to sacrifice everything you know. That's the deal."

Amy started to speak and stopped. She understood deals. Probably the devil had explained them to her the day before she was born. She saw that he was serious and that was not a quality she liked in him. Her whipping boy had grabbed hold of the strap. And he was a strong sonofabitch. But exactly how strong she needed to know.

"What if I say no?" she asked.

"I'll take the Farallon and jump overboard and get to my boat. I'll disappear with Jimmy. You'll never hear from us for the rest of your life."

"You're bluffing."

He shrugged. "Try me."

She acted wounded. "Why are you doing this to me? Is it because of the other night? I explained all that. You talk about testing my love. What about your love? If you loved me you wouldn't force me to make such a horrible choice."

"The horrible choice is to commit murder. I told you, I'm not a murderer."

"But you kidnapped my son. Yeah, go ahead, say he was your son as well. That is bullshit. You lied when you said you knew Jimmy was yours when you stole him. How do I know you're not lying now?"

"This is a simple plan. What is there to lie about?"

"How do I know? You throw this in my face at the last minute. Why can't we just go ahead with what we planned?"

"I told you why. I don't want to kill David. Besides, we could be seen on the deck. One backward glimpse and Gilbert could put us both in jail for the rest of our lives. Do you want to risk that?"

"Gilbert won't see anything."

"Those are just words. In any murder, if something can go wrong, it usually does. You're out of your league when it comes to this stuff. Trust me, I know."

She wrung her hands. "But our son will grow up an outcast."

"He'll grow up with his parents. That's the important thing. He doesn't have to be an outcast. We can move to another country. We have enough money to do whatever we want."

"Three million is not much nowadays."

"When someone talks that way, no amount of money is enough."

"Why didn't you tell me about this ahead of time?"

"It would have spoiled the drama."

She was angry. "How can you joke about this?"

"You accuse me of being a coward. It takes courage to make a decision. I'm asking you to make one. But the decision to kill your husband is a delusion. Murder is just another cop out. What I'm offering you is a life free from tyranny. You have lived in fear of David for too long. Now you can escape. He will not search for you if he thinks you're dead." Matt stood and hugged her. "Come with me, Amy. This can be a great adventure. I'll take care of you. Don't be afraid."

She looked up at him with a tear-streaked face. "But I am afraid."

"I was afraid when it came time to leap from my plane. But you know what I thought?"

"What?"

"I thought of you. Then I was able to jump."

She trembled in his hands. His hatred of a moment ago was replaced by a wave of love. Her voice came out small and vulnerable.

"But I'm not you. You're a genius. I'm just a stupid girl."

He kissed her forehead. "We're not so different. After all that's happened, that's got to be the reason we're still together. Go back upstairs. Return to bed if you want, as long as you don't wake David. You have thirty minutes to make up your mind. If you're not back down here by then, I'll be gone."

She pulled away and studied his face. "You're not bluffing."

He shook his head. "I can't afford to bluff anymore."

She left and he put on his wet suit and checked the power supply in the Farallon. He laughed softly to himself. This time he was sure he saw the light in her eyes. She would come with him, he knew it. She really did love him.

Ten minutes later his cell phone rang. He had the volume down low.

"Hello?" he said. Why would Amy call?

"Simon? It's Kathy." She sounded out of breath.

He had forgotten he had given her the number. "How are you?"

"Fine. How are you?"

"Great. Hey, would it be okay if I called you later? I'm sort of busy right now."

"No. We have to talk now," she said.

"What's the matter? Are you sick again?"

She sighed audibly. He thought he heard a motor in the background.

"I'm not sick. But I'm not far behind you. Maybe a quarter of a mile."

Matt swallowed. "Excuse me?"

"I'm following your boat."

"What? Why?"

"Because you're in danger. Amy's setting you up."

A knife made of ice went through his chest.

"Who are you?" he whispered.

"My name's Kelly Fienman. I'm an FBI agent. I know your name is Matt Connor. I was initially assigned to the case surrounding the kidnapping of Amy's child. But I'm no longer working on that case, not officially. This might be hard to believe but I'm here as a friend. I know what you've gone through and I want to help you."

He did not feel merely disoriented. It was as if his head had suddenly detached from his neck and fallen on the floor. He was afraid to move, afraid he might kick himself in the face. He had to strain to speak.

"You're FBI. You cannot be here to help me."

"I'm a renegade. No one at the Bureau knows about you and Jimmy. They think you're dead and I'm perfectly happy to leave them in their ignorance. You have to believe me. I've risked a great deal to help you. What I'm doing now could destroy my career. I could go to jail. But I've done this for you because I care about you. I can't let you kill David."

"I have no intention of killing David."

"Matt, I bugged your apartment. I know your plot in detail."

"You bugged my apartment? When?"

"On Monday, when you were out walking Jimmy."

"Wow."

"Matt," she began.

"No," he interrupted. "You only heard what I told Amy. I'm not going to kill David. I'm not a murderer. I'm not a kidnapper. Jimmy's my child. I'm his rightful father."

"I know that about Jimmy. But if you're not going to kill David, why are you secretly stowed aboard his boat in the middle of the night?"

"I'm here to test Amy. To see if she loves me."

"She doesn't love you! It's what I tried to tell you the other night. When you love someone, you don't keep betraying them."

"No. You don't understand Amy. The two of us spoke a few minutes ago. I have set it up so we can disappear without a trace. She only has to trust me and everything will be all right."

"Did she say she will trust you?"

"Not exactly. I just sprung it on her. She has to think about it. But I know she wants to be with me."

"Matt, you're a brilliant man. You're a good man. But when it comes to Amy, you're a complete idiot. Also, you've compromised everything you believe in to stay with that bitch. No decent woman plots to murder her husband."

"David is an asshole."

"The world is full of assholes. Amy is one of them. They don't deserve to die. Matt, listen to me. You have to get off that ship."

"I'm going to get off. In about twenty minutes."

"How?"

"I have it all worked out." He paused. "But I don't know if I should be telling you this."

"I could have arrested you a dozen different times if I wanted. Right now I'm the only friend you have in the world. Tell me how . . . oh shit!"

"What's the matter?"

"Amy just came on the deck with David! They're standing at the rear of the boat!"

Matt suddenly felt very small. "So?"

"She's going to kill him! Stop her!"

"No. He just woke up is all. She won't kill him. She wouldn't do that to me."

"I can see them both in my binoculars! She's pointing down into the water! She has him leaning over the side of the boat! Trust me, she'll push him over the side!"

"No."

"Matt! She's setting you up!"

He might have gone into shock right then. Later on he was not sure. In the last year he had performed a number of complex feats under extraordinary pressure. He had never failed the test. But in that moment he felt his world topple. Everything he knew was false. Kathy was Kelly. Amy's love was not love. And he was about to go to jail for a murder he had planned but never intended to commit. Kelly was right, it was crisis time, and he could not react. He could not even speak.

The moment stretched forever and ran into a stone wall.

"Your loving girlfriend just pushed her husband overboard," Kelly said quietly.

Matt drew in a ragged breath, straining to get control of—at least— his body. "Can you see him in the water?" he asked.

"No."

"How long will it take you to reach here?"

"*You* are pulling away rapidly. But I can reach David in two minutes."

"I can get to him in less time. I'll see you there."

Matt did not give her a chance to respond. He tossed his equipment into his bag and grabbed his Farallon and rushed out of the storage room. He ran right into Amy. No sorrow on her face now; she positively glowed.

"What have you done?" he demanded.

She acted innocent. "Nothing."

"You just pushed David overboard!"

Curious to see such innocence transform into wrath in the space of one second.

"I did it for us!" she swore. "Because you were too much of a wimp to do it!"

"Damnit! Now I have to save him!"

She grabbed his arm as he turned. "You save him and you ruin us both!"

He stared at her. "I don't care anymore, Amy. I just don't care."

Then he was gone, up the stairs, out onto the deck, and in one mighty leap, he went over the side of the boat. If Gilbert saw him, he would have appeared as a flying wraith. Saltwater engulfed him like a bath thrown on a dreaming man. The Farallon smacked his face as he hit the surface. The most crucial thing was to get his bearings. David would have fallen into the wake of the ship, but without any moonlight even that was difficult to find. The ocean was as black as an underground lagoon. He couldn't even find Kelly's boat. Secretly trailing them, she was probably running without lights.

So she was an FBI agent who was risking her career to protect him? That was sort of cool in a way. He didn't know why he believed her since she had obviously lied to him from the moment they had met. Maybe it all came down to an inherited flaw: he was a sucker for a pretty face. He was curious how she had managed to find him.

But David—he had to save the jerk's life. He could not make the mother of his child a murderer. Perhaps David was so drunk he would not know Amy had shoved him overboard. Matt still had on his disguise. He could pretend to be a lifeguard out on late-night patrol. David was pretty stupid, he might fall for it. Especially if an FBI agent who happened to be sailing by supported his story. Then again, if Kelly had worked on the kidnapping case, David would recognize her. What the hell, he would worry about the details later.

Matt powered up the Farallon and raced in the opposite direction of the *Stardust*, which was already close to vanishing. He ran the underwater propulsion device on the surface. He did not have a face mask, and he made no effort to look underwater. But he had his diver's light out and panned the area in front of him. The churned foam was already settling into the expanse. Matt estimated David to be three hundred yards behind the spot where he had jumped into the water. Yet it was possible the current created by the *Stardust* had swept the bastard along. There was even a chance David was aware of the gravity of his situation and was swimming after the *Stardust*. Matt desperately hoped to find David on the surface; his only hope. If David had gone under, their chances of rescuing him would be close to zero.

A calm night. Yet he did not hear David shout for help.

Without landmarks, he had to time his estimate of how far he had traveled. When he had gone what he thought was three football fields, Matt paused and searched in every direction. He was surprised Kelly had yet to show, but understood that at night it was difficult to guess distance over water. If her binoculars were powerful, she might have trailed the *Stardust* by as much as a half mile and not realized it.

Matt could not find David. The strength of the panic that swept over him stunned him. For over a year he had thought about little else than hurting the guy. Now he felt sick to his stomach because he could not save him. That was the reality about death, though—it dwarfed all other human preoccupations. Amy had said she had put Valium in his liquor. He had probably been semicomatose when she had shoved him overboard. The shock would have been overwhelming. A lungful of seawater and he would have sunk. Still, Matt searched.

"David! David!" he shouted.

Kelly showed a minute later. Her ship was without lights. There was a short on the control board, she explained. She could not turn them on.

"I don't even have a flashlight," she called to him in the water. "I was looking for him back a ways."

"Is that where he went in?" Matt shouted back.

"I don't know! You have a light. Do you see anything?"

"No. I better come aboard. My light will work better if I'm out of the water."

Kelly lowered a ladder. He was aboard with his equipment in less than a minute. But that was a lot of wasted seconds when they were talking about a drowning man. Matt ordered her to return to the spot she had originally searched. She was the one who had seen David go overboard. Her estimate of David's location would be more reliable than his.

Still, there was nothing. While Kelly steered left and right and shouted until she was hoarse, he raked the light over the surface. The *Stardust*'s wake was history—he couldn't find bubbles, never mind foam. He began to wonder if they were even near the correct spot. As a last resort he had Kelly kill the engine and remain silent. The night settled over them like a smothering blanket. He stood beside Kelly as the boat faintly rocked from side to side. The stars were bright holes in a black canopy. There was no worse tomb than the sea. It buried what it swallowed.

Chances were David would never be found.

"I have a GPS." He held up the phosphorescent display on the instrument. "We should note our location."

"Are you giving up?" she snapped.

"Yes."

"I don't want to give up. I know you hate him. You don't care if he dies. David! David!"

"Kelly." He tried to stop her. She shook him off.

"Leave me alone! David!"

He grabbed her and held her firmly. "I do care, honestly I do. But we're too late. He's dead."

She lost her strength and sagged in his arms. "This is my fault. I could've stopped this. I should have stopped this."

"Why didn't you?"

"I wanted to give you a chance to redeem yourself."

"I don't understand."

She lowered her head and sighed. "I need a few minutes."

They sat across from each other. He felt it prudent to save his flashlight batteries. The night was black enough to see the outline of their souls. Kelly wept quietly and Matt could not think up a single thing to cheer her. It was not as if he could reminisce with her about what a great guy David had been. But the fact of his death, so near to where they sat, began to sink in. Matt feared he had no place to put his hate. He was afraid it might turn onto Amy.

He could not believe what she had done.

He realized most of his disguise had washed off in the water.

Eventually Kelly began to talk. She told about being called out on the kidnapping case, meeting Amy and David, the long wait for the ransom demands. It fascinated him to hear what the FBI had gone through the day he snatched the money out from under their noses. It made him feel both guilty and absurdly pleased.

But there were gaps in Kelly's narrative. She explained how she figured out how he was still alive, but went to great lengths to hide other aspects of her investigation. He wondered if it had anything to do with the injuries she had sustained. He was not sure how the timing of all these events overlapped.

"I didn't get to Catalina until nine o'clock," she concluded. "I had a hell of a time finding you. Finally I spotted you hanging out at the old casino. I considered stopping you right then. But I wanted to see what you'd do." She gestured to the sea. "Because of that decision, David died."

"David died because Amy killed him. But I gave her the knowledge to kill him. I'm more to blame than you."

Kelly shook her head. "I'm a law enforcement officer. If I had upheld the law, he would still be alive."

"Why was it so important for you to see what I would do next?"

"I told you, I care about you. I moved into the apartment complex to understand you better. My husband dumped me. Amy dumped you. You're a wanted kidnapper, but in a strange way, I sympathized with your plight. I didn't want to just put you in jail."

"You went to a lot of trouble for a stranger," he said.

"The first time I saw your picture in the paper—beside the article explaining the circumstances of your death—I didn't feel you were a stranger."

"Why?"

"There was something in your face. I can't explain it."

"Are you going to put me in jail now?"

"No."

"Maybe you should. What happened tonight can get you in serious trouble. Let the blame fall on me if it must, I don't care anymore."

"I'm not going to do that."

"Then you have to forget about tonight. Neither of us was here. We leave my original plan with Amy in place. To the cops, to the FBI, David just got drunk and fell overboard."

Kelly shook her head. "I can't do that. You kidnapped your own child and you had reason to do so. I can bend the law for a moral dilemma. But Amy murdered her husband out of greed and malice. She has to pay for what she has done."

"How are you going to prove it?"

"My word against hers. I'm an FBI agent. I saw her kill David."

"How are you going to explain being out in the ocean in the middle of the night?"

"Let me worry about that," she said.

"It might be better for all concerned if I just take off with her."

"Are you crazy? She just tried to set you up for David's murder."

"You don't know that for sure. I was the one who switched plans on her."

"Matt! One day she'll shoot you in the head and you'll try to defend her. That girl is rotten to the core. You can't be thinking of still staying with her."

"Well, no." He paused. "What do you suggest?"

"How were you going to get off the *Stardust*?"

"I have anchored a boat about five miles in front of us, slightly south. With Amy, I hoped to bail overboard and ride the Farallon to it. Just disappear, make it look like she was the one who died."

"You honestly believed she would go for that?"

"Yes. She might have if I hadn't sprung it on her at the last second. Killing David might have been a panic reaction."

"Amy does not panic. Amy schemes. If you even talk to her again, she will try to pin David's murder on you. She will do so anyway."

"Are you going to arrest her?"

"Yes."

"She could go to jail for life."

"One can only hope. Matt, you have to let her go. I guarantee she'll try to convince everyone you're still alive. She'll take the police and FBI to the apartment complex."

"No one there will recognize me as Matt Connor."

"You know better than that. You'll have left hair or scraps of skin in your place. You'll have to clean it thoroughly, every blessed inch. Then get your son, get the money, and get out of town."

"There are loose ends. Amy might suspect you were the Kathy I talked to."

"Unlikely. Why would she make the connection?"

"I would," Matt said.

"She's not as smart as you. She'll be up for first-degree murder and she'll focus on you. She'll make herself look like a fool. Also, I have an ace in the hole. I might be able to convince my partner he was with me tonight and saw Amy push David overboard. That would seal her fate."

"He must be a hell of a partner."

"He'll want to protect me. He knows what I've gone through lately."

"The bad man? The one who hurt you?"

She hesitated. "Yes."

"Who was that guy? Is he still alive?"

She shook her head. "I can't talk about him right now. We need to find your boat and get you on your way. Just promise me you won't try to contact Amy ever again."

Matt hesitated. "I'll stay away from her."

"You swear to God?"

"Yes."

She patted him on the shoulder. "You're free now. You can put this nightmare behind you. Don't worry about Amy, she'll get what she deserves. I'll see to it."

"You can't let her go?" he asked.

"No way."

They located his boat a half hour later. The GPS led them straight to it. Matt turned on his light and lassoed the ship with a spare rope. He was able to transfer his equipment without having to get wet again. Kelly wanted him to get back to the marina ahead of her. She believed Amy would opt for silence when she was arrested. She intended to push Amy in that direction because she wanted to give Matt as much time as possible to clean up his apartment and get out of town.

"Shampoo the carpet if you can," Kelly said as they were about to part. "Use plenty of chemicals. Remove my bugs. They're on the living room lamp, behind the kitchen painting, and under your bed. You'll have a few hours at least. Amy will get a high-priced lawyer who won't allow her to say a word until he's present."

"You'll immediately accuse her of pushing David overboard?"

"Yes. I'll have to in order to arrest her."

"What if your partner refuses to back you up?"

"David is missing. Plus, as far as Carl Techer will be able to tell, Amy was the one who set up this whole trip. She was the one who insisted on going back early. With my finger pointed at her, things will not look good for Amy. Don't worry, I'll be all right."

"I do worry. I hate that you were dragged into my life."

She smiled and hugged him. "I don't."

He held her tight in the center of the swaying boat. The wind had stirred; irritating waves chopped their flank. A sorrowful moon had appeared; it hung on the horizon like a broken plate. Kelly squeezed him hard and quickly kissed his lips as they parted. He was surprised at the sparkle in her eyes.

"You should have been my partner," she said.

"Instead of one of the bad guys?"

She kissed him again, for a second longer. Was her kiss better than Amy's? His head was in a whirlwind. He only knew that he hated to let her go.

"Call me. Okay?" she said, as she stepped back.

"Sure, Kathy. I mean, Kelly."

"You better get another alias. You've worn Simon out."

"No. You wore him out. But you saved Matt."

"Matt saved himself. Take care of yourself. Give my love to Jimmy."

"Will I see you again?"

She sniffed and wiped her eyes. "I don't know."

Another hug, another goodbye. He climbed into his boat. As he rode away, he saw her wave. He did likewise and thought he heard her call his name. But already the shock of the night's events was settling in, and he realized the seriousness of Amy's plight. He would probably never see her again.

The very thought brought intolerable pain.

CHAPTER SIXTEEN

Kelly crept toward the unearthly glow of L.A. as seen from the sea at night. The wind and chop continued to increase. Her stomach complained. She had to call Charlie but feared using her cell phone. If Amy's case went to trial, her lawyer could subpoena the phone records of the witnesses to her crime. It was these pesky little details that could mess up the rest of one's life. She would have to wait until she could get to a pay phone.

At the harbor she got a break. No one was around when she docked the boat. No witnesses to worry about. She left the marina before calling Charlie from a phone beside a deserted gas station. Sounded like she woke him.

"Charlie. I need your help."

"Why am I not surprised?"

"I need you to listen to a story I have to tell. Please don't get mad at me."

He yawned. "I'm listening."

She gave him the straight scoop. To get his assistance, she dared not lie. Charlie would interpret the latter as an act of betrayal. He did not interrupt once. She worried he might have fallen asleep. No need for concern—her tale was sufficiently shocking. She ran out of words and there was a long pause.

"Are you done?" he asked.

"Yes. Don't yell at me."

"No need. I'm going back to sleep. I'll visit you in jail in a few days. Bye."

"Wait! I need your help."

"Really? Odd, but you don't act like a person who needs anyone's help. In fact, you behave precisely like the megalomaniac Slate accused you of being. How could I possibly help such a person?"

"Charlie, I don't have time for this. Amy murdered her husband. I cannot let her get away with it. I need you to back up my story."

"How?"

"Say you were with me tonight."

"You want me to lie?"

"Yes."

"Why?"

"I'm on a leave of absence. You're in charge of this case. If you explain that you've been following Amy because you suspected her of acting in collusion with the kidnappers, the court will believe it."

"Why would I have you with me?"

"We're partners. Even while on a leave of absence, I like to hang out with you."

"You don't need me."

"Vicki will eat me alive if you're not there to back me up."

"Vicki's a vegetarian."

"I'm in trouble here!"

"True. You rented a boat to go over to Catalina. I wasn't with you. There's a witness."

"You went over earlier on the ferry."

"I don't have a ticket stub."

"We can find one at the marina. People throw them away."

"Why would we follow them over to Catalina of all places?"

"You wanted to go over for fun anyway. That's another reason I came along."

"Sort of a business and pleasure trip?"

"Are you making fun of me?"

"No. I'm making like a defense lawyer."

"Yes. Business and pleasure."

"And we just happened to witness a murder?"

"Yes."

"Were we expecting to see a murder?"

"No."

"Then why were we following their boat back to L.A.?"

"We were following them, period. When they left, we left."

"Sounds weak."

"What do you suggest?"

"I have two suggestions. The first one is to tell the truth."

"I can't do that. Matt will get arrested and I could too."

"I understand. My second suggestion is to drop the whole thing."

"What? Matt said that."

"And we both know how smart he is. Amy's life is not worth yours."

"She murdered her husband! You only say that because David was an asshole."

"The reverse is closer to the truth. You only protect Matt because you like him. But Matt committed serious crimes. He kidnapped a child and stole lots of money. He's at least as guilty as Amy. And I for one do not appreciate that this guy I've searched for all this time will get to walk—just because you happen to have a crush on him."

"That's not it, seriously, Charlie. I protect Matt because he's essentially innocent. Amy is completely guilty. I cannot let her go free."

"We have laws so that we don't have to make these decisions ourselves. But as far back as the Acid Man, you have taken it upon yourself to decide how these laws are to be enforced. You're a romantic. You're insightful. You're also an idiot. You shouldn't be an FBI agent."

She sighed. "I don't disagree. But what am I supposed to do now? Amy cannot go free. You see how unfair that would be."

"To take her down could cost us both our careers. Is she worth it?"

"To me she is." Kelly paused. "I shouldn't put you on the spot like this. Forget it, I'll bring her in myself. You go back to sleep."

"Okay."

"Charlie?"

"You're so full of shit. You know I cannot hang you out to dry."

"Will you help me?"

"Yes. If you'll answer one question. Did you sleep with Matt?"

"I slept with him twice. We never had sex. One night was because I was very sick. He took care of me. The other night was because, well, he was losing his mind."

"I'm losing my mind right now. Do I get to sleep with you?"

"Maybe. When this is all over."

"I have another question. Are you sure David is dead?"

"Yes. How could he be alive?"

"It's summertime. The water is cool but not freezing. He could survive for an hour or two if he was in good shape. At least a few boats must have come back from Catalina this late. Maybe someone picked him up."

"But we searched for him. He went under."

"From what you said, you didn't search long. You could have been looking in the wrong place."

"I wanted to look longer. But Matt said he must be dead."

"Who hated David more than Matt?" Charlie asked.

"Point taken. I don't think it's an issue."

"What is this Matt like anyway?"

Kelly considered. "He's very mysterious."

She returned to the marina. Charlie met her in the far corner of the parking lot forty minutes later. Using a pay phone, they called the police and Coast Guard. Kelly had no trouble conveying where David went overboard. Matt had given her his GPS before splitting. The Coast Guard moved to dispatch a boat. The police would arrive in minutes. Kelly and Charlie asked a security guard where the *Stardust* was docked. Walking toward the boat, Charlie was in a foul mood.

"The police are already asking why we didn't call sooner," he said.

"We just got back to shore."

"Why no cell phone?"

"You didn't bring one. Neither did I."

"Vicki knows I sleep with my cell phone."

"We're not talking to her tonight."

"That's what you think. She's our boss. We have to wake her. I want to be the one to arrest Amy."

"Fine. I want her to remain silent. Give Matt more time."

"Damnit!" Charlie stopped and glared. "We're not going to bend over backward to protect this guy. We say we don't know anything about him. That's the extent of our helping him. Understood?"

There were times when Charlie could not be pushed. "Understood."

He shook his head. "Why am I doing this for you?"

"Because you love me. You love justice. This is just."

"This is illegal. You're a loose cannon. I don't love that about you."

She put her palm on his heart. "She cannot go free."

"Do you have your gun?" he asked.

"No. Will I need it?"

They resumed walking. "She did just murder someone."

The *Stardust* was impressive, long and sleek. Kelly assumed they were all still aboard, but that was not a given. She was curious to meet the powerful Carl Techer, who just happened to be suing the FBI because of their botched ransom surveillance. Vicki said he was an older version of David's prick. As they walked up the plank, they were met by Captain Gilbert Perkins—the Gilbert Amy had spoken of. He was still at work swabbing the deck. Tall and blond and dressed in white, he looked like a hospital orderly who kept a surfboard in the closet. She smelled alcohol on his breath. Charlie flashed his badge.

"FBI. Are Amy and Carl Techer here?" Charlie asked.

"Yes. What is this about?"

"Go get them."

"They're asleep."

"Wake them," Charlie said.

Amy was the first to arrive. Maybe she had not been sleeping well. She wore a dark red robe over her pajamas. Her calm impressed Kelly. Amy had obviously learned long ago how to use the natural innocence of her face to best advantage. Gilbert was still digging up the old guy.

"Agent Fitzsimmons, Kelly. What's this about?" Amy asked.

"Where's David?" Charlie asked.

Amy looked around. "I don't know. Gilbert just woke me up. David wasn't there."

Kelly could not contain herself. "You know where he is. My partner and I trailed your boat tonight. We saw you push him overboard."

Amy paled and her lower lip trembled but she kept the face.

"I don't know what you're talking about," she muttered.

Carl Techer appeared seconds later. His hair was dark and there was way too much of it; the thing was an expensive wig. He moved with more authority than his son. His eyes were a steely blue that reminded Kelly of ice water. He looked fit for his age, but there was a slight quiver to his mouth and cheeks. Wall Street's money had yet to figure out how to buy time. The man had to be in his late seventies. He wore the same color robe as Amy. That was odd.

"What's going on here?" he demanded, a strong rasp.

Charlie held out his badge. "FBI. We regret to inform you that your son has been murdered. Your daughter-in-law pushed him overboard approximately three hours ago, in the middle of the ocean."

Mr. Techer snorted. "David's not dead. He's sleeping down below."

"Mr. Techer," Kelly said gently. "David's not aboard your boat. Both my partner and I saw Amy push him overboard not long after you left Catalina. We were trailing you and we attempted to rescue David but we were too late." She added, "I'm very sorry to have to tell you this."

Mr. Techer looked to Amy. "What are they talking about?"

She gestured helplessly. "I don't know. Gilbert woke me up a few minutes ago. David wasn't there."

Gilbert appeared on deck. "I can't find David anywhere."

Mr. Techer was bitter. "Who are you people to come here at this time of night?"

"We're two of the agents assigned to the kidnapping of your grandson," Charlie said. "We were trailing your party tonight because we've suspected for some time that your daughter-in-law was personally involved with the kidnappers. We have no direct proof of that at this time, and it may have nothing to do with the murder of your son. But we're here to arrest her." He drew his gun and pulled out his handcuffs. "Amy Techer, you are under arrest for the murder of your husband, David Techer. Please put out your arms while I handcuff you and read you your rights."

You have the right to remain silent. You have the right of an attorney. If you cannot afford one . . . Mr. Techer tried to stop Charlie from cuffing Amy but Kelly held him back. Mr. Techer shouted that he would find Amy a lawyer and get to the bottom of this nonsense. Amy cast the old man a pleading look as Charlie and Kelly led her away. Kelly wondered what the deal was between those two. She stayed close to Amy's side as they walked toward the parking lot. Two black-and-whites had arrived. Charlie had made the arrest because he had supposedly witnessed the crime, but as Amy's offense did not yet fall under FBI jurisdiction, she would be turned over to the LAPD.

"You know I had nothing to do with the kidnapping of my son," Amy hissed.

"I advise you to remain silent," Kelly replied.

"You know!"

Kelly couldn't resist. "I know more than you dream. You're going to fry, girl."

■

VICKI HAD Kelly and Charlie in a room at the police station in Santa Monica. The type of box where prisoners were interrogated. The walls peeled green and the overhead light could have been used in an epileptic test center. Vicki made them repeat their story several times. Kelly did not appreciate the harsh treatment but Charlie played it cool. At least Vicki was not taping. She had some sense of loyalty.

"This sounds like a bullshit story," she said as she leaned into the corner. Kelly had never seen her in sweatpants before, no makeup. The bags under her eyes needed coffee. They had awakened her an hour ago. Charlie spread his hands.

"This is what happened," he said. "The guy's dead."

"I believe that much."

"And what exactly don't you believe?" Kelly asked.

"Don't get self-righteous, Fienman," Vicki snapped. "I don't know everything that happened last night, but you're scaring me again. You're not even supposed to be on the job."

Kelly shrugged. "I went along for the ride."

"How long you been riding this particular wave, Charlie?" Vicki asked.

"How long have I suspected Amy? From the beginning."

"You keep your opinions to yourself. Why did she kill her husband?"

"For money," Charlie said.

"Is that why she helped kidnap her own kid?"

"Maybe," Charlie said.

"I don't buy it," Vicki said.

"Why not?" Kelly asked.

"Stupid question. You have no proof."

Charlie spoke. "David's dead. We saw her push him overboard. Later, we can sort out how his murder might relate to the child, Jimmy. For now, Amy Techer is guilty of murder one. What other proof do we need?"

"Her lawyer's going to rape you guys."

"Hope he's good-looking," Kelly said.

Vicki scowled. "What's your problem? I'm trying to help you."

"Do we need help?" Kelly asked.

"Did anyone ever tell you that your attitude sucks, Fienman?"

"Dirty Harry would take that as a compliment," Kelly said.

Vicki simmered. She was no fool when it came to schemes. Yet they might have convinced her, despite her reservations. There was no obvious hole in their story. Why would they lie? Not even Vicki, for all her street smarts, would suspect the whole truth. It was too preposterous.

"Where's Amy now?" Charlie asked.

"They've detained her," Vicki said. "That's all. She hasn't been booked. She hasn't made a statement. I hear a lawyer's coming."

"Do you know who?" Charlie asked.

"Somebody expensive. Mr. Techer's in her corner."

"Curious," Kelly said. "Amy just murdered his son."

"She was probably banging father and son," Vicki said.

"I wouldn't put it past her," Kelly muttered.

"If she has the kid, I wonder where she keeps him?" Vicki said.

Charlie and Kelly chose to remain silent.

Vicki let them go a short time later. Kelly and Charlie regrouped in a coffee shop down the street. Caffeine and sugar—breakfast of chumps. Charlie had jam with his toast and Kelly ate a doughnut, her first since the Acid Man had performed exploratory surgery on her intestines. She felt reckless—a half dozen digestive enzymes would take care of the lard. Charlie kept shaking his head as he ate.

"She knows we're hiding something," he said.

"She only suspects. It's her nature."

"Did you need to piss her off?"

"That's my nature. Hey, she should be giving us a medal."

"That's why you keep getting into these situations. I should just buy a box and pin them on your chest."

"Don't poke my breasts," Kelly warned.

"Did you let Matt touch them?"

"No. He touched my scars though. I was embarrassed."

"How did you explain them?"

"I told him this black guy named Charles whips me when I misbehave."

"I wish." He drank his coffee like he was swallowing medicine. "They will book her, won't they?"

"They have to. But come Monday, she'll be out on bail."

"No way. We're talking murder one, two eyewitnesses."

"In the middle of the night, in the middle of the ocean. Two witnesses that had no right being there. And there's no body, don't forget that rather crucial point. Before this is all over, her lawyer will be pointing the finger at us for the murder."

"You think Mr. Techer's going to buy her freedom?" she asked.

"I know he won't blink when it comes to a million or two in bail."

"Do you think she's doing him?"

Charlie nodded. "Matt knows how to pick them."

■

FOR KELLY the weekend was long. She had her daughter to watch but didn't have Tony. All she had to do was say the word, though her ex had changed tactics. Now he acted cool. When he dropped Anna off he hardly spoke. Probably thought he had begged enough. She was tired of all the games.

Matt was not answering his cell. That was not necessarily a bad move on his part. For his sake, she hoped he was long gone. As far as she could tell, Amy had not raised his name to the police—that would not last. For her own selfish reasons, she felt abandoned. She missed hanging out with Matt. He had brought a crazy edge to her life.

Kelly seldom thought of David. The indifference made her feel guilty.

The Coast Guard did not find his body.

Amy did not appear before a judge until the following Tuesday. Kelly and Charlie came for the show. Carl Techer was present, along with Stan Trent, a fiery import from the Bay Area who wore suits from Italy and a smile from the North Pole. Trent had won eight huge murder cases in the last ten years, lost none. He had even gotten a client named Gage Huntly aquitted, and Gage had chopped off his mother's head and stored it in his ice cream truck after dipping her hair in chocolate syrup. Vicki said Trent could defend the Devil before a jury of Pat Robertson supporters, and still win.

Barry Pallor was the judge, two hundred and fifty pounds of legal insight and personal frustration. He was on his fifth wife; she was a prison guard. Number four had been a lawyer; she was forever suing him for back alimony. Pallor was rumored to be soft on pretty women and hard on blacks who looked like his second son—which was the reason wife number three was no longer around. Pallor was white Irish.

Amy appeared fittingly wounded. Trent played hardball. He pushed Pallor for reasonable bail. He read off his reasons as if they were stock quotes: the accused had no motive; she had never been convicted of a crime before; she had suffered enough with the recent kidnapping of her child; the agents who had witnessed her supposed crime were of dubious character. Kelly liked that last one but it annoyed Charlie. The guy the District Attorney's office had sent over argued like a munchkin before the wicked witch. He was so inept Charlie wondered aloud if Carl Techer had already managed to pull strings higher up the food chain. Paranoia, perhaps, but they were in Pallor's court, and with all those exes he had plenty of alimony to pay. Maybe he could be bought. Amy managed to raise her head a few times to bat her long lashes. Pallor seemed to like the look of her.

Bail was set at eight hundred thousand. Amy was free, for now.

She smiled at Kelly as she left the courtroom with her family. Mocking.

"What does she know?" Charlie whispered in her ear.

"She's going to put it on Matt," Kelly said.

"I wonder."

"What?"

"What if Matt helps her?" Charlie asked.

Kelly dismissed the notion. But when she failed to reach Matt over the next two days, she began to wonder herself. Amy knew how to project innocence in the midst of irrefutable guilt, and Matt had the discrimination of Don Quixote when it came to playing the hero. Pallor had ordered Amy not to leave town, but who tracked her? Kelly figured if Amy had Matt advising her on how to vanish, they could blink and the girl would be gone. But Kelly consoled herself that even Matt was not that stupid.

Until Amy did disappear.

CHAPTER SEVENTEEN

Matt told Amy to meet him in Century City. She had called an hour after she got out of prison. He was not sure why he chose the spot. They used to see a lot of movies there, go to the restaurants. Fond memories—did he think they would protect him? Yet he doubted she would try to trap him. She was the one in the box. Now she needed his help. Even if she thought to betray him, she would bide her time.

Amy disarmed him the moment they met. She burst out crying. What was he supposed to do, yell at her? He hugged her instead, whispered in her ear that everything was going to be all right. Of course, a normal person would have screamed in *his* ear that he was comforting a monster. He was curious how she would talk herself out of this one. She could have shot the President of the United States and brought the First Lady tea and cookies the next day and gotten away with it. Sitting on an outside bench, she launched into her prepared speech.

"I know you told me you didn't want to kill David. But after you gave me that ultimatum, I freaked. You threw everything we had planned out the window. When I went back upstairs to our cabin, David was sitting up awake. He started yelling at me about sneaking off to talk to Gilbert. I never told you he was jealous of him. He had been thinking of firing Gilbert for some time. When he yells at me like that—for no reason—I just feel so much hatred. It came over me strong right then. But I hid it, I smiled and told him that I had seen some dolphins swimming in the water behind us. I grabbed his hand and insisted he take a look. That's how we ended up on the deck."

"Going to see dolphins is a long way from committing murder," Matt said.

"There were no dolphins, not then. I just wanted to get him out of our cabin. I half expected you to rush out of the shadows and push him overboard. But you didn't, and David dropped his anger and tried to kiss me. I pushed him off but he kept insisting. After all I have put you through, I couldn't bear the thought of you seeing that. I knew I had to finish it once and for all. Then an amazing thing happened. A bunch of dolphins suddenly appeared in the wake. Acting all excited, I pointed them out to David. He was still pretty stoned. When he leaned over to see them I just, you know, gave him a little shove."

Matt felt that was the stupidest lie Amy had ever tried to run by him in her life.

"You lifted him up by the seat of his pants and threw him into the water."

Amy switched from victim mode to annoyance. "I did it as much for you as for me. Your ultimatum was bizarre. I didn't see how it could work. But right then I had David exactly where we wanted him. I couldn't pass up the opportunity. Not for a second did I imagine you would try to rescue him."

"I wasn't able to rescue him."

"Matt! He would have killed us both if he discovered what we've been doing almost every afternoon. He was not a nice man."

"He did not deserve to die."

"Who deserves anything that happens to them? All I am saying is that David is the last person on earth you should feel sympathy for."

"Except for the minor fact that he was just murdered." Matt stared at her. "You haven't felt *any* guilt over his death?"

Amy hesitated. "Of course it bothers me. When I was in jail, it was all I thought about. He was a lousy husband but he was a good father. He had his qualities. But on the whole he was a horrible person. He would have ruined our lives. The way I see it, it was him or us. And I chose us."

"You think I was a coward not to do it myself?"

"I'm not saying that."

"You don't have to say it. You think it. You should have thought a little deeper before you murdered your husband. I warned you. What can go wrong usually does."

"Who could have imagined that we were being followed?"

"They probably thought you had something to do with Jimmy's kidnapping."

"Do you think they followed me to the apartment?"

"No. They would have arrested us both. They would have wanted me more than you."

Amy shook her head. "It's so weird Charlie and Kelly just happened to be there."

"They're smart agents. They might have misunderstood what you were up to, but they knew you weren't being straight with them. I warned you about that as well."

"Don't keep saying I told you so. It doesn't help."

"I understand."

Amy took his hand. "You have to help me."

"What kind of help are we talking about?"

"Don't act like that. I'm facing life in prison. My lawyer, Trent, is supposed to be the best. But he'll need something to work with if he's to get me off."

Matt spoke quietly. "Have you told him about me?"

"Of course not! I wouldn't do that. How can you even ask?"

"Because of what you just said. You're facing life in prison. Anybody might crack under such pressure. The closer the trial gets, the greater the pressure will get. You're smart enough to know that if you bring me up, you'll throw a wrench into the whole works. You might be able to mess up the prosecutor's case enough to create reasonable doubt. Don't look so offended, you must have thought about it."

"I swear to you, I haven't."

"I don't believe you. That's why I want to warn you that I've removed every trace of evidence from my apartment. The police can scan that suite with a microscope and they won't find a single hair or scrap of my skin."

Amy turned on the tears again. "Why are you talking to me that way? You're supposed to love me. I would never betray you to the police. It doesn't matter to me that it was your plan that got me in this horrible situation."

"I never planned to kill David. Oh, maybe for a day or two. But then I came to my senses. I refuse to take responsibility for what you did. Don't try to hang it on me, Amy."

"I just told you I'm not! Look, let's stop fighting and figure out what we can do."

"There's only one way out of this mess. You have to jump bail and disappear with Jimmy and me."

She froze. "I would be a fugitive."

"True. But that's better than spending the rest of your life in jail. Anyway, with money, life on the run isn't so bad. We leave the country and we can lead a normal life."

"Where would we go?"

"Anywhere." He did not want to specify just yet.

She thought a while. His suggestion had not surprised her. In jail, she had no doubt worked every angle. "Do you really think I'll be convicted?"

"Probably. Even if you try to bring me into the picture. Don't get mad—I have to say it! Two FBI agents saw you push David overboard, not me. Their word will carry infinite weight. You'll get life without parole. I don't care how expensive your lawyer is. The jury won't care either."

"You sound so cold."

"I'm being realistic. Come with me, we'll have fun."

She continued to struggle. "When?"

"Right now."

"That's ridiculous. I have stuff at home I have to get."

"Is Carl staying there?" he asked.

She hesitated. "Yes. But he goes to bed early. When he's asleep, I can pack and sneak out. You can pick me up."

"How do you know your house isn't being watched?"

"Do they do that?" she asked.

"They can. It's another variable I'd rather not deal with. We can buy clothes on the road."

"But I have all my jewelry and stuff. It's worth a lot of money. You'll be able to tell if they're watching the house. You can check it out, call me on my cell, tell me if it's safe. Otherwise, I want to get my stuff."

"Then you'll come with me?"

She took a breath and squeezed his hand. "I'll come, if you'll have me. I'm really sorry about all this, Matt. I know I've screwed up your life."

"To put it mildly." He was amazed how happy he felt right then. Amy was back in his life again. He leaned over and kissed her and she responded warmly. When they were through, he sat back and shook his head. "You're trouble."

"I'm a handful," she agreed. "Where's Jimmy?"

"In a safe place."

"Where?"

"You'll see him tonight." She knew he did not trust her. "What time should I come by?"

"Midnight. That will give me time to pack after Carl passes out."

"Keep your cell close. I'll ring twice as I cruise by. Don't answer, just be ready."

"No problem." She paused. "What do you know about that Kathy woman you talked to at the apartments?"

"I told you about her. She's a psychologist, in the middle of a divorce." Kelly had underestimated his girlfriend. Another reason to get Amy out of the country. He could not let Kelly get buried by their problems.

"What did she look like?" she asked.

"Oh. She was blond, short, a little chubby."

"I thought you said she was pretty?"

"She is pretty. Just slightly overweight is all. Why do you ask?"

"Just wondering," Amy said.

■

AFTER AMY left for home, Matt's newfound relief was tempered by old anxieties. It was noon; he had twelve hours to kill. Jimmy was in Fresno with Lupe—a hideaway he had never shared with Amy. The boy had been there since before Catalina. The money and diamonds were there as well. He had never let Amy see it all. His trust in her was not exactly at an all-time high. He spoke to her with love, but he knew that at some point near the start of their trip, he was going to have to test her love.

Test it in a way that would resolve all doubt.

He had lost his disguise and had yet to replace it. But he did not want to leave the city only to have to return. He killed most of the day watching a succession of movies. One was about the kidnapping of a rich wife who was cheating on her husband. He found the story implausible. Hollywood was seldom able to convey the subtlety that drove the insane. In the end everybody was setting each other up. The popcorn was good, though, the theater used real butter.

Near twelve he made his way into Brentwood. In reality he did not believe the police would spare men to watch Amy. That was the purpose of bail—to set a financial and psychological wall against fleeing. Family was supposed to serve a similar goal. The latter was not a small matter when it came to Amy. She was still close to her father and sister. He did not underestimate that bond. She could try to talk him into another plan. But there was no other plan possible that did not involve the resurrection of Matt Connor.

He scanned the neighborhood carefully before slowing in front of her house. He rang twice and she answered. It was these little deviations from their arrangements that made him nervous.

"I'm ready," she said.

"Hurry. I'm out front."

She appeared a minute later with three large suitcases in tow. He had to get out to load them in the trunk. He did not tell her that they could not travel with so much stuff. She would have to learn that her new life was an austere one. The lesson could wait. He was happy just to have her in his car. As they pulled away from her house, she leaned over and kissed him.

"You're my knight in shining armor," she said.

"You're my Guinevere," he replied.

Guinevere and Lancelot. And poor Arthur.

They headed north toward Fresno. Amy asked where they were going, but did not seem interested in his response. As he drove the long stretch of Interstate 5, she snuggled close and dozed. He could not resist reaching over and touching her soft face. It never seemed to disturb her. There was nothing in life that brought him more joy than watching her sleep beside him.

He kept an eye on his rearview mirror. A few times he imagined they were being followed. There was this one car—it appeared to stop when he did. Headlights were not always easy to tell apart. He might have just been paranoid.

Dawn was around the corner when they reached Fresno. He was in and out of the trailer in minutes. To hide his changed appearance, he told Lupe he'd had cosmetic surgery. He wore a hat, dark sunglasses, and heavy bandages on his face. He also told Lupe she could stay there as long as she liked. He had paid for the place through the next year. She gave him and Jimmy a big goodbye kiss. But he did not invite her outside to meet Amy. The less Lupe knew the better.

Jimmy was overjoyed to see them. He chatted in an alien tongue as the sun rose. Amy was in great spirits. There was no denying how much she loved her son. With the three of them together, Matt felt a profound sense of comfort. The morning air was free of yesterday's stress. The Connors against the world—they were embarking on a great adventure. His fatigue melted into euphoria. The warmth of the sun felt like magic on his heavy eyes. Amy offered to drive but he told her to relax with Jimmy. Soon the two of them were back asleep.

He kept the dough in the trunk. Amy had asked to see it.

No, he had told her.

He did not want her to see that it was only a third of the ransom.

He was not a complete idiot.

A test, a test . . . Something would present itself.

After Fresno, he turned east toward Tahoe. He considered stopping beside the lake for a couple of days to rest but something drove him deeper into Nevada. Eventually they had to head south and cross the border, but he figured the later the better. The police and FBI would intensify their watch on the border for the next month. But they would not be able to afford to keep it up forever.

The line of sand between Mexico and Texas would be the place to leave the U.S. He had studied the area not long after snatching Jimmy. Security was a joke if a person had money, particularly if one was heading south instead of north. Too many miles and not enough honest border agents. Until they left the country, his plan was to camp out in the middle of nowhere and let the days pass. It was summer, nights were warm, and the three of them needed a break.

That same day they drove all the way across Nevada before cruising into a small town in western Utah called Susanville. He had not had time to buy camping equipment, and Amy was desperate for a shower. A motel room paid for with cash did not sound risky. Coming up on another sunset, they stopped at a Motel 6 and registered under the name Jones. He had a few cheap IDs left to burn. But he would have to buy quality passports and credit cards in Mexico if they were going to fly. In the end he had his sights set on New Zealand.

"Can you get us diapers and milk?" Amy asked as they unloaded their stuff in the room. "I saw a Seven-Eleven on the corner as we came into town. Our room has a small refrigerator. Get a loaf of bread and some butter as well. You still eat cheese sandwiches?" It was odd, but he felt reluctant to leave them.

"Too many of them," Matt said. "Do you want fruit if they have it?" Amy ate tons of apples and melons—one way to stay slim. He had to be careful while they traveled. Unless he worked out an hour a day he put on weight. But he could jog anywhere.

"Whatever they have." Amy set sleeping Jimmy down on the spare bed and turned to hug him. "You must be exhausted. Why didn't you let me drive?"

"You can drive tomorrow."

She buried her face in his chest. "Are they looking for me?"

"Yeah. Don't go out for a walk. Don't talk to people. They'll have your picture all over the TV."

She squeezed him tighter. "I don't care. I feel safe with you."

He stroked her hair. "You are safe."

The words followed him out the room and down the street. In the 7-Eleven he felt restless. The clerk had to go in the rear to get the size diapers he requested and Matt had to restrain himself from yelling at the guy to hurry. He tried to identify the source of his anxiety. He had felt *watched* all day. The narrow vista his rearview mirror had afforded the last twenty hours had not soothed his nerves. He had not always seen a vehicle behind them, but there was this one white car—if indeed it was always the same car—that appeared to come and go. If someone was trailing them, he was a pro. He would have to have binoculars and extraordinary patience. Luck as well—Matt was no fool when it came to being tracked.

Yet it must be paranoia.

Where could *he* have picked him up?

At Amy's house for one place. If someone knew her, he might have figured she would run. But who understood her that well besides Carl or Kelly? Carl had plenty of cash—he could have hired people to keep tabs on his daughter-in-law. Yet why had he gone to all the trouble to get her out of jail? True, his doubts in her innocence might have grown since he wrote the check for her bail. From what Matt had heard, Carl was a horny devil with a high credit limit. He believed that loyalty could be bought for the same price as sex.

When all was said and done, though, it was not logical. If Carl had tagged Amy, he would have stopped her the second they had picked up Jimmy rather than risk losing his grandson. Kelly was an even less likely suspect. Granted, he had promised her he would not see Amy again, but

Kelly would have no pressing motive to trail him a thousand miles. She wanted Amy to pay for murdering David, but she was more concerned that he get away free. Also, Kelly would have tried talking to him. She had his cell number. He had planned to call her himself, when he had a spare moment. No, Kelly was not in that white car, there was no such car.

But what if there was another person out there who knew Amy?

Understood her like he did. Saw what drove her.

The moment he turned his back, that person would come for her.

"Forget the diapers, I don't need them," Matt called to the clerk. Suddenly the walls of the convenience store were no different than the prison bars he had once feared. He practically ran from the 7-Eleven onto the quiet Main Street of Susanville. There was not a soul on the road, and had there been one, they would have called the police the moment they saw his crazed face. It was half a mile back to the motel and it felt like a light year.

The evening sky shone with unearthly clarity: Venus a hard diamond in the west, the mountains a black silhouette in the east. As he ran the four blocks to the motel, it was as if a world of questions spun in a universe without answers. Mere intuition did not drive him. His panic was the product of deep gestalt. Somehow, he knew the missing element in Kelly's explanation of how she had found him had magically reappeared. He had no idea how it connected to his sudden fear, he only knew the association existed. Kelly had spoken of a bad man who had done bad things. She had said she had stopped him. But she had not sounded sure of herself.

Plus there was truth beyond subconscious links.

While they had unpacked, someone had parked in the motel lot.

In a white car. Funny how he had only just remembered.

With the walk up the road, and the frantic run back, he had been gone a total of ten minutes. In that time a monster had sprung. When he burst into the room, he found Amy tied to the bed. Roped to the four corners and spread like an animal that had been chosen for gutting. A circle of duct tape gagged her mouth. Her shirt and bra had been removed. The only light in the room was a weary glow from the bathroom. The sight of Amy's bulging eyes and ashen face skewered his already tumbling brain. He registered the fact that Jimmy was still asleep on the other bed, and that there was a fourth person in the room. But he did not instantly react to the threat of the intruder. He could not move because he did not understand. A hooded figure held a vial above his girlfriend's naked chest, a priest completing a sacrament. The vial was polished silver. It caught the feeble light from the bathroom and transformed it into a hypnotic spark usually glimpsed in celebratory moments. Even the cloth over the guy's head did not immediately register as a disguise. The hood was white, very clean. Didn't good guys wear white, Matt asked himself? He simply could not believe what was happening.

His paralysis lasted perhaps two seconds.

He rushed toward the hooded figure as the guy turned to toss the contents of the vial his way. An image of Kelly's scarred abdomen flashed in his mind. The liquid in the container could not be healthy. Instinct told him to raise his hands to take the brunt of the concoction but he overrode it. Instead, he dropped to the floor—his momentum caused him to roll forward. Out of the corner of his eye he saw a steaming mist pass overhead. Even before the stuff hit the mirror attached to the chest of drawers, he knew it to be highly corrosive acid.

And the guy had been about to pour it on Amy's chest.

Several things happened simultaneously. Matt smashed into the guy's legs and an explosion of melting glass and damp fire erupted four feet away. The hooded figure fell close to his right side and Matt felt a unique sensation along his other side—a torturous burn ignited under a canopy of rain. The half-spent drops of acid had bounced from the mirror and raped his flesh. He did not know how badly he had been hurt; he would have to worry about it later. His position was awkward—it was difficult to turn over and rise. Already the guy was back on his feet. From his position on the floor, Matt was trying to estimate the guy's height when he caught the tip of a boot on his jaw. A friendly kick in the face. Matt saw red; blood swelled over his chin. The guy tried to kick him again.

Matt grabbed the guy's boot and twisted. His assailant screamed and staggered to the side. Matt jumped up quick. Off to his left the mirror melted into a puddle of soggy ash. Smoke rose from the ruined wood.

The stink was oppressive, possibly fatal. Matt feared to breathe, but the guy had regained his balance and needed attention. Matt kicked him hard in the balls. The guy grabbed his jewels, but did not double up as much as Matt would have preferred. It was only then Matt realized the guy had on gloves. No doubt special gloves that could weather corrosion. The guy reached over and grabbed the contaminated chest of drawers and toppled it toward the floor. Matt had no choice but to leap back. The room was not large. He ended up tripping onto the bed, on top of Amy.

The stumble was enough. The guy ran out of the room.

Matt stood to go after him. Then Jimmy cried and he changed his mind.

The following minutes were almost as crazy as the previous ones. Using his Swiss Army knife, he cut Amy's binds and tore the tape off her mouth. He tried to hug her to reassure her but she pushed him away and grabbed Jimmy. She huddled in the corner of their son's bed. When he tried to touch her, she recoiled. Her eyes were swollen; her breath came in hysterical gasps. With the fumes from the acid, he wanted to get her and Jimmy out of the room. He tried telling her of the danger but she stared at him like he was Jack the Ripper. In the end, the best he could do was ventilate the room by opening all the windows and turning on the fan. He tried to prop open the door and she shrieked. It broke his heart to see her trembling like that.

Fortunately the fumes from the acid abated swiftly. He figured there was no significant danger in breathing the air. But the room continued to stink—overcooked chemicals mixed with scorched wood. He was relieved Amy's flesh had not been touched by the gruesome brew.

His left side was sore but he did not need a hospital. Judging by the damage the vial of liquid had done to the chest of drawers, they were talking about an extremely active acid. The drops that had splashed on his side had burned through his clothing and the top layers of skin. No question he would be left with a few scars. He suspected the drops had been minute, however. A few grams of the stuff probably would have eaten into his internal organs. He wondered who in the world manufactured such corrosive material.

310

He shuddered to think what would have happened if he'd been one minute late.

Outside, the white car was gone.

No one came to check on all the commotion.

After thirty minutes he was able to coax Amy into their car. She huddled over their son and wept quietly, which he took as a good sign. She was coming out of shock. He loaded their luggage quickly and pulled away with the motel door left open. He felt no need to leave cash to pay for the damage.

He drove two hours farther into Utah. He took only back roads, and knew for a fact they were not being followed. During that time Amy hardly spoke. Then again, what was there to say about the bizarre attack? Yet Matt continued to feel certain it was tied to Kelly's past. Acid was one of the few things on earth that could have created the type of scars on her abdomen.

Why had this person come after Amy?

What connected Amy to Kelly? Was it him?

Close to midnight he stopped at another motel. He was not exactly sure where they were and didn't care. Amy continued to hold on to Jimmy as if he were a shield. She no longer pushed Matt away but made it clear she wanted to sleep alone. The room had two beds. He was not surprised when she passed out seconds after lying down. Amy had the unique ability to blot out everything and sleep.

While they slept, Matt took his cell into the bathroom and called Kelly.

"Matt! Where are you?"

He spoke softly. "Are you alone?"

"Yes. I was in bed. Is Amy with you?"

"Yes."

"Damn." She sounded disappointed.

"I know what you're going to say."

"Does it matter what I say? Half the cops in California are looking for her. Never mind the FBI."

"We're not in California."

"I figured as much. Don't tell me where you are. I just want to know that you're all right."

"We're fine, for now. But we were attacked this evening."

"Attacked?"

He described the incident from beginning to end. He gave as much detail as he could. But when he finished she did not even reply. He had to prod her to speak.

"That's impossible," she gasped.

"Is it the same person who hurt you?"

"It can't be. I shot him in the back of the neck. He's paralyzed from the neck down."

"Says who?"

"Says his doctor. He's a quadriplegic."

"I would check on that diagnosis if I were you."

"Matt. How did this person find you?"

"I was going to ask you the same question."

"I have no idea."

"The guy must have picked us up when I swung by Amy's house. He must have known her address. How's that possible?"

Kelly hesitated. "The person I crippled was given the FBI file on the kidnapping of Jimmy Techer."

"This guy is FBI?"

"No. He's a serial killer. But we . . . well, I used him to help find you."

"Kelly. This guy is crazy. How could you have *used* him?"

"I'm sorry, I was desperate to find you. And this man, besides being nuts, is also brilliant." She added quietly, "Without his help, I never would have found you."

It took Matt a moment to swallow her excuse. Yet he did not think she was lying. "It's all right, it's done. Why is he after Amy?"

"I'm not sure. Like I said, it can't be him."

"It has to be him!"

"Okay. Let's say for a second it is him. He would want Amy because she cheated on you. That's what drives him, or at least that's what drove him in the past. It's possible he admires you for what you've accomplished so far. At the same time, he thinks you lack the will to completely punish Amy for her sins."

"Her sins?"

"He sees every woman who betrays her spouse as a sinner."

"Are you saying this guy is trying to do me a favor?"

"In his own mind, yes. If it is, in fact, him."

"Can you ask him not to bother?"

"I'll check on his whereabouts the second I get off the phone. Are you in a safe place now?"

"Yes. I took steps to make sure we weren't followed. But I took steps to begin with. Whoever this guy is, he's smart."

"He must have an accomplice," she muttered.

"What do you call him?"

"The Acid Man."

"Nice. I don't know if I buy the accomplice idea. It would be hard to find two psychopaths in this world with such similar tastes in torture."

"It's the only explanation," Kelly insisted.

"Do you have any idea who it might be?"

"Yes. How strong was he?"

"He was a grown man. But I don't think he was as strong as me. He ran at the first chance."

"Did he wheeze?"

"Not that I noticed. Tell me who you think it is."

"No. You'll just go after him."

"Damn right. Better hit him before he hits us again."

"It doesn't work that way. I can't tell you who this person is. It was a freak occurrence he was able to get to you and Amy in the first place. It won't happen again. Besides, I'm going to take care of this situation once and for all."

"You'll need my help."

"You're the one who needs help. Look who you're traveling with. The police and FBI think you're dead. You can move around without fear. But with Amy beside you, you're exposed. Someone will spot her."

"I'm aware of that. I'm taking steps."

"That's only half the problem. Amy herself is more dangerous to you than the authorities. She was born to hurt you. Even if she doesn't want to betray you, she will. She can't help herself. Trust me, it's her nature."

"People can change."

"Amy will never change! And you swore to me you'd stay away from her."

"I'm really sorry about that. It's true, you did so much for me and I gave you my word. But for good or bad, I love her. I can't let her spend the rest of her life in jail."

"She's a vampire."

"We'll see. Besides, you cannot go to trial. That story you cooked up with your partner won't hold up under close examination. You were so anxious to help me and get back at Amy that you underestimated the number of loose ends. I've been thinking about them all day—there's just too many holes in your account. Amy's jumping bail helps you as well."

"I know the law better than you. I'm willing to take my chances in court."

"You shouldn't have to take any chance on our account. My problems with Amy are my problems. You have your own life to live. But you have to let me help you with this Acid Man."

Kelly chuckled sadly. "You give good advice, but you never listen to it when it is offered to you. Amy is your dragon, this guy is mine. The sad truth is, from here on out, we probably can't help each other. We have to face our fears. I'll stop the Acid Man. You get away from Amy."

"I've given some thought to the matter. We'll see . . . we'll see what happens." He swallowed. "They're asleep in the next room. I better go."

She sighed. "Take care of yourself."

"Thanks. Be careful, Kelly."

Matt broke the connection, and sat alone with his thoughts.

CHAPTER EIGHTEEN

Kelly sat a long time in the dark after talking to Matt. His call had awakened her from a dream about Mai Mai. Only this time she was the treacherous wife, and she turned into a fish. When the phone rang, she had awakened shivering. And she was still cold, still scared.

There was reality and there was speculation. Obviously the Acid Man must have a partner, and yet, Matt had cut to the core of why the

Acid Man *could not* have an accomplice. Gene Banks was simply too strange. Who else, on the whole fucking planet, was capable of burning a hole in a woman's chest?

An interesting question. There were two dark answers.

His father. His brother.

Or was there a third answer?

She had asked about the strength of Matt's assailant because she suspected that Dr. Fred Banks had from the beginning brewed the acid, and had vicariously enjoyed the thrill of his son's exploits. A few facts supported the theory. Fred Banks had moved close to his son around the same time his son had begun to kill. He was a chemist and had the knowledge and skill to make the acid. He had suffered the same trauma as his son. He had in fact suffered it more directly than his son.

Plus he was a strange man. He had millions and yet he chose to end his days in a broken-down house. His emphysema was so bad he couldn't draw in enough oxygen to talk, and still he smoked like a fiend. What kind of doctor would do that? Had the whole illness routine been an act? Perhaps the guy was fit as a fiddle. Why had he run the moment Matt had him face-to-face? He could be fit, but still old enough and wise enough to know that Matt would kick his ass.

Kelly dialed Dr. Fred Banks's number. No answer.

More sitting in the dark. More speculation.

The brother was a question mark. Kelly had tried to find him and had come up with a dubious PO Box in New York City, nothing more.

"Where is Scott these days?"

"Forgive me. When he learned what happened, he asked that he not be brought into the matter. He has a good job and a well-adjusted lifestyle. For his sake, I would prefer to leave it at that."

"Does he have anything to do with his brother?"

"No. They have not spoken in years."

More lies? She suspected Scott Banks had changed his identity years ago. She had checked. He didn't pay taxes under his given name. He didn't have credit cards. He was a nobody born of a ruined family. The younger brother of a clever devil. Dr. Banks had said Scott did not trust Gene but maybe the reverse was true. He might have looked up to him.

Kelly was dying to call the Acid Man, see if he was at home. Impatience was an old weakness of hers. She had to force herself not to act impulsively. Calling now could alert him that she was in contact with Matt, give him an edge she might need. Tomorrow morning she could have the local FBI agent check with his around-the-clock help, get the information that way.

Kelly got out of bed and went online and tapped into her office files. The agent in the Midwest who had followed up on the case had made a notation on the doctor who had operated on the Acid Man. Of course Kelly knew the hospital where the doctor worked—she had spent plenty of time there. She was able to dial the number from memory. Even when she identified herself as an FBI agent, the hospital operator did not want to page Dr. Jack White. Seemed the guy was an asshole, at least when it came to being disturbed in the middle of the night.

"This is an emergency situation," Kelly said impatiently. "Lives could be at stake. You're to page him until he calls my number. Is that understood?"

"But he left strict instruction that he wasn't to be disturbed. He's not on call."

"We're not talking about sick people here. This is a criminal investigation. If you force me to explain again, I'll see that you're arrested."

That got the woman's attention. Kelly instructed her to have Dr. White call her other number. That way she was able to keep the operator on the line to make sure she was not forgotten. The doctor was stubborn. He did not respond until paged a dozen times. He started out by insulting Kelly but she cut him off quick.

"I don't have time for your attitude," she said. "This is a serious matter. You are to answer my questions clearly and honestly. Six months ago you operated on Professor Gene Banks. When he arrived at the hospital, he had a bullet lodged in his neck. It was I who put that bullet in him. I was also a patient in your hospital for some time. Does this ring a bell, Dr. White?"

He spoke dryly. "I remember him as well as you. What do you want?"

"What I am about to tell you is highly confidential. You're not to discuss it with anyone. That includes your wife or kids or associates at the hospital. You know Gene Banks had security around him in the days after his surgery. What you do not know is that he was a serial killer. His MO was very unique, and yet it has resurfaced in another incident in the last twenty-four hours. What I need to know is if it is medically possible he has regained the use of his limbs."

"No."

"You sound so certain. Haven't there been cases where people are paralyzed and then regain the use of their arms and legs?"

"Not in a case like this. The bullet you put in his neck tore through his spine at the seventh cervical vertebrae. I remember exactly where it was lodged."

"So what you're saying is that his spine was not merely bruised, but severed?"

"Exactly." Dr. White yawned. "Anything else?"

"Yes. Did you attend to Gene Banks after his operation?"

"I kept tabs on him."

"Did you know that when he completed his rehabilitation he had some use of his right hand?"

"Yes."

"Is that unusual?"

"Yes. Not physically impossible, though. But to suggest that he's now up and walking around is impossible. The man you're looking for cannot be the same man I operated on."

"Thank you for your time, doctor."

The moment Kelly set down the phone, she called Dr. Fred Banks again. Still no answer—no machine either. Her last talk with the Acid Man continued to haunt her. Tomorrow was July fourth. She'd had no intention of seeing him again so soon, yet he had been certain she would come.

"I told you. July fourth. A hero's day. Will I be seeing you?"

"I'm not sure I'll be finished with my business by then."

"You'll be finished. Neither you nor Matt will disappoint me."

The only explanation for his confidence in his prediction was that he had known ahead of time that he would do something to force her hand. The attack on Amy? How could he have predicted she would kill her husband? Then again, perhaps he'd had Amy under surveillance for some time. Her murdering David could have been insignificant in the greater scheme of things. The idea was disturbing. Who stalked whom? Kelly recalled the scratches on her own lock. Perhaps the Acid Man or his associate had watched Amy at the apartments—watched them all.

"I'm losing it," she muttered.

Gene Banks had known her private cell phone number, information the Bureau alone possessed. Did he have an ally inside? He had plenty of money. Almost anybody could be bought. If that was the case, every time she used FBI resources to further her investigation he would know. He might even know that she had just accessed his file.

"No!" she cried as she paced her apartment. She hadn't returned to the Malibu complex since Matt had split. She had not felt safe there. Amy could always have sent her lawyer sniffing. But now Kelly felt even more vulnerable in her original apartment. Opening her drawer, she pulled out her Glock to see if it was loaded.

She set it on the stand by her bed and tried to lie down and get some rest. It was probable she did pass out, at least for a couple of hours. But then she bolted awake as if struck by another remark from her conversation with the Acid Man. It was almost as if he had hissed it into her ear while she slept.

"We have a bargain. Independence Day is six days away. I would like to celebrate my freedom then. Close all the files so to speak. I'm sure you understand why."

July fourth was the day Mommy had died—that was obvious. But his use of the word *files* was more subtle. For one thing he used the plural. Also, she had given him a file that related to Amy. And tonight Amy had almost died. Coincidence?

"Hardly," she gasped.

It went deeper. In the Acid Man's own life, Amy was insignificant compared to Julie. His wife was key—he had told Kelly as much before he had tried to kill her. He had said he could not leave the country as long as Julie was alive. When Kelly coupled that perspective with his confidence that she would be with him July fourth, she realized that he had practically shouted at her that he was going to kill his wife the same day. That was why he had spoken in the plural. The files belonged to the women who had cheated on their men. There was perverse logic in the timing. Julie had behaved like Mommy. Julie should die the same day as Mommy.

Kelly reached for the phone and called Julie Banks and Michael Grander. It took a long time before Michael answered. He sounded sleepy. "Hello?" he mumbled.

"Michael. This is Kelly Fienman. Sorry to call so late. I've been worried about you and Julie. Is everything all right there?"

"Yes. Everything is fine. Why?"

"Julie's there? Is she okay?"

"Yes. She's right here. She's sleeping beside me. What's up?"

"Don't wake her. I'll explain later. I'll be in your area tomorrow, late afternoon. Mind if I stop by?"

"You're always welcome. Has something bad happened?"

Kelly hesitated. If she explained that there had been an attack that copied Banks's MO, then Michael would press her for details. He might call the police, or even the FBI, and she would be forced to tell what she knew about Matt. She could not risk that. The best she could do was to get to their house quickly. It was a gamble.

"I'll explain tomorrow. Go back to sleep. Again, I apologize for waking you."

"No problem," he said.

Kelly booked a flight to Ohio. The plane, a nonstop flight, left at six in the morning. She would arrive at her destination in the early afternoon. Then she would have to rent a car and drive at least an hour north. Alone, she thought, why did she keep acting like she had to go alone? She almost called the airlines back to make a reservation for Charlie, when something stopped her.

"You saw Banks."

"How did you know?"

"I have my ways. Don't worry, I'm the only one at the office who knows."

"Charlie?" she asked the walls.

The Acid Man had known stuff he should not have known.

Was her old and trusted partner talking to someone?

She did not call the airline and change her reservation.

■

THE PLANE ride turned out to be a reality check. Kelly sat beside a little Hispanic girl named Maria who had lost her mother in a car accident two years before. Maria was the same age as Anna; they even looked alike. Kelly chatted with her for hours; it brought up a deep longing for her daughter. She was forced to face the fact that her bold decisions were intrinsically selfish. Charlie had tried to tell her that. Heroes made lousy partners in business and in love. The courage to face death was not always a virtue. It could be the ultimate cop-out. If she died in a noble cause, she didn't have to face the boredom of day-to-day existence. It was partially the plainness of her previous life that had driven to her to become an FBI agent. And that same reason had been there when she had rushed off to confront the Acid Man. Yet she knew there were deeper rewards than those offered by dangerous thrills. When Maria spoke of her dead mother, she had tears in her eyes and Kelly had to hide her own grief.

What kind of life would Anna have without her?

She missed Tony. He had made poor choices, and his timing could not have been worse, but he was a decent man. Once she had been happy with him, and that happiness could return if she gave him another chance. She had to drop her bitterness and forgive. A simple prescription, but she knew it would take tremendous strength. Anna and Tony were real. Matt was a fantasy; a very dangerous one at that. Like many heroes, he had journeyed into the underworld. He had convinced the world he was dead. But he had not returned stronger. She did not believe he could ever leave Amy.

Once again the Midwest was an oven. The tall grass and mindless reeds which lined the highway seemed impossibly resilient. Without air-conditioning she would have melted. Her head throbbed—she had slept poorly. She had taken four Tylenol and her brain had snickered: gimme something stronger, babe. Some of those blue Percocets. But she dared not dull her senses. Today she reclaimed her life. Or else her life ended.

Trenton was her first stop. Parking in front of Dr. Fred Banks's house, the place looked like a bed-and-breakfast for coma patients. Pain gripped the paint and wood like a cloud of regret neither wind nor confession could eliminate. At the end of his tale, she had not felt sorry for Dr. Banks. Why? Because he had lied? Because he had given the world his murdering son, and warned no one? As she walked toward the front door, she felt pure dread.

She knocked and there was no answer. Unlike with Michael and Julie, she had not called ahead of time. She did not know the old man's schedule. Maybe he was out of the house. The afternoon sun was hot and ugly. She paused to wipe the sweat from her forehead and check her gun. Knocking again, she felt her impatience grow. She decided to break in, what the hell. It was not like he would sue her.

But the front door was unlocked. Sticking her head inside, she called out, "Dr. Banks? Are you there?"

No reply. Drawing her gun, she stepped inside and shut the door behind her.

The silence of despair. The house was so still she felt reluctant to inhale. The air was thick with imagined odors—they pierced her brain before her nose. Moving from the living room to the kitchen, she kept calling for the good doctor. The place gave her the creeps.

In the end she had to go upstairs. She didn't really want to because she had an inkling what she would find. There was an aura of death that extended beyond the five senses. She found him in bed lying flat on his back. His arms laid by his side; his eyes were open. His blue jeans and red flannel shirt were not pajamas. He had not lain down to die.

After checking the rest of the house to make sure she was alone, Kelly knelt by his side and put on a pair of plastic gloves. He was still warm. Rigor mortis had not yet set in. He had been dead less than six hours. Today of all days—made for a hell of a coincidence. Closing his eyes, she noticed a prescription jar on the table beside his bed.

Vicoden—a reasonably strong painkiller. A hundred-tablet jar—all gone. There was a pitcher of water handy, and a glass. Was this suicide? She studied his wrists and thought them bruised. But old people's skin was often black and blue. They were always bumping into things. If he had been smothered, his killer was skilled. She didn't know what to make of it. She was not a coroner, nor did she want to call one. If she did she would be forced to remain on the premises and answer too many questions. Later would be time enough.

Kelly searched the house. She did not know what she was looking for so she didn't find it. But there were interesting papers: financial statements that recorded huge balances; old letters from Gene Banks telling his father about the birth of Robert; a picture of Gene and Julie on their wedding day. Kelly found the latter so tragic she almost wept. She had never noticed before that Julie wore a ruby instead of a diamond on her fourth finger.

Kelly feared for Robert's future.

On the verge of leaving, Kelly found *the* syringe. She knew that's what it was—the one Dr. Banks had stabbed into his wife's heart the night she had died. It was in the dead man's desk in the study, bottom drawer on the left. Wicked needle, long and thick, with a half-filled plunger just waiting for another seizure. The liquid would have evaporated, over the years, but he had placed a plastic cap on it. Otherwise, he had saved the thing in exactly the same condition it had been in when his wife had died.

The fluid had not colored over the years. It might be worth testing.

Kelly slipped the syringe in her pocket and left the house.

CHAPTER NINETEEN

As Kelly drove toward Michael Grander's home, Matt and Amy were camped deep in Bryce Canyon National Park, Utah. Daylight-wise, it was an hour earlier for them than it was in Ohio. Even with the holiday weekend, they had seen no one in over four hours. Matt knew the park well—it had been his favorite rock-climbing destination since he was a teenager. Particularly in the heat of the summer: the hard red rock, the sculpted riverbeds, the magic of timeless vistas—he loved it all. The sun seemed brighter, the sky larger. Perhaps the isolation erected a bridge to another dimension, he did not know.

It was not only because Amy was a fugitive that he had chosen a secluded spot to set up camp. When he was in nature, he disliked being around people. He felt there was something intrinsically incompatible about humanity and untouched beauty. When he fell asleep beside a gurgling stream with a million stars in the sky, he felt at one with the universe, and almost, but not quite, believed in God.

He had bought camping and rock-climbing equipment before they had entered the park, and plenty of other supplies. He was certain they had not been followed. Yet Kelly had spoken of the Acid Man with superstitious fear. Matt believed there could be another attack, and he wanted to see his enemy coming from far away. Of course, if he believed everything Kelly had to say, he was already sleeping with the devil.

Not today, though; Amy was her old self, even better. She refused to talk about what had happened in Susanville, but she showed no signs of lingering trauma. They had spent the first couple of hours becoming familiar with their gear and playing with Jimmy in a nearby stream. Matt had taken them to the exact spot he and Amy had visited almost two years ago. He had thought the happy memories could be rekindled.

The afternoon was great. After playing with their son, and putting him down to rest, they made love on the bank of the stream, then dozed in the shade in each other's arms. But he spent at least half the time awake, staring at her face.

And he thought about a lot of things while she slept.

When she awoke he told her he wanted to go rock climbing.

That evening. The two of them. Before it got dark.

Her eyes flashed with interest. That would be lovely, she said.

CHAPTER TWENTY

The shadows lengthened across the Midwest. When night came, there would be fireworks. Kelly had called Michael and Julie again—they were expecting her. She found she was driving slower than usual. She should have been in a hurry, since the main reason she had come to Ohio had been to protect them. But her head was filled with doubts. Just when she believed she had the Acid Man figured out, she realized she knew no more than the women he had killed.

Agent Richards, who had followed up on Gene Banks, had only

called back a few minutes ago. Kelly decided *not* to ask her to check on where the Acid Man had been the previous night. As it was, Richards already thought she was weird, probably obsessed with the psychopath. Kelly figured she would know the truth soon enough. Plus, once again, she didn't want Banks to know she had spoken to Matt. And Banks *would* know if Richards called to check on him—the guy had a sixth sense.

Kelly wondered if she was going to kill him.

There was a question all profilers were taught to ask about a serial killer: what did they do? Obviously they murdered, but beyond that, what was their pattern? It surprised her how seldom she had bothered to examine the Acid Man's fundamental ritual.

He sought out women he believed to be unfaithful. He seduced them, tortured them, then killed them. He let the whole world see what he did by taping the murders. But he didn't let anyone see what he did with the women's bodies.

Why?

The obvious answer was that he was trying to hide something. Because if the bodies were located, this something would come to light. And since he did not want the bodies found, that meant he still had his secrets, perhaps even fears. Yet what did a man who begged to die have to fear? The paradox disturbed her.

Kelly dug deeper. How did he seduce women? He was handsome and charming, but his main tool was his clever lies. That was the cornerstone of his technique. He lied to women. Kelly almost felt like shouting the sentence out loud.

He lied to women!

Yet for some reason—ever since he had pointed his gun at her in his apartment—she had believed he was telling her the truth. He had seemed to care for her. In a way, he had made her feel special. But the women he had killed must have each felt the same to have risked so much to be with him. Kelly began to see her relationship with him in a new light. He had provided her with several extraordinary insights, about herself as well as Matt. But had all of that simply been part of an elaborate manipulation?

What was his ultimate goal?

He said he wanted to die. What if that was just another lie?

And if that was the case, did it mean . . . he wanted her to die?

"God, he sounded so convincing," she said aloud as she drove. She wanted to continue the mental examination but she was near Michael and Julie's house. Christ, if nothing happened tonight she would look like such a fool. Julie could call the local FBI office and report her for scaring them for no reason. There was something about that woman that gave her the creeps. Kelly wondered what a guy like Michael saw in her, besides her beauty.

Michael was out front with Robert, playing Frisbee, when she drove up. Robert appeared pretty athletic for a six-year-old. He caught a fast one from his stepfather. The steaming thermometer had yet to acknowledge the setting sun. Getting out of her car, her hot skin longed for California. She was envious of their attire—they both had on shorts and tennis shoes. Michael's tan muscles and natural handsomeness reminded her of Matt.

Robert stopped and stared as she approached. Michael rubbed his head and told him to get his mother. Robert did not run in the house but around the side. Michael tossed the Frisbee as she neared. She caught it with one hand. He was impressed.

"You must have been an athlete," he said.

"A frustrated one," she said. "I played basketball in high school."

"I was a cyclist. Used to pedal all over the place."

"Where did you grow up?"

"Idaho. Beautiful country out there."

She fanned herself. "I don't see how you guys stand this humidity."

"It's only bad a couple of months out of the year."

"Then the other months it's freezing."

He laughed. "We get the seasons. But you're not from the West Coast, are you?"

"No. I'm originally from Boston."

"You don't have much of an accent."

"I'm one of those people who can blend in anywhere." She looked west, toward the cloud-streaked sky—red rivers chased from the sky by a growing gray hand. In the bewitching light, the dark silhouette of the Acid Man's garden looked like a collection of shrunken elementals preparing for battle. Odd to think how a man who cared so much for plants could destroy human beings so easily. She added, "I hope I'm not disturbing your holiday weekend."

"We didn't have any major plans. But Julie—she's concerned. I'm sure you can imagine why."

"What did you tell her?"

"Nothing. Only that you were stopping by again." He paused. "What happened?"

"A couple were attacked in Utah yesterday. The assailant tried to kill the woman by pouring acid on her chest."

Stricken, Michael took a step back. "How is that possible?"

"We don't know."

"Was the woman hurt?"

"No. But the guy with the acid got away. Do you know if Gene Banks left his apartment yesterday?"

"How could he leave? He's a quadriplegic."

"So he says. We don't know that for sure, not anymore. If he is confined to his wheelchair, then the attack makes no sense."

"Do you think we'll be attacked? Is that why you're here?"

"It's a possibility. Especially today. It was forty years ago today that Gene Banks's mother died."

"Why is that significant?"

"He might have killed her."

"He would have been ten years old then."

Kelly nodded. "He had a rough childhood."

Michael was flustered. "What am I supposed to tell Julie?"

"The truth."

"I'm confused. *Who* are we in danger from?"

Kelly hesitated. "I honestly don't know."

"But if it's Gene—" he began.

"I think it would just be best if I stayed the night," she interrupted, trying to deflect how confused she was about what was going on. "If that would be all right?"

"I'll have to talk to Julie." He paused. "But don't you think you should at least check on what Professor Banks is up to?"

She nodded. The question was logical. "I'll go see him at some point. Where exactly is Julie?"

"She's swimming in the pond out back. Here, let's go get her."

They went around the side of the house. Along the way, Michael asked why the FBI had not sent out a local agent. He obviously thought her interest in the case a little too personal but was too polite to say. She brushed aside the question.

Julie was coming out of the water when they arrived. The woman was naked, and although she carried a large towel, she was not exactly covering herself. Ordinarily Kelly had nothing against skinny dipping, but Robert was all eyes. Michael might have sensed her discomfort. He took the boy inside and once again Kelly was alone with the wife of the infamous Acid Man. Julie dried herself slowly, taunting her to admire her fabulous body.

"Is the water cool?" Kelly asked.

Julie gestured to the pond, which was oval shaped, a hundred yards across at the narrowest point. "It's already too warm. And the water isn't what it used to be."

"What's wrong with it?"

Julie dried her ears. "It's kind of sticky."

"You must wonder why I'm here."

"I do wonder about you, Kelly."

"The feeling is mutual."

"You suspect I knew about my husband's activities. You're mistaken."

"Where were you last night?" Kelly asked.

"Here. Why?"

"A couple was attacked in Utah. Acid was involved. Do you know anything about that?"

"No."

"You don't look terribly surprised."

"Utah is far away. It can have nothing to do with Gene."

"How can you be so sure?"

"For obvious reasons. Why are you here? To protect us?"

"Yes. July fourth is a significant day to Gene. I believe there is a connection between what happened in Utah and you guys. I'd like to stay tonight, if that's all right with you?"

"If Michael doesn't care, I don't care."

"Tell me about Gene's brother, Scott?"

"I never met him."

"He didn't come to your wedding?"

"No. Gene said the two of them had a falling out years ago."

"Over what?"

"He never said."

"Did he talk about him at all?"

"No."

"Do you know where he lives now?"

"No. Ask Gene's father, Dr. Banks."

Kelly did not want them to know about her visit to the old house. Technically speaking, her entering, searching, and stealing—it was all illegal. Also, she had yet to report the man's death.

"Do you know anything at all about Scott?" Kelly asked.

"I know Gene loves him very much."

"How do you know this?"

"I heard it in his voice."

"When he talked about him?" Kelly persisted.

Julie ignored the question, wrapped herself in her towel. They walked toward the house. "Can I get you something to eat? To drink?"

"A cold drink would be nice," Kelly muttered, feeling frustrated.

The house was old colonial. Exquisite wood floors, rugs from Persia, soft brown wallpaper, a few nice antiques. The grandfather clock in the living room kept time like a pulse. No air-conditioning, though—they could have baked cookies on the coffee table.

Kelly took a chair by the front window and felt the outside darkness deepen. Michael brought her a glass of Sprite with plenty of ice. From where she sat, she could keep an eye on the long driveway that led up to the property. Her gun felt tight in her shoulder holster and she took it out and laid it on her lap. She apologized to Michael and Julie.

"I'm not trying to be dramatic," she said.

"It must be a pain to wear that thing," Michael said.

"You get used to it. Where's Robert?"

"Playing video games in the den," Julie said.

"My daughter loves them. Her favorite is *Raven*."

"Robert has that," Julie said, nursing a tall iced tea. She had changed into a casual red dress.

"How's your drink?" Michael asked.

"Fine." Kelly sipped. She wasn't that thirsty, after all.

They talked. Julie surprised her by chatting freely, at least making a pretense of being sociable. They discussed academic politics and space flight and the deciphering of the human DNA. The grandfather clock tick-tocked and time went by. Julie went to check on her son and found him passed out on the floor. Julie said he had been playing all day in the sun. Kelly was still surprised. At that age, she could not have gone to bed without seeing fireworks. But perhaps she was the one who had ruined their plans. In the distance she heard the boom of explosive powder. There was still a faint glow in the west. The real fireworks would start soon.

At one point there was a lull in the conversation. Michael turned on the TV and watched the news. Julie reached for a magazine and yawned. Kelly was left to stare out the window. The ice in her drink had disappeared. So had the last year of her life. She tried to remember how she had felt the morning before Slate had introduced her to the Acid Man. It was like trying to recall a past life. The thought reminded her of that story, "The Tears of Rati."

"It was said the karma of the three was so entwined that they would have to take another hundred births together to resolve it."

Triangles were tricky. She need look no further than the couple in front of her. She wondered what it would be like to be them—a part of such pain and despair. True, she was a vital element in the drama as well, but she had come later. She had not been a cause, merely a victim, and a savior.

It still annoyed Kelly that Julie had never thanked her for saving her life.

It was stuffy in the house. Julie continued to yawn and talked about going to bed early. Michael was unusually quiet. The TV was his world. Kelly set her drink aside and ran her fingers over the barrel of her Glock. Even in hell, she imagined, the steel would feel cool. It troubled her that the Acid Man had held her gun. Fortunately, he had mocked her by placing it on the table beside the bed where he had tied her down. That had been his single biggest mistake.

But had he made other mistakes? When he had talked to her perhaps?

"*But I need to bring Julie and Michael back here and show them your body. The acid works swiftly. Since he will be first, he needs to see how it will be for him.*"

The remark had always bothered Kelly. It did not fit into the Acid Man's basic scenario—punishment for those who betrayed. She had not betrayed her husband. Yet he had explained that he needed to kill her for the sake of Julie and Michael. He needed her as an example of the horror they were about to face. That rationale had always struck her as weak. Julie was the source of his pain. She was all that mattered to him. Michael was merely a pawn in the betrayal. Yet Banks had insisted Michael had to see ahead of time what was to befall him.

Naturally, Kelly could understand how he could hate Michael as much as his wife. She had despised Tony's new girlfriend. Nevertheless, it didn't add up. It should have been enough for Banks to kill Michael in front of Julie. And a disfigured FBI agent did not belong in the equation at all. A bullet in the brain of the brave girl should have been enough. Banks had deviated from his established pattern when he had tried to burn a hole in her heart. And change was unusual for a serial killer. In their sick minds, there were only so many options and that was it.

Michael flipped to CNN. Julie kept yawning.

Kelly wanted to speak to Michael but didn't have the energy.

Why didn't the Acid Man tell them where the bodies were?

What was he hiding? Not the condition of the bodies themselves, surely. Had he chopped the women into pieces or disemboweled and stuffed them with straw, it wouldn't have mattered to the Bureau. He knew that, he was a smart guy. So if it was not the state of the bodies he wished to conceal, it must be the location. It must be that the place they were buried revealed something secret he wished to keep hidden. Kelly tried to imagine what it could be and ran into a wall. Even if the women were buried here—in his garden, for example—what would that tell them?

On the other hand, his wife continued to live here, with her lover.

Her lover—supposedly the reason the Acid Man had killed in the first place.

Dr. Fred Banks continued to haunt her. His dead eyes staring at the ceiling that had sheltered him and his wife and his children decades ago. She thought of what he had told her, and what he had kept to himself. It still bothered her that, at the end of his life, he had moved within five miles of his son's home, to be close to his grandson. He had acted like he saw Robert regularly. Yet he had never met Michael Grander, not once.

It just didn't make sense. The whole family, were they all liars?

But why would Dr. Fred Banks go out of his way to lie to her about Michael?

He must have met him at least once, Kelly told herself. Probably lots of times.

Michael continued to watch TV. He drank coffee, black. He did not take milk or sugar. "Michael," she said to him.

He looked over. "Yes?"

"Did you ever meet Dr. Fred Banks?"

"No. Why?"

"Just curious."

"Did you talk to him?" he asked.

She hesitated. "Yes."

"What did you talk about?"

"Gene's childhood. Do you know much about it?"

"No."

"It's scary." She paused. "Why do you live here?"

"It's a nice place. Why should we move?"

"Because Gene lived here. Because he now lives only half an hour away."

Michael shrugged. "That doesn't bother me."

"Really?"

"Why should it? The doctors say he's paralyzed."

"That's interesting."

He turned off the TV. "Why is that interesting?"

"Most people would find it hard to live here." Kelly noticed that Julie had dozed off in her chair. Dropped her head with the magazine in her hands. Her long dark hair hung like a doll's. All serial killers without exception saw their victims as objects. "Julie?" she called softly. "Julie?"

"Let her sleep," Michael interrupted. "She's exhausted."

"I understand." Kelly coughed; she had a funny taste in her throat. She had barely touched her drink. "You were here last night when I called?"

"Yeah. Why?"

"You know phones nowadays. You can forward your calls and all that."

"I was here," Michael said.

"I believe you." She had believed a lot of things for a long time. Practically every word the Acid Man had fed her. She was in the Midwest because of him. She was in this house for that reason. Perhaps that's what he had wanted . . .

Nine months ago, to show Julie what was going to happen to her, the Acid Man had only needed to kill Michael. He had not needed to mutilate the brave FBI agent. Why had he done so? She kept asking herself the question over and over again.

Perhaps that was her problem.

What if she was framing the question backward?

Or what if she was simply asking the wrong question?

What if the Acid Man had never intended to kill Michael?

Michael studied her. "What's wrong?"

"Nothing."

"You're sure?"

"Yes."

He stood. "I have to get something in the kitchen."

"All right," she said.

The second he was gone, Kelly crossed the living room and knelt beside Julie. Grabbing the woman by the hair, she raised Julie's head and checked her closed eyes. White marbles, the pupils were rolled back. Julie had been drugged.

Kelly returned to her seat. She put her finger on the trigger of her gun.

Nine months ago would not repeat itself.

She was ready. She waited—a minute, two.

She did not see the gun until it had extended a foot through the window. He had come at her from the outside. She had not anticipated that.

There was ice in her head. Emptiness in her heart.

She could not believe it was happening again.

"Hand me your gun slowly, the barrel pointed toward yourself," he said.

She did as she was told. Michael stuffed the gun in his shorts and easily climbed through the window. He crouched on the floor in front of her. He looked rather pleased with himself. She had never seen that cockiness in him before.

"You know," he said.

She acted innocent. "I don't understand."

He smiled and pointed his gun at her forehead. "What is my name?"

He would just shoot her. "Scott Banks," she whispered.

He lowered the gun. "Very good. How did you figure it out?"

"An asshole smells like an asshole."

"Gene told me you had a sense of humor. I'll have to tell him what you just said. He'll like that."

"Does he like you fucking his wife?"

"He doesn't mind."

Kelly nodded to Julie. "Did she know you were his brother?"

"No. The cunt never suspected."

"Is that all she is to you?"

"What is this? A counseling session?"

"I assume you're going to kill me in a few minutes. You can indulge my curiosity for that length of time. Is that too much to ask?"

He gestured with his gun. His body language had undergone a metamorphosis. The sweet man she had known as Michael Grander was gone. The guy who gloated in front of her was worse than white trash. Only it was not that simple. He had not lost his sophistication, he had merely chosen to hide it. The distinction was important and made sense to her. He probably didn't have a genuine split personality—those were rare. He had lived a double life so long, it was just easy for him to switch from one personality to another. He acted like he had just lost forty IQ points, but it was an act. He could be as smart as his brother. Yet unlike Gene, Kelly sensed crudeness in Michael. She was furious that she had not seen it earlier. Just two minutes earlier.

"What do you want to know?" he said.

"I asked your brother this question. Why?"

"What do you mean?"

"You were a baby when your mother died. You were not directly affected by the trauma she caused your father."

"You're asking why I don't mind killing?"

"Yes."

He shook his head. "I don't know if Gene would want me telling you that shit."

A revealing remark. He only did what his brother allowed.

"Gene won't mind you talking to a dead woman," she said.

He snickered. "All right, shoot. What's your question?"

"Your childhood. How did your brother influence you? What kind of stuff did you guys do together?"

"You mean, weird stuff?"

"Yeah. Did you torture animals? Other kids?"

"Sure."

"Tell me about it. Tell me about the kids. When was the first time?"

He scratched his head. "I was about six. There was a girl who lived two blocks over. Her name was Brenda—she was ten or eleven. Gene and I talked her into going to an abandoned barn with us. She was kind of wild. I think she wanted to kiss my brother. Anyway, when we got to the barn Gene slapped her around a bit and then we did her."

"What did you do to her?" Gene would have been sixteen at the time.

"We fucked her and then we killed her."

"You were six. How did you fuck her?"

His eyes flashed with anger. "That's none of your business."

"How did you kill her?"

"Stuck a needle filled with vinegar in her heart."

Kelly repressed a gasp. She had not forgotten the needle in her pocket. But she had overlooked it while driving to the house, preoccupied as she was with her analysis of the Acid Man's psyche. The cap had fallen off, and as a result, the metal portion of the syringe had punctured the bottom of her pocket and was now pressing against her bare leg. The half-filled plunger was still in her pocket. Had the needle not poked through the material and sunk deep into her pocket, Michael—Scott—probably would have noticed it.

"How many girls did you kill?" she asked.

"I don't know. Six or seven. Usually, Gene would borrow our dad's car and put their bodies in the trunk. We brought them here. We weighed them down and dumped them in the pond. That's why Gene bought this property when he got older. It had been abandoned for some time."

"Did Gene dump the five women he killed with acid out there?"

"Sure."

Kelly understood. Gene had refused to reveal the whereabouts of the bodies because it indirectly pointed a finger at his brother, who refused to leave the land.

"Did you ever stick a needle in a girl yourself?" she asked.

"He let me when I got a little older."

"Did you enjoy it?"

"Sure."

"Gene taught you that it was a fun thing to do?"

"It was fun. He didn't have to teach me."

"When you were young—after killing the half-dozen girls—did you and Gene stop killing for a while?"

"Gene did. He didn't start again until he went after those rich cunts. But I lived in New York for a spell. I got around."

"How many did you kill?"

"I don't know. A few."

"Did you always use a needle?"

"No. That was Gene's thing. I cut them up. Whores, they were all whores."

"Are you a graduate student in literature?"

"Yeah."

"Were you also a chemistry major?"

"I have a master's in chemistry, like my father."

"You made the acid."

"Gene wanted the stuff. I made it for him."

"Did you kill your father today?"

"Yes. Smothered him."

"Why?"

"He knew too much."

"Did you try to kill Matt's girlfriend last night?"

"The guy walked in on me. He was a tough sonofabitch."

"Why did you want to kill Amy?"

"Gene told me to. He said she was no good."

"You followed them from Amy's house?"

"Yeah." He acted bored. "It's getting late."

"What made Gene start killing again?"

"Didn't he tell you?"

"He said it was because Julie had an affair with you."

"That was why he did it."

"I don't understand."

Michael was restless. He stood and waved his gun.

"I'm tired of these questions. We've got to move things along. You were hung up on where we put all the bodies. Now you get to hang with them. How do you want it? I can shoot you in the head or you can drown. It's your choice."

"How about you let me go?"

"That's not an option."

"Then I would prefer to drown. Are you going to kill Julie as well?"

"Yes. Got to do it." Keeping the gun on her, he backed to a desk and pulled out a roll of duct tape. Using his teeth and his free hand, he yanked off a two-foot piece. "Stick out your hands."

There was no point in arguing with him. His eyes had gone remarkably flat. He could have been a six-foot-tall insect for all the emotion he showed. He could shoot her in the head and not blink. She stuck out her hands. He was as skilled as his brother. He wrapped them tight without disturbing his aim. He went to cover her mouth and she shook her head faintly.

"That isn't necessary," she said.

"All right." He glanced at Julie, who had toppled sideways on the couch. "I better take care of you first. Stand up. You run and I shoot you in the lower back. Then you die very slowly. Understand?"

She stood. "Yes."

He retreated to the same drawer and pulled out a box of green garbage bags. She understood his routine. He would seal her in the bags with heavy rocks and wade out into the pond and let her go. The simple disposal method was effective—Kelly knew from classes at Quantico that it often took decades for plastic to disintegrate. Yet there must have been some leakage. Julie had said the water felt sticky.

Obviously the brothers planned to leave tonight. With all their files closed.

Michael took her by the elbow and led her outside and across the grassy field toward the pond. She considered going for the needle but it was in an awkward position—especially in relationship to her bound hands. He had her in his left hand, a Glock in his right—the same type of gun as her own.

He had been in her apartment in Malibu. He had swapped guns with her. He had probably wanted her weapon as part of a backup plan, in case he had to shoot Matt in the head after pouring acid on Amy. Then the bullet and the gun would have been traced back to her. Those twisted brothers, they thought of everything.

Underfoot the grass was thick. She stumbled three times and he yanked her back into line. Christ to the cross—but there was a huge difference. Her death would serve no purpose. Her terror was almost outweighed by her bitterness. Once again she had rushed in like the big hero and in the process had fucked up royally. If Charlie could see her now, he would die. God, if she hadn't had the audacity to mistrust her old friend. He would be with her now—on top of these jerks—and Michael and his weird brother would probably be dead.

Night had fallen; the black sky hung over the pond and failed to reflect back a single star. It might have been her imagination, but she smelled rotten eggs. Hydrogen sulfide—she remembered her college chemistry. She noticed a structure off to the right, at the edge of the property. The odor came from that direction. Probably a laboratory set up by the brothers to mix their love potions. And Julie never went in there once?

What a perverted mind Julie must have. Would Michael wake her up before he killed her? This woman he pretended to love? Kelly tried to console herself. Maybe her self-loathing was unwarranted. There was no way to understand such minds. Maybe had Charlie come, he would have died as well.

Ten feet from the water, Michael forced her to lie on the ground. She stayed on her back; she needed to see him. The grass was damp and smelled infectious. The night buzzed with insects. She remembered the swarm of mosquitoes that had hovered over Julie's head the last time she had visited. She was shocked to see a similar cloud above Michael. It was as if nature shouted:

"There are demons here, watch out!"

Only she had failed to listen.

He snapped open a green bag and tossed in a few rocks. Kneeling, he pulled the bag over her legs. It reached past her waist; she managed to keep her arms outside. He drew out a long piece of duct tape and circled her torso. Then he stood and searched for more rocks. The next bag would go over her head. He would cover her with two or three layers. He would not need to drown her—she would smother.

She tried not to cry. She was so scared.

"Scott," she said softly.

"What?" He sounded impatient. The neighborhood rocks were small. He feared she would float to the surface come morning.

"I want you to fuck me," she said.

He stopped and stared down at her.

"Why?" he asked.

"You fucked Brenda. She was your first. You fucked Julie. I don't want her to be your last."

He knelt close, his eyes shiny black dots. Already, he breathed heavily. "You messing with me?" he demanded.

"No." She moved her hips suggestively. "Take the bag off. Take your dick out. I'm wet, you have to fuck me before you kill me. That's the best time to do it, you know it is."

He sat back on his heels and chuckled. "You really are a cunt, aren't you?"

She licked her lips. "We're all cunts. Get your dick out. I want to see it. I bet you're already hard."

"I ain't stupid. I know you're just trying to buy yourself some time. But it ain't going to help you none, and I'm going to fuck you anyway." He began to unbutton his pants. "But you're going to love this."

"I know it."

He was erect. He was smart, but not as complex as his brother. He was a straight-out-of-the-book psychopath. He got off when he killed. As he struggled to get his pants down to his ankles, she tested the limits of the duct tape and managed to reach in her pocket and draw out the needle. The night protected the move but could it save her?

"Fucking cunt loves it," he whispered to himself. He was in a hurry to mount her. He momentarily forgot the plastic bag, and then angrily tore it away. No matter—he had a whole box left. He reached to rip off her pants.

"Kiss me," she said.

He froze. Obviously, he didn't often get that request.

"What?" he said.

"Kiss me before you fuck me."

"Why?"

"Because I want to taste you. I know you taste good."

He chuckled again. "How do you know?"

"Because I smell you. Please, let me taste you. Kiss me."

He sneered. "You're still thinking you're going to escape. Well, I'm not just going to kiss you, I'm going to bite your cunt tongue and suck your cunt blood."

He moved close, a bear outside the tent. His breathing was heavy; she smelled his sweat. He had her straddled. In the distance she heard the machine gun sound of a rain of fireworks. The shadow of his head blotted out the sky. The stars went out—so far away, and he so close. Her syringe floated in a handful of perspiration. One last chance—she had to get a grip!

"Open your mouth wide," he whispered as his black face descended.

"I'm opening it, babe." She was fortunate he still had his shirt off. When Gene and Scott had injected the vinegar in their victims, they had probably pinned them down on the ground. Easy to hit the heart that way. She was literally stabbing in the dark, but at least the absence of his shirt removed one obstacle.

"Fucking cunt," he said as his breath brushed her cheek.

Her wrists were tightly bound and the mobility of her fingers was questionable. It was hard for her to twist the needle completely upward. At the last second she doubted she could do it. His lips touched her lips. She felt his tongue . . .

Kelly panicked. She jerked upward with the needle, not sure where the tip was headed. The flat of her palm was wedged against the base of the plunger. The needle appeared to sink into his flesh. She was sure the syringe had emptied but his reaction stunned her. One moment he was kissing her, and the next he let out a grunt and calmly sat back on his heels. He looked down at the needle stuck in his chest. It was rammed to the hilt below his breastbone. The angle appeared deadly— the needle should have gone into his heart. It was his reaction that devastated her. He did not look the least bit hurt.

"What did you do to me?" he muttered, sounding confused.

She didn't answer. Just waited.

Then the vinegar hit him, the acid in his heart. He leapt to his feet and tore away the needle. Throwing it to the ground, he put his hand over his chest as if trying to plug a leak. The puncture was minute—it was what she had pumped inside that mattered. He drew in a sharp gasp and seemed unable to let it go. It was as if he had swallowed the air in his lungs and it had squeezed into his bloodstream. Convulsions rent his body, and he danced like a scarecrow on fire. He tried to curse her, to scream. Most of all he wanted to say his brother's name. He wanted Gene to help him. But it was clear he did not have the breath for it.

Still, he managed to pull out his gun and point it at her.

"No!" she cried.

He fired. The bullet struck harmlessly between her legs. Tremors shook him from head to foot. Once more, he tried to take aim. He was only two feet away; she thought he would hit her. Moving fast, she rolled right and swept his legs out from under him. She ended up flat on her back again, this time with him on her left side. But he was having trouble getting up. Best of all, he had dropped his gun. He pointed a shaky arm at her.

"Bitch," he mumbled.

He toppled backward and lay still.

Kelly sat up, tore off the duct tape with her teeth. Once free, she picked up his gun and cautiously knelt by his side. No pulse at the neck, no air moving in and out. He was dead.

"Bastard," she muttered.

She left him where he had fallen. But she took the other gun from his belt. When she was back inside and had some light, she saw that the gun he had put to her head was *her* gun. He had definitely been to her apartment in Malibu. She did not have to stretch her imagination to figure out why.

Kelly checked on Julie. The woman appeared to be breathing normally. The same with Robert; the kid snored peacefully. She brought them both blankets and pillows and tried to make them more comfortable. Neither appeared in danger—they would probably sleep through the night. Hopefully she would be back before morning. Later, there would be time to explain the true identity of Michael Grander.

Kelly collected both guns, the needle, the roll of duct tape, and left the house.

CHAPTER TWENTY-ONE

The cliff was not the edge of the world, but the drop over the side could still kill. Three hundred feet straight down to a stream just four feet deep. Amy did not appear to remember, but it was the same cliff she had practiced on during their last visit to the national park. Once she had conquered it, she had felt like a real rock climber.

Right now, though, they were just goofing off. It was not the time for serious rock climbing. It was near dark and they had Jimmy to watch. Only one of them could go over the side at a time.

Amy rappelled down first. The rappel system had four basic elements: an anchor; a rope; a means of applying friction to the rope; and of course someone to rappel. The spot Matt had chosen to explore was ideal because they had a huge boulder on top. It was a perfect anchor; it weighed a ton. Matt had bought three one-hundred-yard lengths of rope—each with a tested strength of one thousand pounds. He made Amy a diaper sling with ten feet of webbing—which helped secure the rope to her body. She was unable to use his harness because it didn't fit her. Also, the webbing worked well on smaller people.

Matt reminded her how to use the double carabiners to brake, and away she went. He was impressed she didn't look down before going over the side. Whatever her faults, she was no coward.

"How does it feel?" he called. Jimmy was back at the tent, crawling in the rock and sand, playing with colored blocks. Matt could keep an eye on both at the same time. Amy had already dropped down fifty feet, close to a natural ledge. He would have preferred she slowed down. Her smile shone up at him.

"It's better than sex!" she shouted.

He groaned. "Don't be in such a hurry. Your rope is doubled. You won't be able to reach the bottom."

"That's not fair! I'll have to climb back up!"

"Remember that," he cautioned. "Don't exhaust yourself."

"Yes, Daddy!"

He laughed. He loved to see her having a good time. In reality, he was not too concerned. If worse came to worse—if she lost her strength or nerve—he could rescue her. The double carabiners had a built-in safety feature. If someone slipped and fell, they automatically jammed the rope. A climber had to deliberately feed the metal loops plenty of rope in order to keep going downward. A sudden fall—of some distance—was next to impossible. Still, he followed her closely. She had been through a lot the last few days. Reckless moods and rock climbing did not exactly mesh.

Amy descended another ten feet and rested for a couple of minutes on the ledge. Then she boldly dropped down another sixty feet. She dangled away from the side, her inexperience showing. Rather than finding footholds with the tips of her shoes, she kept kicking herself off the stone wall. That was all right for a while. But if she couldn't find a series of spots to lever herself up, he would have to pull her up by force. No problem—she only weighed a hundred and five pounds. He could pull her up with one hand if he had to.

"Stop kicking and you'll stop spinning!" he called.

"I like to spin!"

For the next ten minutes he let her tire herself out. Ten minutes using practically every muscle in one's body could be a long time. She was panting when he finally took mercy on her and grabbed the rope and pulled her back up to the ledge sixty feet below. Leaning her head on the wall, she closed her eyes and struggled for breath. He knelt by the edge.

"Having fun yet?" he asked.

She looked up, not smiling. "I didn't need your help."

"Sure you did. Want me to pull you up the rest of the way?"

She shook her head. "I can make it."

"Whatever you say."

It took her twenty minutes to make it back to the top. By then she was drenched in sweat and her mood had changed. But she insisted she was fine and wanted him to try it out.

"I don't know, it's getting late," he said.

She unhooked her diaper sling. "What's the matter, scared?"

"Hardly. A cliff like this is nothing to me. You've seen what I can do."

She handed him the rope. "I forget. Show me."

"So I still have to prove myself to you?"

"Of course. Show me what a man you are."

He stared at her, thinking of their nap together a little while ago.

"Okay," he said.

Matt did not have to make up a diaper sling. He had bought an actual harness to secure to the rope and carabiners. Squeezing his legs and hips into it, he rechecked the knots on the webbing that circled the boulder. Amy stood quietly nearby. Jimmy continued to amuse himself beside the tent.

He went over the side easily and reached the ledge within seconds. They were losing the light. It was a crazy time for indulging in such a sport. But it had been his idea to begin with. Puffy orange clouds rode the western sky. The blue sky was changing into a hard violet. Staring straight up, he saw Amy lean over the edge, her face almost lost in the shadow cast by her long hair.

"Tired already?" she asked.

"Just getting my bearings. I'm going down a little farther."

"I'm watching you."

Matt eased off the ledge but kept in contact with the hard wall with the tips of his shoes. He fed rope into the carabiners, descending in two-foot jolts. Far below he heard the noise from the stream, and thought how exquisite it had been to make love to Amy on the smooth stone, the clear water inches away, the sun blazing overhead. A line from a book he had read passed through his head: *You never know when it is the last time.*

A lot of truth in that remark. Who would know?

He reached the end of the rope. He was midway between the top and the bottom, hung like a puppet on strings of his own design. He could not see Amy anymore. He called out, "Amy!"

She must have gone to check on Jimmy.

No problem. There were no problems.

Except his girlfriend had lied and cheated on him. She had stolen his son. She had murdered her husband. She had fled the law. Sure, there were problems but they were not insurmountable if only he could trust her.

"Amy!" he shouted.

No reply. She must be checking on Jimmy.

No damn problem, he kept telling himself.

Matt *imagined* he felt a tug on his rope. He was not sure because it did not feel as if she was trying to pull him up or even trying to get his attention. To do the latter all she had to do was stick her head over the side and call down. He did not understand why she had gone off for so long.

He felt another peculiar tug on his rope.

He decided to climb back up. Something was not right.

He climbed quick. His old skills had not rusted. His feet had an intelligence all their own. He found numerous tiny footholds; his leg muscles were strong. He reached the ledge sixty feet below the edge of the cliff in one minute. He breathed hard but he was in control and life was still good.

Then something extraordinary happened. His rope went slack. No, actually, it went so slack that it floated off the side of the cliff. The end hit his face as it casually fell to the ground, far below.

The end Amy had cut with a knife. It just flew right by him.

If, by chance, he had not been standing on the ledge, he would have flown with it.

Matt stood there and realized, finally, that all his questions had been answered.

"Amy?" he said quietly. Amazing how she heard him this time.

Her face peeked over the edge. "Matt?"

"What happened to the rope?"

She stared. "I don't know."

"Did it break?"

"I don't know."

"Can you throw me down another rope?"

"Do you want me to?"

Matt had to think about that. He hauled up the end of the rope. No rock burn here, cut clean with a knife. She watched him study the rope.

"What's the matter?" she asked.

"I'm stuck here."

"I know."

"If I hadn't reached this ledge when I did, I would be dead now."

"I know." Obviously she was not in the mood for conversation.

He sighed. "So what are we looking at here, Amy?"

"You know."

He got angry. "I know, you know. What are you doing?"

"I can't live like this. I can't spend the rest of my life on the run. I can't go to jail." She sounded sad. "I'm sorry."

Somehow her response did not surprise him. "You plan to call the cops when you leave. You'll tell them where I am. They'll come and arrest me. You'll tell them that you killed David because I've been holding you psychologically hostage for the last few months. Using your son to threaten you. You'll explain that I faked my death and then returned to life and stole Jimmy. You figure it'll be your word against mine. But you're pretty sure I'll have no credibility because I did in fact fake my death and kidnap Jimmy. Correct?"

"Yes."

"But the same alibi would have worked even better if I was dead right now. That way you wouldn't have to argue with me in court. Right?"

"Yes."

"Thank you. I just wanted to get the facts clear."

"Matt . . ." she began.

"Don't say it."

"I'm sorry."

"How can you do this to me?"

She was going to cry, poor thing. "I told you, I can't live like this. I can't do this to our son. He deserves to grow up in a stable home."

"With a murderer for a mother?"

"I wouldn't have murdered David if you hadn't set it up."

"You begged me to set it up! And right now you tried to kill me!"

"I'm sorry."

"Great! You've apologized and all is forgiven! Look, I'm not Jesus Christ. I'm stuck here. The cops will soon be on their way. I can't go to jail, either."

"I don't want you to go to jail."

"Right. You would prefer I was dead."

Now she wept. "No! I love you! I know that sounds stupid right now, but it's the truth. It kills me to do this to you. If there was any other way . . . What can I do?"

Matt spoke quietly. "You can throw me down another rope. You can let me go. You can take Jimmy and go to the police and tell them everything you were going to tell them as if I were still stuck here."

"You would never let me take Jimmy."

"I wouldn't stop you. You're his mother."

She considered. "I don't think the cops would believe me."

"You'll have Jimmy. That will be proof enough."

"Not total proof."

"You're a great liar. You'll convince them."

"I don't know. I can't risk it."

"But you're willing to risk me?"

"Matt."

"Never mind, I understand. It wouldn't be like having me in person to parade in front of the jury. You have thought this through."

"Yes."

"When did you think all this up?"

"Does it matter?"

"Yes. It matters to me."

She hesitated. "Since that night I left in the car with you. I knew then I couldn't handle it. I've been waiting for an opportunity. When you suggested rock climbing, I felt I had to jump on it."

"What happened last night had nothing to do with your decision?"

"I would like to say it did."

"But you wouldn't want to lie to me?"

"Matt. Don't make this harder than it has to be."

He burst out laughing. "I hate to spoil your party, Amy, but this is already pretty fucking hard. How can I make it any worse?"

She stood and wiped at her damp eyes. "There's nothing to say. I know you're going to hate me forever. You have every right to. I've lied and betrayed you again and again. But I'm not lying to you now when I tell you that I love you." She turned away. "Take care of yourself, Matt."

She disappeared. He was alone.

CHAPTER TWENTY-TWO

As she neared the Acid Man's apartment, Kelly thought of the line from Dante's *Inferno: "Abandon all hope ye who enter here."* The words were supposed to hang above the gates of hell. Privately, she had always thought the quote silly. Hope seemed to cause most human misery. If hell was devoid of it, so much the better. Yet, as it came time to face her old foe, she found new meaning in the words. She had everything going for her. His brother was dead, his big secret was revealed. The element of surprise was hers. Still, she felt as if she were descending into hell. He brought despair, that man, he was a necromancer.

No ghosts flickered on his windowpanes. Scott would have warned Gene as early as last night that she was coming to the house by the pond. But had Scott called while she was at the house? Somehow she doubted it—he had seldom been out of her sight. Yet Gene would still be waiting for a call from his brother. He would be wondering what had gone wrong. Her element of surprise might already be compromised. For that reason she decided to go in the back way.

One of the windows that overlooked the lush woods was ajar. Putting her gun in her mouth and using a garbage can as a stepladder, she reached up and pulled herself inside. As her feet touched the living room carpet, she half expected to take a bullet in the chest. Quickly she moved the gun into her right hand. Her heart was a hammer—it kept pounding a single note of fear. Dread held her like a claw stretched from an open coffin. Too many times at night she had imagined him in this very apartment.

Yet she saw little. It was pitch dark inside; it took her eyes time to adjust. The hospital bed in the corner—she concentrated in that direction but detected nothing. The place was silent as a sealed tomb. Could he already be gone?

Kelly blinked and saw images that did not exist. Creatures she had only imagined who lived and worshiped with him while he plotted his black deeds. They were no more real than her dreams of being a hero. Descending deeper into the apartment, she felt as if she was on the verge of interrupting a demonic seance. Surely, she thought, he must conjure some sort of demons to be possessed by such perverse desires. No human being could have killed the way he did and still remain human.

She did not know he was present until he spoke. Two feet away.

"You may turn on the light if you wish," he said.

Her nerves shrieked and she stumbled backward. In that instant she could have shot him without meaning to. Whether lucky or something else, she stumbled into a lamp. Another antique, a small prop with a stained-glass hat. She felt for the switch. The light came on yellow and soft.

He sat in his chair before her, a green blanket resting on his lap, his hands hidden beneath it. He started to speak but she did not give him the opportunity. With her gun in his face, she stepped forward and threw aside the blanket. Nothing underneath except pajamas. He was defenseless? If he had known she had already killed Scott, he would have been hiding in the shadows.

Or was that true? Did he know and not care? Did he have a contingency plan already in place? She wondered where the around-the-clock care was. The rest of the apartment appeared empty.

"How are you this evening, Kelly?" he asked.

She took a breath. "Fine."

He gestured to her gun. "Is that necessary?"

"You tell me."

He nodded to a chair. "You must be tired from your travels. Have a seat."

She sat down. He bumped the knob beside his right hand. A motor whirled; the chair rotated so that they sat face-to-face. His skin was remarkably pale and cold looking, reminding her of a deep-sea fish that had arisen from the ocean floor to greet the next Ice Age. Yet his blue eyes shone; he could not cloak his razor-sharp mind. She lowered her gun so that it pointed at his heart.

"Where is your help?" she asked.

"I paid them to take the night off."

"Your help is also your guard, per the terms of your release."

"I paid them handsomely. Relax, we're alone. How are you?"

"Fine. I just saw Julie and Michael."

"They told me you were stopping by. Pleasant visit?"

"Yes. It was good to see Robert again. He's growing up nicely."

The remark about his son was calculated. She believed he cared for his child. She thought hearing the name might put a dent in his armor. She needed to see inside him. Did he know his brother was dead? Unfortunately, he betrayed nothing.

"I'm happy to hear that," he said. "How is Julie?"

"As pretty as ever."

"And Michael?"

"He appeared kind of distracted. I don't know what was the matter."

"Did you tell him you were coming here?"

"No. Why?"

"Just curious. How was your flight?"

"I sat beside a little girl who reminded me of Anna. It made me realize how much I miss my family." She added, "My husband's trying to get back together with me."

"Are you going to take him back?"

"Should I?"

"If you love him. That's the only question that matters." He paused. "You cannot pretend to be a hero forever."

"Is that what all this is? Pretend? I thought I was here to slay the dragon. Or do you want to change the conditions of our deal?"

"We'll go ahead as planned. But I thought we might talk a bit first."

"What do you want to talk about?"

"How is Matt?" he asked.

"Fine. As far as I know."

"Have you spoken to him lately?"

"Yesterday afternoon. I'm sure you watch the news. Amy jumped bail."

He was pleased. "After murdering her husband. We both saw that coming. The two of them are together?"

"Of course. What do you think? Will it work?"

"She'll destroy him. Or he'll have to destroy her."

"I told him the same. You and I are beginning to think alike."

"You flatter me. Did he tell you where he was?"

She was casual. "I think somewhere in Nevada."

"Has Tony left his lady friend?"

"He says he has. Should I believe him?"

"That is also the question, isn't it? When you've been lied to the way you have, trust comes hard. But you two share a daughter. There's no reason to think you cannot share your lives once again."

What he just said went against everything he supposedly believed in.

Kelly leaned forward and taunted. "Unless I end up in jail."

He shrugged as best a quadriplegic could. "You'll never go to jail. I'm sure you've thought up the perfect way to kill me so as to make it look like an accident."

"Maybe. I'm going to poison you."

"How?"

"Potassium choride."

"Not very original."

"Sometimes the old ways are best. Even with a thorough autopsy, it's difficult to detect." She held up the needle she had plunged into his brother's heart. She had wiped it clean on the road, put water in it. "Especially when the solution is injected directly into the heart."

His eyes widened. "But you'll have the problem of the puncture wound."

"It will be tiny. You're paralyzed and ill. I don't think a coroner will take the time to notice. There's no reason to suspect foul play. I'll wipe away any blood."

"I'm disappointed. I assumed you would come up with something more exotic."

"What do you care? You'll be dead."

"True."

She pulled out her roll of duct tape. "I think we should get started."

He stared. "All right. I see you're in a hurry. Why the tape?"

She stood and holstered her gun. "You might convulse when I inject the solution. I don't want you to bruise yourself. It's better if I tie your arms down. You don't mind, do you?"

"No. But it's unnecessary. The musculature in my arms is ruined. They couldn't shake even in the middle of a spasm. It's physically impossible."

She set down the needle on a nearby coffee table and tore out a piece of duct tape, using her teeth in place of scissors. Taking a step closer, she stood and looked down at him. "Nevertheless, I would prefer to bind them to the arms of your chair. If that's all right with you?"

He nodded. "That would be fine. I'm just grateful you have come. All this has been a nightmare for me. I'm glad it will soon be over."

She knelt by his side. "It has been a nightmare for me as well." He had slight use of his right hand. Best to deal with that first. Stretching the tape through the arm of his chair, she leaned close and began to wind it around his wrist. Her Glock bumped against her ribs. She looked over at him and nodded. It would be over soon.

But then he reached out with his left hand and snatched the gun from her holster. Cocking the hammer, he put the barrel to the side of her head. The steel against her skin was as cold as his eyes. Like him, she was a student of mythology. They both understood that the dragon was immortal as well as a liar. They were in the same position they had been months ago.

"Tell me more about your visit with Julie and Michael," he said.

CHAPTER TWENTY-THREE

It had been his idea, Matt reminded himself as he stood on the narrow ledge and watched as night stole over the arid landscape. She loved him, she would not try to kill him. But try she had, only a few minutes ago. At least he finally knew where he stood with her. Never mind that it had taken him three years to wake up and smell the coffee.

But she had failed to kill him. He was alive and angry. What a bitch! He had risked everything to save her and still she had betrayed him. He swore she was not going to get away with it. He was not as helpless as she believed. For one thing he had started out as a free-rock climber before he had moved on to equipment. She did not know that. She had never seen him without a rope or carabiners. Also, before going over the side he had changed out of his hiking boots into rock-climbing shoes. The upper portion of the shoes were unusually flexible. The soles were made of a compound developed to create a sticky bond between the shoes and the rock. That gave him a formidable tool. Finally, he had a small block of gymnastic chalk in his pocket, which improved one's hand grip, especially in hot weather. Rock-climbing purists did not approve of chalk. They felt it messed up the natural environment. But at the moment Matt couldn't have cared less.

He had a job in front of him. Another reason it had never occurred to Amy that he could scale his way out of his predicament was because there was an overhang between the ledge where he stood and the edge of the cliff. The bulge would have literally forced him to hang upside down. A highly skilled climber might have tried it, but he wasn't that guy. Luckily, a hundred feet to his left, the overhang disappeared. He did not know what sort of handholds and footholds waited for him over yonder, but it was not as if he had a lot of choices.

He could hear Amy packing their gear. She had brought a couple of unfinished paintings from home—most of her paint supplies—and she had Jimmy's toys spread over the rocks. Still, she would be gone in fifteen minutes.

Just the fact that she was packing annoyed him. Another person in her situation would have bolted from the park. She was not worried about him anymore, maybe she had never worried about him. But he suspected she wanted him to hear her packing. She wanted to torture him.

Matt chalked his hands and started left. He used an approach to rock climbing called three-point suspension, in which a person moved one hand or foot at a time while the other three limbs remained stationary. The key was to remain in balance over the feet before releasing a handhold and reaching for the next one. The technique was elementary but it was not like he was trying to impress Amy.

He did well for several minutes, then ran into a problem. The light was failing fast and the cliff wall was relatively smooth. The next clear handhold was four feet over—a crack in the rock—and there didn't seem to be a decent foothold below it. Four feet was beyond his reach. He would have to jump to reach it, and if he missed, he would die. He considered going down and then cutting over but the prospect was depressing. In poor light, to search for holds below one's feet was extremely difficult.

Matt jumped and caught the crack with his left hand. He had a second where he was sure he was a goner. He flayed helplessly; it was the scariest moment of his life. But he got his right hand up quick and regained balance.

The next stretch of rock was rich in cracks and bumps. He had to caution himself not to hurry. He focused on the basics. He paid attention to his footwork and balance to reduce the need to rely on his arms. He stood erect over his feet and fought the tendency to lean forward and hug the wall. He kept his arms outstretched to avoid hanging on bent arms, which was the single most tiring position in existence. Mostly, he struggled to stay calm. It was a long way down to the shallow stream.

He was a few feet from the top when he made a beginner's mistake. He gave in to the temptation to reach forward and pull himself onto the ledge. The correct technique was to continue to walk his feet up the rock and use what was called *down pressure* with his hands near the edge of the ledge. In other words, he should have ignored that he was near his goal and kept going as usual. When he lunged and grasped the ledge, he lost his balance and his footholds. He ended up hugging the side of the cliff with his feet kicking uselessly in the air. At that point he could see Amy packing the car and had to fight the urge to call for help. Like she would run over and say you poor dear, let me give you a hand. Most likely she would stroll over and kick him in the face.

A well placed bump two feet from the ledge saved him. As he pulled himself up, he was forced to lie on his back for two whole minutes to catch his breath. Had Amy ran over and tried to stab him in the chest right then, he couldn't have stopped her. Sweat dripped from every pore in his body and was absorbed by the thirsty rock. He had been on the wall for thirty minutes total and was completely dehydrated.

Amy was absorbed in packing. He stood and walked back to the place where he had gone over the side. He was not surprised to see she was leaving the rope and the knife behind. She was not smart when it came to details. Of course she would have a story for the police to explain how she had escaped the evil and cunning Matt Connor. Too bad no one was going to get to hear it.

Matt picked up the knife and walked toward the car. He made no attempt to hide his approach. He was too exhausted and disgusted to bother. She did not look up until he stood at her back. Perhaps she smelled him; she had always had an incredible nose.

She raised her head and turned around. He smiled.

"Hi, Amy. What's happening?"

There was pleasure in the moment. Her pupils swelled like camera lenses. A hailstorm could have struck—she looked both frozen and bruised in the same instant. Her legs seemed to turn to sand. He thought he would have to reach out to catch her to keep her from falling, not that he would have bothered. She staggered and bumped against the trunk of the car. Jimmy was inside, probably asleep, secure in his infant seat. His mother was a ghost. As her eyes darted to the knife in Matt's hand, she must have thought he was going to kill her. Still, she was Amy and she had a story ready.

"I was just going to go back for you," she said.

"I know. You would never have left me. You love me."

"Matt. I do."

He offered his free hand. "Can we go for a little walk?"

She trembled. "Where?"

"To the edge of the cliff."

"Why? What are you going to do?"

He grabbed her arm. "I'll show you."

"Matt! No!" She struggled but it was useless. "Don't do this!"

He pulled her close and whispered in her ear. "Trust me. It's your only hope."

There must have been something in his tone. Perhaps it was absolute conviction. She had never heard that coming from him before. Perhaps it was the blade he put to her neck. She went limp and he was able to lead her back to the edge of the cliff. He nodded to the spare rope on the ground. There was a full three-hundred-foot bundle they had not used.

"Take that and tie it to the webbing," he said.

"Why?"

"I want you to climb down to the ledge."

She shook her head quickly. "I'm not doing that."

He tightened his grip on her arm. "You have no choice."

"You're hurting me!"

"Amy. If you don't climb down to the ledge, I'll throw you off the side."

Her face was bitter; imagine, after what she had just done to him. It reminded him of the night he had caught her with David. "You wouldn't dare," she swore.

Matt yanked her to the edge. She screamed but there was no one to hear her. He pushed her so that she was hanging at a forty-five degree angle over the ledge. Naturally, she started to struggle. One foot slipped and went over the side. It was hard to hold onto her.

"Matt! No! No! Don't! Matt!"

He pulled her back to safety and spoke in a cold voice. "Tie the rope to the webbing and climb down to the ledge. Hurry, I won't give you another chance."

Now she knew he was not bluffing. He let her go and she fell to her knees and began to knot the rope onto the webbing that circled the boulder. She shook so badly, he had to help her. Weeping like a child, she trembled in his arms as he pulled her back to the edge.

"I can't do this," she gasped. "Don't make me do this."

"The ledge is only sixty feet down."

Her big brown eyes pleaded. "But I might fall!"

He nodded. "You could fall if you're not careful. But a few minutes ago, you didn't care if I fell. You didn't care how long and how dark I fell when I caught you with David. That's your problem. You only think of yourself. My problem is the opposite. I only think about you. But I'm tired of that and I'm tired of you. Go over the side now or I throw you over. Either way, I don't care."

She fell to her knees. "Please! I'm the mother of your son!"

He pulled her back to her feet. "Not anymore you're not."

"Matt!"

He gripped her arm. "Last chance, Amy."

She heard his voice. She saw his face. Absolute conviction.

"Okay," she whispered.

There was scant light left but it was not an obstacle. Amy's shoes had excellent soles—he had picked them out for her that morning. And with the rope, she did not need any other equipment to reach the ledge. Summoning her nerve, she went over the side. The overhang caused her a problem—she went briefly airborne—but she slid past it and was on the ledge within a minute. He tried to pull up the rope. She refused to let it go.

He cut the rope with his knife and threw it down to her.

She let out a groan and slammed it to the ground.

"I'm going to leave now with Jimmy," he said. "When I'm far from here, I'll stop and call the police and tell them exactly where you are. I have a device that'll allow me to mask my voice. It's possible they won't be able to rescue you until morning. You can survive until then. The ledge is wide enough to sit down on. You might even want to lie down, although I don't suggest sleeping. You'll be arrested and returned to L.A. I'm sure you'll have a great story for the cops but it won't get you far. Two FBI agents saw you kill your husband and you jumped bail. Your father-in-law will confirm that you went to the trouble to pack all your valuables before you split. You won't find Carl supportive this time. You won't be able to talk yourself out of this one. And if you try bringing me up, the police and FBI will laugh. They'll never believe I'm alive. You'll go to jail and you'll stay there for the rest of your life. You'll never see Jimmy again. When he's older, I'll tell him his mother died in an accident." He paused. "Do you have anything to say for yourself?"

She wept. "I'm sorry. Please don't leave me here."

"You're sorry I caught you with David. You're not sorry you fucked him behind my back. You're sorry those two agents saw you kill David. You're not sorry he's dead. You're sorry I escaped from the ledge. You're not sorry you put me there." He paused. "And you know what? I'm not sorry that it ends this way. Somehow, it all seems fitting."

"Matt! Please! We can start over! It can be good again!"

He knelt and stared at her. She was not tall, and trapped on the side of the cliff she looked even smaller. A caged animal, nowhere to run. No teeth left to bite with, her claws gone. He felt a pang of sympathy but it was not strong.

"You don't want to try to climb up as I did," he said. "I barely made it, and I knew what I was doing. Sometime in the next few hours you might panic. The urge to escape will come over you. Don't even think about it. You'll get a few feet and you'll fall. I only tell you this because I'm a nice guy. To be honest, I don't care if you live or die."

She grew hysterical. "But you need me! I need you! You're the only one I can really make love to! Please, let me make love to you one last time! Matt, I do love you!"

He stood. "May I ask you a question?"

She stopped. "What?"

"My middle name is James. Did you know that when you named our son?"

"Yes! Yes! I named him after you!"

"I was lying. I don't have a middle name." He added, "But I researched David. His middle name was James."

For once she had no response.

"Goodbye, Amy," he said.

He walked backed to the car.

CHAPTER TWENTY-FOUR

A night of deception. A monster one foot away. A gun to her head. On her knees before the Acid Man, Kelly sucked in a breath and stared him in the eye.

"May I sit on the couch?" she asked.

He withdrew the gun. "No tricks."

"No tricks." She eased back slowly. The cushions felt like quicksand. She had to cough to speak. "So you have the use of your arms."

He kept the gun pointed at her heart. "Yes. You shot me in the seventh cervical vertebrae. That's the cutoff point between having the use of the arms and being totally paralyzed. For two months after my surgery, I was a complete quadriplegic. But as the swelling in the spinal cord decreased, I began to regain the use of my arms."

"A fact you kept carefully hidden."

He nodded. "A case could be made for a complete cripple—even a serial killer like myself—being spared a trial. Being put under house arrest rather than thrown in jail. The extreme nature of my handicap helped grease the wheels of my comfort, so to speak."

He chose his words carefully. *Grease* was slang for *bribe* in certain quarters.

"I always wondered why you didn't have a trial," she said. "Slate gave me the reasons. You were no danger to anyone. The cost of keeping you locked in a federal prison would be prohibitive. You had humiliated and murdered the wives of prominent men who wanted the case to go away. All these reasons were logical. I suppose most people fell for them. But I never did. Your father was a rich man. Obviously he shared that wealth with you. Tell me, Professor Banks, how many people did you have to bribe to avoid the death penalty and life in prison?"

He was pleased at her insight. "Two major players in the FBI. Three judges on the federal level. A handful of cops on the local level."

"How much did all this cost?"

"They knew what I was worth. They bled me dry. Ten million."

"Did Slate take any money?" she asked.

"No. He is a man of principle. He wouldn't take a cent."

"But he knew about it?"

"Sure. But the reasons he gave you were still logical. No one wanted to see me brought to trial. The publicity would be too messy for all concerned."

"Not for me."

"Still wanting to be acknowledged as a hero?"

"Perhaps. Did you pay Charlie any money?"

"Your partner? Don't be silly." He chuckled. "I had you suspecting everyone."

"How did you get my cell number? How did you know my husband left me?"

"Oh, that information. There was one other man in the FBI that I paid off. Do you know Agent Lentil?"

Kelly felt disgust. "I know him."

His tone hardened. "What happened at Michael and Julie's house?"

"At Scott's house?"

He blinked. "You know."

"Aren't you proud of me?"

He waved the gun. "Talk."

"I discovered you had a brother. I went looking for him but couldn't find him. But then I began to put a few facts together and it was obvious. Unfortunately, I asked Scott revealing questions and tipped my hand. He drugged Julie and Robert and tried to kill me." She shrugged. "But lucky me, I managed to inject a syringe filled with vinegar into his heart."

The Acid Man went very still. "He's dead?"

"Yes."

His grief was real. Her admission was a sword through his chest. He struggled to catch his breath. In the process she was surprised he did not pull the trigger. He bent over and his aim wavered.

"How did you overcome him?" he gasped.

"Your brother was a textbook psychopath. You know that. You ruined him at an early age. He was predictable, and as a result he was easy to manipulate. When I spread my legs, he got all excited and I killed him." She added, "I didn't enjoy it."

The Acid Man wiped at his eyes with the gun. His right hand was still tied down.

"I regret having involved Scott in my personal difficulties," he said quietly. "When I was a teenager he was the only friend I had. I had no one else to share my pain with."

"Sounds like you guys shared more than pain."

"You spoke to my father?"

"Yes. What did he know about all this?"

"He knew my brother was sleeping with my wife. That's all."

"You lie. He wasn't totally innocent. He suspected a lot more than that."

"My father was a good man."

"But he wasn't your father, was he? I read the pain in Dr. Banks's face. Your mother's affairs were more numerous than he wanted to admit, even to himself." Kelly paused. "Do you know who your real father was?"

He hesitated. "The milkman."

"I understand."

"Do you? As a child I saw her with this man that was not my father. She did little to hide the affair. Twice, I saw them fucking. Then I began to see I looked like the other man. I was seven years old at the time."

She nodded. "Your father was everything to you. You were your father's son. And when that was taken away from you, you were no one."

"No one," he whispered, sinking inside.

The answer to the riddle. Who could have committed the crimes he had? Only a soul who had lost all identity. He was a hollow vehicle capable of channeling energy from the bowels of the earth. She half believed him possessed. He looked as if a demon sat inside him now. His pale face shone with a purple light. Perhaps a trick of reflection. In the distance she saw a firework burn to nothing in the black sky. The demon withdrew—the man before her merely looked exhausted.

"I'm sorry," she said.

He glanced up. "Why are you sorry?"

"Because I have learned your secret. You lie."

"We all lie. No one more than a woman."

She stood. "I can't argue with you. I have lied to you."

He shook the gun angrily. "Sit back down!"

"No. I have to finish what I came here to do." Taking a step forward, she picked up the duct tape she had dropped when he had stolen the gun from her holster. She hardly noticed when he raised the gun toward her head and put pressure on the trigger.

"You know I'm not afraid to kill," he said.

"That gun belongs to your brother. It's not loaded." Reaching around to the back of her belt—beneath her shirt—she pulled out her own gun. "But this one is."

He froze. "How?"

"I spoke to your doctor last night. He insisted you were completely paralyzed. But he was pompous and I didn't trust him. I read more about the seventh cervical vertebrae and learned what you just explained—it is the cutoff point for feeling in the arms. When I was here last, I noticed you had kept your weight-lifting equipment. Specifically, I noticed you had kept the equipment that developed upper body strength."

He lowered his gun. "Clever."

"Thank you." She tore off a piece of duct tape. "We can do this the easy way or we can do it the hard way."

He was indignant. "You're not going to kill me."

"Wrong. I am going to kill you."

He snorted. "You'll go to jail."

"You wanted me to go to jail for life. You had your brother steal the gun from my apartment. The same day I was supposed to come here to put you out of your misery, Scott was going to shoot Julie in the heart with my gun. Scott would have been here to stop me from hurting you, but I would still have been blamed for the death of your wife. The poor, obsessed FBI agent who couldn't get over what the Acid Man had done to her. The girl just lost it. Naturally, the prosecution would have had access to all the records of my travels to the Midwest. All files closed, huh?"

"You cannot get away with killing me. You'll be the first one they'll suspect."

"I'll make it look like a suicide."

"Your bottle of potassium chloride? You're inexperienced when it comes to this business. The coroner will spot that immediately."

"I'm not going to use potassium chloride. That was another lie."

He looked worried. "What then?"

Kelly slipped on a pair of gloves.

She smiled as she came closer with the tape. "A new and improved screw."

He squeezed the trigger but the gun just clicked. Then he dropped the weapon and, using his left hand, tried to turn the wheelchair away from her. She did not mind—there was nowhere to go. Coming over his head, she stretched the tape across his mouth and pulled it tight. Always important to consider the neighbors. He tried to tear off the gag but she grabbed his hand and pressed it down onto the arm of the wheelchair. She had watched his videos closely. Tearing off more tape, she began to wrap his arm in place. The muscle strength in his arms was poor. He must still have partial paralysis. It took her only a minute to finish. His eyes bulged—she had seen the sight before.

"You look like one of your victims," she said.

His voice came out muffled. Did he beg for mercy?

She quoted. "'The instinct to survive is not as strong as people think. Pain is more daunting than life. The sick and depressed crave extinction. Even content souls wonder about death.'" Pausing, she withdrew a small screwdriver and file from her pocket. "What a crock of shit, huh?"

He fought to explain. She was not listening.

Kelly knelt and began to undo the screw at the base of the tiny bulb that controlled his chair. Because the FBI and the doctors knew he had slight use of his right hand, she worked on that side. When the screw was halfway out, she picked up the file and began to sharpen the edges. He talked gibberish the entire time but it didn't bother her. She had planned this for a long time. She knew what had to be done. When she was ready, she sat back and looked at his face.

"You bribed your help to leave you alone for the night. That is a verifiable fact. But my presence here will never be known. Before I leave, I'll clean up. I'll not leave so much as a hair. I'll return to Julie's house and wake her. I'll act like I was just attacked by Scott. She won't know any better. No one will know that you didn't spend this last night alone slowly opening the veins in your wrist."

There was blood in his face now. Soon it would be on the floor.

Kelly took his wrist and—slightly loosening the duct tape—rubbed the skin over the razor-sharp screw. Pressing down hard, the flesh caught and tore. Deeper layers of tissue became visible around the silver spike. He resisted but the effort was feeble. Blood spurted out, first in a dribble, then in a strong rhythmic pulse. A hole in the heart. A hole in the vein. Either way a person died. Sitting back, she watched as the puddle grew beneath his wheelchair. The stain was not far from the stain her blood had made on the floor.

Ten minutes went by. So much blood.

He stopped struggling and fell silent.

"You're bleeding badly," she said finally. "Soon you'll lose consciousness. If you promise not to call out, I'll remove your gag. Agreed?"

He nodded. She tore the duct tape off his mouth.

"I underestimated you," he gasped.

"I learned from you."

"How to lie?"

"How to kill. There's a part of you inside me."

"That you hope dies when I die."

She nodded. "You said it yourself. I can't live with you in the world."

He glanced down at his ruined wrist and his lip trembled. "This is hard."

"It was hard for the women you killed. Did you care?"

He stared at her. "I care about you."

"Why me?"

"How can I explain? You are the opposite of Julie but you stir similar feelings in me."

"You don't feel for your wife. You gave her to your brother."

"You're mistaken. You think I spent my whole life killing. After my troubled youth, I tried to live a normal life. True, I had difficulty with relationships with women. They never lasted long. But I never gave up the hope of falling in love, and when I met Julie my prayers were answered. The day we got married was the happiest day of my life."

"Then you told your brother to fuck her."

"I asked my brother to test her. I did not expect her to fail the test. I told the truth when you first came here. When I saw her sucking on Scott's penis, a part of me died."

"It was already dead. Who tests their own wife?"

"I had to know. You can understand that."

Kelly shook her head. "Julie is a blank. Why were you attracted to her?"

"What do you get when you pour one empty glass into another? There was an alchemy to our relationship. When we were alone together we were complete." He studied his blood loss. "Oh my."

"You didn't need to kill those women."

He raised his head slowly. "I feel dizzy."

"Tough."

"I could not kill Julie. I had to do something."

"You ordered Scott to shoot her tonight."

He sighed. "True. But you know how special tonight is."

"You put vinegar in your father's needle."

"She was no good."

"You took the vial of epinephrine from your father's bag. You emptied it and replaced it with white vinegar. It was acid he accidentally injected into his own wife's heart the second time she had an attack."

"So? She hurt my father."

"Your excuses bore me."

He looked weary. "I'm a dragon. You're a knight in shining armor. You're victorious. The victor should not gloat."

"Want me to kiss your ass?"

He drew in a ragged breath. "In olden days, when a dragon was defeated on the field it had to grant three wishes to its conqueror. Let us reverse that tradition and have you grant me three wishes."

"Such as?"

"Wish number one. Bandage my wrist. Apply a tourniquet. Let me live."

"No. You're too dangerous alive."

"You have exposed all my devices. I'm harmless now."

"No."

He appeared in pain. "Wish number two then. Let me talk to Matt."

"Why?"

"Since you told me about him, I've wanted to meet him. I feel a special kinship with him. We've both suffered. That's why I sent Scott to help him with Amy. Do you have his number?"

"Yes."

"There's a phone on my coffee table. Let's call him, see how he is doing."

Kelly hesitated. Her gut didn't want the Acid Man getting anywhere near Matt, yet it was a fact the monster would be dead within minutes. Since he had already been attacked once by the family, perhaps it would comfort Matt to hear the death rattle in Gene Banks's voice, and know the threat was finished.

"I don't know if he'll talk to you," she said.

"He'll talk to me."

Kelly picked up the phone. She had memorized Matt's cell numbers. She dialed the one he had given her just before Catalina. She was surprised when he answered.

■

TO GET to the camping spot Matt had chosen for their hideaway, he had taken a winding dirt road that was so close to nonexistence that it could vanish in a cloud of dust. Driving down the steep terrain in the dark was a harrowing experience. He wished they had a parachute as well as four-wheel drive. But eventually they ended up on a sane road that ran alongside the same stream that stretched beneath the ledge where he had stranded Amy. He stopped the car and turned off the engine beside the water. Craning his neck, he tried to spot her but it was too dark. Jimmy stared at him with large brown eyes. It spooked Matt how much his son looked like Amy.

"Do you miss her?" he asked.

Jimmy looked sad.

Matt was surprised when his cell phone rang. For a moment he thought it must be Amy. "Hello?" he said.

"Matt, this is Kelly. How are you?"

"Fine. This is a pleasant surprise. How are you?"

"Great. Are you alone? Is Amy there with you?"

He hesitated. "Amy's not with me. But Jimmy's here."

"Where is she?"

"Let's just say you'll read about her in the papers." He added, "But I didn't hurt her. You have to know that."

"Of course. I know you. As long as you and Jimmy are all right."

"We'll be all right now, thank you. How's the Acid Man?"

"He's sitting two feet in front of me. He wants to talk to you."

"What?"

Kelly lowered her voice. "He's dying. He'll be dead in a few minutes. Talk to him, it can't hurt."

"All right."

A raspy voice came on the line. "Matt Connor?"

"What can I do for you?"

"First off I would like to apologize for that fright you had last night in Utah. Kelly says she's told you about my history. I was just trying to help solve your girl problems."

"I can take care of my own problems."

"I understand. I overheard what you said to Kelly right now. I take it Amy is no longer in the picture?"

"She has left the picture. What exactly can I do for you?"

The man chuckled. "Nothing. Just wanted to say hi to a fellow warrior. You may not know this, but you and I have fought similar battles. I admire your style. I only wish I could say I was as successful as you. I wouldn't be in the predicament I'm in now."

"Are you really dying?"

"Kelly is bleeding me to death. Tough chick, wouldn't you say?"

"Yes. But inside she has a heart of gold."

"Good to talk to you, Matt. Watch out for those women. They can kill you."

"I know."

The Acid Man gave the phone back to Kelly.

"Matt," she said softly. "How's your heart?"

"It went the way you predicted. She was no good. But we're okay."

"You'll do great." She added, "I wish I didn't have to say goodbye."

He understood. "We were lucky. Our paths crossed at a critical time and we were able to help each other. I'll remember you for a long time."

"I'll remember you until the day I die." She sniffed. "Love you."

"I love you, Kelly. Take care of yourself."

He set down the phone and sat for a long time in silence. Jimmy sensed his mood and remained quiet. The night was warm and comforting. So was the sound of his heart as it beat in his chest. At least now it could heal. He decided to drive back to the West Coast and see his mother. He would explain everything. She would be overjoyed to see him. Perhaps she would travel with them to New Zealand. She had always wanted a grandson.

In the distance he heard a scream. A woman falling.

The scream did not last long. The silence returned.

A tear rolled over his cheek but he did not wipe it away.

"Mama," Jimmy said softly.

He messed up his son's hair. "Don't worry. We're better off without her."

Matt started the car and drove away.

■

KELLY ALSO sat in silence after setting down the phone. The Acid Man gave her a moment. He did not have many left. His breathing was labored and he was having trouble keeping his head up. Shivers shook his torso. Bleeding to death was no fun.

"Thank you," he said weakly.

She stared at his open veins. How his blood continued to pump from his body.

"I never killed anyone until tonight," she whispered.

"How does it feel?"

"It was a relief to kill your brother. He was such an asshole. But with you it's different."

"How so?"

The truth shocked her. "It hurts."

"Kelly. It does hurt."

"What is your third wish?"

He struggled. "May I kiss you?"

"Why?"

"Love knows no reason. Nor does hate. I suppose that is the lesson of my life."

"What is my lesson?"

"You know. When we first met we spoke of *The Lord of the Rings*. I told you that you were Eowen—the great female warrior. She was wounded in the final battle but she found love. She was able to go home."

Kelly was thoughtful. "Frodo was the tale's real hero. He tried to go home but his wounds were too deep. He could find no peace."

The Acid Man choked as he swallowed. His voice came out thin as a reed.

"You'll find peace. The dragon will haunt your dreams no more."

She came close to his side. "Do you die in peace?"

He looked at her with fading eyes. "No. But maybe I'll return in another age. The line between the hero and the villain is often slight. Perhaps we'll meet in that time, and our roles will be reversed."

Lines from her thesis. Perhaps he had read it.

She leaned over and kissed his forehead. "Perhaps."

He died minutes later. Her eyes burned, but there were no tears.

Later, she called Tony as she drove back to Julie's house.

He sounded happy to hear from her.

"How are you?" she asked. "How's Anna?"

"Fine. We miss you. When are you coming home?"

"I'm on my way right now," she said.